set it right

JULIA WOLF

Playlist

"Parachute" Hayley Williams

"In A Lake" Mitski

"The View Between Villages" Noah Kahan

"The Night We Met" Lord Huron

"Strange" Celeste

"Never Really Mine" The Lumineers

"Drag Path" Twenty-One Pilots

"Your Rocky Spine" Great Lake Swimmers

"Meet Me In The Woods" Lord Huron

"The Great Divide" Noah Kahan

"Missing Piece" Vance Joy

"If We Were Vampire" Jason Isbell

"Rivers and Roads" The Head and The Heart

"The Night We Met" Amber Run

Listen on Spotify

Chapter One

Zara

Three Years Ago

At twenty-three years old, it was hard to believe I'd just snuck out of my parents' house for the first time. Back in high school, I'd never even thought about doing it. Then again, my house had been the hangout spot. If anyone had snuck out, it would have been my friends to come over.

That felt like centuries ago.

I wasn't superstitious, not like my dad, but I had planned to abide by the old-fashioned wisdom of not seeing my groom before the ceremony.

Except...

It was nearing midnight, and I was having doubts about the whole thing. The air was warm and heavy, the kind of Oregon summer night that hummed with crickets and distant traffic, and my skin felt restless. I just needed—

A hug would have been nice. Jackson holding me, telling me he loved me and everything would be perfect, assuring we were doing the right thing.

He'd give that to me. He'd been revving to get married since we'd met in college, and I'd been swept up with him in his excitement.

It was hard not to be flattered when a man was genuinely obsessed with you—when he wanted to be around you, always, and filled your days with compliments—when he planned an elaborate proposal and over-the-top wedding.

Until tonight, I hadn't had time to stop to think for even a minute. Lying in my childhood bed, staring at the ceiling, ruminating over conversations from our rehearsal dinner, questions about our plans for the future, it struck me this was going to be my life. From here forward, everything I did would have to be discussed with Jackson.

Dreams I had growing up would never happen. I was on a path I had never seen for myself. A future I'd never daydreamed even once.

Sure, I loved Jackson. We were *in* love. But I'd always thought I'd have a marriage like my parents. My father barely let my mother's feet touch the floor, and she was his soft place to land, always.

Jackson urged me to be independent. Which was...great. Really great. Independence was fantastic.

But sometimes, a girl wanted to tuck herself into her man's lap and have him feed her dinner.

At least, I thought I wanted that. If I tried with Jackson, he'd laugh me right out of the room. That wasn't to say he didn't take care of me, just not in that way.

Still, we loved each other a lot, and that counted for something. Plus, family was as important to him as it was to me, even if *his* family always seemed to take precedence over mine and my dad hadn't stopped giving him the side-eye even after all our years together...

My flip-flops slapped against the soles of my feet as I half-walked, half-jogged the two miles to the house Jackson had rented for the weekend. The pavement was damp from earlier rain, and the air smelled faintly of grass and ozone. Being out alone after midnight in only my pajamas wasn't the smartest decision I'd ever made, but I had to do this.

There was no way I could walk down the aisle tomorrow without having one more conversation with Jackson.

I needed him to promise me I wouldn't lose myself in him. I had to hear him say he understood I wouldn't be ready for kids for several years. I really hoped he grasped my need for adventure and exploring nature and would help me nurture that, even if he didn't have the same need.

We'd talked about all this plenty, but when I thought back to those discussions, I couldn't remember Jackson ever giving a straight yes or no. He was good at dancing around answers until I forgot I'd asked for something in the first place.

I knew he loved me. He told me multiple times a day. And if I didn't go through with this marriage...well, I couldn't bear to think how he'd react.

My feet hit the ground harder as I sped up, the puddles on the sidewalk splashing my bare legs. I just needed to see him, then I'd know.

The screened-in front porch glowed, warm-yellow light spilling out into the night. Voices and laughter broke through the otherwise stillness. Jackson's brothers were with him, so I shouldn't have been surprised, but their presence made my plan of sneaking in and out more daunting.

I inched across the wet lawn, sticking to the shadows. I really didn't know what I was doing, lurking around like a thief in the night. Was this what I'd come to? It couldn't have been a good sign. Surely, my mother hadn't done anything like this the night before her wedding.

A burst of laughter stopped me in my tracks, but I could see Jackson, Owen, and Randall clearly enough from where I stood.

The fourth man made my stomach lurch.

What was Cormac Kelly doing here?

He sat with the boys like they were all old friends, easy and familiar. While it was true he and Jackson had been roommates in college, they weren't close anymore. I hadn't thought so anyway. I hadn't even known Cormac was in town.

He wasn't supposed to be here.

The ringing in my ears faded, replaced by a low murmur. Cormac was speaking now, and the sound of his voice hit me with a sharp, unexpected wave of nostalgia.

"You need to be sure."

Jackson chuckled, sounding loose as a goose. "I told you, I've got it all figured out."

"Sounds like you do," Cormac replied, shoving his thick hair away from his face. "But I don't see it working out the way you think it will."

"Ah, you don't know Zara the way I do." Jackson tipped his beer into his mouth, and I flinched.

He shouldn't have been drinking—not this late. He'd had more than his fair share at the rehearsal dinner and had sworn he wouldn't be hungover tomorrow. Watching him drain the bottle, I wondered, not for the first time, how often his promises had been made with the best intentions and broken just as easily.

Cormac leaned forward, steepling his elegant hands between his knees. He'd always been almost...graceful with his movements. Given he'd been six feet tall by twelve years old, that wasn't easy. But he'd never had an awkward, gangly stage. Not to me, at least. All these years later, when everything else had changed, he still moved the same.

"That's true." Cormac tapped his fingers together. "I haven't known Zara for a while, but I do know you, man, and I've been listening to you all night. It seems you're making a big mistake."

The words landed hard, knocking the air from my lungs.

Randall, Jackson's oldest brother, cupped his hands around his mouth. "Booooo. Keep that sensitive shit to yourself, Mac."

Owen, the middle brother, burped so loud it echoed, making him laugh like it was the funniest thing he'd ever heard. I wasn't surprised. Owen was an overgrown frat bro. He and Randall constantly tried to get Jackson to go out drinking with them, and most of the time, succeeded.

After the wedding, things would be better. We'd be moving a couple hours away, outside Jackson's brothers' sphere of influence.

"Jackie knows exactly what he's doing. He's got it handled," Owen declared.

Heat traveled from my cheeks to my chest, wrapping around my heart. I shouldn't have been hearing any of this, but my feet had taken root in this spot.

"No—wait"—Jackson quieted his brothers— "maybe Mac's got a point. Let's hear him out. Who do you think would be a better match for Zara—*you*?"

Cormac shook his head. "Absolutely not. You know that's not what I'm saying. Zara and I were only ever friends, and that was years ago. I'm concerned about you. That's all this is."

Cormac was concerned about Jackson marrying *me*? That hurt more than it should have. He was right, we had been friends once, a long time ago. Who did he think he was, barging in now, putting doubts in Jackson's mind?

"Zara's a good girl," Randall said. "She'll be a good wife to Jackie."

"Right? Sweet and docile," Owen added. "Just how I like 'em."

That burned. Sweet. Docile. I pressed my lips together, my nails digging into my palms. Was that how they saw me—was that how *Jackson* saw me?

Jackson groaned. "Don't talk about my girl like that, and never say anything like that in front of her."

"Sure." Owen clapped his shoulder. "My lips are sealed, baby bro."

Jackson turned back to Cormac. "My decision was made the moment I slipped the ring on Zara's finger. I appreciate your concern, but I've got this. My marriage may not look like your parents', but I know how to make her happy, and she sure as hell makes me happy. We're good, man."

That should have put an end to it, but Cormac wasn't convinced. "I really think, after what you said—"

Randall jumped to his feet and instantly stumbled into the side table, taking down the lamp and a few beer bottles. The brothers erupted into hysterics, and all I could do was stare at Cormac in the dark, wondering what I'd ever done to him to make him feel this way about me.

He'd traveled all the way from Wyoming to try to convince Jackson he was making a mistake marrying me—

I couldn't breathe. My feet sank into the damp earth. A dog barked two doors down. Above me, an absurd number of stars scattered across the sky. I pressed my hands against my stomach and wiggled my toes to make sure they still worked.

When a light flicked on in the house next door, reality snapped back into place.

What was I doing?

Tomorrow was my wedding day. I should have been in bed. If I'd stayed there, I wouldn't have heard my first best friend say those things about me. I wouldn't know what Cormac Kelly really thought.

Now, there was no unhearing it.

Laughter and the clink of glasses followed as I stumbled back to the sidewalk and turned toward my parents' house. My feelings were bruised. My heart ached. Cormac and I had been thick as thieves. Even though that had faded years ago, I'd believed our friendship had meant something.

My pace picked up. Tomorrow was my wedding day. My *wedding day*. No one was going to take that from me, especially not Cormac Kelly and his unwanted opinions. He could stuff them in his saddle and ride his high horse right back to Wyoming.

Jackson and I were getting married, and we would make this marriage work.

Come hell or high water, we were going to be happy together.

Chapter Two

Zara

MY SUITCASE WAS STUFFED so full, I was scared the zipper was going to break and I'd be buried under an explosion of clothes. My car wasn't any better, filled to the brim with everything I'd need for the summer.

"I'm beginning to think you're not coming back," Zane said, throwing himself on my stripped bed.

I brushed my hair out of my face with a sigh. "Don't worry your pretty little head. This is a summer job. I have no interest in experiencing Wyoming winters."

He raised a doubtful brow. "Your suitcase says otherwise. Do you really think you need two pairs of heels?"

I scrunched my nose, contemplating, then nodded decisively. "You never know what could come up. I'm not going to be working all the time."

"Still..." he swung his crossed leg, his flip-flop dangling perilously, "it's *Wyoming*—and not even Cheyenne. Though it is a stretch to call that a city."

I put my hands on my hips. "Since when are you such a snob? It's not like Portland is the paragon of glamour."

He flicked his fingers. "I just can't see you so far from the coast. It doesn't make sense. Can you explain this very abrupt decision one more time? Since you're leaving me with Mom and Dad, I need to be able to talk them down when they start climbing the walls with worry about you."

My brother was nothing if not dramatic, but that didn't mean his point wasn't valid. We were a tight, close-knit family, and our parents were the definition of overprotective. I loved them. Really, truly loved them. Since I'd split from Jackson, they'd been superheroes, offering nonstop support, checking on me every day, making sure I wanted for nothing.

That was why I needed to go somewhere I could breathe on my own. No matter how well-intentioned, sometimes their concern was suffocating.

I sat beside him, laying my head on his shoulder, and he reached for my hand, threading our fingers together the way he always did.

"You know how much I've always loved the Kelly ranch," I said. "The summers I spent there were so uncomplicated."

Before things got heavy. Before I grew up and made a string of bad decisions. I wouldn't have said it was the last place I was happy, but it might have been the place where I could dial back into those days—when I was sure of who I was and where I was going. I needed that more than anything.

He huffed. "Because there's nothing there."

I poked his side. "Exactly, Zaney. Nothing but cattle, horses, and endless blue sky. That's the point."

He shuddered. "All that land creeps me out. I went once—never again."

My brother was a city boy. Funny, since our mom was a nature lover. But our dad only spent time outside to be with her, so I guessed he'd inherited that gene from him.

When we were ten and eleven, they'd shipped us off to spend the summer with their college friends, Lock and Elena Kelly. Zane had been completely miserable, but I'd lived my best life on their ranch, getting dirty and exploring with the Kelly kids. The next summer, Zane's refusal to go back was adamant, while I couldn't wait to return—which I did, every summer until I was sixteen.

I lifted my head, drinking in my fill of his face. Zane had our mom's blue eyes and long lashes, hooded by our dad's heavy brow that always seemed a little suspicious. His bronze skin was so smooth it was almost unreal, even up close.

My brother was a beautiful person, inside and out, and I was going to miss him more than anyone. I'd been missing him for years, though, all of my own doing. My life with Jackson had become so chaotic, I'd distanced myself from pretty much everyone, not wanting them to see and question and know. I'd been embarrassed and ashamed—still was, to be honest—and had barely been able to face any of them. The second I walked out on Jackson, I was lucky my parents and brother had immediately opened their arms to me. If they hadn't...I didn't want to think about where I'd be.

Still, I needed more...different. The last six months, they'd propped me up. It was time for me to figure out what standing on my own two feet felt like.

I dug my teeth into my bottom lip, considering my words. "I need this reset—a summer away from everything, so when I come back, I'll be ready to start fresh. If I had to do it now..." I shook my head, "I can't even think about what that would look like. I'm not there yet. And a lot of my best memories happened during the summers I spent at the ranch."

"Mmmhmm." He didn't seem convinced, and I wasn't sure there was anything I could say to make him so. "You could reset with Steven and me, you know. That offer will always stand."

A blond head poked through the doorway. "Did I hear my name?"

Zane held his hand out and wiggled his fingers, beckoning his husband closer. "I was reminding Zara our guest room is permanently open to her."

Steven crossed the room, taking Zane's hand. His thumb went straight to Zane's wedding ring, rubbing the smooth surface. "That's true, honey. We love having you at ours."

I hopped up, giving Steven a hug. He was an incredible hugger. Only a few inches taller than me, but stocky, with massive arms capable of lifting extremely heavy objects. He put them to good use now, wrapping me up tight.

"I'm most definitely going to take you up on that when I come back from Wyoming, since I'll be homeless."

Steven was a foreman at one of the docks our dad operated. A few years ago, Zane stopped in to have lunch with him, laid eyes on Steven, and never looked away again. They might've looked like an odd match on the outside, but besides my parents, I'd never seen another couple so in love.

Another reason I had to get out of here: I was still in my bitter divorce stage and refused to infect them.

Zane cleared his throat. "The offer might be rescinded if you don't take your hands off my man."

I squeezed Steven tighter. "But he's so good at hugging." Zane growled, and I laughed, releasing Steven. "All right. You can have him back."

The two of them helped me pack the rest of my bedroom. I hadn't lived in this apartment long, so there wasn't much, and everything I did have was going into storage while I figured myself out.

Just as we were deciding whether to reward all our hard work with pizza or Chinese, our parents showed up carrying bags from my favorite Mexican place.

Mom bustled into the kitchen, brushing kisses on my, Zane, and Steven's cheeks. Zane followed to help her dish the food onto paper plates as Dad greeted Steven, clapping him on the shoulder and kissing the side of his head. "How's my favorite son-in-law?"

"I'm your only son-in-law now," Steven quipped.

Dad didn't miss a beat. "Nothing changed. You were always my favorite."

"Amir, be nice," Mom called from the kitchen.

He grumbled under his breath. "No need to be nice to that piece of shit, Zadie. Least our girl came to the realization before wasting any more of her life with him."

She sighed. "Do we even need to talk about him?"

I waved. "If I get a vote, we never mention my very bad taste in men again. I'm aware my picker is broken. It's in the shop being serviced."

My dad came to me, taking me by the shoulders. With my mom, brother, and me, he was a gentle man, but as I'd gotten older, I'd become aware outsiders had a different impression of him. Even at sixty, he was an intimidating presence. Tall and strong, his dark eyes were a black hole when he wasn't focused on the people he loved, and his resting expression was a scowl. But he always looked at me like I was precious and treated me the same.

"Nothing about you's broken, baby girl. You got caught up in something, and maybe a little turned around, but that's not your fault." He leaned down, kissing my forehead. "You'll take the summer, get your head on right, and see you were never the problem."

I sucked in a shaky breath, my head falling to his shoulder. "Thanks for saying that. I was sure you were going to try to talk me out of going."

"If I thought it'd do any good, I would." His chuckle was a low rumble. "You've got your mind set on Wyoming. I get that. Only thing I worry about is you making the drive alone. Not a fan."

"I'll be fine," I said, hoping I sounded more certain than I felt. It would be a long drive, farther than I'd ever done...the kind of trip I'd imagined taking with Jackson one day. And while I'd be doing it alone, at least I could play any music I liked without worrying about him complaining and eat all the junk food I wanted without judgment.

"You will be." He pulled back, tipping my chin up. "You're gonna get out there, have your big adventure, find your path again, and set it right."

"I hope so," I whispered.

"I know so, Zara."

Chapter Three

Zara

A THOUSAND MILES LATER, I rolled down Main Street in Sugar Brush, Wyoming.

Everything looked the same...but smaller, like the town had shrunk while I'd been away. The wide sidewalk still stretched beneath rows of storefronts, their windows gleaming in the late afternoon sun, polished to lure summer tourists inside. Diagonal parking spots were mostly filled with dusty SUVs and trucks sporting out-of-state plates. Sugar Brush wasn't Cheyenne or Cody, but the hot springs and surrounding ranch land drew a steady trickle of visitors every year.

It was why I was here.

Snagging one of the last open parking spots, I cut the engine. The silence rang in my ears, but relief sagged through me. My lower back throbbed, my legs ached, and my brain felt like it had been rattled loose inside my skull. Two days in a car would do that to a person. Tomorrow morning, I'd report to the ranch. Tonight, I planned to eat something hot and fall face-first into a motel bed.

But first, I needed to stretch my legs and remind myself I was human.

Pushing my sunglasses up my nose, I strolled along the sidewalk, peeking in windows and noting the changes. There were a couple cute boutiques that hadn't been here when I was a teenager, but the five-and-dime was exactly the same.

The pink door of Sugar Rush Bakery was new. I peered inside, spotting my old friend, Phoebe Kelly, behind the counter, smiling at a customer.

Despite my bone-deep exhaustion, I couldn't stop myself from going inside. I hadn't seen Phoebe since my wedding, and...well, a lot had changed since then.

Her rich-brown eyes lit up as I made it up to the counter. "Zara! You're here. What—oh my god."

My lips trembled as I smiled. "Hey, you. I heard this is the place to get yummy sweets. What's good?"

Ignoring the question completely, she darted around the counter and wrapped me in a fierce, sugar-laced hug. I closed my eyes as I sank into her, my body giving in to her comfort.

"Oh my god," she whispered. "I knew you were coming, but not today. It's so good to see you, Z."

Moisture gathered behind my eyelids, and I squeezed them shut to keep it there. "You too. I missed you."

She pulled back, keeping me at arm's length as she looked me over. "I wish I could say you look good, but you kinda look like death warmed over."

A laugh burst out of me. "I feel that way. Two days in a car and barely sleeping in cheap motels will do that to a person."

She grimaced. "Okay, no. We're fixing that. Do you still like tea and honey?" She steered me toward the pastry case, its shelves half full of croissants and muffins and glossy fruit tarts. "Take whatever you want. Several things, actually. Deacon claims he's getting a gut from being *forced*"—she made air quotes— "to eat my leftovers. You'll be saving my poor husband."

I laughed. "I'm sure having to eat your baking is pure torture for him."

She rolled her eyes. "It is. He just hates it." Then she wrapped her arm around my shoulders, pulling me into her warm, soft side and laying her head on top of mine. "Did I say how happy I am you're here?"

"You implied it." I closed my eyes, relishing her closeness. Phoebe was only a couple years older than me, but she reminded me of my mom in a lot of ways. Her gentle heart and never-ending kindness. Soft hugs and sweet nature. "I'm happy to be here."

As soon as the words left my mouth, I realized they were true. Sugar Brush, Wyoming, was supposed to be an escape from everything that had gone wrong, but now that I was standing in the town I'd loved as a kid, it hit me just how good it was to be here.

Maybe this really was what I needed to set it right and get back to myself.

Phoebe boxed up way too many pastries while one of her employees made me a cup of tea. Just as I was about to carry my goodies to a table, the bell over the door tinkled, and a rangy man with strawberry-blond hair walked in, a chubby toddler perched happily in his arms.

Phoebe abandoned me immediately, greeting them with kisses. I recognized Deacon Slater and little Abigail from photos, but seeing them in person made my chest ache. Deacon looked at Phoebe like she'd hung the moon, and Abigail's toothy grin was pure joy.

Phoebe brought them over, introducing them to me. Abigail had the Kelly family brown eyes and her daddy's rose-gold hair. She clung to Deacon, giving me a shy wave that made my heart skip.

"Nice to have you in town." Deacon was gruff but sincere, and he held on to Abigail like she was the most precious thing in the world—besides Phoebe.

"I'm glad to be here and finally meet you guys. She's even cuter in person. I can't get over it."

Phoebe sighed. "Isn't she? Wait until you see Hannah's kids, and Cay's little squish."

I shook my head. It was hard to believe wild Hannah Kelly was a mom of two and stoic Caleb Kelly had settled down, gotten married, and had a baby. Life had really moved on while I'd stagnated in a dysfunctional marriage and job that...

Well, we'd leave it at that.

I clutched my tea to my aching chest. "Your mom sends my mom pictures daily. She's so jealous I get to hang out with the Kelly grandkids all summer."

Phoebe poked my arm. "I know you're going to be busy working, but you better make time to hang with me."

"I will. Promise. I could use some girlfriend time."

Her gaze flitted over me, so soft and concerned I had to look down at my steaming cup.

"I bet. I'm here to talk or distract or whatever. And if you need snuggle time, Abigail's pretty amenable once you get to know her."

That made me smile. "How could I refuse an offer like that?"

Phoebe had to wait on a few customers, so I said my goodbyes to Deacon and Abigail and carried my tea and pastries down Main Street. As Gray's Diner came into view, my stomach rumbled. Living off gas station junk and fast food the last few days, a real, hot dinner was exactly what I needed before I passed out in my motel room.

I pulled open the door and went inside. The smell of french fries and onions hit me with a wave of nostalgia, sending me back a couple steps. I could almost picture Phoebe and me sitting at the counter, sipping milkshakes, giggling over boys.

I turned my head, finding the corner booth where I'd spent hours with Cormac, trading comic books and telling each other our secrets.

Not every secret, though. Some I'd kept to myself.

And right up until the night before my wedding, I'd wondered how things would have turned out if I hadn't. That was when every question I'd ever had was answered. Cormac Kelly had once been my best friend, but I'd never been his. That much I knew to be true.

I forced my gaze away from the booth before I could spiral into the melancholy I'd left in Oregon, scanning the other side of the diner.

Everything stopped.

My heart. Time. The earth.

As if conjuring him with my thoughts, my eyes landed on the man I'd been trying to shove out of my mind. Even worse, he looked incredible. The sleeves of his crisp white dress shirt were rolled up, a few buttons at his collar left undone, exposing the golden skin of his throat. His wavy hair was longer now, darker in the low light, and his smile was easy as he laughed at something the woman across from him said.

My mouth was desert-dry, and my tongue was too big to do any kind of swallowing. The air around me grew suffocatingly hot, and my pulse rushed in my ears. I shouldn't have felt this...this panic. It didn't make sense. I'd washed my hands of this man and the way he'd made me feel a long time ago.

Had it really only been three years since he'd sat at the back of the chapel, watching me marry Jackson—since he'd tried to talk him out of marrying me? If only Jackson had listened...

A tap on my shoulder made me flinch.

"Table for one?" a teenage waitress asked, menus stacked in her arms.

"No," I blurted. "Sorry. I can't stay."

She shrugged, already turning away.

What was I doing? I had to get myself together. I couldn't have a panic attack every time I saw Cormac. Chances were it was going to happen quite a bit this summer. We wouldn't be working together directly, but we'd both be on the ranch and in this town.

That didn't mean it had to happen this very second.

I pulled in a breath and headed for the exit, taking one last look at Cormac—which turned out to be a fatal error. His pale-blue eyes clashed with mine, flaring with what looked a lot like shock. I tripped over my own feet and stumbled, nearly dropping my box from Sugar Rush.

I righted myself just in time, clutching the pink box carefully. Then heat rushed up my neck, and another wave of panic shot through me.

Cormac was halfway out of his booth.

Nope.

Absolutely not. I was *not* ready for that.

I yanked the door open and burst out onto Main Street, the bell jangling behind me. My sandals slapped against the sidewalk, my heart hammering like I was fleeing a crime scene instead of a man I hadn't spoken to in years.

Get it together, Zara.

I didn't stop until I reached my car and slid into the driver's seat. Then…I just sat there, forehead resting against the steering wheel, breathing like I'd run a mile.

I squeezed my eyes shut, willing his image out of my mind. The way his eyes had gone wide. The way his body had instinctively moved toward me. The fact that, even now, some traitorous part of me had taken note of the breadth of his shoulders and how stupidly gorgeous he'd grown to be.

I straightened, forcing my pulse to slow. I was tired. Emotionally wrung out after too much nostalgia and not enough sleep. Of course, seeing Cormac Kelly—Cormac *of my childhood*, Cormac *of every "almost"*—had rattled me.

Anyone would've been thrown.

But I wasn't that girl anymore, and that wasn't why I was here. I wasn't eighteen and tangled up in what-ifs. I wasn't twenty-three, making the worst mistake of my life. I was here to work, reset…breathe again.

Next time I ran into him, I'd be ready. I'd smile politely. Say hello like he was any other person from my past—not the ghost of the life I'd never gotten to live.

I wouldn't trip.

I wouldn't bolt.

I definitely wouldn't panic.

Chapter Four

Cormac

"ARE YOU OKAY?"

"Yes." I forced my attention back to the woman across from me. "Sorry. I thought I saw someone I knew."

Someone I'd known a long time ago.

I'd been braced to see Zara Vasquez again—this summer, sometime, inevitably—but not tonight. Not like this. Not sitting in Gray's Diner, across from a woman who'd said yes when I'd asked her out, doing my level best to give her the courtesy she deserved.

Victoria lifted one perfectly shaped eyebrow, her glossy lips curving. "Was it a ghost?"

I huffed out a quiet laugh. "No. A friend of the family. From years back." Reaching across the table, I took her hands, her skin warm against mine. "Nothing to worry about. Please—finish your story."

Victoria resumed talking, her voice animated as she picked up where she'd left off. I nodded in the right places and smiled when she smiled, wanting to be present. I owed her that.

She was good company. Lovely, sharp, easy to be with. We'd met a couple months ago on the resort side of my family's ranch. I managed hospitality operations, and she worked in the spa. I usually avoided dating anyone I worked with, but our roles didn't really overlap, so it had felt safe enough to take the chance.

She was great. Beautiful and lively. Amenable. She hadn't complained about a casual dinner at the diner, even if her designer heels looked wildly out of place on the scuffed linoleum.

I should have been paying attention.

Instead, all I could think about was how wide and startled Zara's eyes had been, more than halfway to panic. The way she'd bolted the moment our eyes had met.

Was that how it was going to be? Was she planning to spend the entire summer ducking corners and sprinting for exits to avoid me?

Maybe it would be better if she did.

I smiled at Victoria as she spoke, my gaze drifting to the corner booth. *Our* booth. The one Zara and I had claimed so thoroughly, we'd carved our names into the underside of the table, laughing as if we were doing something scandalous instead of stupid.

"Now it's ours," Zara whispered, eyes shining.

My heart thudded so hard I worried she might hear it. "Gray will kill us if he finds it."

She laughed and kicked my foot under the table. "Tell him it was my idea. I'll take the blame, Maccie."

I shook my head. "No one would ever believe that."

Everyone loved Zara. It was her fifth summer in Wyoming, and each time she showed up, the town became brighter and more alive.

Or maybe that was just me.

She shrugged. "I'm leaving in a couple weeks. What are they going to do, ground me when I'm back in Oregon?"

I nudged her foot with mine. "Do you really need to remind me you're leaving?"

She poked her bottom lip out. "Don't be sad. You know I can't stand it when you're sad. You're only meant to be happy."

"How am I supposed to be happy when my best friend is going to be a thousand miles away?"

I winced inwardly, sure I'd revealed too much. But Zara only smiled, resting her foot fully on top of mine.

"I like when you say I'm your best friend."

Heat rushed to my face. "You know you are."

Her head tilted, that familiar, knowing smile playing on her lips. "Yeah. Besties for life. To the river and back."

"To the river and back," I echoed.

If Gray had ever noticed, he'd never said a word. Not then. Not in all the years after.

Then again, I didn't even know if they were still there.

That summer had been the last time I'd sat in that booth.

And the last time Zara Vasquez had set foot in Sugar Brush.

Nothing had been the same since.

Chapter Five

Zara

By morning, I felt more human than zombie. On my drive out to the ranch, I nibbled on Phoebe's pastries, getting more and more excited about what was to come. I'd be spending the summer working as an outdoor adventure guide for guests at the resort side of the ranch. It was pretty much my dream job.

If only I hadn't spent four years getting my accounting degree and busting my butt to become a licensed CPA.

It wasn't like being an adventure guide was a career, anyway. This was just a summer thing before I found a real job. In an office, at a desk, staring at a computer all day...

I shook off the thought. There was no sense going there now. Not when the sun was shining, horses were grazing at the fence line, and some of the most beautiful country I'd ever seen was outside my window.

I parked in the staff lot and found my new boss's office in the main resort building. I knocked once, then again when I didn't hear anything over the hum of voices somewhere down the hall.

"Come in," a voice called.

I pushed the door open, and Javier Morales rose from behind his desk, gracing me with an easy smile. We'd met through several video calls. On screen, he'd been handsome in a rugged, distinguished way, with salt-and-pepper curls and crinkles around his eyes. In person, he was tall and broad-shouldered, looking like a man who belonged outdoors instead of an office.

"Zara," he said warmly, his Spanish accent faint but unmistakable. "At last, in three dimensions."

I laughed, some of my nerves loosening. "It's nice to finally meet you in person."

He crossed the room and shook my hand. "Welcome to Kelly Ranch. How was your drive?"

"Excruciating," I said honestly. "But I'm glad to be here."

"We're glad to have you."

He gestured for me to sit, but only a few seconds passed before he was on his feet again. "Actually, paperwork can wait. Come. You should see where you'll be working before I bury you in schedules and liability waivers."

We stepped out into the hallway, sunlight pouring through massive windows framing the landscape like art.

"I know you spent time here in the past, but this side of the ranch is more curated than what you're probably used to," Javier said as we walked. "The guests want wilderness—but not too much wilderness. They like to feel brave without actually being uncomfortable."

"I can relate," I said, though I hadn't felt very brave in recent years.

He laughed, a deep, easy sound. "You'll fit in just fine."

Then he showed me the equipment room, where there were neatly organized racks of helmets, harnesses, and neatly coiled ropes, running his hand along one shelf. "You'll be responsible for daily safety checks. We're obsessive here."

"I appreciate that." I eyed the color-coded tags. "I can be safety-obsessed too."

"Good. That's what I like to hear. You'll lead beginner and intermediate hikes most mornings, trail rides three afternoons a week, and rock climbing rotations depending on demand." He pinned me with a serious look. "If you see a guest pushing beyond their limits, you shut it down. I don't care how much they paid."

"I won't hesitate," I said, meaning it. This wasn't my first rodeo. I'd worked at summer camps and as a nature guide in Oregon. The clientele here might've been in a higher tax bracket than I was used to, but I was pretty certain I could handle them.

Outside, he led me along a winding path that dipped toward the river I'd once thought of as *ours*. My and Cormac's. A group of guests passed, laughing, one woman waving enthusiastically at Javier.

"Do you know everyone staying here?"

"I try. People remember how you make them feel, and our guests like to feel important."

We stopped at an overlook, the land dropping away into jagged, uncompromising peaks. It wasn't lush like the forests back home. There was no soft green canopy, no gentle shade. Here, the earth was stripped bare and sun-bleached, only stubborn trees clinging to the soil. Far below, a river cut through like a blade, carving its path without apology.

It was beautiful in its brutality, tugging loose memories of scraped knees, windburned cheeks, and the happiest days of my childhood. I'd been sure those days had been sealed off behind adulthood and responsibility. For a long time, I'd believed I'd never stand here again.

Yet, here I was, boots planted in the hard, craggy dirt, sky stretching endlessly overhead, so blue it almost hurt to look at.

That river...I'd raced to it more times than I could count. Not this section, though. Cormac had taken me to areas only the family ventured to. In the shallow, narrow parts, we'd waded to our knees, splashing one another. Other times, we'd soaked in the natural hot pools. We'd fished and swam and cooled our toes. And some days, when summer had begun to wane and we'd try our best not to count the days until I'd be leaving again, we'd whisper, "To the river and back," as a promise.

"I still can't believe I get paid to be here," I said quietly.

He chuffed. "Probably not enough for all the work you're going to be putting in. You have to love it for it to be worth it."

"I do." I turned to him, determination steeling my spine. "I will."

We continued our tour of the grounds, Javier introducing me to two other guides and pointing out trailheads. By the time we circled back toward the main building, I was past ready to get started.

I followed him to his office and signed the last of the paperwork, my wrist aching by the time we reached the final page. Javier was midsentence, explaining something about schedules, when a light, decisive tap sounded on the door.

"I hope you're finished, Javier," a familiar voice said. "I'm here to steal Zara from you."

I was out of my chair before he could answer, a smile breaking across my face.

Elena Kelly stood in the doorway, elegant and beautiful, her silvery-blond hair swept into a perfect knot at her neck.

"Come here."

The second I was close enough, her arms wrapped around me in a fierce, enveloping hug, squeezing the breath right out of my lungs.

"I'm so glad you're here," she murmured. "*So* glad."

"Me too."

She pulled back, holding me at arm's length, blue eyes sharp and assessing as they swept over me from head to toe. "I can't believe you're a grown woman. Weren't you just a tiny baby?"

I laughed. "Only twenty-six years ago."

Elena and my mother had been best friends during college, and despite living in different states, they'd maintained their friendship all the years since. They'd been present for each other's milestones, cheered for victories, and supported one another through grief and difficult times. At this point, they were family.

Javier lifted his hands in surrender. "I'll release her into your care," he said with a smile. "Zara, take the rest of the day to settle in. We start early tomorrow."

Elena drove us to the family area of the ranch, far from the resort. The guest cottage I'd be living in was tucked behind Elena and Lock's house. Close enough, I wouldn't feel alone, but separate enough for it to feel private.

"It's not much," Elena said as she unlocked the door. "We built it for my parents when we first moved here. After they passed, it's mostly stayed empty, aside from the occasional guest."

"I love it." Dropping my suitcase, I turned in a slow circle.

The space was small and bright, with picture windows everywhere, framing views of the barn in the distance and open land beyond. Months in a beige, forgettable apartment, this was a breath of fresh air.

"It's perfect," I added. "I've been living in the blandest place imaginable. This feels like a gift."

Her gaze softened, just slightly. "You're welcome to stay as long as you like. Even after the summer ends. There's no time limit."

But there was. Already, September loomed, heavy and inevitable. I didn't like how quickly the thought made my stomach dip.

"I know," I said carefully. "But this is just a break."

She huffed a laugh. "If you think Javier is going to make your new job a break, think again, honey. He's fair, but incredibly tough. I've seen his guides dragging their bodies back home after a long day…"

I grinned. "That doesn't scare me. Sounds like the other guides should toughen up."

She tilted her head. "Oh dear, I see your father in that evil little smile. Zadie's sweetness didn't cancel out Amir's black soul, did it?"

I burst out laughing. I knew my dad's past was more than a little checkered, but Elena had been there to witness it up close and personal. "Post-divorce me is trying to get more in touch with that side."

She slipped an arm around my shoulders, drawing me in. "A little grit is good. It keeps your head above water when things get rough." Her voice gentled. "Just don't forget you're allowed to have a tender heart with the people who would never hurt you."

I leaned into her, missing my mom acutely in that moment. "That group feels a lot smaller than I used to think."

She hummed, unconvinced. "You might be surprised."

Then she straightened, crossing the room to the refrigerator. "Now, back to business. I stocked you with a few groceries, but I will not allow you to cook your own dinner your first night here. Get settled. Unpack. I'll see you at five."

My eyebrows shot up, though I wasn't sure why I was surprised Elena was taking charge. She had always been a force of nature. "Five? Okay. Thank you, Elena."

She nodded once, decisive. "Of course. You're always welcome at my table. Don't wait for an invitation. None of my children do."

Lock and Elena Kelly's house hadn't changed much since I was a kid. A few toys were scattered across the living room floor now, evidence of grandchildren, but the bones were the same. Warm and comfortable, the kitchen was still the heart, anchored by the massive table Cormac had once told me was magic.

I arrived right at five, and was greeted by Lock, who was even bigger than I remembered. His arms were tree trunks, and his chest was as broad as the doorway, but he folded me into the gentlest hug before shuffling me into the kitchen where his wife was preparing dinner. Elena didn't stand on ceremony and put me right to work chopping vegetables.

She moved around me, seasoning chicken and checking her rising dough, folding me into the scene like I was a regular guest.

"Is anyone else coming?" I asked.

"It's a crapshoot these days with everyone married with kids. Well, everyone but Maccie. But he's busy with his new girlfriend, so who knows? Maybe he'll settle down soon too." She lifted a shoulder. "I make more than enough, though, just in case. If there are leftovers,

Lock takes them for lunch." She bumped my shoulder with hers. "He won't retire."

I laughed. "My dad won't either."

That made her groan. "Don't I know it. Those two are bad influences on each other. I swear, they're waiting each other out."

Lock wandered over and kissed the side of her head. "Says the woman who still works forty hours a week."

Elena frowned. "Why in the world would *I* retire before *you*? You expect me to sit at home all alone every day? I'd get into so much trouble."

He slipped his arm around her waist, resting his jaw against her temple. "You'd rather us get into trouble together?"

She tipped her head to the side, peering at his scruffy face. "You know very well that's exactly what I want."

"Hmmm." He pressed a kiss to her cheekbone. "I'll think about it."

Feeling like I was intruding on an intimate moment, I dropped my gaze to study the carrot I was chopping, my stomach churning.

Jackson and I had never been like this, even as newlyweds. Even before things had gone so far south we had no hope of bringing them back, I'd known our relationship wasn't right. Not right for me, at least. I had always wanted this type of intimacy—to look at my husband the way my mom did my dad, and Elena did Lock.

I couldn't really remember why I'd settled for him, except he'd asked, and I'd been so sad about so many things, I'd said yes. The night before our wedding, when I'd had too many doubts to ignore, I'd been on the edge of backing out.

Then Cormac had to go activate my stupid, stubborn pride.

If not for overhearing that conversation, I would ha—

"Hey! Is everyone dressed? I'm here."

My knife paused midslice.

As if I'd conjured him by thinking about him for the second time in as many days, Cormac strolled into the kitchen, devastating me right down to my toes.

It wasn't how much older he looked, or how ridiculously handsome he was in his navy-blue suit, or even the way his thick brown waves fell almost to his shoulders.

The moment his pale-blue eyes landed on me, the light vanished, and his easy smile turned off like a switch had been flipped.

All because I was standing in his parents' kitchen.

He couldn't even hide how much he didn't want me here.

I'd never been able to figure out what I'd done to make him hate me this much, but my stupid, stubborn pride had been reactivated.

This summer I'd find out.

Come hell or high water.

Chapter Six
Cormac

The Past...

"It's bad, Maccie."

I gripped the phone, wishing I could shove myself through it so it was her hand I was holding instead. "I'm here. Tell me."

Zara sniffled, her breath shuddering. "They won't tell us the truth. I know they're pretending it's not as dire as it seems. But cancer is bad enough, right? She has to have surgery. Like, right away. And I—"

I heard her panic. I understood it. If it were my mom, I didn't know how I'd handle it. As it was, I was choking back tears. Zadie Vasquez was the nicest woman I'd ever met. She didn't deserve this. But I couldn't get lost in my own feelings. Zara needed me to be strong for her. I had to be the person she could lean on.

"Your dad won't let anything happen to her. He's got the best doctors, doesn't he?"

What did I know? I was almost eighteen and had lived in the same small town my whole life. But I spoke like I knew everything because she needed to hear it. It made me feel better to say it too, even if we both knew it was only wishful thinking.

"Yeah. I think so. He doesn't sleep, and he's always making calls. I think my mom's more worried for him than herself, which is crazy." She let out a wet, humorless laugh. "If she dies, I don't think he'll survive it."

"She's not going to die, Z."

"You don't know that," she whispered.

"I do. I'm sure of it."

She didn't say anything for a long moment then sucked in a ragged breath. "Can you keep talking to me? Tell me something good. Anything, Maccie. Just don't hang up."

"I won't hang up. Promise."

Seeing her shouldn't have hurt like this. It'd been so long, so many years since we were friends...since she was the most important person in the world to me. We'd barely been more than kids, but dear god, I couldn't even pretend seeing Zara wasn't a direct punch to the gut.

I slipped my balled hands in my pockets. "Oh. Hi."

She waved her knife. "Hi, Mac. Long time no see."

Her deep-brown eyes darted over me, away, then back again. She seemed nervous, which didn't sit right on her. Zara had always found a way to fit in wherever she went. Hanging with the ranch hands, charming Gray at the diner, making frat boys trip over themselves on our college campus. Now, she looked like she wasn't sure she was in the right place.

"Yeah. A real long time." *Three years since I watched you marry a man nowhere near worthy of you. Did you see me? Did you care I was there?* I cleared the thickness from my throat. "I guess you're here."

"Seems like it." She looked down at the chopped carrot on the cutting board. "It's still kind of surreal."

Surreal was a good word for it. I never thought I'd be standing in this kitchen, talking to Zara like no time had passed. Yet, here she was, golden in a tank top and cutoff shorts. Purple shadows streaked beneath her eyes, and new lines around her mouth made me think she hadn't gotten enough sleep and had done too much frowning recently.

My dad opened the fridge and peered back at me. "Want a beer, kid?"

Hell yes. Drinking beer in my parents' kitchen was normal. Getting lost staring at the girl I'd been crazy about as a teenager wasn't.

"Sure," I replied.

He glanced at Zara. "You too, sweetheart?"

It took her a beat, but a sweet smile spread across her lips. "Yes, please. I'd love a beer."

I forced myself to move forward, crossing the wood floor to my mother. Her eyes, which matched my own, slid over me. Her mouth was pressed into a tight line as she studied me.

"Hey, Mom."

With a sigh, she opened her arms. "Come here, kid."

She squeezed me a shade too tight, my bones creaking in her embrace, and whispered, "Try, Maccie. Please try."

I froze, my breath getting stuck in my lungs until she hugged me a little harder, forcing it out. I'd never spoken to her about any of this, but she knew. Maybe it was her mom witchcraft, or maybe I had a habit of wearing my heart on my sleeve. Either way, she had always seen right through me.

Sighing, I nodded.

"Okay."

The beer helped. Sitting at the table, getting some distance, even if it was just a few feet, helped even more.

Dad sat down across from me, cradling a beer. "Good day?"

"Busy, like always." I rolled my bottle between my palms. "The Keller party arrived. They kept me on my toes all day."

He grimaced. "Is Mrs. Keller hounding you already?"

"You could say that. She's trying to rope me into going on a trail ride with her." I sighed. "I'll probably relent. I always do."

Some of our guests thought the staff came as part of the exorbitant rates. The Kellers had been coming every summer for the last decade, and Mrs. Keller was...attached to me. She spent more time hanging around the front desk, trying to chat with me, than enjoying the resort's amenities. Fortunately, not all guests were as needy as she was. Otherwise, I'd never get my job done.

"You should take her on one Zara's leading," my mother said. "Check the schedule."

My gaze landed on Zara. She was already looking at me, her brow pinched, and I cocked my head, curious about her expression. I was still wondering why she'd bolted out of Gray's at the sight of me too, but had decided to add that to the stack of things I'd never ask.

The corner of her mouth quirked, and my gut plummeted, reminded too much of the old days, back when summers went way too fast and the time in between crawled.

"Do you remember how to ride?" I asked.

"I do. Riding in Oregon isn't quite the same, but I'm pretty sure I can manage." She grabbed the end of her long ponytail, wrapping the silky black strands around her fingers. "You might want to come along, just to make sure I'm up for the job."

"I'm sure you're up for the job in general. Handling Mrs. Keller is another story. You'll need me there for that."

"Is she terrible?"

"Needy. Very, *very* needy." I set my beer down and rested my elbow on the table, turning my body fully toward her. "The resort is a whole other ball game to the ranch. I hope you're prepared for it."

"I think I'll be okay. I can manage assholes with egos as big as their wallets—especially when I get to be outside all day while doing it." She picked up her beer, peering at me as she took a long pull from the bottle.

I couldn't stop the smile tugging at my mouth. "You used to say you'd live outside if you could."

"That hasn't changed." Her tongue darted out to lick her upper lip. "I just stopped dreaming of that ever happening and accepted my fate as an office drone."

My mom made a disgusted noise. "You're too young to give up your dreams."

Zara laughed. "I feel about a hundred. But I don't think dreaming of spending my life outside is very practical."

"Dreams don't have to be practical." My mom turned on the gas stove and grabbed a pan. "God, how boring would it be if I fantasized about wearing granny panties, eating salad for every meal, and going to bed at a sensible hour? I might as well crawl into my grave."

Dad chuckled. "You'd still be sexy in granny panties."

I closed my eyes, letting out a heavy breath. "Really? Not only is your son here, but we have a guest."

He knocked me on the shoulder with the back of his hand. "Your mom brought up panties. It can't be helped."

"Besides," Mom added, "Zara isn't a guest. She's family."

"I think you guys are sweet," Zara said. "You remind me of my parents, so I'm used to it."

Mom folded her arms. "Thank you, darling. At least someone appreciates having parents who adore each other."

I tossed my hand out. "I appreciate it, I promise. I'd just like to acknowledge it's a little gross sometimes."

Zara's soft burst of laughter drew my eyes straight to her. I hadn't heard that kind of laugh from her in so long. Years, really. The kind where her cheeks flushed and her eyes shone.

She shook her head, bringing her beer back to her lips. "I think we had this exact conversation when we were fifteen."

Dad grunted. "Nice that some things don't change."

"Yeah." Her smile faded slowly as she gazed at me from across the kitchen. "Most do. It's a nice surprise to uncover things that haven't."

My mom put her hand on Zara's shoulder. "The carrots are good, darling. I've got this. Why don't you go sit down and enjoy your beer?"

Since arguing with Elena Kelly was useless, Zara reluctantly crossed the kitchen and took a seat at the table opposite me, her beer clutched in both hands. She leaned back, sliding down in her seat, looking small and tired. So damn tired.

It irritated me more than it should have, but this was all wrong. Everything about the situation: the dark circles under her eyes, my tied tongue...that slightly darker freckle on her cheek—a glaring reminder of the days I spent staring at it, imagining it would be the first place I kissed her.

"You said you've been riding back home?" Dad asked.

"I have." Zara sat up, placing her beer on the table. "I haven't been working the last few months. My career is a mess—actually, my life in general is a mess. The only thing that made sense was to plant my feet in nature. I started hiking again, and that led to getting back to riding. Before I got here, I was going out a few times a week and teaching lessons."

"You stopped hiking?" The words were out of my mouth before I could stop them, but goddamn, I was too surprised to help myself.

"I did." She tucked her hair behind her ear. "I haven't really been myself for a while."

"Good you're in a place you can be you now," Dad said.

"I hope so." Zara offered him a wobbly smile. "When I was explaining to Zane why I wanted to spend my summer here—"

I laughed. "Let me guess—he didn't get it."

"Of course not." Her laugh was breathy and soft. "Zane would build tunnels between every building in Portland to avoid setting foot outside if he could, and if he could have the summer he spent here wiped from his memory, he'd be more than amenable."

Elena feigned a gasp. "I'm so offended. That boy spent more time helping me in my office than he did out on the ranch. I showed him a fabulous time."

Zara snickered. "Those five minutes were too much for him."

I shook my head. "I think the fly fishing was the nail in the coffin for him. He really didn't like having to be *in* the river."

"That didn't help, for sure, but I think it was pretty much everything." She sighed, a content smile tugging at her lips. "But the thing I told him before I left Oregon was I only have happy memories here, so I thought this would be the best place to really begin my fresh start."

Dad raised his beer. "Hear! Hear! To new beginnings."

She clinked her bottle against his. "Cheers to that."

I tipped my beer toward hers. "To making more happy memories."

She hesitated a beat before touching her bottle to mine. "To happy memories."

Happy memories were good. Trouble was, a whole lot of mine centered around her.

Zara yanked my hand, pulling me into the woods. "Come on, Maccie. You're so slow."

"It's raining. Don't you think we should go back?"

She turned to laugh at me, raindrops trailing along her cheeks. "It's the Pacific Northwest. If we stayed inside when it rained, we'd never get fresh air."

She was smiling for the first time this week, so I wasn't going to do anything to ruin it—not when I had to fly home in a few days and leave her here to handle her mom's treatment on her own.

She wasn't really on her own. She had her family, and they were great. But I wouldn't be able to hug her whenever she needed it, and that was going to suck more than I could put into words.

She led me to the old rope swing by the river—the one we weren't supposed to use because someone's cousin had allegedly broken an arm. Slick with rain, the first time I jumped, it slid right out of my hands, dumping me face-first into the mud.

Zara laughed so hard, she clutched her stomach, wheezing, "Oh my god. If someone sees you, they're going to think you're some forest cryptid."

I raised my muddy arms and groaned, coming for her. "I'm the mysterious Mudman of Oregon, haunting the forests."

She yelped when I got too close and ran for the rope, swinging away with a battle cry.

When she swung toward me, I pushed her harder than she expected. She shrieked as the swing arced over the water, rain flying everywhere, her laughter echoing through the trees.

But she didn't let go.

On the walk home, soaked and muddy and breathless, she slid her slippery fingers into mine like it was the most natural thing in the world.

"To the river and back," I whispered.

She looked at me and smiled, but it was tinged with sadness. "To the river and back, Maccie."

And I held on for as long as I could.

The rest of dinner was as painless as it could have been. My parents carried the conversation, asking Zara about Zane's job as a nurse and his husband, Steven, her parents, the job she'd be doing this summer, neatly skirting around Jackson and her old job, as if they'd all silently agreed it was a land mine best left alone.

I didn't contribute much. I mostly watched Zara. Christ, I couldn't help myself.

Seeing Zara like this—close enough to pass the bread, to hear the quiet hitch in her laugh—hit me harder than I'd been prepared for. It was a true mindfuck. There was no other word for it. Everything I'd been convinced had settled a long time ago was scrambling uncomfortably in my chest.

This wasn't supposed to happen.

I was never meant to sit across a table from her again—never meant to catch her eye and have her smile back like nothing had been broken.

Our carved names were going to be smoothed over, just like time had done to the friendship I'd believed was unbreakable.

So why did I feel like I was back on that rope, swinging wildly and out of control, no idea where I'd land?

By the time dinner ended, my skin had grown too tight for me to sit still another second. I made my excuses and left quickly, the need to get out of that room urgent and overwhelming.

Something had cracked open inside me, and though I didn't have a name for it, I was pretty damn sure it couldn't be shut again. At least not while Zara was on the ranch.

I didn't know what that meant, only that I couldn't ignore it. I knew what I had to do, and hesitating or dragging it out wouldn't be fair to anyone.

Chapter Seven

Zara

After my first day at work, I slept better than I had in years. Javier ran a tight ship and used his guides to the fullest, but that wasn't what had knocked me out cold.

It was spending the day in the sunshine, my feet planted in soil that held nothing but good memories. It was smiling until my cheeks ached, getting nuzzled by gorgeous horses, and feeling like I was exactly where I was meant to be. It was peace, heavy and warm, settling into my bones.

My second day was just as good. I joined another guide, Henrik from Germany, to lead guests on a hike and rock climbing. It reminded me of when Cormac would take me out to his favorite scrambles, him standing on the ground, yelling directions at me as I climbed my way up.

"To the right, Z. Keep your foot where it is and reach out with your right hand."

I hugged the face of the boulder, every instinct telling me to get my butt back on the ground. "I don't think I can."

"You can. I've done it a hundred times. Do you really think there's something I can do you can't?" he called.

I squeezed my eyes shut. "You're manipulating me."

"Maybe. Is it working?"

I bit back a smile. "It might be."

"Do it, Zara. Trust me, all right?"

I slowly exhaled and nodded, reaching out my right hand. "I trust you, Maccie."

I'd trusted him so much, I was sure he would have caught me if I'd fallen. For a long time, he had. Even from a distance, he'd been there, arms wide open.

When my mom got sick, he was the only one I wanted to talk to.

He came to visit after her surgery and held me while I cried out all my worries—worries I'd hidden from my dad and Zane. They'd already had more than enough to bear. But never Cormac. And he'd never made me feel like I was a burden.

Cormac had been a once-in-a-lifetime kind of friend.

I wasn't so sure *I'd* been a great friend to him, though. If I had, he wouldn't have said those things about me.

I'd just finished my third day of work, and exhaustion was seeping into my bones. The good kind where I was melting into my couch with my feet kicked up, eating a sandwich, talking to my brother on the phone.

"Ready to come home?" he deadpanned.

I laughed. "Not even close."

He sighed. "I was afraid you'd say that. They're going to get to keep you, aren't they?"

"I told you, this is just for the summer." I was trying not to think about the end, though—especially since it had just started. "By then, I'm sure I'll be longing for fluorescent lights and my computer screen."

He snorted. "Has anyone ever truly longed for either of those things?"

"I'm sure someone has."

I shoved my sandwich into my mouth while Zane told me about a cantankerous patient he'd been dealing with this week. Then he waxed poetic about Steven's lifting gains at the gym.

"It still boggles my mind you married a gym bro."

"Well...he's hot—and he lets me watch him pump iron. What's there to complain about?"

"As long as he doesn't try to get you to join."

He gasped. "Steven would never. *I* would never. We're both perfectly happy with me trotting around on the treadmill every once in a while."

"Oh, is that what you call running three marathons last year—trotting?"

"That was just for fun." He chuckled softly. "You sound happier than I've heard you in a long time."

"I really am." I slouched farther down on the cushions. "It's only been a few days, but I know I made the right choice coming here."

"As much as I protest, I think you did too." He hesitated, then asked, "And Cormac...what's that situation like?"

I groaned. "I don't know. Being here makes me miss him. Then I remember what I heard him say to Jackson...and how he was in college."

"Right."

"But we were such good friends..." I said quietly. "All the memories are flooding back. He was so good to me, Zane. I really thought we'd be best friends for life. Remember when he flew out after Mom's surgery?"

I fell against his chest—fell and fell and fell until he wrapped his long arms around me, stopping me from hitting the ground.

"You're shaking," he murmured, nuzzling my hair.

I tried to shove myself beneath his skin. "I needed you so badly, Maccie."

"I'm here. I've got you."

I shook my head against his chest. "My dad was crying this morning. He was holding my mom's hand, sobbing his guts out. He doesn't—I didn't even know he could cry like that. That can't be good, right? That has to mean something."

"I think it just means he loves her and hates seeing her in pain." He held me tighter. "I think it means he's scared."

"I'm scared too." A shiver ran through me, making me lean into him even harder. "It's less now that you're here."

"Nowhere else I'd rather be," he whispered.

"Of course. You were pretending to be a little badass about it all. Then that boy showed up, and you fell apart, and he caught you." Zane sniffed. "I'd kinda thought there was something there..."

"It wasn't like that."

Once upon a time, I'd thought it might become like that. When we were thirteen and fifteen, fourteen and sixteen, fifteen and seventeen, the two years between us had seemed like a lifetime. But in my dreamy teenage mind, I'd imagined one day our age difference wouldn't matter. Then my mom got sick, and all my hopes narrowed to one thing: her getting well.

"Mmmhmm. Try to work on sounding more convincing next time," Zane teased.

I laughed. "Really. Cormac was a really great friend. Being here is making me face some things I haven't had to, though, and I'm wondering if it was me who screwed us up. I leaned on him a lot—probably too much."

He pulled in a breath through his teeth. "If that's what made him act like a jackass, good riddance."

"I'm not saying it is. I'm saying I don't know. I feel like maybe I was the jackass for never asking him what happened."

"You had a lot going on."

"I did, but...I think I made a mistake letting our friendship die without even putting up a little fight."

Cormac had been starting his junior year at Savage U when I arrived on campus. He had a whole life and friend group, and even though he'd seemed happy to see me and had welcomed me with open arms, I'd wanted to establish my own life too.

Then, Jackson happened.

He'd found me, caught me, kept me, and I hadn't objected to any of it. I'd gotten so swept up in him. Before I knew it, Cormac would barely look at me, and Jackson had become the center of *everything*.

Cormac and Jackson being roommates that first year had only rubbed salt in the wound. I'd started hanging out at their place regularly, and Cormac had made himself scarce. I'd noticed—how could I not have?—but I didn't do or say anything about it.

Seeing where I'd gone wrong was easy.

I'd chosen a new and exciting boy over all my plans for myself and a friendship that had meant the world to me.

"Huh."

"What was that?" Zane asked. "It sounded like a honk."

"No." I rubbed the center of my forehead. "That was me realizing what a craptastic friend I was in college."

"Hmm."

I sat up. "What was *that* sound?"

"Oh, nothing," he replied airily.

"Okay...but normally if I say something bad about myself, you argue with me."

"Only if you're wrong."

Silence stretched thick between us.

"Zane..." I whispered.

"Zara," he sighed. "I wasn't a fan of who you were with Jackson. You turned into a trad-wife zombie. Everything became 'Jackson says.' It made me wonder if there was anything left that was just you. I'd thought I'd lost you."

My chest ached, and I blinked my burning eyes a few times. This didn't feel good to hear, but I needed it. I never wanted to become that person again.

"I'd thought I'd lost myself too."

"And look at you now," he said gently, "being the most Zara you can be. Seeing yourself now, can you even imagine the Zara you were a year ago?"

"She'd be so jealous."

"Hell yes she would. You're doing this thing, baby, and I know you're going to be just fine."

"You think?"

He sighed. "Didn't you hear me? I said I *know*. Trust me. I'm your big brother."

We hung up, and I sat in the quiet, fresh air drifting through the open window. My muscles were sore, my heart felt tender and raw, but underneath it all, a fresh, green bud was breaking free.

I wasn't quite found, but I wasn't lost anymore either.

And maybe some things didn't have to stay broken simply because too much time had passed.

Chapter Eight

Cormac

Mrs. Keller leaned heavily on my arm. "Oh, darling, are you certain we can't share a saddle?"

"I'm very certain. If I could bend the rules, I would," I promised, not meaning it in the least. There was no universe in which I'd willingly share a saddle with this woman, but she didn't need to know that.

She sighed, her long nails clutching my forearm as we strolled toward the barn. "Oh, Cormac, I know you would. You're such a good boy."

"I have every confidence in your ability to handle your horse. You know these trails like the back of your hand."

After a decade of vacationing on the ranch, the Kellers had done every activity available. Mrs. Keller was an accomplished rider, even if she pretended to be a feeble old woman. If she expected anything more than my arm for support, I might've called her on it, but when it came down to it, there were worse fates than entertaining a spoiled guest.

"Well, of course I do." She flicked her hand dismissively. "Riding with you would just be a lot more fun."

"I'll be close. Don't worry."

My eyes landed on Zara outside the barn, and I lost track of what she was saying. Wearing boots, snug jeans, a T-shirt, and cowboy hat, she looked like she belonged right where she was: surrounded by horses and a couple ranch hands, kicking up dust as she checked saddles, the bright sun beating down on her shoulders.

Her skin was a deeper gold than it had been a few days ago, and the purple beneath her eyes had faded. Seemed the sunshine was doing her a world of good.

She lifted her head, turning in our direction, and her brow rose. Then she noticed the woman clinging to me, and the corner of her mouth hitched.

I shrugged, almost sheepish, heat crawling up my neck.

She turned away, but not fast enough for me to miss her laugh.

My gut rocked like a ship in a bottle. What *was* that?

It felt way too familiar. A tease of years gone by, when laughing at each other had been second nature. We weren't there. I didn't know if we ever would be. But damn, getting a glimpse of our past in the curve of her lips was nice.

"Is that your new guide?" Mrs. Keller asked.

"That's Zara. She's new, but she spent a lot of time on the ranch as a kid."

She eyed me with interest. "Oh, that's nice. Were you childhood sweethearts?"

I frowned at her. "What makes you think that?"

She rolled her eyes and patted my arm. "I might be old, but my vision's perfect."

"I'm sorry," I swiped at my brow, "I don't know what you mean."

"Sure, darling." She squeezed my hand then strode toward Zara with purpose, all her earlier wobbliness forgotten. "Hello! I'm here for the trail ride. Which of these beauties is mine?"

I stayed back, letting Zara handle Mrs. Keller. She wasn't having any trouble with her either. Together, they decided which horse she would ride, and by the time she was mounted in her saddle, Mrs. Keller declared Zara would be a perfect match for her son.

Considering George was close to forty, twice divorced, and a raging misogynist, I didn't agree. Turned out I didn't have to worry either. Zara managed to shut it down without breaking a sweat.

Two other men joined our group. The first in jeans that were dark and stiff, like they'd never met dirt, and boots that were new and shiny clean. The other wore a pressed button-down, the sleeves rolled exactly once, creases still sharp. Some of our guests were true outdoorsmen. Others were cosplaying. I suspected these guys were the latter.

Zara moved between the horses, tightening cinches, adjusting stirrups, murmuring low reassurances that had twitching ears and swishing tails settling under her hands.

"All right," she stated, planting herself where everyone could see her. "Helmets are optional, common sense is not. Keep at least a horse length between you and the rider in front of you, and if you need something, let me know."

"I've ridden before," New Boots said, a little too quickly.

Zara smiled at him with patience. "That's nice. This horse hasn't carried *you* before."

Mrs. Keller snorted.

Zara turned to the second man. "You're on Ranger."

He didn't hide his nerves as well. "Is he well-behaved?"

Zara smoothed her hand up Ranger's sleek, black neck. "He's a great horse for beginners. You'll do fine together."

She stopped in front of me then, Dusty shifting impatiently at my side. Her gaze swept over me once, head to boots, assessing.

"You're good, right?"

"I'm good."

She tilted her head. "You're sure? I'm available if you need help getting up."

Mrs. Keller pressed a hand to her chest. "Oh, do let her help. I'd love to see that."

My pride burned, hot and fierce. I might've worn suits most days and didn't get out here as often as I would've liked, but that didn't mean I'd forgotten how to ride.

"I've got it," I said, swinging into the saddle.

I landed cleanly, and Dusty gave a satisfied huff.

Zara grinned up at me, and I was right back in that bottle, getting rocked something fierce. "I guess you do. What do you think about taking up the rear? I don't want to worry about those guys getting lost."

"I can do that."

"Thanks, Maccie." She brushed against my leg as she passed. Whether it was on purpose, I didn't know, but I felt it all the way to my gut.

"Well..." Mrs. Keller said brightly, "you'd make a marvelous daughter-in-law. My son—"

"No thanks," Zara breezed, still smiling.

Mrs. Keller laughed. "Straight to the point. I like that. Don't worry—your message is received."

With everyone settled, Zara stepped up to her own horse. She checked the cinch one last time, swung up smoothly, and settled into the saddle like it was an extension of her body.

"All right," she said, reins loose, posture easy. "Let's go before someone changes their mind."

She nudged her horse forward, dust rising in the sunlight as the line followed.

The trail narrowed as we left the open stretch near the barn, sage and scrub brushing close enough to our boots, the scent rose warm and sharp in the sun. Zara set an easy pace, everyone falling into it.

Even New Boots, who'd started out too stiff in the saddle, relaxed inch by inch as she called back quiet instructions. A reminder to loosen his grip. A suggestion to let his horse pick its way over the rocks instead of fighting it. The other guy had been asking questions every five minutes, but began to peter out, settling into the rhythm of his horse.

Not noticing how natural and self-assured she was at this was impossible. Like she'd been back when we were friends. Before everything changed.

Mrs. Keller rode near the front, chatting away, and Zara handled her with the same ease she did the horses. When Mrs. Keller worried aloud about a narrow pass, Zara talked her through it. When she complained about the sun, Zara pointed out a bend where cottonwoods threw long shadows and promised we'd stop to rest there.

I stayed at the back like she'd asked, keeping an eye on the line, but my attention drifted forward more often than it should have. It drifted to the loose set of her delicate shoulders and to the way she glanced back often enough to make sure everyone was still with her.

How she laughed when one of the guys made a dumb, self-deprecating joke.

I couldn't picture her going back to an office after this. This was what she was meant to be doing. When she was a kid, her plans had always revolved around moving to Wyoming and riding horses all day.

And mine had revolved around her.

Somewhere along the ride, I realized my shoulders had dropped, the tight knot between them unraveling without me noticing, and my constant mental checklist went quiet. For once, there was nothing to manage. Nothing to anticipate.

I just rode.

Zara finally called a short break near a scenic overlook, and everyone stopped without complaint.

Mrs. Keller sighed contentedly. "I could do this all day."

Zara smiled. "Careful. That's how they get you."

"You're lucky to live here."

"Oh, this is temporary." Zara gave her horse a pat. "I have to go back to reality at the end of the summer."

Mrs. Keller clucked her tongue. "If I were young and unencumbered, I'd make this my reality. Unfortunately, I was burdened by motherhood and marriage at a young age, limiting my choices. George is a lovely boy, but he'd never last a minute outside the city. You, dear, can do anything you want."

"It's not that easy," Zara replied.

Mrs. Keller lifted her sunglasses, giving Zara a long look. "Isn't it, though?"

After the ride, a staff member on a golf cart took the guests back to the resort while I stayed behind, intent on helping Zara with the horses.

If I was around her for more than a few fleeting minutes, I figured I could smooth out the feelings twisted up inside me.

She raised a brow, noticing me lingering. "I'm good here."

"I know you are. Thought I'd lend a hand anyway."

Turning from her horse, she faced me. "All right. I'm not going to fight you. You want to help me do my job, have at it."

She handed me Dusty's reins without ceremony, already turning back to loosen her own cinch.

"Can you walk her out first?" she asked over her shoulder. "She sweated more than usual."

I did as told, leading Dusty in a slow circle through the packed dirt, the late afternoon sun warming my back.

When I brought Dusty back, Zara was brushing down her horse. She'd hung her hat on a hook, and beads of sweat dotted her crease-less forehead. Soft music played from a nearby speaker, and every once in a while, Zara's lips moved with the lyrics.

I loosened Dusty's girth and slid the saddle free, muscles remembering the weight. It felt good to be doing this work. Real in a way my days usually weren't. The leather creaked. The air smelled like sweat and hay and sun.

When the silence stretched on and on and on, I decided it was up to me to break it. After all, I'd been the one to start it.

"You were good out there."

She paused, brush hovering. "At the ride?"

"Leading," I corrected. "Everyone listened to you. Even the nervous guy with a thousand questions."

The corner of her mouth lifted. "He relaxed once he realized Ranger wasn't plotting his demise."

"I noticed."

She set the brush down and leaned her forearms on the fence, watching one of the ranch hands lead a horse toward the wash station.

"How are you, Cormac?" she asked.

"I'm all right. It's been a pretty good day." I moved into her line of sight, hitching my hip on a low gate. Her gaze trailed over me, her brow furrowing. "How about you, Zara? How are you?"

Her chest rose and fell with a deep pull of breath. "It's been a pretty good day for me too. All week has. I'm happy to be here."

"Good. That's good." My pulse thudded in my throat. Why was I nervous? I didn't get nervous. "So coming here was the right move then."

"I think so." Her eyes landed on me and stayed for a while before straying back to her horse. "I might be running away. I haven't decided yet."

"When will you know?"

"I'm not sure it matters. I'm here, so whether I'm running away or 'resetting,' as my dad says, the result's the same, you know?" She paused, flicking her gaze at me. "Well...you probably don't know. You've always been pretty sure of what you want."

"That's not true." My fingers dug into my knees hard enough to bruise. "I'm still figuring a lot out."

"Job-wise…"

"Yeah." My chin lifted. "My job is the one sure thing."

"You like it?"

"Most days." I shot her a tight smile. "The Mrs. Kellers of the world keep it interesting."

That earned a soft laugh. "She wasn't as bad as you made her out to be."

"You're right. She's not so bad. I mean, she has the ability to be a pain in the neck, but mostly means well." I folded my arms across my chest. "Except for pushing her son George on you. I didn't like that. If you ever see him, walk the other way."

"Oh?" Her brows lifted. "Is he that terrible?"

"Worse." I grimaced. "He's like Randall on steroids."

My reference to Jackson's asshole brother brought her up short, the brush in her hand forgotten as she blinked rapidly at a spot over my shoulder. I could've kicked myself. We'd been doing so well, dancing around everything that mattered. The conversation was surface level, but at least we were talking.

And goddamn, I'd missed talking to this woman.

"That's…" it was her turn to grimace, "pretty bad. Randall is the worst of them all. Do you know he started a rating system in his frat house?"

"A rating system?"

"Yeah. He made a fancy chart he'd pinned in their meeting room and had all the brothers rate their hookups based on their 'talents' and 'level of attractiveness.' I wasn't supposed to see it. When I did, I threatened Randall's ability to father children if he didn't take it down." Her mouth pinched in disgust. "In hindsight, I should have kicked him where it counted to save the world from his future offspring."

I barked out a laugh. "Christ, yeah. I can't imagine more Randalls running around out there."

"And yet, you were friends with him."

"I wasn't." I shook my head hard. "If anything, we were acquaintances. And only by circumstance."

She waved that away. "It doesn't matter. I'm the one who married into the family, even after knowing the depths of his depravity. Who am I to judge?" She tipped her head to the side. "Actually, I doubt I'll ever truly know how deep his depravity goes, and I'm fine with that. I'd like to forget them all."

"Seems getting some distance this summer was the right move."

I finally got her eyes again. Bottomless, black pools that had once been easy for me to read were now akin to trying to find my way at midnight: dangerous and mysterious, flying blind without a flashlight.

She released a little breath, giving me the barest hint of a smile. "I really hope so."

Chapter Nine

Zara

CORMAC HUNG OUT WITH me while I took care of the horses, pitching in when I asked. He was being nice, just like he'd been during dinner at his parents' house.

It made me sad.

Not that being nice wasn't a good thing. This...stiff formality was another reminder we were strangers now, and that sucked.

Forcing myself to stop caring about him had been a lot easier when he was states away. With him so close, his smooth, easygoing voice melting like warm wax in my ears, long legs pitched out in front of him, no troubles in the world...playing it cool was a lot more difficult.

If he kept this up, I might get mad. And then...and then, and then, and then I might say something I'd regret.

Or maybe I wouldn't regret it. Maybe biting my tongue was what had gotten me here in the first place. Maybe post-divorce Zara was going to say what she thought, and everyone would have to deal with it.

Since that was probably not the best attitude to have at my job, I clamped down hard on my tongue to refrain from screaming, *"What did I ever do to make you hate me so much?"*

After shutting the last stall, I swiped my hands on my jeans and whirled to face Cormac. He'd stood up and moved to the door, leaning his shoulder against the frame, waiting for me. The sky behind him was bright blue, beams of sunshine radiating around him.

It was sick. Absolutely gross and disgusting how handsome he looked doing nothing special at all. The audacity of this man.

"I'm all done." I breezed toward him, intending to barrel right through him if he didn't move. "I need to go check in with Javier, so..."

He shifted aside at the last second, falling into step with me. "I'm headed in the same direction. I'll walk with you."

"You're actually going to your office today?"

He chuckled. "I am. Spending time with guests is part of my job, but not the majority. I'm sure I have a hundred emails waiting in my inbox."

"You didn't have to hang around after the ride."

"I know. I wanted to, though." His arm brushed mine. "I didn't know what having you on the ranch again would be like. It's not like old times."

We were going there. Cormac had always been one to say what was on his mind. In the early days, at least. When we got to college, it seemed like he'd forgotten how to talk to me at all.

I guessed I had too.

"No, it's not," I agreed. "We're all grown up now."

"We are. It's been a long time since we spent our summers together. Things have changed."

"A lot has changed."

"A lot. Yeah. But not everything." He kicked a rock off the path, dirt billowing in its absence. "History doesn't go away because we stop thinking about it, though. It's still there. It happened. Our names are still carved under the table at Gray's."

"Are they?" I peered at him in my periphery. "Have you checked recently?"

"No," he admitted, his shoulders slumping slightly. "But they never replace anything at the diner, so I'm assuming...hoping."

"You've made me curious. I'm going to have to go to Gray's and check."

His gaze slid over the side of my face. "Maybe you'll stay and eat this time."

I turned sharply toward him, my lips parting.

His cheek twitched, and the corner of his mouth rose.

A laugh sputtered out of me. "Are you calling me out, Cormac Kelly?"

"Maybe." That corner kept rising and rising. "When you saw me, you hotfooted it out of there. Might've given a less secure man a complex."

"Oh, shut up." I gave his arm a shove, but he didn't go anywhere. "I'd just driven a thousand miles all by myself. I was *not* prepared for a reunion scene. Plus, you were on a date with your girlfriend. Me interrupting was the last thing you needed."

"Ah. You ran away for my sake."

"Yep. You should be thanking me." I folded my arms and did my best to frown at him. My efforts were thwarted by his stupidly sweet smirk. "Don't look at me like that. I'm trying to be serious."

He huffed a laugh. "Why would you want to go and do that?"

Something light and long-lost filled my chest, bubbling up to my throat. My heart quickened, and my scalp tingled. What was this?

I couldn't put a name to it, except that it was familiar in the same way as catching the scent of childhood out in the wild. Instant nostalgia and floods of memories of laughter, skinned knees, and reckless days so strong and out of place, it was disorienting.

It didn't last any longer than it took to reach the resort, but that was okay. Knowing I could have it, even if only for a little while, made it worth it. It meant I might have it again one day soon.

Cormac held the door for me, laughing at something I'd said about Javier's color-coded clipboard system. The lobby was relatively empty, only a pair of guests sitting together on one of the plush leather couches.

Cormac placed his hand on the center of my back, guiding me toward reception. We drew near the desk, and his pace stuttered.

Melanie, a pretty young brunette, stood, her chin tipped up as she leaned toward the blond woman perched on a stool beside her.

Wait a minute. I recognized this woman from Gray's Diner. This was Cormac's girlfriend—and wow, was she gorgeous. Her blond curls were as perfect as her makeup, and her black suit was tailored within an inch of its life. Elena had mentioned her name.

Victoria.

Cormac drew in a breath, his hand falling from my back.

Victoria straightened when she saw us, her eyes flicking to his face before sliding to me. Any trace of warmth vanished, replaced with something sharp and assessing. Melanie's expression followed suit, her smile going tight at the corners as she took me in, from my dusty boots to sun-warmed cheeks.

What was that about? I'd met Melanie once, and she'd seemed cool. I was rethinking that now. Maybe there was some line between the guides and the inside staff I wasn't aware of. I'd have to ask Henrik about that.

Cormac cleared his throat. "Hello, Melanie. Victoria."

Victoria hopped off the stool. "Hey." Her voice went honey-sweet as she stepped around the desk, moving into his space. She brushed her hand over his chest, settling on his arm. "Can I talk to you for a second?"

"Right now?"

Her lips pursed. "Yes, please."

"Sure. I don't have much time, but I can spare a minute." He took a retreating step and rubbed his nape as he turned to me. "I'll see you later, all right?"

"Of course." I smiled, not sure what was going on. "Thanks for all your help today. I really appreciate it."

Melanie's eyes flicked to my smile, and her hard gaze sharpened. Her gaze slid back to Victoria, and a silent exchange passed between them. I couldn't read it, but it didn't seem particularly kind.

Without looking at me again, Victoria hooked a finger into the belt loop at Cormac's hip and nodded toward the hallway leading to the management offices. "It won't take long."

"All right." He tapped on the desk, pinning Melanie with a look. "Visits with friends need to happen during breaks. Even if guests aren't around, there's always something to do."

She nodded. "Sorry. I—"

He waved her off. "No need to be sorry. Just keep that in mind."

Cormac's eyes darted to me, like he wanted to say something to me too. Then he shook his head, following Victoria without another word.

I watched them go, the familiar line of his shoulders disappearing down the hall with a woman who looked perfect at his side, while I stood there smelling like hay and horses, feeling like I'd wandered somewhere I didn't belong.

Melanie cleared her throat.

"Can I help you with something?" she asked, her tone clipped enough to sting.

I blinked, thrown. The shift was so abrupt, it took me a second to catch up. There must have been an invisible line on the floor I'd missed and crossed without realizing.

"No," I said slowly, searching her face for a clue I wasn't finding. "I'm all set."

I turned and headed for Javier's office, my boots echoing too loudly against the wood floor, my thoughts tangling over themselves. No matter which way I looked at it, I couldn't figure out what any of that interaction had been about.

Deciding it didn't concern me, I shoved it out of my mind.

Chapter Ten

Zara

My first afternoon off, I ventured back to Main Street to do more exploring. After a short stroll and stopping in a few cute little shops, I ended up in Sugar Rush again. For a Sunday afternoon, the place was buzzing, with only a few empty tables.

Phoebe lit up when I made it to the counter to order. "Hey, you. It's good to see your face again."

"You too." I leaned over the counter to brush a kiss on her cheek. "God, you smell good. Do you roll around in sugar in the back?"

She laughed. "That's all natural. It comes from my pores."

"Why do I believe that?" I pushed my hair off my shoulders as I glanced at the bakery case. "What should I order? I'm starving. My stomach is eating itself."

"Trust me to pick a few things?"

"Yes. Please. I have decision fatigue. If you could make some for me, I'd love you forever."

She gasped, one hand flying to her cheek. "You don't already?"

I waved my hand back and forth. "To be honest, it's touch and go."

That made her giggle more. "All right, you. Go find a table. I'll bring something over in a minute."

I reached into my purse for my wallet. "I have to pay."

She rolled her eyes. "No, you don't. Besides, I'm planning on joining you. Your company is payment enough."

I would have argued getting to sit with her would be another treat, but there was a line forming behind me, and I didn't think I'd be able to talk her out of it anyway.

I claimed an empty table near the front window. The next table over, a man appearing to be in his fifties pecked away on his laptop. A group of women were playing some type of card game at the table in front of me, speaking softly. Teen girls were clustered around another table, snickering over something on one of their phones. The door chimed as customers went in and out, not remaining silent very long.

Phoebe appeared a few minutes later, carrying a pink box and two iced coffees. She sat across from me, wiping her hands on her frilly apron, and smiled.

"It seems like your shop is doing really well," I said.

"Oh, it is. It helps to be the only game in town—and that I kind of know what I'm doing." She flipped open the lid of the box. "I've created addicts out of the whole town. They can't resist my baked goods."

I snorted a laugh. "Is that what you're doing with me—giving the first hit for free so I'll keep coming back?"

"Absolutely." She nudged the box closer. "Pick your poison. I put one of almost everything in there. If you want a suggestion, I highly recommend the carrot cake muffin. There's cream cheese frosting inside."

"Sold." I lifted the muffin out of the box, surprised and intrigued by how heavy it was. My mouth was watering so much I could barely peel back the wrapper before taking a massive bite. "Mmm...ungh."

Her brows lifted. "That good?"

"Yunggg." I covered my mouth to muffle my moan. It might've been my hunger speaking, but this was the best thing I'd ever tasted. I took another big bite as soon as I swallowed the first.

Phoebe was more polite, taking delicate nibbles of a chocolate cookie that looked so good I had to stop myself from snatching it from her. Luckily, there was another one in the box.

Once I got a handle on myself and was able to behave like a normal human being, we updated each other on our lives. We'd never fallen out of touch, but it had been a few years since we'd seen each other in person. Phoebe became almost euphoric talking about becoming parents with Deacon. She said he was the sweetest, most protective dad, and Abigail absolutely melted in his arms. She was only slightly jealous of their bond. Mostly, she adored watching them together.

I was slightly jealous hearing how wonderful her life was, but I was able to set aside my feelings about the disaster of my own life and revel in her happiness.

Her soft-brown eyes swept over me. "Please tell me if I'm being insensitive. I only know a little bit about what happened with your marriage, and maybe you don't want to listen to me gushing about mine. You can tell me to shut up at any time."

I reached across the table to squeeze her hand. "First of all, I would never tell you to shut up. Second, if you want to know, all you have to do is ask. It's not a secret."

"Okay..." She rested her chin on her fist, "what happened, Z?"

So much. Yet, when it came down to it, it was pretty simple.

I took a deep breath and launched into the worst decision I'd ever made.

"I married a liar enmeshed with his family. There were no boundaries between Jackson and his brothers—to the point where it was like we were in a four-way marriage. I tricked myself into thinking they were extremely close, like Zane and me, but this was way beyond. We rarely had a second of alone time, and when we did, nothing I shared with him remained private. After we got married, we were supposed to move an hour away from them, but I quickly came to realize that was never going to happen. I don't think Jackson *ever* intended to move and only said it to placate me and get me down the aisle."

Her nose crinkled. "That sounds awful. My family is close too, but they know when to back off."

"Your family is lovely. They're nothing like his." I blew out a breath. "I might have put up with it. Actually, I know I would have. I was determined to make it work no matter what."

She shook her head. "That stubborn streak."

"A mile wide." I smiled ruefully. "No one wants to get divorced, but it's even worse when you're thinking about it on the honeymoon."

"No..." She pushed the bakery box all the way to my side of the table. "You deserve a cookie—or twelve."

I picked out the chocolate one I'd been eyeing and took a bite. It was just as good as I'd imagined.

"We went to an all-inclusive resort in Mexico. It was so pretty and romantic. Then, on day two, Randall and Owen showed up with their parents. Jackson pretended to be surprised, but he'd known they were coming the whole time." I leaned close, whispering, "We had sex *once* that whole week. The rest of the time, he spent getting plastered with his brothers."

Phoebe choked on her iced coffee, her cheeks flushing red. "*One time? And you stuck it out?*"

"Right? Go me. I wish I could tell you it got better. Jackson convinced me to work for the construction business he was starting with Randall and Owen. I had a really good job with a tech firm, but he said he needed me, so I gave it up to run the books for them."

I pressed my fist to my forehead. "I worked for them for a year before I discovered what they were doing. It was a mess, and they'd tangled me in without me knowing. They'd raised money from private investors and were making the company look healthier than it was by counting what wasn't there yet."

Phoebe nodded, listening intently, so I went on, spilling it all.

"I handled the internal books. I didn't have access to the investor accounts. When I finally realized what they were doing, there was no explanation Jackson could have given that would have been enough." My throat thickened as I tried to swallow. "One of the worst parts was he didn't try. He basically shrugged, expecting me to continue playing along. It felt like he'd literally shaken me out of a stupor. And once I was awake, I couldn't force myself back to sleep—my eyes were open to *everything*."

Phoebe fell back in her chair, her lips parted. "Wow. This guy...in what episode does he die?"

I hadn't thought I'd be able to laugh about this, but a big, bright burst of humor rocketed out of me, making all my limbs buzz. A few heads turned in my direction, but Phoebe kept her eyes on me, light filling them as she grinned.

"Maybe in the spinoff," I said. "I'm not his emergency contact anymore, so I don't have to worry about that."

"At least you can joke about it now."

"I honestly didn't know I could, but yeah…" I wrapped my hands around my cup, the condensation cool on my palms. "When I lay it out like that…it's ridiculous. I don't know what I was thinking. I had massive doubts, saw the red flags, yet I still went through with it."

"Even the smartest people can be dumb sometimes. I once dated a guy who turned out to be married. In retrospect, I should have seen the signs, but I kept my blinders on. All you can do is try to forgive yourself and learn from it."

"I'm working on the forgiving part." I broke my cookie in half and brought it to my lips. "But I learned my lesson all too well."

"I bet you did. The bright side is it can only go up from here, right?"

I groaned, rapping my knuckles on the table. "Knock on wood when you make statements like that."

With a laugh, she knocked on the table too. "Sorry. I don't know what I was thinking."

I waved the other half of my cookie. "For another one of these, I'll forgive you."

I was in a good mood after spending time with Phoebe. Carrying my pink box filled with pastries back to my car, I was almost feeling optimistic.

Until I pressed the ignition button…and nothing happened.

Absolute silence.

I gripped the steering wheel, letting my forehead fall against it. This couldn't be good.

It took me a minute to gather myself, then I climbed out of my car and popped the hood. My dad had made sure I knew how to change my oil and a flat tire, but that was as far as my mechanical skills went. I had no clue what I was looking at, only that I couldn't see any glaring problems.

With a groan of frustration, I kicked the front tire. "What good are you, car?" I wound my foot back and kicked it again. "This is your one job, and you can't even do it. I should send you straight to the junkyard."

I geared up for another kick when a roll of laughter broke through the air.

"What did your car do to you?"

Startled, I jerked midswing. My foot caught awkwardly on the pavement, and the world tilted. I let out a small, undignified gasp as I stumbled sideways...

Running straight into solid warmth.

A strong pair of arms wrapped around my waist, stopping my fall just short of disaster. "Whoa, whoa," Cormac said, low and close. "I've got you."

For a heartbeat, I forgot how to breathe.

He gently steadied me on my feet, his hands lingering long enough to make me acutely aware of where they'd been. "Sorry," he added. "Didn't mean to startle you."

My heart was racing like I'd sprinted a mile. I kept my hands on his forearms, partly for balance, partly because I wasn't ready to let go. "Did you really have to show up while I was in the middle of a full-blown temper tantrum?" I asked weakly. "As if I don't have enough to be embarrassed about."

"Nothing embarrassing here." His brow furrowed with concern. "Is something wrong with your car?"

"Yes." I let go of his arms to shove my hair off my face, and he released my waist slowly, like he didn't trust me to stand on my own two feet. Fair, since I'd almost toppled only a minute ago. "It's not starting."

"Hmmm." Hands on his hips, he peered under the hood. I wasn't sure he knew more about cars than I did, but his confident stance and serious expression as he examined its inner workings made him look incredibly competent. "I'm not seeing anything glaring. Did it make a sound when you tried to start it?"

"Silence." I stepped beside him, my arms folded. "That can't be good, right?"

He huffed a quiet laugh. "Usually, yeah. Could be a dead battery. Could be the ignition." He pulled his phone from his pocket. "I'll call Scott. He's closed today, but he can tow it to his shop and take a look tomorrow."

"Oh, you don't have to do that. I can find someone."

His eyes flicked to mine, narrowing a touch. "Someone other than Scott, the guy who owns the only shop in town?"

"I—" My stubbornness flared then fizzled just as quickly. He was helping. There was no reason to fight it. I exhaled. "Thank you for helping me, Maccie."

"Anything you need, Zara." He looked down at his phone, thumb moving over the screen. "You don't even have to ask."

He sounded like he really meant it. And there was a time when I'd believe it with my whole heart.

That may have been a long time ago, but here we were. All grown up, standing toe-to-toe, and Cormac was holding out his hand, just like he used to do.

I still couldn't make sense of this man and the man I'd overheard on the night of my wedding, and looking at my dead car, I wasn't going to be able to solve the mystery today.

I had the rest of the summer for that.

Even as I hoped that would be long enough, I already knew it wouldn't be.

Chapter Eleven

Cormac

ZARA SAT IN MY truck, a sullen expression on her face and a box from Sugar Rush in her lap. I twisted in my seat, looking at her. The freckle on her cheek. The point of her chin. Her eyebrows were different now. Sharper. But her hair still swirled around her face the way she'd always hated and I'd once studied like a treasure map.

Finally, she turned toward me.

"I'm grumpy."

I chuckled. "Yeah. I see that. It sucks your car is making trouble, but Scott'll get it working in no time. Fortunately, you don't need it most of the week."

She wrinkled her nose, blowing out a heavy breath. "I don't need it most days, but I *did* need it today."

I drummed my thumbs on my steering wheel. "Okay. I've got time. Where else do you need to go? I'm glad to take you."

"No." She shook her head. "That's okay. You've already done more than enough."

"All I did was make a phone call. No skin off my back."

A soft laugh puffed from her lips. "You sounded like your dad there."

"That seems to be happening more and more often lately." I shrugged. "There are worse things, right?"

"Your dad is wonderful, so yes, there are far worse things." She pushed her hair behind her shoulders and looked down as she stacked her hands on top of the box. "I'd planned to hit Grocery Barn on the way back to the ranch, but I can ask Javier or Henrik to drive me another day."

"Why?"

"I don't want you going out of your way for me."

"Zara...you just said it yourself, Grocery Barn is on the way back. Plus, I was planning to go myself. I ate crumbs out of the pantry last night. You're lucky you weren't there to see it. *That* was embarrassing."

Her mouth tipped upward as she shook her head again. "Shut up. I absolutely refuse to believe that."

"You don't know my late-night habits. When I get hungry, I get a little feral."

She flipped open the box and held it out to me. "Then you better eat a cookie before you start gnawing on the steering wheel."

I picked out a chocolate chip cookie. "Thanks for looking out for me."

When we got to the grocery store, we each got our own carts. Zara zoomed away from me with barely a backward glance, but I caught up to her in the snack aisle. She was holding two bags of pretzels, her brows knitted in concentration. I pulled up beside her, peering over her shoulder.

"What's the decision-maker?"

She jumped, both bags flying out of her hands. I managed to snatch one out of the air while the other landed in her cart.

I laughed, putting the one in my hand back on the shelf. "I guess that was it—decision made."

She poked my bicep twice. "Stop sneaking up on me. My heart can't take it."

I held up my hands. "All I did was walk up to you. There was no sneaking."

"You're too light on your feet for your own good." She grabbed the bag from her cart and replaced it with the one I'd put back. "I like this brand better."

I raised an eyebrow. "Does it taste like spite?"

She flipped her hair back, a smirk curving her mouth. "My favorite flavor! It fuels me."

I grabbed the same pretzels and tossed them in my cart. "I've always heard spite's a good motivator. Thanks for the suggestion."

She laughed and tried to muffle it with her hand, but I didn't miss it. "Shut up, Maccie. And don't follow me. Grocery shopping is private."

We met up again in the bread section, Zara once again weighing two options. I made sure to make a lot of noise as I approached, reaching around her for my usual brand. I still earned a frown, but nothing went flying this time.

"This store doesn't carry my bread," she muttered.

"I'm going to guess it doesn't carry a lot of what you're used to. People around here like keeping things simple. If you want to order something specific, let Pam know. She'll get it for you."

Her brow crinkled as she looked up at me. "Pam?"

"The manager. My grandmother has her order her favorite chardonnay by the case."

"She does?" Just like that, her brow smoothed, and light glinted off her inky irises. "I haven't even asked how your grandparents are."

"Wily as ever." I rubbed the back of my neck. "I...uh, live with them."

"You do?"

"Yeah. It's a recent event. I was living in town and commuting to the ranch, but in the winter, that can get tricky. They have this big house, and it's just the two of them, so when my grandmother suggested it, I thought, why not? It works well for us. They live on the main floor, and I have the upstairs to myself. Half the time, they're traveling anyway, so—"

"Mac." Zara laid her hand on my chest, and my heart jumped wildly behind it. "You don't have to explain it to me. We lived with my grandfather when I was growing up, remember? If he were still alive, I'd move in with him in a heartbeat."

I cleared the clog out of my throat. "I remember, yeah. A lot of people don't really get it. I should have known you would."

Victoria had been...well, repulsed wouldn't have been too strong a word. I should have called it then. That was pretty much an irreconcilable difference. I'd kept trying, but the writing had been on the wall from the very start. I couldn't say I was disappointed it hadn't worked out. And the way she'd behaved at work this week had only cemented my decision. Ending our short-lived relationship had been the right move—along with my resolve to never date a coworker again.

Zara hit my cart with hers. "Anyway, I'm going to find Pam to ask her to order my bread. Meet you up front?"

"I could come wi—"

She raised her hand, a hint of a smile tracing her lips. "Grocery shopping is private, remember?"

I chuckled, bemused. "All right. I'll just...uh, linger here for a few minutes."

"Perfect."

Zara put up a cursory protest as I took her bags and loaded them into the truck. Then I opened her door for her and waited until she was buckled to close it, and the look she gave me was loaded with something I couldn't pin down. Something like confusion, but that wasn't it. Loss? Maybe...yet that didn't really fit either.

There was a time when I'd thought I could read Zara like a book, but that was years ago. Another life. I had to remember that. We were different people now, with a metric ton of experience and baggage shaping who we'd become.

When we were on our way again, Sugar Brush thinning out behind us, she rubbed her palms along her legs and sighed.

"Pam's nice."

I glanced over. "Yeah. Most people around here are."

"I forgot that—what it's like to know everyone you come in contact with. It's...I don't know if it's comforting or claustrophobic."

"Yeah." I drummed my thumbs on the wheel. "It's a perspective thing. When I was younger, this town felt like an ill-fitting suit—like I couldn't take a full breath or move my limbs properly. Then I went to Savage U, where everyone was a stranger, and missed the hell out of it."

She huffed a soft laugh. "There were no Pams in Savage River, that's for sure. Portland either."

"There's no place like home."

"I've heard that somewhere before." She shifted in her seat, pulling her leg up so she could face me. "Tell me everything that's happened in Sugar Brush the last couple years."

I cocked my head. "Everything? You don't know?"

"Only what I've heard from my parents. I want your version."

"All right." The easiest thing to talk about was my family. They'd been up to a lot. Built lives, found happiness. "All my siblings are parents now. Caleb's got Jesse, of course. He's fifteen and the smartest person I know. Now he's got little Desmond with his wife, Alice, too. If you take a trip to the library, you'll likely meet her. She's the head librarian and knows pretty much every book ever written. She wrote her own series that's finally getting published."

"Wow. That's incredible. Sounds like Caleb landed himself quite the catch."

I had to laugh. "He did, no thanks to himself. He almost screwed it all up by missing what was right in front of him. Fortunately for him, Alice gave him another chance."

She leaned in, elbow on the console, chin on her fist. "Tell me more."

"Hannah got married to Remi a few years back. Have you heard of Remington Town? He left Wyoming to become a pretty well-known conflict photojournalist."

"My mom showed me his books a couple years ago. I recognized a lot of his pictures. He was Caleb's best friend when they were kids, right?"

"Right. When Remi came back after his dad died, he and Hannah got together. None of us saw that coming, but they're perfect for each other. They've got Silas and Brooks. Silas takes after Hannah, as wild as they come. Brooks is a mellow little guy. He just watches his big brother wreak havoc."

I saw her smile in my periphery, soft and unguarded. It settled into me like muscle memory. "God, I can't wait to meet Silas and Brooks. Desmond too. I'm sure he's adorable. Jesse was so cute when he was little. I already know I'm going to love them all."

"Hard not to," I agreed. "I'm sure you'll see them sooner than later, especially if you come over for Sunday dinners."

"I don't want to intrude or wear out my welcome."

"You have to know my parents consider you family, Zara." The words came out easily because they were true. "There's no possible way you could intrude. You could move yourself into their house, and they'd welcome you, no questions asked."

Her hand fell away from her chin, sliding back to her lap. "I kind of did that when I was hired for the summer."

"Pretty sure they offered you the guesthouse."

"*I'm* pretty sure my mother called your mother and asked."

I chuckled. "Proves my point. That's a family thing to do, isn't it?"

The wind picked up as we drove, buffeting the truck just enough to remind me how exposed this land was. There was nowhere to hide out here. I wondered if she felt it too, the way this place stripped you down to the essentials.

"I guess it is. If I had a house, it would be wide open to Zane and Steven's kids."

"Think they'll have any?"

"Oh yeah. Probably not for a while, but for sure. They'll be incredible fathers."

"I see that." I snuck another look at her. "Want me to keep going?"

"Please."

"Phoebe and Deke Slater got married a few years ago and had Abigail. Deke's a carpenter and Joy's nephew. You know, of Joy's Elbow Room. Actually, I don't think you ever went in there."

"I didn't," she replied. "I was too young, but I was always curious."

I nodded. "You'll have to check it out before you go home. It's a dive, but the beers are cold, and the burgers are pretty fantastic. I've been known to win a game or two of pool there."

"I never mastered pool. You'd certainly beat me if we ever played."

The road ahead was straight as an arrow, not another car in sight, the sky stretching wide and pale above us. I let myself look at her longer. Her night-sky hair draped over one shoulder. Her gaze soft and bright as it rested on me.

We'd taken drives like this plenty before. Back when she was too young to have a license, we'd meander down the endless, empty roads outside of town, windows down, dust curling behind us, music blasting so loud it rattled the doors.

Then later, during my visits to Oregon, when things were grim and she needed to get out of her house so badly, she looked seconds away from screaming or bursting. We'd borrow her mom's car and wander unfamiliar roads, rain streaking the windshield, neither of us caring we were lost. All that mattered was we were together, putting distance between us and everything else.

That wasn't what this was.

But it was impossible not to feel the echo of it in my chest.

Instead of bringing it up, I said, "I could teach you."

"Maybe I'll take you up on that." Then she nudged my arm, and the brief contact sent a ridiculous jolt through me. "You told me what your siblings have been up to. What about you?"

"Me? There's not much to tell. I've been working a lot. Last year, I took over as the lead of hospitality operations. That's taken most of my time and attention. You met Mrs. Keller—you can imagine the kind of extra tasks I have to pile on my already full plate. We have a dozen Mrs. Kellers a season."

"I *can* imagine. I know what it's like to get buried by work and not take time for myself. I hope you're at least making time for Victoria."

I jerked so hard the truck drifted over the yellow line, tires humming in protest before I corrected. My heart kicked hard against my ribs. "What?"

She straightened in her seat. "Victoria...your girlfriend. Are you okay? Was I not supposed to know about her? If you're keeping it a secret, her dragging you into your office was probably not the most subtle thing she could have done."

She'd surprised me that day. Her behavior had been out of character and unprofessional. Allowing her an audience had been the only choice I'd had, but I hadn't liked it.

She'd had some vague work thing she'd wanted to discuss—nothing I'd needed to be involved in. Then she'd asked me to have dinner with her.

As friends.

I still wanted to kick myself for allowing our short relationship to happen. I could only blame loneliness and a long dry spell.

"It's not a secret. It's not anything."

"What do you mean?"

I pulled in a deep breath. "We dated for a short time, but it didn't work out."

"Oh." She tapped her fingertips on her knee. "Does she know that? Because it seemed to me—"

"Yes, Zara. She knows."

I was firm but as kind as I could have been with her in my office. We weren't a match. No sense in moving forward with anything, no matter how casual—not when my head was somewhere else.

I wasn't a man who played games like that.

Thinking about one woman while with another wasn't me.

And as long as Zara was here, thinking of anyone else would be impossible.

Some things really never changed.

Chapter Twelve

Zara

THE LAST CLIMBERS HAD just been picked up to head back to the resort, but the sun was nowhere near quitting. My shirt clung to my back, sweat and chalk ground into the fabric, and my forearms trembled as I fed rope through my hands, looping it into neat coils.

I was done guiding for the day, but I still had to organize everything before I could leave. Crash pads were stacked and dragged into place, their vinyl scuffed and warm under my palms. I clipped shoes together, knocked grit from helmets, and put away rope.

I was halfway through looping the last one when Henrik slapped my shoulder.

"We're going to Joy's tonight. Are you coming with us?"

"Who's 'we'?" I asked.

He ticked off a good portion of the guides. "Martina, Nancy, Gregor, Chitra, Mikey, me, *you*...and if we're lucky, Javier will join us."

I had a feeling he'd asked everyone, but those were the only ones he'd snagged. As tired as I was, I understood those who'd bowed out. If he weren't looking at me with his big, puppy dog eyes, I would have begged off too. All I wanted to do was shower off this sweat and dirt and curl up on my couch with a fat sandwich.

But Henrik was convincing.

"It sounds like I don't have a choice."

He cackled, his sweaty blond hair falling away from his deeply tanned face. "That is right. You do not. We'll leave at six. Meet at the bunkhouse."

I tossed the rope at him. "If you finish collecting the rest of the gear, I'll buy your first drink."

"You have a deal, buddy."

Joy's Elbow Room was fantastic. Rugged and a little beat down, but clearly cared for. Life flowed through the worn floorboards, the scuffed oak tables and chairs—the long stretch of lacquered bar lined with vinyl-topped stools, their seams split from years of elbows, boots, and long nights.

Cowboys and ranch hands crowded the bar, hats tipped back, dust clinging to their jeans. This wasn't the kind of place you had to change out of your work clothes to patronize, and I loved that. It made it all more real.

Glowing beer signs hummed against wood-paneled walls, casting soft neon halos over couples tucked into corner tables. An old juke-box played country songs I didn't know all the words to, but recognized anyway. In the back, dartboards bore the scars of questionable aim, and two pool tables sat under hanging lights, felt worn thin but brushed clean.

If I lived in Sugar Brush full time, I would have made this place my haunt. I could picture myself coming here, saying hi to the regulars, picking out a song from the jukebox I'd never heard, learning a few lyrics one verse at a time.

I'd never thought of myself as a bar girl. Jackson and his brothers had regular boys' nights—and days, if we were being honest and true. They'd go out drinking and watching sports, but that had been his thing. I'd had book clubs and coffee shops. Solo shopping trips and binge-watching shows from twenty years ago.

It had been fine. Okay, even. Sometimes, pretty good. I'd never wanted wild nights out on the town in spangly dresses, spending too much on fancy drinks. That wasn't me.

But this?

In another life, this could've been me.

When I got back to Oregon, I'd make Steven and Zane go with me to some divey bars and see if they fit me better. I wasn't going to be complacent about my life anymore.

Henrik placed a tray of shots on our table, snapping me out of my thoughts.

"All right, my friends. No guests were lost, injured, or got dead this week. I call that a success. Let's make a toast the German way."

He held up his shot glass, waiting for us to pick up our own. "We make eye contact. This is very important. If you don't, you'll have one hundred years of bad sex."

A chorus of protests went up as everyone complied. I locked eyes with Chitra, then Nancy, then Henrik, who looked far too pleased with himself. But, hell, I'd already lived through an entire marriage of bad sex; there was no way I wanted to be cursed with more.

Henrik continued. "We clink glasses and say, '*Zum wohl.*' Can you say that?"

We practiced working our mouths around the German phrase until Henrik was satisfied we had it down. Then we all raised our glasses, chanted, *"Zum wohl,"* as we clinked, and tossed back the burning shots of vodka.

Shuddering, I slammed my glass onto the table and picked up my beer, chasing the flames down my esophagus. Henrik laughed at my reaction and plopped down between me and Javier.

"Oh, my friend." He draped his arm on my shoulder. "I did not know you were such a beginner. You will be drunk in no time."

I shoved him off, pinning him with a glare I didn't mean. "I'm not getting drunk tonight."

I'd had half a beer and one shot, and I was already slightly tipsy, but he didn't need to know that.

He hummed, unconvinced. "Okay. If that's what you would like to believe, I will not argue. Come play darts with me. I'm very bad. There is a small chance you can beat me."

I took my beer with me, dropping it on one of the high-top tables near the darts. At first, we followed the rules as best we could, then after the first round, we started making up our own. Chitra and Nancy joined for the blindfolded throwing competition—the blindfold being Henrik's hand, and Gregor and Mikey trampled us during the hand-holding round.

Henrik and I couldn't stop laughing long enough to aim at the board. That might have been due to the second shot he'd fed me, or when he whispered in my ear that he thought Javier was a "Hot and spicy salt-and-pepper daddy." I'd suspected I wasn't Henrik's type from the beginning, but having it confirmed made it easier to be physically close to him and let my guard down.

When we lost yet again, I wrapped my arms around his neck and buried my face in his broad chest. "We should dance now."

"Oh yes." He took me by the waist and dipped me so low my head went fuzzy. "Do you think Javier likes to dance?"

I let my arms fall back as my hair brushed the floor. "I don't know. We can ask him."

He brought me back upright faster than I was ready for. Splotches of pink painted his cheeks.

"No, no. Zara, we can't ask him."

I patted his rosy cheek. "Don't worry, Hen-hen. I won't give you away. Your secret love for our boss is safe with me."

His brow dropped. "It's only a summer crush. You should find one of your own. They make the summer far more fun. How about Gregor? I do not understand half the things he says, but his red hair is very nice."

Gregor had a thick Scottish accent and pretty, flaming-red hair, but I didn't foresee myself falling for him. Not even a little bit.

"Why do I need a summer crush when I've got you?"

His smile spread wide, and he rocked me wildly side to side. "I'm not going to kiss you, my friend."

I snorted a little laugh. "That's the best kind of crush."

"I disagree. I will find you a suitable man who might kiss you." He scanned the bar behind me. "Ah. I've found the perfect guy for you. He looks even better out of a suit."

My reflexes might've been a little slow, but the hairs on the back of my neck immediately stood on end. Henrik spun me and dipped his mouth to my ear, pointing toward the man sitting at a table on the other side of the bar.

Cormac, Caleb, and another man I suspected to be Remington Town were having dinner. Henrik was right, Cormac did look even better in a fitted tee and jeans. The tattoo peeking from beneath the short sleeve of his shirt did even more to add to his appeal, and that wasn't fair. He'd always been beautiful…

But now…

Henrik giggled with maniacal glee and spun me in the other direction, making my already dizzy brain turn like an out-of-control top.

Then he whispered in my ear, "I've decided, Zara. Cormac Kelly is going to be your summer crush."

That made sense. Why should this summer be any different than any of the others I'd spent in Sugar Brush?

Chapter Thirteen

Cormac

By the time the plates hit the table at Joy's Elbow Room, Caleb, Remi, and I had already covered ranch logistics, Remi's latest photography project, and Jesse's upcoming summer camp. Caleb and I had dinners like this regularly—though less often since he'd gotten married and had another kid—with Remi or Deke tagging along when they could.

Caleb had barely touched his burger when he finally wiped his mouth with his napkin and said, almost as an afterthought, "Oh. Forgot to mention, Des is walking now."

I froze, then slowly set my burger down. Remi and I exchanged a look before I barked out a laugh. My brother was an enigma. I'd looked up to him all my life, but there were times—like now—I wasn't sure I'd ever fully understand how his brain worked.

He and Alice had been worried Desmond wasn't walking yet at almost eighteen months. So worried they'd had him evaluated and were gearing up to start therapy.

"You waited until we were half done with our dinner to drop that news?"

Caleb shrugged. "I told you. Does the timing matter?"

Remi slapped him on the shoulder. "Big news, man. We wanna celebrate with you."

"How long's he been walking?" I asked.

Caleb dipped a french fry in ketchup. "Kid got up on his own about a week ago. Saw Jesse playing with his favorite toy, got mad, and decided to do something about it. He waddled across the living room to take it back, and once he saw he could get things done faster walking than crawling, he's been a stumbling, upright little beast ever since."

I blinked at him. "A week? He's been walking a week?"

Remi chuckled under his breath. "A week. Makes sense."

Caleb pulled out his phone, swiped on it with his thumb, and turned it to face us. A video of my nephew started playing, arms raised above his head, sending up a battle cry as he hauled his chunky little body across the living room to get to a laughing Jesse. Jesse caught him and hugged him tight until Desmond wiggled and demanded to be let down so he could stagger around like a tiny, angry drunk.

I grinned at the screen. "That might be the cutest thing I've ever seen. I'm mad you've delayed me from seeing this in person, though."

Caleb took his phone back, tucking it away. "I figured I'd give him some time to get steady before the hordes descend. Wasn't sure he was ready for an audience."

Remi leaned back in his chair, draping an arm over the back. "Please tell me your parents know."

Caleb lowered his chin, giving him a long look. "Alice called them five minutes after she stopped sobbing."

"And they came right over?" Remi asked, though we both already knew the answer.

"They did." Caleb's mouth twitched. "Good thing Des is used to being stared at by a throng of tall people. Kid took it in stride. I think he was curious why everyone was crying, though."

"To be fair, it's a big deal," I said.

Caleb nodded. "It's a big deal, yeah. I'm relieved my wife can put away her worries. I didn't like what it was doing to her when I had no way of fixing it."

Remi smiled knowingly. "Ah, parenting. Put away one worry and another falls in its place."

Caleb grunted. "Give me some time to feel good about where we are."

Remi patted his shoulder again. "Feel good, Cay. You've got two healthy, happy boys and a beautiful wife."

"And two parents who cry tears of joy when their grandkids do something miraculous like walking," I added.

"Yeah," Caleb agreed. "I've got it pretty damn good, don't I?"

I reached for my beer, still smiling as I replayed the video of my nephew in my mind, when a loud burst of laughter cut through the din of conversation.

I turned, taking a closer look at the group I'd vaguely noticed in the back near the darts. A few tables covered in pitchers of beer and shot glasses had been pushed together, and gathered around were faces I recognized. I didn't know all their names, but I spotted Javier talking with a woman who was a guide at the ranch.

Something deep in my stomach shifted as I scanned the rest of the group. Another raucous laugh drew my attention farther back, to a massive blond man who looked more like a Viking than a cowboy. He swayed like a ship in a storm, his cheeks ruddy and eyes like glass.

But he wasn't dancing on his own.

He had Zara by the hands, spinning her out and back in, his laughter carrying as she stumbled into him, breathless and smiling. She laughed too, hair slipping loose from behind her ear, her free hand bracing against his chest as they found the rhythm together.

My chest tightened.

"Isn't that Zara?" Caleb said.

I didn't look at him. Couldn't pull my eyes away.

"Yeah," I said, my voice rough, unfamiliar even to me. "That's her."

"How's that going?"

I shrugged.

Remi glanced back at Zara, then to me and Caleb. "Is there a story there?"

He'd left town before Zara had started spending her summers here, so he'd missed...everything. Not that he would have noticed a little girl ten years younger than him.

"She was a childhood friend," I said. "Her parents went to college with ours. She spent a lot of summers on the ranch."

Caleb filled in the details I hadn't. "She was Mac's first crush. Kid was so smitten he didn't know what to do with himself."

The first few summers, that was true—a crush that faded when summer ended and picked right back up when it returned. Describing what came later that way, however, would have been a lie.

But I didn't need to get into any of that. Not now...or ever. What good would it do?

"We were friends for a long time, then we weren't."

"She got married," Caleb supplied.

Remi raised a brow. "Still married?"

"Nope," Caleb uttered. "Free as a bird, as far as I know. Spending her whole summer on the ranch, just like old times." He eyed me like he could see through me. "Is it, Mac? Like old times?"

I swallowed hard just to sound normal. "No, Cay. It's not like old times at all."

Six Years Ago...

"Hey, man. I'm Jackson."

I took his offered hand, shaking it. "Hey. Cormac. Nice to meet you." I moved back from the door, letting him into the apartment. "Do you need help?"

He dropped an overfilled duffel bag at his feet. "Nah. My brothers will be by with the rest of my stuff later. It's not much, though." He grimaced. "Sorry, I'm not bringing anything to the table. I can go out and buy whatever we need..."

"It's cool. I think we've got it covered. Let me show you your room."

This wasn't how I pictured my junior year of college starting. Tim, Rye, and I were supposed to be sharing this apartment—guys I'd known since we'd all been wet-behind-the-ears freshmen. Then Rye had to do abysmally his last two semesters and get kicked out of school, leaving Tim and me on the hook for a three-bedroom apartment.

That we'd found Jackson had been dumb luck. He'd needed a place to live this year, and we'd needed a third roommate. Kismet. I didn't know the guy, but Tim had met him while I'd been in Wyoming for the summer. He'd declared him cool, so I'd gone with it.

So far, so good.

He dumped his duffel on the stripped mattress and looked around the room. "It'll do."

I chuckled. "It's not fancy, but anything's better than a dorm, right?"

"No question."

I leaned against the doorframe as he started to unpack. "You said you have brothers?"

"Two. Randall and Owen. We're pretty tight."

"Cool. I have a brother and two sisters. We're thick as thieves."

He raised a brow. "Sisters? Will they be coming around?"

Warning bells sounded in the back of my mind. That he'd picked up on the mention of my sisters but had ignored the fact that I had a brother rankled me. But I pushed it away. Last thing I needed was to look for trouble where there wasn't any.

"They're past college age, and both live back in Wyoming."

He whistled. "Wyoming? I've never met anyone from Wyoming. How'd you end up in California?"

"My parents went here. I kind of always knew I wanted to come to Savage U." My phone vibrated in my pocket, alerting me to a text. "One second."

Zara: Hey, Maccie. Guess where I am?

Me: Hmmm…Mars?

Zara: Close. I'm currently sitting on my bed in my very first dorm room.

Me: You're here! Never thought it'd happen. Welcome to college, Z.

Zara: I didn't know if it would happen. But I'm here. I'm really here! Only a few tears were shed when my parents left.

Me: That's surprising.

Zara: They were holding back for my sake. I'm one-hundred-percent sure they had a mental breakdown after they drove away.

Me: Because you did too?

Zara: Oh yes. Definitely. I'm fully recovered now, though.

"Girlfriend?"

I lifted my head, the smile I didn't realize I was wearing slowly slipping off my face. "No. My childhood friend just moved into her dorm. She's a freshman this year."

"Cool. Sorry for assuming. You were just smiling at your phone like it was more than that."

"Zara's just a friend." But I hoped...one day...

"Zara," he repeated. "I like that name."

Distant alarm bells rang again, but I tuned them out. Jackson was being friendly. Curious. It wasn't his fault I was protective of Zara. He'd understand what we were to each other soon.

Me: Hey, do you want to meet up for dinner? It's been a long time since I've seen your face.

Zara: Let's wait a little while, okay? I want to get to know the girls in my dorm and find my way before I start leaning on you too hard.

Me: You could never lean on me too hard.

Zara: I could and have, and you've let me because you're such a good friend, Maccie. We'll hang out soon. Just give me a little time to settle in, all right?

Nothing in me wanted to agree with her. I wanted to tell her she could make friends at the same time we stayed close. But I knew her. When her mind was made up, she wouldn't change it, and pushing would only make her dig her heels in.

Me: All right, Z. Text me whenever. Glad you're here.

Zara: I'll text you soon. Promise.

Chapter Fourteen

Cormac

CALEB AND REMI HAD to get home to their families, but I lingered at the bar, having nowhere to be. It wasn't long before Zara approached, taking the stool next to mine.

I spun my lukewarm beer between my palms. I'd been nursing it for a while. "Hey."

"Hey yourself." Her shoulder brushed mine as she settled onto her seat. She was wobbly and unbalanced, so it took her some time. "I was waiting for you to come say hi to me, but you never did."

"You looked like you were having fun. I didn't want to interrupt."

"Pfft." Her teeth dug into her bottom lip as she blew away my concern with a puff of vodka-scented air. "Why would you think I'd stop having fun if you came over? You could've joined in the fun, Maccie. You seem like you need to have fun."

I chuckled, but it was only surface-level amusement. "You're probably right."

She leaned toward me again, her midnight eyes rounding dangerously. "You know, in all the years we knew each other, we never once danced. I've only known Henrik a few weeks, and he danced with me all night."

"I'm not sure if what you two were doing counts as dancing."

"Ah!" She held up a finger. "You were watching us like a little creeper, but stayed away. Why's that?"

Despite myself, I laughed. Drunk Zara was as cute as she was confrontational.

I'd only seen her drunk once, when her mom was sick and she stole a bottle of rum from her parents' liquor cabinet. I'd stayed sober while she'd drunk herself numb. When I'd brought her home and carried her inside, her dad had been there. Waiting.

Amir's glare pinned me right where I stood. "Did you drink?"

I shook my head. "Not a sip."

"Did you touch her?"

"Never. I would never."

He raised a hand. "I know. Had to ask anyway."

"I know."

His gaze softened as he looked her over, passed out and curled in my arms.

"Oh, baby girl," he whispered, brushing her hair from her face. "You're going to be okay."

"She is," I promised. "I think she just really needed to take a break."

His jaw rippled, and he jerked a nod. "If it gets to be too much for her—for you—I need you to tell me. No matter what."

It had never been too much, though. Not for me.

"We never had a chance to dance," I said.

"No, I guess we didn't. We should've made the chance. That was a real missed opportunity." Her head fell heavy on my shoulder as she sighed. "I'm sorry for calling you a creeper. That wasn't nice of me. I'm feeling a little mean tonight."

"Directed at me?"

"Pretty much. A little at Jackson too. He never took me dancing either. Or even out to bars. He always went drinking with his brothers while I stayed home watching reruns. What kind of life is that, Maccie? I was twenty-three and twiddling my thumbs, waiting for my stupid husband to come home. Why'd I let that happen?"

This was the most I'd ever heard about her life with Jackson, and I wasn't sure if I wanted her to keep talking or never hear her utter his name again.

"It sounds like you're more than a little mad at him."

"It sounds like that, doesn't it?" She picked up my hand and brought it close to her face. Her brow puckered as she studied it. "You have the longest fingers I've ever seen. Did you know that? They're like ten inches long each."

"Maybe not quite that long."

"No, I think they are. We should measure them." She slid her fingertip along my index finger. "Do you have a ruler?"

"Can't say I carry one on me."

"That's a shame." She let out a huff. "Oh well. We'll just have to agree they're ten inches."

"If that makes you happy."

Her head shot up from my shoulder so fast her eyes went fuzzy and unfocused. "I'm not really mad at Jackson anymore. I was for a long time, but now...I'm just mad at myself. I can't even remember why I loved him. He wasn't who I was looking for. Not really."

"Who were you looking for?"

Why'd I ask that? I didn't want to know. The answer would never be what I wanted. Even if it was, even if, by some chance, she'd ever wanted me, she'd married someone else. Had built a life with someone else and cast me out of it.

That fact remained.

And yet...

I couldn't stop being curious about her.

She wouldn't leave my mind. My memories. She was entrenched in my past, stuck deep in my heart, woven into the core of what made me who I was. Impossible to shake off when she was a thousand miles away. Even worse when she was on the stool beside me, her small fingers wrapped around mine.

And she didn't even know. Not any of it.

"Someone like my dad. I don't mean that in a weird way—I mean the way he'd lay down his life for my mom." She made a claw with her free hand, right over her heart. "A lot of people think he's scary, but he's *so* soft with her. Zane and I too. His love is a flannel blanket, and the way he cares for us is like Bubble Wrap. Jackson's love was like...he stuck me in a too-big cardboard box, taped it up, and sent me off, hoping for the best. If things were smooth, I was fine, but if *anything* went slightly off course, I was bouncing around, flipping upside down, ping-ponging off the sides with the tiniest layer of protection."

I nodded. "He was careless."

"Yes." She slapped her hand down on the bar. "Yes. What I can't figure out is why I thought that cardboard box would ever be enough."

"Maybe it was—until it wasn't."

Her lashes brushed the apples of her cheeks as she blinked at me. Green neon reflected off the deep, shiny pools of her eyes. They were hazy but fathomless. And her sadness was there, right at the surface, diluted only by all the alcohol swimming in her blood.

"You're so smart," she said softly. Sadly. "I wish you hadn't stopped speaking to me."

"I didn't stop on purpose. It wasn't a decision I made. We just...burned out."

Her eyelids fluttered closed. "I was swept up and didn't see it coming. One day, you just weren't there anymore."

"Kinda how I felt about you, Zara. You were there, then you were gone." With him. Always, *always* with him.

"Then you hated me."

"No." I curled my fingers tighter around hers. "That isn't true. I've never hated you. Not even for a second."

Furious. Lost. Heartbroken. But hate?

Never.

Not Zara.

Her eyes snapped open. "Then why—"

Heavy arms fell across our shoulders, cutting off whatever she was going to say, and Henrik's face appeared between us.

"Hello, my friends. Enough serious talk. It's time for spinning."

Zara's laugh tinkled. "I don't know. If I start spinning, I might not stop."

"What's the problem?" Henrik pulled her hand from mine. "Come on. I promise to catch you. Or maybe Mr. Kelly will do that job."

She let him pull her off her stool, but reached for me, tugging on my sleeve. "Come on, you. We're long overdue for that dance. No time like the present to make it happen."

We were long overdue for a lot of things.

"Where are we?" Zara murmured against my chest, her eyes cracking the slightest bit.

"Home." I shifted her in my arms and punched in the code on the front door. "You can go back to sleep."

She nuzzled against me, broke through my sternum, and gnawed at my heart. Or maybe it only felt like I'd been flayed open.

"Okay, Mac. I'm pretty tired."

I closed and locked the door behind me. "I know, Zara. I'm tired too." I kicked off my boots and headed up the stairs, her limp body heavy and perfect in my arms.

She'd bounced between Henrik and the other guides, singing to country music and throwing darts like confetti. She'd danced and laughed and drank more while I'd mostly sat and watched. Seeing her happy and free had unraveled some of the knots I'd carried for a long time. And even though I hadn't been the one to make her feel that way, for now, it didn't matter.

We'd danced too—in the loosest definition of the word. By the time she'd grabbed my hands and pulled me toward the jukebox, she was stumbling more than keeping any sort of rhythm.

Still, she'd made me smile. I'd found glimpses of my friend. The way she'd reached for me, and reached for me, and reached for me whenever we parted. Poking me. Slapping her hands right over my heart. Showing me to all her new friends, telling them I was her *first* best friend. The air under her feet, the galaxies in her eyes. Light, light, *light*.

Knowing those parts of her were still there soothed me. Sweetened the bitterness I'd had too long on my tongue.

And at the end of the night, when Zara proclaimed she could dance no more, it had been nothing less than natural for me to scoop her up and carry her to my car.

This was why I'd stayed stone-cold sober, so I could be the one to watch over her and make sure she got home safe. Only in the darkness of my guest bedroom, with Zara tucked under the covers, sighing in her sleep, could I admit that to myself.

I took one last look at her, shadows dancing over her peaceful face, hair like an oil spill across her pillow, then I backed away, quietly closing the door.

In my dark room, under my warm blankets, I blinked at the ceiling. No matter how tired I was, sleep wouldn't come. The deep, visceral ache in my chest was too present. Impossible to breathe through or ignore. It kept me up. Kept me staring at the ceiling.

I rubbed the words carved in ink on my collarbone—a memory attached to my skin—and wondered if this would ever end.

Would it hurt forever?

Tears welled and spilled over, no matter how many times I blinked them back. Streaming along my temples onto my pillow. Silent trails of grief as I lay frozen, unable to move on.

Why the fuck couldn't I move on?

My fingers curled into my sheets, gripping them so hard I wouldn't have been surprised if they were shredded by morning. I was *angry* at myself, the situation and, if I were honest, *her*.

For existing. For being here, in my home, where I'd brought her. For falling for a man who never deserved her. How easily she moved through the world. Through life. Even when she failed and things weren't going her way, she still laughed, danced, and touched.

This was *my* problem, and I hated myself for my anger. I had no right to it. I was the one who couldn't shake these feelings. I'd tried. Had even thought they were fading. Then something would remind me of her—a wedding invitation in the mail. Christmas card from her parents. A song, a meal, the earth, the wind, my home—and she'd be there. I'd remember everything and be right back where I'd started.

She's just a girl, I told myself.

My girl, I argued.

But she wasn't. Not my girl. Never my girl.

Frustration sat heavy in my chest, making my breath short. I was panting, close to clawing off my skin. Was the ceiling falling? Had it moved?

I turned my head, finding the moon out my window. Big and bright, so full, it was nearly bursting. Close enough to touch, but always out of reach.

I sucked in a breath. Sweat beaded along my hairline, and my heart thudded in my ears.

Broad, endless sky. Pinpricks of light scattered through. So many stars, they'd never be counted. In the distance, cattle wandered, their faint and familiar sounds never being anything other than home.

Another breath, this one easier.

Across the hall, she slept. Safe and free from all her troubles. My grandparents were downstairs, tucked away in their bed. My parents down the road one way, my brother and his family the other. Everyone was in their place. Even me.

I closed my eyes, and they stayed that way, even as more tears trickled out.

The weight lifted gradually until I stopped thinking about my next breath.

Not all at once. Not merciful. It was slow. One notch at a time.

I pressed my palm flat against my sternum, over the place she'd smacked earlier, laughing. My heart was still beating too hard, but it was no longer trying to escape.

Just knocking.

Just alive.

You're here.

The moonlight cut a pale rectangle across my floorboards. I traced it with my eyes. The worn knot in the wood near the dresser. The shadow of the oak outside, branches swaying steadily in the summer wind.

The world was not ending.

My lungs figured that out before my head could.

Another breath. Deeper this time. I held it until my lungs stretched uncomfortably then let it go. The tight band around my ribs loosened. The buzzing in my fingertips dulled.

I dragged a hand over my face and rolled to my side, turning fully toward the window. I didn't have to solve anything tonight. I just had to make it to morning.

Life would keep moving, the way it always did. And I would move with it.

Like I always did.

Chapter Fifteen

Zara

Oh, was I ever a fool.

I'd drunk enough last night to wake in absolute misery, but not so much I couldn't remember most of what I'd done. I was in Cormac's guest bedroom. I couldn't quite recall him putting me to bed, but there were snapshots of him carrying me to his car and whispering for me to sleep well burned in my mind.

This was not great.

I sat up, and the room tilted. Breathing deep through my nose, I waited on the edge of the bed until I was mostly certain I wouldn't lose the contents of my stomach.

I was surprised to find my phone charging on the bedside table, along with a bottle of water and painkillers. After checking the time, I poured two pills into my hand and swallowed them along with half the water. As my mind became less hazy, it dawned on me Cormac had done this. He'd plugged in my phone and left the water and medicine.

My throat tightened with a sudden surge of emotion and a deep, unbearable sense of loss. This boy...this man now, had always been good. To me. To everyone. He still was. No matter what had happened to drive us apart years ago, he was still Cormac. And I had missed him more than I ever thought possible.

Another deep breath, and I pushed to my feet, making my way into the en suite bathroom.

Once I'd washed off my smeared makeup and scrubbed my teeth with the toothbrush Cormac had left for me—of *course* he'd left a toothbrush for me—I ventured into the hallway.

If I'd thought I could have gotten away with sneaking out, I might have tried, but voices filtered up from downstairs. A man's deep voice...and a woman's.

My stomach went wobbly again. There was a ninety-seven percent chance that voice belonged to Cormac's grandmother, Lily. As much as I'd love to see her, the circumstances weren't great. At all.

Still, there was no use hiding.

I found a wool cardigan in the guest room closet to cover my sparkly top and wove my tangled hair into a braid. Only then did I tiptoe down the stairs and slowly make my way into the kitchen, following the scent of freshly brewed coffee and cinnamon.

I stopped in the entry, one foot stacked on top of the other. "Good morning."

Cormac's grandfather, Connell, looked up from the plate he was dishing. Still broad and tall. He'd aged since I'd last seen him, but he'd done it well. There was a twinkle in his soft-brown eyes, and his spine was straight as an arrow. His silver hair was neatly combed, and his chambray button-down was tucked into jeans that were probably older than me. His silver belt buckle gleamed at his soft middle, but not shinier than the gold wedding ring on his left hand.

"There she is," he said gruffly. "Good morning, darlin'."

Lily pushed up from their round kitchen table and came toward me with outstretched arms. I nearly choked on tears at the sight of her, so beautiful and healthy and alive. She was in her eighties, but it didn't show. She was so elegant, with skin that looked like it had to feel like velvet, a sleek blond bob that brushed her shoulders, and a pale-gray cashmere lounge set.

"Hello, beautiful," she said, taking my hands in hers. "Cormac said you might not be feeling your best this morning, but you look absolutely stunning."

"Good morning, Lily," I said thickly. "It's so good to see you."

And to my utter mortification, my eyes pricked with tears that did not go unnoticed. Lily sighed and pulled me into a tight hug. My cheek pressed against hers, confirming her skin was as soft as I'd imagined.

Did Cormac have any idea how lucky he was to have his grandparents? My last year of high school and first year of college, I'd lost my grandmother and two grandfathers like dominoes, one after the other, and I still missed them like nothing else.

"I'm so glad you're here, sweetheart," she murmured before pulling back to look me over. "We've missed you on the ranch. Summers haven't been the same without you running around with our Cormac."

"I'm sorry for being weird." I swiped my eyes with the back of my hand. "I'll blame it on the hangover and being really happy to see the two of you."

She waved me off. "Nonsense. You have nothing to apologize for. Come. Sit down. Connell made cinnamon rolls. They're the perfect cure for a hangover. In fact, I'd venture to say they'd cure almost anything."

His chuckle was a roll of thunder. "I wouldn't go that far. Coffee, Zara?"

"Please," I replied. "If it isn't any trouble."

"No trouble." Lily took her seat and directed me to the chair across from hers. "Cormac rarely lets us take care of him these days. He fusses over us like we're *his* children. It's a pleasure to be the ones who fuss."

Connell deposited a steaming mug in front of me and topped off Lily's before bending to kiss her temple.

After I doctored up my coffee and took a few sips, my mind cleared enough to ask, "Is Cormac sleeping?"

"Oh no," Lily answered. "Our boy is an early riser. He's out for a run. He should be back soon, though."

"A run." The thought made my brain hurt. "He's disciplined."

He'd always been that way. Cormac had taught me how to run when I was twelve. We'd started slow, just to the river and back, and had gradually added distance. His legs were twice the length of mine, but he'd stayed by my side the whole way without complaint. I hadn't done a lot of running lately. Maybe this was the summer I'd get back to it.

Just...not when I was hungover.

"He is." Connell placed a gooey cinnamon bun in front of Lily and me before taking the seat at the head of the table. "He has a gym in one of the spare rooms upstairs, but he mostly does his running outside. It's rare he misses a day."

Lily crinkled her nose. "Even in the snow. It's barbaric."

Connell patted her hand. "That's your California showing. Cormac is a Wyoming boy, born and bred. He's heartier stock. Cold weather doesn't slow him down."

Breakfast with Connell and Lily was a delight, despite my tilt-a-whirl stomach and the low throb in my head. The coffee and cinnamon bun helped, but it was their company that really eased me through the morning. They told me about their travels, which were far and wide. They held hands and looked at each other like the secret of the universe was within their connection. And when it came time to ask me about my life, they didn't dance around my divorce. Lily was frank, and Connell was gentle, but by not avoiding it, it became less of a *thing* and just another event in my past.

It made me think of how my own grandparents would have treated me.

If he were alive, my grandpa would have taken me on hikes in our woods to hunt for morels. He'd have let me be quiet with him or talk about anything I wanted.

My grandma would have sat me on the floor in front of her and brushed my hair until I fell asleep with my cheek on her knee.

Granddad might've taken me for a milkshake and a drive. He'd have cussed Jackson out and stood by me while I threw shells into the ocean, giving me space for my anger.

I missed them something fierce, but sitting with Lily and Connell, accepting their brand of comfort, was almost as nice. It wasn't the same—how could it be?—but it settled a little piece of my wobbly insides.

The back door creaked open just as Connell launched into a story about getting stranded in Lisbon. A rush of cool morning air slipped into the kitchen, along with the steady thud of running shoes on the mudroom tile.

I didn't turn at first. I didn't have to look to know it was him.

"Morning," Cormac called, slightly winded.

Then I looked.

That was my first mistake.

He filled the doorway between the mudroom and kitchen, chest rising and falling in slow, controlled pulls of breath. His shirt was twisted and tucked into the back waistband of his black shorts, and a fine sheen of sweat coated his skin, catching the light streaming through the kitchen windows.

His hair was damp and pushed back from his forehead. My gaze followed a droplet sliding from his temple down the side of his neck before disappearing along the ridge of his collarbone.

That was when I saw something I hadn't expected.

Script inked in dark lines. Words I couldn't read from where I was sitting, but they followed his shape. Lower, his bicep flexed as he reached up to drag a hand through his hair, revealing a black-and-gray landscape wrapped around the muscle.

I averted my gaze, very carefully studying my coffee.

"How many miles today?" Lily asked.

"Five," he replied, stepping into the kitchen fully. "It's going to be a beautiful day. The sky is clear."

Clear.

Unlike my head. Why wasn't he putting his shirt on? He definitely should have.

Connell tapped Lily's hand. "Want to take a walk with me?"

"If it's along Main Street and ends with a glass of wine at Joy's, I'd be delighted."

His smile was warm and indulgent. "That's exactly what I had in mind."

Cormac crossed to the sink, the muscles along his side stretching and shifting as he reached up to grab a glass from the cabinet. I swallowed. Hard.

He turned on the tap and filled the glass, then braced one hand on the edge of the sink, drinking it down in long pulls. His throat worked as he swallowed. A bead of water escaped the corner of his mouth, tracking over his sternum.

I absolutely did not follow it with my eyes.

Except I did.

When he finished, he refilled the glass and tipped his head back slightly, eyes closing for a second as he drank. His skin was flushed from exertion, golden and alive. There was a small scar beneath his ribs I didn't remember. And when he turned, he revealed ink stretching across his back. Another tattoo, this one bigger.

Lowering the glass, he finally looked at me, his gaze flicking over my borrowed cardigan, my braid, then my face. Something shifted in his expression. Not quite a smile. Not quite concern.

"You're up," he said.

"I am. Not us up as you, but I'm up," I replied, aiming for breezy and landing somewhere near breathless.

"How're you feeling?" He pushed off the counter, turning to face me fully.

"Alive," I said. "Marginally."

"That's always a good sign."

He stepped closer to the table. I tried not to stare at the tattoo along his collarbone again and failed miserably. I was curious, wanting to know what it said.

"When did you get those?" I asked before I could stop myself.

His brows lifted. "The tattoos?"

Heat flooded my face. "No, the...yes."

Lily hummed into her coffee.

"A few years ago. The one on my arm's for the ranch. My back-piece too."

I glanced at his arm again. Now that he'd said it, the lines resolved into something that looked like the ranch's gate with barbed wire threaded around it.

"And the words?"

He lifted his hand to his collarbone, fingers brushing below the ink.

"A reminder," he stated simply before pulling his T-shirt from his waistband and tugging it over his head.

Lily pushed her chair back. "Connell, darling, didn't you say you wanted to show me that article about that vineyard in Argentina?"

Connell stood immediately. "I did."

They couldn't have been more obvious as they made a swift exit, sneaky little smiles on their faces. It was adorable and sweet and made my chest pang for my own grandparents once again.

When we were alone, Cormac slowly exhaled. "You don't have to look like you're about to bolt."

"I'm not."

"You keep eyeing the door."

So I don't look at you...and your muscles...and all the changes I wasn't around to see happen.

"You took care of me last night," I said softly.

His jaw flexed. "Yeah."

"Thank you."

"Zara." My name sounded different. Deeper. Rougher around the edges. "You don't ever have to thank me for that."

My heart gave an unsteady thud.

"I should, um"—I gestured vaguely toward the hallway—"let you shower."

The corner of his mouth tipped up. "Probably a good call."

He stepped closer as he moved past me, the heat of his body brushing my arm. My breath caught, and he paused at the edge of the kitchen, looking back.

"Once I'm dressed, I'll drive you to the guesthouse, then we can go pick your car up from Scott."

"You don't have to."

"I know I don't," he replied. "I'm going to, though."

"I'm not going to argue with you."

He nodded. "Good. It'd be a waste of time." His gaze dropped briefly to my mouth before returning to my eyes. There and gone. "I'm glad you're here."

Then he disappeared down the hall, and I found myself staring at the doorway long after he was gone, my pulse fluttering in my throat.

I'm glad I'm here too.

Chapter Sixteen
Cormac

ZARA LEANED HER HEAD against the passenger window, her golden legs stretched in front of her, fingers tapping to the rhythm of the road. The sunlight caught in the fine hairs on her thighs, and I had to drag my eyes back to the highway before they lingered too long.

She didn't seem to be in the mood to talk, and that was fine by me. After last night, I was stuck in my head. The run had helped burn off some of the edge, but sitting in the truck beside the source of my internal upheaval had brought me right back to where I'd started.

That always seemed to be the case around Zara.

Out of nowhere, she said, "You know, you never told me."

I raised a brow, glancing from the road to her, trying to read her profile. "Told you what?"

"What you were doing in town last weekend, when you found me making a complete fool of myself in public."

"Ah. When you were beating up your car." I drummed my thumbs on the wheel. "I was headed to Sugar Rush."

She sat up, turning toward me. "But...I'd just come from there."

"Right..."

"That means you couldn't have gone there. I would have seen you."

"I ran into you before I made it," I explained.

Her mouth parted, and a little puff of air blew out. "Mac"—she huffed, indignant—"I screwed up your plans. You didn't get to see Phoebe."

I shrugged off her concern. "Not a big deal. I see her pretty often. Your situation seemed more dire than my need for a muffin. Plus, I ended up with a cookie anyway, so I can't complain."

She smacked my arm, but it landed as light as a butterfly. "That's it. After we get my car, we're going to Sugar Rush and I'm buying you whatever you want. The whole pastry case is yours. Well, unless there are Danishes...or have your feelings about Danishes changed?"

"They haven't changed, and that's not necessary."

"Yes, it is. You rescued me last weekend, then last night, and you're doing it again today. I'm going to start feeling pitiful if you don't let me do something for you."

Zara's stubborn streak still ran as strong as it always had. If I tried to deny her, she'd dig her heels in and wind up winning in the long run. Since I was in no mood to argue—especially when I already knew the outcome—I took the path of least resistance.

"All right. We'll do things your way."

My sister was a little too thrilled to see Zara and me arriving together. She didn't know everything. No one did. But she'd been around for the height of our friendship...and had seen the aftermath of the ending. It came as no surprise she would think we were mending fences.

And maybe we were.

Zara ordered damn near one of everything and insisted she'd pay for my coffee. At that, I'd made a lame attempt at arguing, but only because I knew I'd lose and she'd feel good about winning.

Her victorious little dance and smile had made it worth it.

While we waited for our order, Phoebe kept darting glances at us. I couldn't begin to imagine what she thought she was seeing, but if it was anything other than a hungover woman and a man so emotionally raw it *felt* like a hangover, she wasn't seeing us.

With no open tables, we took our drinks and box of pastries out to my truck without much discussion. Zara closed her eyes as she sucked down her latte, and I flipped the box open, claiming the carrot cake muffin I'd been craving for a week.

Zara opened her eyes and turned toward me. "I haven't been drunk like that since college."

I pressed my thumb down on my leg, gathering the crumbs I'd dropped. "It's always fun while it lasts."

Her mouth curved as her eyes went hazy. "It was a really good night. I'm glad you were there. We haven't had fun together in a long time."

"You were having plenty of fun without me."

"I was. Henrik is a big, lovable oaf. I'm pretty sure it's impossible not to have fun when he's there." Tucking her leg under her, she leaned across the console like she was sharing a secret. "Don't tell anyone, but he has a crush on Javier. He called him a hot and spicy salt-and-pepper daddy."

I sputtered a laugh. "Oh, that's rich. Did he say that to Javier's face?"

"No, no, no." She covered her giggle with her hand. "Only to me, which is why you can't repeat it. Henrik would die, and Javier probably would too."

I cocked my head. "Maybe he'd like it. You never know."

"True." She grinned, and I did too. "You never know that side of people. Javier could be a total daddy."

I leaned back against my door and folded my arms, considering it. "I see it. I don't necessarily want to, but I do."

"Exactly." She examined the contents of the pastry box, picking out a lemon bar after some consideration. "Closed doors are a great thing."

I laughed softly. "They are. It's okay to have some questions unanswered."

"Sure. I guess that's true." There was doubt behind her words, and for a beat, her mouth opened, like she had more to say. Then she closed it, shaking her head, and took a bite of her lemon bar.

"Good?" I asked.

"Mmmhmm." She wiggled in her seat, a little happy dance of pleasure. The move was so Zara, I couldn't stop myself from smiling.

"You're doing your dance."

She went still and looked down at herself. "I was?"

That made me laugh. "You didn't notice?"

"Not at all." Her teeth dug into the bottom curve of her grin. "Leave it to you not to miss anything."

"Anyone who spends any time with you would notice." While that was probably true, it was a deflection. There wasn't much about Zara I didn't notice and catalog. It was how it had been when we were younger, and I guessed it still was that way.

She hummed softly and changed the subject. "Your grandparents seem like they're doing really well."

"They are." I scrubbed my hand along the scruff I hadn't bothered shaving this morning. "As far as I'm concerned, they're immortal."

She flinched, and I felt like an asshole. I'd never known anyone else as close to their grandparents besides Zara. I got that flinch. Felt it deep in my chest.

"Wouldn't that be nice?" she said softly.

"I try not to think about the alternative."

The Past...

Zara's name lit up my phone for the second time. I looked around, searching through the throngs of people for a place I'd be able to hear her. Finally, I set down my beer and headed outside. By the time I'd found somewhere, the call had dropped, so I dialed her back.

"Maccie," she gasped.

My heart stilled. "Your mom?"

"No. My-my-my grandma's dead."

"Shit." I fell back on the porch step, wishing like hell I was more sober. "Oh god, Zara. I'm so sorry."

"She wasn't sick. I don't know—how, Maccie? How can she just be gone? My mom needs her. God, how's my mom going to deal!"

My head was spinning. I hadn't even wanted to come to this party. It had been Tim's idea. I should have been home and sober, so I could think clearly, but he'd made the point that I'd done that all freshman year and needed to live a little this year, and I'd let myself be convinced.

Zara cried and cried, and my heart broke. There was nothing I could do. She needed a hug. Why wasn't someone holding her? Where was Zane? Her dad?

Without warning, the door to the house opened, and a few bodies spilled out. Someone yelled my name. Elbows and knees bumped into me. I nearly lost my grip on the phone.

"Where are you?" Zara asked, her voice wobbly.

"Nowhere important. I want to talk to you."

"Maccie!" Tim called from the side yard. "Get your pretty cowboy ass over here. Kayla misses you."

I groaned. "Look, I'm going to—"

"No, I'm sorry for calling so late. Of course you're busy. It's fine. I need to go be with my mom anyway."

"I'm here, Zara," I rushed out. "Talk to me."

"I have to go. We'll talk tomorrow, okay?"

And she was gone before I could say anything else.

Both of us went quiet. Any minute, I expected her to climb out of my truck and get into her car, but she stayed, looking out the window, sipping her coffee. Having nowhere to be, I let myself relax as best I could.

Zara's breath got stuck in her throat, and she sat up straight, her brow furrowed as she studied me.

"You okay?"

"Yes." She nodded a few times. "I need to ask you something."

"All right. Ask me anything you want." I might not have liked the question, but if she wanted answers, I'd give them to her.

"While I agree it's best to leave some questions unanswered, I can't let this one go. Last night, you said you never hated me. Not once."

"That's true."

She looked down at her hands clenched in her lap, her shoulders rising as she sucked in a deep breath. When she let it out, she raised her head, pinning her dark eyes on me, accusation and hurt swirling in them.

"Then why did you try to talk Jackson out of marrying me the night before our wedding?"

For a second, I didn't understand.

The words hit my ears, but my brain refused to process them.

I stared at her, certain I'd misheard.

"I—" My throat closed, and I swallowed, but it didn't help. "What?"

How could she know about that night?

Chapter Seventeen

Zara

I HADN'T PLANNED ON asking him that. Long ago, I'd decided to let it be the punctuation at the bitter end of our friendship.

But that was before spending time with Cormac these last few weeks and finding out he was still the same guy he used to be. So sweet and tender, funny and kind. He'd bend over backward without a second thought. Even after everything, he'd dropped everything to help me last weekend. Last night. Today.

I didn't know how to reconcile the things I'd overheard him saying with the man in front of me.

And from his befuddled expression, he didn't understand what I was asking.

"I was there that night. Outside." My heart thudded, and I pressed my hand against my chest. When that didn't work, when it seemed like it was trying to beat its way out, I stacked my other hand on top. "I couldn't sleep, and I was having doubts. Cold feet, I guess. I snuck out of my parents' house and ran to the house Jackson was staying at with his brothers. I thought if I saw him, he'd remind me why we were getting married. He'd calm my nerves, hold me for a while, and I'd be okay. When I got there, he was out on the porch with Randall and Owen, so I...well, I eavesdropped."

As I spoke, the pinched muscles in Cormac's face went slack little by little until understanding struck. Then he jolted like he'd been shocked, his body folding in on itself, chin dropping to his chest.

"He'd texted, asking me to come over for a drink." He rubbed his cheek, eyes sliding to the side to stare blankly out the window. "They were drunk when I got there, reminiscing about college."

"When I showed up, you were telling him you were concerned about him. You were trying to talk him out of marrying me, Mac."

It still hurt. Even if, in hindsight, it would have been a favor if Jackson had listened to him—if he'd stood me up at the altar instead of saying vows he hadn't meant to keep.

Cormac's brow furrowed. "I don't remember the conversation exactly, but I think I said how things were going to be different now, with you two getting married. The brothers thought that was funny. Jackson seemed to think you'd give him free rein, just like in college. He—"

He stopped himself, his worried gaze dragging up to mine.

"Just tell me all of it."

"It's not nice," he said carefully, eyeing me like a wounded bird.

"I need to know." My hands were balled tight, nails digging into my palms. "I have to, Mac. Say it."

He tipped his head back, taking a great, deep breath. When he spoke, his words were measured and slow, each one intentional, to cause the least amount of damage. Because that was who he was. That was Mac.

Something I'd let myself forget because it was easier that way.

"I don't know what he got up to in college. Not anything concrete, at least. There were rumors, but I'd never seen anything myself.

If I had, if I'd had any sort of evidence, I would have told you, even if you would've hated me after."

My nails dug in harder. "He was cheating?"

His throat bobbed as he swallowed hard. "It's what I heard. I don't know for sure, Zara. You know what it was like on that campus. Word traveled and got distorted. I can't say with confidence he did the things they said, but it wouldn't surprise me."

"Okay." I nodded, blinking back tears. That shouldn't have been such a sharp jab to the gut. Jackson and I were long over. I'd come to terms with him not being a good man. But...I thought...well, I really hadn't known. I'd never guessed. I should have. In retrospect, I should have seen it. "I feel pretty dumb for having no idea. He did a lot of things I didn't like, but I never thought that was one of them."

"It might have only been rumors," he said softly.

I shuddered, looking up at him. "But it probably wasn't. And the night before our wedding, he was bragging to you and his brothers about continuing his college ways?"

"Basically, yeah." He dragged his fingers through the side of his hair, tucking a lock behind his ear. "I tried, Zara. I thought if I framed my objections as concern for him—that *he'd* be unhappy—he might've listened. It was a long shot, but I really did try. It gutted me to think about you being married to a man who didn't deserve you."

It took me a long time to find the words I wanted to say. Cormac had flipped everything I thought I knew upside down. How had I gotten things so very mixed up?

"I don't think I wanted to see it," I finally said. "I felt like I was losing, and losing, and *losing*. I'd already leaned far too heavily on you, so I'd decided to hold on to him as tight as I could instead. For a while, he really was good to me. Things hadn't changed until I was in so deep I couldn't tell up from down."

"You had some rough years. I don't blame you for seeing him like a life raft, but I promise, you never leaned too heavily on me. That was never a thought in my mind."

"I know that now…I'm not sure I was exactly rational back then." I blinked at him through wet eyes. "How can you not blame me? After everything…"

He sighed, long and rough. "You were really young, Zara, and you'd been dealt a crappy hand. I would have never have picked Jackson for you, but I could see why he appealed to you back then. He worked to land you and keep you. You got all his time and attention. That had to have felt good."

"It did. Of course it did."

"He sure as hell was pleased with himself," he muttered, an edge of bitterness lacing his words.

"What does that mean?"

His jaw rippled then relaxed. "I think it was like a game to him, winning you. Not that he didn't have real feelings, but I'm pretty sure that's how it started."

"Why am I not surprised? He loved nothing more than winning." I let my head fall back on the rest. "There must be something about that man for you to have been friends with him…for me to have fallen for him."

"We weren't ever friends."

I raised my head. "What do you mean? You lived with him."

"By chance. Tim and I needed a third roommate last minute, and he stepped in. We weren't friends, Zara."

"But he..." I shook my head, trying to clear my jumbled thoughts. "When we met in class, he said you'd told him all about me."

Cormac turned his head, staring out the window. The corner of his jaw twitched, and his hands rubbed back and forth over his jeans.

"The day he moved into the apartment, you texted me. I guess I was smiling at my phone because he asked about it. All I gave him was your name and that you were my best friend."

"And then he found me," I whispered, filling in the rest. "He sat down beside me in class, and when I told him my name, he was almost giddy. I thought it was because he liked me. But...it was because he knew I was yours...and he—"

"You weren't mine," he bit out, then slowly exhaled. Facing me again, he nodded. "I don't know what went on in his mind. I'm going to guess meeting you was a coincidence, but going after you once he did was a calculated effort."

I groaned, covering my face with my hands. "God, I wasted so much time with him, and for what—a game? I'm a real idiot."

"Hey. You aren't." He reached across the cab and gently squeezed my shoulder. "I don't doubt he loved you. How could he not?"

The words were soft. Earnest.

And they wrecked me.

Without thinking, I tilted my head and brushed my cheek against his wrist, chasing the comfort the way I used to when we were teenagers and the world felt too sharp. His skin was warm and familiar.

"I can't believe you're still defending me," I said. "After everything."

His hand stilled on my shoulder.

"That's really, really sweet of you to say," I went on, my voice wobbling despite my attempt to steady it, "but it's okay to admit I was stupid."

He huffed out a breath, pulling his hand back. Not abrupt but deliberate, and the loss was immediate. Despite the day's heat shining through the windows, cold air rushed in where he'd been.

"Don't think you'll ever hear me saying that."

I studied him. The way he shifted toward the door. The way his shoulders squared, like he was bracing against something—against *me*.

A slow, nauseating realization began to bloom in my chest.

All those years, I'd carried this version of him in my head that had been entirely fabricated. I'd made up this whole story of being such a terrible friend to him, I'd caused him to hate me so much he'd tried to sabotage my wedding.

That wasn't what had happened.

Not even close.

He'd been trying to protect me.

And I'd chosen Jackson anyway.

"I'm sorry." But the words felt too small for the weight of what I'd done. "For believing the worst about you. For shutting you out. For"—my throat closed—"not even asking."

He gave me a sharp nod. "It's water under the bridge now."

It wasn't. I could see that. Water under the bridge wouldn't have made him withdraw from me, and the space between us felt as barren as the Arctic. As icy too.

"It doesn't feel like it," I said quietly.

"Look," he said, his voice rougher now, "I'm glad we cleared the air. It's good for both of us." He turned the key in the ignition, and even though I wasn't ready to leave yet, the engine roared to life. "Makes it easier to move on."

Move on.

The words hit harder than anything else.

Moving on from Cormac Kelly was the last thing I wanted to do.

I'd just found him again.

Zane and Steven's faces crowded the screen of my laptop, looking so concerned and breathtakingly sweet, my stomach panged from how much I missed them. They'd just patiently listened to me spill my guts for the last ten minutes. I'd hoped to find some clarity after my conversation with Cormac, but I still had no idea what to do next.

"You apologized, right?" Zane pressed.

Steven looked at him and huffed. "Do you really need to ask? Of course she did."

Zane raised an eyebrow. "She really doesn't like to admit she's wrong, so yes, I do have to ask."

Steven turned back to me. "You apologized, didn't you?"

"I did." I scrunched my nose. "Though I don't think it was as profuse as it should have been considering how very wrong I was."

Steven was the first to try to let me off the hook. "The fact is, Cormac didn't actually know how angry you were at him."

"That's a good point, honey," Zane said. "Really, you should be apologizing to me. I told you that really didn't sound like Cormac, and you told me to shut my big fat mouth."

I narrowed my eyes. "I don't think those were my exact words."

He brushed me off. "It was something like that. We don't have to argue semantics."

"I think we do. Your mouth is perfectly sized, and I'd never say otherwise."

Steven scoffed. "You're both getting way off topic, but that's no surprise with you two."

Zane leaned his head against Steven's. "We're a delight. Just admit it."

Steven kissed his temple. "You are. I would never argue that point. And Zara's right. Your mouth is perfect."

I groaned. "Please, guys. I can't take another second of you being disgustingly in love. It's not the time."

Zane straightened, putting his game face on. "All right. We're here. Tell us what you need from us."

"I don't know. I feel really unsettled, and I want..." I trailed off, my gaze wandering to the window. In the distance, I could see Cormac's house, and I wondered if he was inside. If he'd gone home after our talk. If he was going over everything we'd said in his mind or discussing it with his grandparents. If he'd set it all aside and gone on with his day like nothing had happened...

Steven leaned closer to the camera. "What do you want, Zara?"

Deep down, I knew exactly what I wanted. It felt dangerous to wish for it, let alone to say it aloud, but denying myself would get me exactly nowhere.

So, I said it.

"I want my friend back."

And whatever comes with it.

Chapter Eighteen

Zara

After meeting with Javier to go over the week's schedule and discuss a few staff changes, I found myself knocking on Cormac's office door.

I had no plan. Despite my long talk with Steven and Zane yesterday, I just really wanted to see him.

His muffled voice called, "Come in."

I pushed the door open and stuck my head inside. "Hey."

He masked his surprise well, but I didn't miss the jerk of his shoulders. "Hey to you."

I slipped into his office, shutting the door behind me, and leaned against it. "Busy day?"

Sighing, he clicked his mouse a few times. "Always, but especially this time of year. You're not busy?"

"No, I am. I just finished meeting with Javier. He asked me to help him rework some things on the schedule." I cupped my hands over my mouth like I was telling him a secret. "And it was difficult to look at him without wondering if he's a spicy daddy."

Cormac snorted a laugh. "I had the same problem when I saw him this morning. Please thank Henrik for ruining my working relationship with him."

I saluted him. "I'm on it. I already put him on the kids' hike for the week—his nightmare."

His brow dropped with worry. "Maybe we shouldn't put him in charge of children..."

"Don't worry. He's astonishingly good with them *because* he's frightened of them. He practically backflips to keep them entertained and happy so they don't chew his face off. Besides, a little exposure therapy will do him some good. Maybe."

He chuckled softly, shaking his head. "It sounds like you're helping Javier out."

"Yeah...he can't get out there as much as he'd like. He had knee surgery in the spring, and things aren't as healed as he expected. I offered to pick up the slack since I'm the most familiar with the ranch and have gotten to know the strengths and weaknesses of all the guides."

"It's not too much?"

"No." His concern sent a little curl of delight through me. "It's not too much at all. I like that he trusts me, and making spreadsheets has always been my cup of tea."

"No one has ever said that."

I pointed to myself. "Besides me. I said it."

His mouth quirked, and I was so relieved to see it I could have burst. The way we'd parted yesterday had been heavy. Too heavy. I still had hope we could somehow find our way back to...well, not the way we used to be, but something that resembled it, though.

"So, Zara, what brings you by? Just saying hello?"

"I found I couldn't walk by your office without seeing your face." I pushed off the door and moved closer, stepping around the chairs in front of his desk. "Can I make you dinner tonight?"

He leaned back in his chair, tilting his head to look up at me. "Do you know how to cook?"

I rolled my eyes. "It would be awfully cruel of me to invite you over for dinner and expect you to cook it. *Yes*, Cormac, I know how to cook. You've eaten my mother's cooking plenty of times. I learned from the best."

When he didn't answer right away, I braced myself for rejection. In truth, I probably deserved it. I wouldn't have blamed him for wanting nothing to do with me.

"Okay." He rose to his feet and it was now me looking up at him. "You talked me into it."

All the dread that had gathered in my chest fled in a whoosh of breath. "Oh, good. I had a feeling reminding you how good a cook my mom is would do the trick."

"That was what did it. I'm in it for the food," he said wryly.

"I know. The company is for the birds." Smiling, I backed toward the door. "I'm glad we're on the same page."

"We are." He watched me, humor dancing behind his icy blue eyes. "I'll tolerate you if I have to."

"That's all I ask."

He offered me a warm grin. "See you tonight, Zara."

I smiled back, and if it was wobbly, I couldn't have helped it. "Tonight, Maccie."

As I passed the reception desk on my way outside, Melanie gave me a look so sharp it could have cut glass, but not even a little side-eye could bring my good mood down.

Cormac showed up right on time, carrying a six-pack of beer. "An offering."

"Very kind." I took out two bottles and placed the rest in the fridge. "There was talk of a virgin sacrifice, but I prefer this kind of offering."

He chuckled as he slipped his utility knife from his pocket, flipped out the bottle opener, and popped our tops off. It was so smooth and effortless, my hands went clammy and I had to swallow a few times.

"It's a good thing my grandparents keep our fridge well stocked. I don't know any virgins. We'd have spent all our time hunting instead of eating."

I laughed, loving that he was playing along. "That really would have been a shame. I've gone to all the trouble to make my mom's pasta primavera—my dad's favorite meal of hers."

He leaned his hip against the counter, his beer hanging loosely between his fingers of one hand, the other tucked in his jeans pocket.

"Is there anything I can do to help?" he asked. "Or should I stay out of your way?"

"Stay out of my way and look handsome," I replied, going back to the stove to stir my pasta. "That shouldn't be too difficult."

When I glanced over my shoulder, he was staring at me, a deep crevice between his eyebrows. Had I messed up already? Calling him handsome had been kind of flirty, but he'd done the thing with the bottle opener and scrambled my mind a little. It was his own fault.

"How was your day?" I asked, trying to get things back on track.

"All right." He straightened and took a long pull of his beer. "A few fires had to be put out. A guest accused housekeeping of stealing their wedding ring."

"Oh no. What happened?"

"She forgot she'd put the ring on her necklace so it wouldn't get damaged while she was rock climbing. It was around her neck the whole time."

"Did she apologize?"

He huffed. "Of course not. We comped a bottle of champagne to smooth things over."

"And the housekeeper?"

"She was given a paid day off and a gift certificate to the spa."

That made me smile. "I had a feeling you were a great boss. Too bad you can't flick the guest on the forehead."

He smiled back. "I wish I could. A spray bottle would work too. 'Bad guest. Bad!' And they'd stop their entitled behavior."

"Not before batting your favorite mug off a ledge and watching it fall."

"If only some of these guests were as cute as naughty cats." He shook his head. "Fortunately, most people are happy to be on vacation and become more and more relaxed during their stay and easier to handle."

"And you're good at it."

He raised a shoulder. "It seems I am. For the most part, I enjoy it."

I tilted my bottle toward him. "Here's hoping I feel the same way about my next job."

"Do you know what that will be?"

"No, not yet. I have feelers out, but I'm not in a big rush. I figure I'll really dive into applying and interviewing when I go back to Oregon. I don't really have the time or inclination to think about it right now."

My phone's ringtone cut off his reply. Frowning, I checked the screen, not recognizing the number. Most likely, it was a sales call, but I decided to answer just in case.

"Hello?"

"Zara Vasquez?"

"Yes?"

"Zara, my name is Ryan Mercer. I'm a licensed private investigator calling out of Portland. Do you have a moment?"

My spine went rigid. This couldn't possibly be good.

"A private investigator?" I repeated, forcing a small laugh. Cormac's gaze on me sharpened. "That sounds...dramatic."

A soft chuckle met my attempt at levity. "I promise it's far less exciting than movies would have you believe. You're not in any trouble, and I don't own a trench coat. I just have a few questions regarding a former business associate of yours, Jackson Hale."

The kitchen suddenly felt smaller.

Cormac set his beer down quietly.

"I'm not married to Jackson anymore," I said carefully. "And no longer have anything to do with his business."

"Yes, I'm aware," Mercer replied smoothly. "Again, this isn't about your personal life. My client was an investor in Mr. Hale's company. He's attempting to reconcile certain discrepancies in the financial reporting and hoped you might be willing to provide clarification."

"Discrepancies?" I echoed.

"Accounting ones," he clarified. "Numbers not quite lining up. As I understand it, you handled internal financial documentation."

"I prepared internal summaries," I explained. "I didn't control or have access to investor funds."

"And that's exactly the kind of distinction we're hoping to understand," he replied. "My client simply wants to know what happened to his investment. We're not accusing anyone of anything. I'm gathering information."

Cormac was watching me, barely blinking.

"I don't know what I can tell you," I said, tightness creeping into my voice.

"That's why I'm calling you," Mercer responded gently. "I think you can tell me quite a bit. Cooperation tends to make these matters resolve more...efficiently."

My pulse ticced in my ears.

"Is your client pursuing legal action?"

"My client is exploring his options. At this stage, we're simply gathering facts. I'd very much prefer to note in my report you were open and forthcoming. It tends to reflect well."

Reflect well.

It wasn't a threat.

It wasn't *not* a threat either.

"I'm in Wyoming," I said.

"I'm aware of that."

That landed harder than anything else. He knew where I was? Had he been looking for me?

"To make things easier for us both, I can fly out to you. That is, if you'd be comfortable meeting in person. I find these conversations are clearer face-to-face. We could have coffee. There's a shop in your town, Sugar Rush. What would you say to a meeting there?"

This was...not anything I had expected. I'd left Jackson's company more than six months ago. Why was this coming up now?

"I need to think about it."

"Of course." His tone never wavered. "I'll send you my credentials via email so you can verify them. I want you to feel entirely at ease, Zara. My client's only interest is the truth."

When I didn't say anything, he added, "Thank you for your time. I look forward to speaking with you."

I lowered the phone slowly, and Cormac stepped closer, reaching around me to turn off the burners on the stove. Then he placed his hands on my shoulders, drawing my attention to him.

"Zara," he said carefully, "who was that?"

Chapter Nineteen

Cormac

Jackson was an even bigger piece of shit than I'd previously believed. Since I'd considered him the lowest of the low, that was saying something.

Zara talked and talked, spilling everything that had gone on with his company. Reading between the lines, he'd brought her on to provide cover for the underhanded practices he and his brothers were getting up to. It didn't surprise me she'd left both him and the company as soon as she discovered what they were doing. If nothing else, Zara had always been honest.

But it killed me the man who'd been supposed to love and honor her had put her in this position. She'd done nothing wrong, was trying to move on and start fresh, and had a PI wanting to come here and *meet* with her.

That wasn't going to happen.

By the time she finished telling me everything, she was more incensed than freaked out, which was something, I guessed.

We were face to face. Her cheeks were flushed, and her eyes were shining—not with tears but deep wells of anger. And she had every right to be pissed off. Hell, I was angry for her and hated that Jackson was still rearing his ugly head from a thousand miles away.

My fingers twitched from the desire to reach out and gather her in my arms. I held on to the edge of the counter instead, though it did nothing to abate the desire to comfort her. It seemed that was something that was never going to go away.

"You want to sit down? Take a break for a minute?"

"No." She flipped her hair away from her face and took a deep, steadying breath. "No, I'm fine, Maccie. I promised you dinner, so that's what we're going to do."

Then she gave me a light shove. "Get out of here. You're distracting me."

I couldn't help but laugh. "*I'm* distracting you—not the phone call from the PI?"

She waved me off. "That was ten minutes ago. You're my current obstacle."

I held up both hands. "I'm only standing here, being handsome."

That got me another shove. A laugh too. I liked both. For a moment, it felt like old times, when things were easy and uncomplicated.

"And it's distracting," she said. "Go away."

I went, but the house was so small I couldn't go far. I took a seat at the table right outside the open kitchen and watched Zara plate up our dinner. It took everything in me not to jump up and help her bring the plates to the table, but the razor-sharp look she shot me helped keep me in my seat.

She carried the plates over a minute later, chin tipped high, like she was waiting for me to comment.

I didn't dare.

She set the plate in front of me, and steam swirled up, catching in the soft overhead light. Pasta twisted with ribbons of zucchini and yellow squash, bright pops of cherry tomatoes, flecks of parsley. It smelled like garlic and butter and something citrusy.

It smelled like summer. The best memories of my life—and they all featured her.

Zara slid into the chair across from mine. "If it doesn't taste as good as it should, please keep it to yourself."

"I'm sure it's great, and I'm hungry enough it doesn't matter."

We both took our first bite at the same time. I didn't mean to close my eyes, but I did.

"Why are you making that face?"

I swallowed and looked at her. "Because it tastes exactly like your mom's."

Her expression changed instantly, the sharp edges dulling. "It does not." But her mouth rose in victory.

"It does." I twirled another bite, studying it like it held proof. "There's lemon in here, right?"

Zara blinked at me. "Only a little."

"Yeah." I nodded once. "She made it the exact same way."

For a second, we were little kids again. Sitting at her family's kitchen table during one of the times we visited them in Oregon. Our moms chiding us for "eating like wolves." Zara kicking me under the table for taking the last piece of bread.

My chest tightened. There was no place in my memories Zara hadn't touched.

She smiled, softer now. "You always liked it."

"Still do."

Silence settled between us, but it wasn't heavy. Not at first. Just the quiet of forks against ceramic and the hum of the fridge behind her.

I shouldn't have accepted her invitation tonight.

I shouldn't have been sitting at her table, eating her food, laughing like we hadn't detonated our friendship years ago—like I hadn't spent half my life wanting something I couldn't have.

I knew what this was doing to me.

Every minute across from her was a step backward. A reminder of what it felt like to belong in her orbit. To be the one who made her laugh. The one she confided in. The one she looked at like that.

I told myself I could handle it. I was grown now. I could sit across from Zara and not fall straight into the same hopeless place I'd been at sixteen and eighteen and twenty.

But the truth was, my feelings for her weren't any smaller. They hadn't faded. If anything, they'd sharpened with time. Cutting away the dreaminess of childhood until all that was left was the crux. The blunt reality of desire and wanting. Of a friendship that would always be more...but only for one of us.

She tucked her hair behind her ear, unaware of the war happening across from her. "You're being quiet."

"Just eating."

"You're thinking," she corrected.

I huffed a breath. "I'm always thinking."

"I should hope so, but that's not what I meant."

Of course it wasn't.

Her gaze swept over me, curious and open. There was none of the heaviness I carried, and I was glad for that. I would hate for Zara to feel the way I did.

But I wasn't going to dive into any of this. Not now. Not ever. Quite frankly, thinking about it over and over and *over* was exhausting.

"Are you going to talk to the PI?"

She put her fork down and wiped her mouth with her napkin. "I don't know. I don't want him to come here. Sugar Brush is mine. I'd hate anything having to do with Jackson to touch it. Maybe talking to him on the phone will keep him away."

"Do you have any information to share with him?"

"I can tell him what I told you, but I don't know how helpful that will be. As soon as I discovered what was going on, Jackson removed my access to every company account. I have a few things saved on my laptop, but nothing damning as far as I can tell."

I nodded. "If you do decide to speak to him, let me know. I'd like to be there when it happens."

Her brow crinkled. "Why?"

"This isn't something you should have to deal with on your own. If you were back home in Oregon, I really doubt your dad or brother would allow that."

"You're right. If my dad knew a PI was calling me, he'd flip, so chances are, I wouldn't tell him."

I let out a curt laugh. "Luckily, you don't have to decide whether to tell me. I was here, and I'm all in."

She tossed her napkin on the table, slumping in her seat. "Here we are again, huh? I seem to always be the damsel in distress, and you ride in like my knight in shining armor."

I flinched at her acerbic tone. "That isn't how I see things, but if you don't want my help, I won't give it."

"No, wait." She shot forward, resting her hand over mine. "I didn't mean it like that. You're great. The best, really. I just hate myself for putting you in the position to come to my rescue. For once in our lives, it would be nice if we were on an even playing field."

"I've known you since we were babies, Zara. My first memory of you is when I was four or five. You had a purple bow that did nothing to hold back your hair, and you were filthy, muddy from hunting morels with your grandpa."

Her fingers curled over mine. "Were you visiting us?"

"Yeah. You came bursting out of the woods when we were unloading our rental car. You ran so fast and were so excited to see me, you knocked me down on my butt. I wasn't so sure about you, but by the end of our visit, I was a Zara convert. My mom said she had to pry us apart when it was time for us to leave. I don't remember that. It's the purple bow, mud, and tackle crisp in my mind."

"I bet our parents have pictures."

"I bet they do." I flipped my hand over so I could hold hers. "Point is, we've known each other forever. I'm no knight, and you're no damsel. We're lifelong friends who've gone through tough times. Both of us, whether you know it or not."

Her chest rose as she inhaled. "I wish we hadn't stopped talking."

"That's as much my fault as yours."

She nodded, rubbing her lips together. "We should have had a conversation like this a long time ago."

"I don't know if we were capable."

"Right." Her shoulders curled forward. "I was so damn sad, Mac. I didn't make the right choices because of that. Marrying Jackson aside, my biggest mistake was letting our friendship go without putting up a fight."

I ran my thumb across her knuckles. The skin on the top of her hand was even softer than it looked, but her palm was calloused, rougher in some spots than others, from climbing and riding and adventuring.

"I should have replied to your texts."

"Yes. You should have." Her fingers threaded through mine, holding on tight. "I get why you didn't."

They were still there, on my phone. When Hannah's house almost burned down a few years ago. When Phoebe was injured. After Hannah had her first baby. When Phoebe got married. Zara checked in on me. On my family.

> **Zara:** Maccie…my parents told me what happened to Hannah. Is there anything I can do? For her? For you? Please, tell me. I'm thinking of you guys.

And:

> **Zara:** Please tell me Phoebe's okay. I can only imagine how terrified *you* all must have been. Are *you* okay, Maccie? If that were Zane…oh, you must have been so scared. If you need to talk, I'm here. No questions asked. Spill it all to me.

And:

> **Zara:** You're an uncle again! I saw the pictures. Silas is the cutest! My mom showed me a picture of you holding him. You look so happy, Maccie. Just beside yourself. I really hope you're happy. I mean that.

And:

> **Zara:** I wish I could have come to Phoebe's wedding. I hear there wasn't a single dry eye in the house. She deserves the best. I'd say I hope Deke is good to her, but who am I

> kidding? You Kellys wouldn't have let him
> get near her if he wasn't. I know you won't
> rep*ly*, but I wanted you to know I'm thinking
> of you and happy for your family.

And:

> **Zara:** Hey, Maccie. Good news: I'm engaged!
> Jackson and I are getting married. Can you
> believe it? I never thought I'd get married
> this young, but he asked, and who am I to
> say no? *Kidding!* I'm excited. Maybe you'll
> be happy for me? Maybe you'll come to the
> wedding? I wish you would. I miss your face,
> even after all this time. You know, you could
> reply. It would be great if you did.

And finally:

> **Zara:** If you had told me back when I was
> 15 there would be a day you and I would
> walk right past each other without exchang-
> ing a word, I would have laughed. But it
> happened today, at my wedding. We're not
> friends anymore, huh? I'm stupid for think-
> ing there was a chance after all the silence.
> Message received, Cormac. Loud and clear.

I'd typed and deleted a thousand responses. I'd sent none. Nothing I could've said would have been right or honest enough for me.

So I'd let it die. It hadn't been easy, but it was the best I could do back then.

"I'll text you back this time. When you go, if you send me a message, I'll reply."

The corners of her mouth lifted. "Good. I'd really like it if you did. We can't be muddy kids anymore, but we can remember what it was like when we were."

I cocked my head, doing nothing to hold back my smile. "I don't know. I think you could borrow a bow from Hannah. Though...I'm not sure you could tackle me to the ground anymore."

She gasped. "Are you kidding me? I could take you down in a heartbeat. I might be short, but I'm strong, and your center of gravity is way too high."

That got me laughing. "All right. If you want to believe that, you can."

"We can go outside right now, Cormac Kelly. I'll prove it."

My shoulders shook at her fierce expression. She meant it. Hell, she probably would knock me right off my feet. I wouldn't put anything past this woman.

"I'm good," I choked out. "I concede."

When it came to Zara, there was not a chance I would win.

I was finally learning to accept that.

Chapter Twenty

Zara

My smile had lasted longer than I'd expected. Cormac had gone home, the dishes had been cleared, my face was shiny and clean, and the lights were off.

Lying in my bed, I faced the wall of windows, and slowly, it slipped away.

The view from here was the same as the living room, with Cormac's house in the distance. The lights were off downstairs, but one still shone upstairs. Was that his bedroom? Or did he still like having a night-light glowing all night like he had as a kid?

Was he awake? If he was, was he thinking about our conversation? *I'll text you back.*

He should have texted me way back then. Why'd he let me go?

Why had we had to let each other go at all? I'd lost so much in such a short period of time, I'd never expected Cormac to be another loss on top of far too many.

He hadn't fought for me, but I'd pulled away first.

It was my fault.

I'd been stupid and young and a little flighty.

But mostly, I'd been afraid.

Six Years Ago...

My heart thumped in my chest like a door knocker as Cormac wove his way through the student union food court, heading straight toward me. I hadn't seen him in person in months. I'd let myself forget what this felt like: to be the only person in a crowded room and the sole recipient of his smile and attention.

I stood from the table I'd found for us, and he wrapped me in his long arms, pressing my face to his chest. His heart was dancing the same wild rhythm as mine.

"Hey, you," he murmured into my hair. "It's so good to see you."

"Hey, Maccie." I rubbed my face back and forth against his soft T-shirt, inhaling his scent. It would always smell like home to me. "Did you get taller?"

He chuckled and slowly released me, taking the seat next to mine. "Maybe. I'm not really counting." His eyes swept over me, warmth and happiness radiating out of him like sunshine. "Look at you, college girl."

I tugged on my Savage U T-shirt. "It still feels like I'm playing a part. I can't believe I'm really here."

"I kind of can't either." He picked up my hand and held it between his. "I'm glad you finally decided to hang out with me. I was beginning to think you were too cool for me."

"The opposite. Do you really want to be seen with a lowly freshman when you're a junior? I'll destroy your reputation."

He barked a laugh. "What reputation?"

Right after he'd asked me that, a group of pretty girls walked by, all of them cooing at him. A minute later, a couple guys clapped him on the shoulder and asked him about some party happening this weekend. And a minute or two after that, a guy and girl stopped to ask him about a study group.

My stomach twisted tighter and tighter each time. I wasn't used to this. Cormac had always been mine during our visits. Sharing him made me feel like a top spinning out of control.

People gravitating toward Cormac made sense. Hands down, he was the most wonderful person I knew. Of course I wasn't the only one to see it, but my irrational, jealous mind wanted to bundle him up and run away with him so I could have him to myself.

We were supposed to be best friends, but we'd never been a regular part of each other's lives. Not in person for an extended period. What if he saw right through me? What if everything changed?

My fingers clenched in my lap, and my eyes started to burn. What was this? It wasn't a good feeling, and I always felt good with Cormac. If things were off or teetering in the wrong direction, he'd always been the one to set it right.

"You should come with me," he said, knocking me out of my mental spiral.

"Where?"

He looked at me funny. "The party Ben and Cam were talking about. It should be fun."

Ben and Cam. The guys who'd stopped by a few minutes ago. The ones he'd introduced me to, putting his arm around me and telling them I was his best friend. His Zara. And they'd already known who I was. They had both lit up when he'd said my name. It should have made me feel better. Why hadn't it made me feel better?

When I didn't answer, he rushed out, "If you don't want to be stuck with me all night, you could bring some of your new friends. I'd like to meet them."

I sucked in a breath, wincing internally at how ragged it sounded. "I'll let you know. I'm not really sure what's going on this weekend."

He slowly nodded. "Right. You might get a better offer."

I forced a smile. "You never know. I've got to keep my options open."

His laugh sounded just as forced. "Hopefully I'll make the cut."

I never made it to the party. Jackson had asked me to go out with him that day in class, and nothing had been the same after that.

My hands balled into fists at my sides. The moon glinted off the weather vane on top of Cormac's roof. My eyes filled, and my stomach churned with regret.

So much regret.

A tear slid down my cheek, then another. I curled onto my side, clutching a pillow against my middle, and stared at Cormac's house until my eyes burned.

I should have gone to that party. I should have been brave.

I was so scared of losing him, I'd made it happen.

I had him back now, and I wouldn't let him slip away again. I didn't know if we could ever get back to where we were before, but something with Cormac Kelly was better than nothing at all.

Once the dam had burst, I'd become somewhat of a pest. I could admit that. The thing was, when I said I had missed Cormac, I'd meant that down to my very core, where my feelings for him resided.

Cormac was on the phone when I wandered into his office. He raised an eyebrow in question but nodded toward the chair in front of his desk. I sat down, setting my lunch bag in my lap. As he spoke to someone arranging a company retreat, I placed the sandwich I'd made him on his desk and unwrapped mine.

It would have been good manners to wait until he was off the phone to start eating, but I'd led a sunrise hike this morning and was absolutely famished.

Cormac continued talking and typing on his keyboard, throwing me a puzzled glance every once in a while. I liked listening to his professional voice. If I'd been on the other end of it, I would have agreed to sign any contract, sight unseen. He was that smooth and convincing.

By the time he hung up, I'd finished my sandwich and had moved on to peeling a clementine. He picked up the sandwich I'd brought him, waving it back and forth.

"What's this?"

"Turkey and provolone."

He turned it over in his hands, bemused. "You made me a sandwich?"

"Yes. I figured it would be rude to eat in front of you if I didn't."

"That brings up the question of why exactly you're eating in my office at"—he checked the time on his watch—"eleven a.m."

"If it's the time you're questioning, I've been up since four. I was so hungry I was close to gnawing off my own arm."

"Okay…" He nodded. "Understandable. Why my office, though?"

"I wanted to hang out with you."

He leaned back in his chair, the sandwich still in his hands. "That's…okay. I, uh…have some calls I need to make. In fact, I'm late for one right now. I don't think I'll be the best company."

I lifted a shoulder. "That's fine. If you don't mind me being here, I can be quiet." I tucked my legs beneath me, getting comfortable. "You can do your work. I don't mind."

His mouth twitched, but he didn't quite smile. "If that's what you want…"

I nodded. "I want—but only if I'm not bothering you."

He gave me a long look, the corners of his eyes pinching and relaxing. "Stay. You're not bothering me at all."

So I stayed.

Two days later, I found myself at loose ends a little after three. I didn't feel like going home yet, so I stopped by the resort café for a coffee and treat and took them to Cormac's office.

Melanie gave a little huff as I passed reception, but I barely noticed.

Cormac was reading something on his computer when I peeked inside his cracked door. Not wanting to disturb him, I silently slipped inside, placed the coffee I'd bought him on his desk, and took up my spot in the chair across from him.

He spent another minute or two reading before looking away from the computer screen, his gaze volleying between the iced coffee dripping condensation on his desk and me.

I smiled, holding up the paper bag in my lap. "Cookie or brownie?"

He cocked his head, a line carving deep between his brows. "Uh...hi?"

My grin widened. "Hey, Maccie. You choose: cookie or brownie? It's not Phoebe's baking, but the resort café is pretty good."

He rocked back in his chair, sliding his fingers through his hair. "You brought me coffee?"

"And a cookie or brownie. If you don't choose soon, though, I'm going to do it for you."

He frowned, and I frowned back. His deepened. So did mine.

Then he cracked. A soft chuckle rolled into deep barks of laughter, pulling me right along with him. Snickers devolved into giggles. I couldn't even have said why we were laughing, but it felt so incredibly good.

He wiped his eye with the heel of his hand. "Let's split them. Half of each."

"You're such a great negotiator. They should send you to resolve every hostage crisis and trade disagreements between countries."

"I don't think I have enough talent not to cause an international incident. I just learned a lot from watching my mom handle four kids without breaking a sweat."

I placed his half of the brownie and cookie on a napkin and slid them across his desk. "You've done her proud."

He bit the corner of his brownie, looking me over. "Seems you making an appearance in my office is becoming a thing. Twice in one week, huh?"

I patted the rock-hard arm of my chair. "It's comfortable in here."

He hummed, slowly eating his brownie. I sipped my iced latte, forcing my gaze to the window behind him. Did he ever spin his chair around to take in the view? Or was it comfort enough knowing the land his family had owned for generations was at his back?

"I appreciate the coffee and treats. Unfortunately, I can't be much of a host, though. I have work I need to get through before the end of the day."

I brought my gaze back to him. He wasn't wearing a tie today. The top two buttons of his crisp, pale-blue shirt were undone, revealing the peachy skin of his throat and divot at the base.

"I'll be quiet like I was the other day," I said, studying the way his throat bobbed when he swallowed. I didn't think I'd ever noticed a man's throat quite like I was his.

He let out a soft breath. "All right. But if you keep showing up like this, I'm going to get used to you."

I almost asked if that would be so bad, but stopped myself. Of course it would. I was leaving in a couple months. Getting used to me was the last thing Cormac needed.

I showed up again Friday morning, all my reasoning to stay away overthrown by my need to see him. It was selfish, but there was nowhere else I wanted to spend my time before taking a group on a trail ride.

When I walked in, he didn't seem surprised.

"Hey, Maccie."

"Morning, Zara." His fingers sped over his keyboard, his gaze never wavering from his screen.

I settled in my chair, pulling out my phone to return a text from my group chat with Zane, Steven, and my parents. Zane had titled it "The Vasquez Family Hang." The last message was from my dad, telling Zane to use his words because the pictures he continued to send didn't mean anything.

The pictures were GIFs that never failed to confuse our father.

I laughed to myself, even as my chest panged with something like homesickness, though that wasn't quite the right word. There was nothing about Oregon I especially longed for, but I missed my family badly.

"What's the smile about?" Cormac asked suddenly.

I put my phone down on my lap and looked up at him. "A while back, my dad tried to ban Zane from sending GIFs in the family group chat."

He raised his eyebrows. "Was that difficult for Zane?"

"You have no idea. GIFs are my brother's main form of communication. It was the closest they'd ever come to having a rift between them."

"They worked it out in the end?"

"They did. Zane's now allowed to use GIFs as long as he follows them with words."

Cormac chuckled. "Sounds like a fair compromise."

"Everyone thinks my dad's a hard-ass, but if Zane had pressed it, Dad would have folded like a wet tissue. He's miserable when either of us is unhappy."

"I expect you had to stop him from murdering Jackson then."

Groaning, I rubbed my face with my hands. "You have no idea. He wasn't pleased when he found out all I'd hidden from him either. Luckily, my mom talked him down. But...yeah, it was touch and go there for a minute."

"I can imagine." After a pause, he asked, "Have you heard from the private investigator?"

"He messaged. I haven't replied."

"Will you?"

"I don't know." I scrunched my nose. "If I ignore it, it won't go away, will it?"

"That's a strategy, but no, I'm pretty sure it won't go away on its own." He tapped his mouse a few times before looking at me again. "What are you up to today?"

"I led a beginner hike this morning and have a trail ride in a couple hours. I was thinking I might be able to hide in here until it's time."

"You might be." He cocked a brow. "You didn't bring me a bribe."

"My company isn't enough?" I teased.

He raked his gaze over me in a way that pricked my skin. "It's more than enough, Zara."

My breath caught as our eyes met and held. Something heavy settled over us, like a warm cloak. Each passing moment tightened it, drawing me closer to him, though I hadn't moved from my seat.

"I'll bring you a cookie next time."

"As long as there *is* a next time."

There would be.

I didn't think I could stay away from Cormac Kelly.

Not anymore.

Chapter Twenty-one

Cormac

I COULDN'T SAY HOW Zara had ended up riding with me to my appointment in Laramie. I couldn't even remember how she'd found out I had one. One minute, she'd popped into my office, and the next, she was beside me in my truck, making me sing along to the song she'd put on.

Not that she'd had to twist my arm too hard.

Saying she'd made me was a stretch. All she'd said was, "Come on, Maccie," and I'd sang like a damn bird. It made her happy. Hell, it made me happy too. Riding down the road, singing my heart out with Zara, wasn't something I ever thought I'd do again, but here we were, enjoying the moment without looking forward or backward.

When the song was over, she turned the volume down and sighed. "Did I tell you Phoebe asked me to help out with the market in the park in a couple weeks?"

"Yeah?" I glanced at her. "Did you agree?"

Phoebe never missed the market Sugar Brush held in the park throughout the summer. Last year, she'd come up with the idea of running a fundraiser for the library market and had dove in headfirst. Our sister-in-law, Alice, was the head librarian, and it was a fact our library was tragically underfunded. Phoebe had donated her baked goods and time, and she'd raised a good chunk of money doing so. And had even bigger plans for this year. It was no surprise she'd roped Zara in for the cause.

"I did. I'm not really crafty or a salesperson, but she said all she needs is a warm body to man the booth. I've got that covered."

I laughed. "I have a feeling Phoebe will have you doing a lot more than that while convincing you you're enjoying every second of it."

My sister had a way about her. Everyone thought she was sweet and soft—and she was—but she tended to get people to do things they would never agree to had anyone else asked.

"As long as I get baked goods as payment, I'm fine with it."

"You might not think a few brownies are worth it when Phoebe's done with you," I warned.

"I heard there might be cupcakes too."

I shook my head. "We'll have to come back to this conversation in a few weeks when it's all over."

"I'll be riding that sugar high all the way through," she shot back.

"You say that now."

I turned down a side street just off Grand, the old brick storefronts giving way to a squat building with blacked-out windows and a sign bolted above the door.

TATTOO

Succinct and to the point.

I parked along the curb and cut the engine, the sudden quiet ringing in my ears.

Zara leaned forward, peering through the windshield. "This is it?"

"Yeah." I rubbed my palms down my thighs. "This is it."

She unbuckled immediately. "Well...are we going in?"

"That's the plan."

"Oh, are you stuck—is that the problem?" She leaned over and pressed the button on my seat belt. "You're free now. Let's go, Maccie."

She pushed her door open, and the wind caught her hair, onyx strands whipping around her face as she stepped out onto the sidewalk. I came around the hood of the truck, trying not to notice how natural she looked standing there waiting for me. Or how much I liked it.

I pulled the door open and held it for her, the bell overhead chiming as we stepped inside.

The place was all dark walls and warm light. Framed flash sheets lined one side, bold traditional pieces mixed with fine-line work and black-and-gray realism. The floors were polished concrete, the whole space both industrial and welcoming.

"Wow," Zara breathed, turning slowly. "I've never been in a tattoo studio. This is not what I expected."

"What did you expect?"

"I don't know. Skull wallpaper. A scary guy named Razor."

A bark of laughter sounded from the hallway. "We had a Razor once," Jett called out as he rounded the corner. "He wasn't all that scary—and only lasted two weeks. Turned out he was allergic to gloves. And by allergic, I mean he kept 'forgetting' to wear them."

Jett grinned at us, wiping his hands on a paper towel. He looked exactly like he always did: dark hair pulled back, ink crawling up both forearms, steady eyes that missed nothing.

"Well, I'll be..." he said, his gaze bouncing between us. "If it isn't Baby Kelly."

"Don't start," I muttered.

"Too late." He stuck his hand out to me first, clasping forearms instead of shaking. "You're right on time."

Then he looked at Zara, and an even bigger smile spread across his face. "And who did you bring me?"

Zara returned his smile. "I'm Zara, Cormac's emotional support."

"Ah." Jett nodded solemnly. "We highly encourage those."

"I'm not sure I require emotional support for this appointment."

She bumped her shoulder into my arm. "You never know when you might need me, Maccie."

"Maccie," Jett repeated. "Adorable."

Then he laughed and gestured toward the front of the shop. "Welcome to my shop. Make yourself comfortable while I get set up."

I slipped my fingers around Zara's wrist. "Come here. I want to show you something."

She followed me to the reception desk, and I let go of her to smooth my hand over the lacquered top.

"It's pretty," she said.

"Deke built this for Jett. He built most of the furniture here, but this is his newest piece."

My brother-in-law had more talent in one finger than most people had in their whole body. His custom carpentry business was still getting off the ground, but each passing year, he got busier and busier, and I was glad he was finally getting recognition.

Zara ran her fingers over the edge. "Wow. Phoebe is a lucky woman. Or is it, like, a cobbler's-kids-have-no-shoes situation?"

I chuckled. "Not at all. I'm pretty sure Deke would build Phoebe the gates of Heaven if she asked. She has several pieces he's made in their house."

"Then I affirm my statement: she's lucky. I guess they both are. She bakes, he builds. What a life."

"They're happy." I rapped my knuckles on the desk. "Are you going to hang out up here or come back with me?"

"Maybe I'll wander down the street and come back. How long do you think you'll be?"

I rubbed my bicep. "An hour, tops. We're just doing shading and a touch-up."

"Okay. I'll be up here when you're done."

"Don't steal anything," I teased.

She gasped. "I would never."

"Mmmhmm. All right."

She shooed me toward the hallway. "Go get stabbed."

I followed Jett to his station in the back, leaving her standing at the flash wall. A couple years ago, Deke had brought me here for my second tattoo, which had been a hell of a lot bigger than my first. Jett had made it so easy, and his company was so enjoyable I got hooked. So far, he'd done my backpiece and the tattoo on my arm.

Jett snapped on fresh gloves and nodded toward the chair. I peeled off my T-shirt and draped it over the back, then settled in and flexed my arm.

Jett leaned in, studying it. "You've been in the sun."

"It's the summer. I keep it covered, but you know…"

"Do better."

"I'll try."

He cleaned the area, the cold swipe of antiseptic sharp against my skin. A second later, the machine buzzed to life, that steady, unmistakable vibration settling me.

As he started in, he glanced up at me. "So…"

I exhaled through my nose. "So…"

"Zara."

"Jett."

He smirked. "You've never brought anyone other than Deke to an appointment. What's the occasion?"

"No occasion. She wanted to come along, so I brought her."

"Uh-huh."

"Zara's a childhood friend," I clarified. "She's visiting."

"And nothing's going on."

"Nothing's going on," I confirmed.

The needle bit into my skin, a familiar sting that barely registered beyond surface level. I'd always liked the sensation. Most of the time even found it easy to sink into.

Jett wasn't letting me sink. "She's gorgeous."

I stared at the far wall. "I know."

"She call you Maccie when you were kids?"

"Yeah."

"And still does. That's cute as hell."

I didn't respond, and he hummed like he'd proven some kind of point and went back to work.

For a while, the only sound between us was the buzz of the machine and the soft drag of paper towels across my skin. I let my mind drift the way it always did in this chair: counting ceiling tiles, tracking the rhythm of the needle, letting everything narrow down to sensation and breath.

It was easy to think here. Or not think at all.

Zara's laugh floated through my head anyway. On second thought, it might not have been in my head at all. She was laughing somewhere nearby, and I couldn't help but wonder what was funny.

A few minutes later, the click-clack of high heels approached Jett's station.

"Hey, boys," Giselle called.

I opened my eyes as she rounded the divider. Jett's mom had been tattooing longer than I'd been alive. Not that you'd know it by looking at her. Silver threaded through her dark hair, and sleeves of ink told half her life story, but other than those subtle signs of age, she could have been a thirty-year-old pinup.

"Hey, Mama," Jett said without looking up. "What's up?"

She tossed a paper towel in the trash. "Just finished up with a surprise client."

"Yeah?" Jett replied absently. "Walk-in?"

"Mmmhmm. Pretty one too." Her eyes flicked to me, amused. "Hey, Cormac. Your friend's a little trooper."

My brain stalled then restarted as I tried to understand what she was saying.

"Friend?"

She tilted her head toward the front. "Zara—the pretty one you brought with you."

"What about her?"

Giselle blinked at me. "Her ink might be small, but she got it right on the bone, and the sweet thing didn't even flinch. I'd love to tattoo more clients like her."

I stared at her. "Wait. You tattooed Zara?"

"She said she'd been thinking about it for years," Giselle continued casually. "Finally decided today was the day."

"Years," I repeated faintly. She'd never said. Not then. Not today. Not even a word. "She didn't mention that."

"Maybe she wanted it to be a surprise." She slapped her hand against her leg. "Your girl will be up front when you're done. Don't worry. I'll take good care of her, honey."

After she left, it took a lot to sit still. Jett threatening to botch the lines in my tattoo was the thing that did it, but my skin was crawling to get out of the chair.

It was a good thing I was adept at waiting for Zara.

I'd been doing it most of my life.

Chapter Twenty-two

Zara

CORMAC BLEW INTO THE reception area like a storm, swiveling around until he locked on me standing with Giselle, the coolest woman I'd ever met. The second we'd started talking, I'd known I'd wanted her to tattoo me.

"What did you do?" he asked.

Giselle gave me a light shove. "Go. Show him, honey. He's chomping at the bit. I don't think he's very good about surprises."

Cormac stalked over to me, scanning me from head to toe. "Where is it?"

I pointed to my hip. "Right here."

He frowned, his brow dropping low. "You didn't tell me you were thinking about getting a tattoo."

"I've been considering getting one for a while, then Giselle and I started talking while I was waiting for you, and I figured there was no time like the present." I pushed up on my toes with excitement. "Do you want to see? It's so pretty."

"Of course I want to see."

I took him by the hand and guided him over to one of the chairs in the waiting area. "Sit. You'll have a better view if you're lower."

His frown deepened, but he allowed me to push him into the chair, putting his face in line with my midsection. I turned to the side and lifted my shirt. Giselle had applied a clear bandage over the tattoo, so it was a little blurred, but still visible.

Cormac leaned forward, his breath a warm breeze over my exposed skin as he read the words floating along the small, winding river.

To the river and back

Our childhood motto. We'd said those words more than hello and goodbye. They'd started as a challenge and had become something more. Sunshine and fun. Laughter and freedom. The best memories. The lightest, longest days that always slipped away too fast.

This time, when I left, I'd be able to touch them, to look down at them or see them in the mirror. And maybe I could get those feelings back, if only for a moment.

He reached out, like he wanted to touch me, but stopped himself, dropping his hand heavily into his lap. His gaze flicked to mine. "To the river and back," he whispered, his voice raspier than before.

"To the river and back," I repeated.

"Let's see this." Jett came around my side and bent to check out my very first tattoo. "Okay, okay. This is cool."

When he straightened, his mom slipped her arm around his waist. "Pretty, right?"

"For sure." Jett peered down at Cormac, who was still staring at my hip. "Hey, man...'To the river and back'—isn't that what you—"

Cormac sprang up from his seat with lightning speed, shaking his head. "It's not." Then he turned to Giselle. "If she hasn't paid yet, add it to my bill."

I tugged his sleeve. "You don't have to."

"I want to." He pulled free from my hold. "We'll head out in a minute, all right?"

He followed Jett to the reception desk, not waiting for my answer. Giselle looked at me with one eyebrow raised, and I shrugged.

I knew Cormac well, but there were times I wasn't sure I understood him at all, and this was one of them. He seemed angry about my tattoo, but that wasn't quite it.

I really didn't know what was going on in his head at all.

Cormac insisted I needed to eat so I didn't get woozy after getting tattooed. We stopped halfway in a tiny town nestled in the Medicine Bow National Forest. The steakhouse looked like a log cabin from the outside, but the back wall was almost entirely made of glass, and the view was breathtaking. A crystal-clear lake sparkling in the sun at the base of a bare-faced mountain was so pretty I had to stop for a moment to soak it in.

"Wyoming isn't real," I said.

Cormac sputtered a laugh, then rapped on the solid table. "Oh yeah? How do you explain this? Feels real to me."

I gestured toward the window beside us. "How can that be real? Explain it to me."

He gazed outside for a moment, his eyes darting over the rocky terrain beyond the lake. "I see what you mean. Doesn't make sense to be able to live somewhere so beautiful. I forget how lucky I am to be here and see this every day."

"You are," I agreed.

He turned back to me, scanning me the same way. "How are you feeling? Any pain?"

"I'm okay. It really is a little tattoo."

His brow hitched with concern. "Did Giselle explain how to take care of it?" He picked up his fork, flipped it over, then moved on to the knife. "If you need any help or have questions, I'm here."

"She explained everything." I reached across the table, covering his fidgeting fingers with mine. "I think I'm good, but if something comes up, you'll be the first person I come to."

He chuffed softly. "I just don't want you hurt."

"I'm not hurt. But thank you for looking out." I tipped my chin toward his arm. "What about you?"

He leaned back, his hand slipping out from under mine. "Ah, I'm fine. Shading is no big deal."

I slowly grinned at him. "You're so tough."

He shook his head and smiled down at his lap. "Not at all, but after sitting through an entire backpiece, I'm pretty sure I can handle anything."

"I still haven't gotten a good look at that one. When are you going to show me?"

His eyes met mine, warm and glacial all at once. "Whenever you want to see it."

"Maybe I'll ask later."

His mouth curved. "Maybe I'll say yes."

Our food was delivered, and Cormac watched me closely, making sure I ate every bite. Then dished more mashed potatoes and buttered rolls onto my plate. When I declared myself too full to eat any more, his frown was as deep as the ocean.

"Are you sure?"

I groaned, rubbing my stomach. "Absolutely. If I keep eating, I'm going to have to unbutton my jeans. I'm not opposed, but I'd rather not in public."

He grunted.

I pushed the remains of my steak toward him. "You can have the rest. And considering I ate ninety percent of the mashed potatoes, you *should* have the rest."

That earned me a scowling glare.

"I'm not eating your food, Zara."

I bit down on my bottom lip, but it did nothing to hide my snicker. The corner of his eye twitched, trying to keep his expression in place. But it was no use. A bubble of laughter floated out of me, and he gave up.

"I'm just trying to make sure you don't faint."

"I know, and I appreciate you looking out for me. It's extremely sweet." I propped my chin on my fists and smiled at him across the table. "I promise I'm good, Maccie. A little tattoo is not going to take me down."

He looked like he didn't want to believe me, but when the waitress came with the bill, he let it go.

Once again, he paid, accepting no argument from me. We walked outside, Cormac's hand light on my back. The summer air was warm but not unbearable, and I wasn't ready to get back in his truck.

"Want to walk down to the lake?"

"I had a feeling you'd want to." He gave the hem of my shirt a tug. "As long as you're feeling steady, I'm game."

I tugged his shirt back. "I'm as steady as they come. Let's go."

He led the way around the side of the restaurant to where a narrow dirt path slipped between two clusters of trees. He kept his hand on my elbow, like he didn't entirely trust my promise that I wouldn't tip over.

"I swear"—I glanced up at him as we walked down a rocky slope—"I'm not going to keel over."

"Good," he muttered. "Because I'm not carrying you back up this hill."

I snorted. "You absolutely would."

He didn't answer, but we both knew the truth.

The trees opened, and the lake spread out before us, even more unreal up close. The water was so clear smooth stones shone beneath the surface, sunlight breaking into shards across the ripples. The mountain loomed on the other side, sharp and bare and impossibly tall against the wide blue sky.

We picked our way across the shoreline until we found two flat stones jutting out just enough to sit comfortably. He lowered himself first, then held out a hand to help me as I sat beside him. Our thighs touched, and neither of us shifted away.

The breeze skimmed over the water and lifted the ends of my hair. Somewhere across the lake, a bird cried out, the sound echoing faintly off the stone. We stayed silent for a while, enjoying the moment.

Cormac leaned forward, forearms resting on his knees, hands dangling loosely between them. His T-shirt stretched across his back, the cotton pulling slightly.

"Is now later?"

He turned his head toward me, brow furrowing. "Later?"

"You said maybe you'd show me your backpiece. I said maybe I'd ask later." I tilted my head. "I'm asking."

"Yeah," he said quietly. "Now's fine."

I shifted off my rock and slipped behind him on my knees, the heat from the sun-warmed stone seeping through my jeans. My fingers hovered at the hem of his shirt, suddenly aware of how close we were.

Of the breadth of his shoulders.

The steady rise and fall of his chest.

"Ready?" I murmured.

He nodded once, and I slipped my fingers under, slowly lifting, the cotton sliding over his skin. Inch by inch, the ink came into view—dark lines and intricate shading stretching across the expanse of his back.

The world narrowed to the curve of his spine beneath my fingertips and the art etched into his skin—the lake and mountain before us fading into nothing but light and wind as I took my first full look.

It was our favorite spot on the ranch, laid out in shades of black and gray. The river...and the stacks of pebbles we always left on the shore to mark our visits. Sagebrush and cottonwoods, rocks tearing through the earth to reach for Heaven. Mountains loomed like giants, the sun beating down on all of them.

Before I could really think about it, I traced the lines with my fingertips. Cormac's spine stiffened, but he stayed utterly still. Tears pricked the backs of my eyes, and I couldn't have explained why if anyone asked.

It was beautiful. Like someone had drawn a dream from my memory onto his skin. I wanted to study it. The way it moved with him when he breathed, when he reached, curled, waved.

"Cormac," I whispered, pressing my cheek against a mountain peak. "I love it."

Through his back, I felt him rumble. He reached around, clutching my knee, and I wrapped my arms around his chest, hugging him tight. My eyes squeezed shut as I rubbed my cheek back and forth then touched my lips to his sunshine.

I hadn't meant to do it. And probably shouldn't have. But I couldn't help it or stop myself.

His heart skipped under my palms. Mine thumped against his back.

"Come here," he gritted out. "C'mere, Zara."

He pulled, and I let him move me. Then I was in front of him, crawling onto his lap, and we held on to each other, my face in his neck, his in my hair.

"I missed you."

His arms tightened, and he inhaled sharply. "Missed you too."

I pressed my lips to his skin, holding them there for a few fluttering heartbeats. His fingers wound through my hair, stroking slowly, making me melt into him. Then he tugged my head back to look at me.

I stopped breathing and stared back, knowing he could see how wet my eyes were. How flushed my cheeks must have been. And probably everything I was thinking and feeling too.

He lowered his face to mine, missing my mouth to touch his lips to my cheek, lingering there for a long time. And then his rough scruff scraped along my cheek, his mouth stopping beside my ear.

"That freckle. Glad it never faded."

I sucked in a shuddering breath, squeezing my eyes shut. "I have a freckle?"

His scruff scraped in the opposite direction, lips touching the same spot again. "Right there. It gets darker as the summer goes on."

"I don't think I ever noticed it."

Of course he had. He was Cormac. My first best friend. He knew me, even after all the distance we'd put between us—the silence that had stretched for far too long. The same boy who'd always been there. Who raced me to the river and back and convinced me I might win, even when his legs were twice as long. The same one who could make me laugh, even with tears flooding from my eyes. Who gave me hope when it was really hard to find. The person I'd missed the most, even when I was so angry at him I told myself I never wanted to see him again.

When he didn't say anything, I opened my eyes. He was close, staring down at me instead of the natural beauty around us. And not just at my freckle—all of me. His eyes roved, taking their sweet time.

We'd hugged each other a lot. We'd been close, but never this way. I'd never been in his lap, in his arms, and we'd never kissed. Not even sweet, brief ones on the cheek.

We were never this. We were kids and innocent and loved each other, but this was a line we hadn't crossed. I'd thought about it. Of course I had. But the time had never been right. We'd been too young, and then I'd been too sad. But now...

I leaned closer, so close his face blurred. And he didn't move back. His breath hitched, and I held mine as I grazed my lips over his.

"Zara," he murmured.

"Cormac," I replied, the syllables pulling our lips together again. His were just as soft and warm as I thought they would be. And when I kissed him with intent this time, he finally let his breath go and kissed me back.

Tentative at first, like he was bracing for me to change my mind. I hooked my fingers into the fabric of his T-shirt and kissed him again, soft and slow, learning his shape.

When my tongue slid along the seam of his lips, he made a low sound in his throat, and his hands slid up my back, holding me where he wanted me.

I smiled into his mouth. I couldn't help it. Kissing Cormac Kelly made me happy. Excited in a way I hadn't been in a long time. Like I was overflowing with bubbles.

He noticed my smile, felt the shape of it against his lips, and his curved to match mine.

"You're smiling," he husked.

"So are you." I licked his bottom lip, getting to know the taste of his happiness...and oh, was it sweet.

His fingers drifted back up into my hair, cradling the back of my head as he deepened the kiss slightly. He was being careful with me. Holding himself back. As if he were afraid he'd scare me away.

There was no danger of that.

The breeze skimmed across the lake and through my shirt, but I was warm everywhere he touched.

I shifted on his lap, angling closer without thinking, and his breath stuttered, his hands tightening at my waist.

"Zara," he breathed again, a warning and plea wrapped into one.

"Kiss me, Cormac."

I tugged on his hair, pulling him down and myself up. I met his lips with my teeth, nibbling and then biting, tugging, until he growled and wrapped my hair around his fist. His tongue slipped into my mouth and finally, *finally* met mine.

Heat bloomed low in my stomach. The first waves of sweetness gave way to something different. Needier. Insistent. It wasn't teasing anymore. Cormac was kissing me like he *had* to, and I could barely keep myself still.

His palm molded over my side, thumb brushing just beneath the hem of my shirt. I arched instinctively, wanting more of him, wanting—

His hand shifted, sliding over the fresh ink on my hip, and pain flared, sharp and bright.

I gasped, jerking slightly. "Ah—"

He froze.

The warmth vanished as quickly as it had come, his hands lifting like he'd touched a live wire.

"Shit." He pulled back, eyes wide, scanning my face. "I'm sorry. I forgot—your tattoo."

"It's okay," I said quickly, still catching my breath. The sting throbbed under my skin. "It's just tender."

His jaw tightened as he glanced down at my hip like he'd personally offended it.

"I should've been paying attention," he muttered. "I wasn't thinking. I—"

"Cormac." I cupped his face, forcing him to look at me. "It was an accident."

But the curtains had already fallen, the heat that had been building cooled in an instant. Cormac looked like he wanted to be anywhere but here.

"We should get you home," he said after a beat, voice rough but controlled. "Make sure you clean it up like Giselle said. Keep it covered."

I searched his face. Part of me wanted to argue. To pull him back into that softness and pretend the world didn't exist beyond this lake.

But the responsible, protective set of his shoulders told me he'd already made up his mind.

"Okay," I said quietly.

He helped me off his lap and onto my feet. I took his hand to pull him up and didn't let go. He twitched and gave a half-hearted pull, but I shook my head, so he gave up trying to get away from me. Threading my fingers between his, I held on the whole walk back.

The restaurant lights glowed behind us as we crossed the parking lot. Cormac opened the passenger door, his hand automatically finding the small of my back again, gentler than before.

I climbed into the truck, and Cormac leaned in, buckling me in himself. I almost snagged his lips when he was close, but he was back to frowning again, and now that I'd tasted his smiles, that was all I wanted.

Satisfied I was safe, he closed the door and circled to the other side.

When he hopped in, I asked, "Should I fasten your seat belt for you? Is that a thing we do now?"

He sighed but couldn't hide the slight curl of his lips. "I've got it."

The mountains faded in the side mirror as we drove, the lake swallowed by trees and distance. The sky stretched on forever above us, daylight fading fast.

Cormac kept his eyes on the road, hands gripping the wheel. The passing landscape blurred in my vision, and my fingers drifted to the sore spot at my hip. My lips still tingled, and my mind couldn't quite believe Cormac was the reason.

Beside me, he shifted, like he wanted to say something but didn't.

I didn't know what to say either. Was this something we needed to talk about? I wasn't sure. But from how stiff Cormac sat beside me, now wasn't the time.

Once the gates to the ranch came into view, I'd come to a conclusion: if this was the only time we kissed, at least it was the sweetest kiss of my life.

Chapter Twenty-three

Cormac

My headlights fanned across the guesthouse as I pulled up. It had gotten dark on our drive back, and out here on the ranch, the only lights came from the stars and my family's houses in the near distance.

Putting the truck in park, I turned to Zara. "Thanks for coming with me today."

"Thanks for bringing me. I had a really good time with you."

I nodded. "I did too."

She reached across the cab and brushed her fingers over my scruff. My heart vaulted into my throat. It wasn't a thought, leaning into her touch. It just happened.

Her palm flattened on my cheek, and I closed my eyes, moving my face back and forth.

"You want to come in?" she asked. "We can hang out, watch a movie or something."

Hell yes, was on the tip of my tongue, following her anywhere she went always my first instinct. Sitting too close on her couch. Breathing her in. Pretending this didn't feel like walking barefoot across hot coals for a few hours.

But that kiss by the lake still burned against my mouth. It hadn't been casual for me. It hadn't been nostalgic. It had been the kind of kiss I was going to spend years trying not to think about.

I forced myself to open my eyes. "I probably shouldn't."

Her hand stilled on my face. "Oh. Well, that's okay. It was a long day."

"It's not—" I scrubbed a hand over the back of my neck. "I just...I have some things I need to do at home."

A small crease formed between her brows. "You don't need to explain. I get it." She pressed the button on her seat belt, releasing herself. "I'll see you at work. Good night, Maccie."

"Good night, Zara."

She climbed out of the truck and shut the door with a soft thud. I stayed where I was, hands gripping the steering wheel, watching her cross the yard. The porch light flicked on automatically, bathing her in a soft gold glow. She looked over her shoulder once and gave me a small wave.

I lifted my hand back.

She reached her door, dug her keys from her purse, and bent slightly to fit the right one in the lock, and all my muscles went taut.

My chest felt like it was being hollowed out with a dull spoon. What was I doing sitting here? Going home now or later wasn't going to hurt any less, and sure as the sun would rise in the morning, I knew I'd regret driving away.

"Fuck it," I gritted out.

Before I could talk myself out of it, I killed the engine and shoved the door open. Gravel crunched under my boots as I crossed the yard in long strides. The night air bit at my lungs, but it did nothing to cool the heat roaring through me.

Zara spun around, eyes wide, the door cracked open behind her. "Cormac?"

I kept walking, colliding with her, pushing her back, my arm snagging her waist. She inhaled sharply, grasping my T-shirt in her fists. Our bodies melded, her head tipped back to see me.

Kicking the door shut, I spun her around and pressed her against it. She blinked up at me with surprise, but no fear or hesitation.

"Zara."

That was all the conversation needed. She pushed up on her toes, and I leaned down, our mouths meeting somewhere in the middle. This time was different. Her lips parted on a groan. I slipped between them, and the sound she made went straight to my bloodstream.

Her fingers twisted the fabric of my shirt, dragging me closer even though I was *right there*. I braced one hand beside her head against the door, the other sliding from her waist to her hip, hauling her flush against me. And god, did she feel so damn good. All sleek, curvy lines, soft in all the right places, smooth strength in others. I was a foot taller, but there was nothing awkward about our fit. We found a way to make it work without any thought or negotiation.

Teeth scraped. Breath tangled. My name broke from her mouth in a whisper. I pulled back just enough to look at her. Her pupils were blown wide, lips swollen, chest rising fast.

"This what you want?" I asked. I had to. This mattered.

Instead of answering, she tugged my shirt up over my head and tossed it somewhere into the dark.

That was answer enough.

Her laugh was breathless and wild as I kissed her again. And when I shifted forward, we stumbled away from the door together, my shoe catching on the edge of a rug.

"Careful—"

We bumped into the side table. Something clattered to the floor and shattered.

"Shit." I turned to see what I'd broken, but Zara caught my face with her hands then my lips with hers, making me forget anything else.

She let out a gasp when I lifted her, her legs wrapping around my waist. My hands slid under her thighs, gripping tight as I carried her forward.

We made it three steps before I hit the back of the couch with my knee. Another couple steps, and I bumped her coffee table then bounced off the corner of a wall. I barely felt any of it. Not with Zara's mouth on mine, her in my arms, her hands roving my torso.

The house was dim, lit only by spillover from the porch light through the front windows and a thin strip of moonlight cutting down the hall. That was all we needed.

Her shirt came off somewhere between the hallway and her bedroom door. I wasn't sure who'd removed it, but it didn't matter. Her skin against mine was the most important part.

In her bedroom, I put her down on her feet, and she wasted no time kicking off her jeans and shoes. Then she dropped to her knees to wrench off my boots and yank my jeans to the ground. She nuzzled against my legs like a cat, making little sounds that came close to purring. Lips and cheeks rubbed my thighs, her hands gripping the globes of my ass to keep me where she wanted me. Pushing up higher, the thin cotton of my briefs was the only thing between my throbbing erection and her dragging lips.

My head fell back against the wall behind me, and the bite of pain convinced me this was real. It didn't make sense. How was it possible

Zara was touching me like this? Slipping her hands down the back of my briefs to draw me closer? Putting her mouth on me, humming with pleasure?

My head swam, and my cock was leaking like a faucet. I didn't know up from down, but I was certain I'd never been this turned on in my life. She hadn't even touched me without fabric between us, and I was so strung tight it was a miracle I was keeping myself upright. God, if she kept going, rubbing against me like she couldn't get enough, I was going to lose it.

If we were going to do this, it wasn't going to go this way.

Reaching down, I caught her under her arms and drew her to her feet.

"Zara," I rasped.

"Cormac," she murmured, her lips wet and shiny in the dark.

Her eyes on mine, she unlatched her bra and tossed it aside. Then she took one step back, hooked her thumbs in the waistband of her underwear, and dragged them all the way off.

Slashes of moonlight made stripes on her perfect skin: a strip across her breasts, a line over her middle, another just below the apex of her thighs. She spun away from me, giving me more peeks. The bottom of her heart-shaped ass. A line of her smooth back. Moon against her inky black hair.

She crawled onto the bed and peered at me over her shoulder, her spine a perfect arch. "Come here, Cormac."

I moved without thought, leaving my briefs on the ground in my wake. I crawled onto the mattress after her, my knees on either side of her legs. Falling onto my hands, I lowered my chest to her back. My lips met her shoulders, the side of her face, her cheekbone, her hair.

She arched her back even more, pushing her ass up to welcome my cock into its valley. Warm and snug, I pressed down, and she rocked against me. And holy hell, I was going to lose it.

She was...

This was...

I sat back on my knees and rolled her. She held out her arms, and I fell onto her again, our mouths finding each other in the dark. I cupped her breasts, traced her waist, her ribs, learned the shape of her curves with the palm of my hand.

It wasn't enough.

Nothing felt like enough.

My mouth moved over her—her jaw, her throat, the hollow beneath it—kissing, tasting, breathing her in. She clung to me, nails dragging down my back, legs wrapping tight around my hips, pulling me closer, closer, like she couldn't stand even an inch of space between us.

Every brush of skin sparked bright. My thoughts were gone—burned away by the heat of her under me. There was only the press of her body, the sound of her breaths breaking apart in the dark, the way she moved against me without hesitation.

She rolled her hips, and my vision nearly whited out. One wrong move, and I would be inside her. Her heat was a beacon, and it was all I could do to resist.

A rough sound tore from my throat. I buried my face against her neck, kissing hard, biting gently. She arched beneath me, hands sliding everywhere at once—over my shoulders, my chest, down my sides.

She mewled my name in a way I'd never heard. Needy and almost frantic.

It hit me like gasoline on a fire.

I caught her face between my hands and kissed her again until we were both panting and the only way through was forward.

Breaking away, I raised my head to look down at her. "Tell me you have a condom."

It took a beat, then her eyes widened. "Oh god. Cormac…I don't. Do you?"

I groaned, lowering my forehead to hers. "Christ, do I wish I did. I'm sorry, but I don't."

"Damn." Her hands fell back on the mattress as she blinked up at me. "I'm not on birth control, but we could be careful. You could pull out?"

"No way." I shook my head. "I'm not taking chances with you. I'd never do that."

"I figured you'd say that." She sighed, and her disappointment struck me in the gut. "I'm sorry. I wanted to do this with you."

Wanting didn't even come close to how I felt. It wasn't going to happen tonight, but that didn't mean I'd leave her like this, frustrated and unsatisfied. There was so much more we could do.

"You don't apologize to me." I kissed her chest and moved lower, sliding my lips along her ribs and hip, careful to miss her tattoo. "Nothing to be sorry for, Zara."

Her fingers tangled in my hair. "Where are you going?"

I peered up at her. "You know where."

One swipe of my tongue along her slick flesh, and I knew I would never taste anything better—sweeter.

Of course. *Of course* she tasted this way. This was my Zara, the girl who was made for me.

"Fuck, sweetheart, you taste so good," I groaned, lapping at her.

"Cormac," she breathed. "I need...I need..."

I pressed a kiss to her inner thigh. "Shhh...I'm going to give you what you need. Let me have it."

Then I buried my face between her thighs, letting myself be ruined.

Chapter Twenty-four

Zara

I COULDN'T SEE STRAIGHT. The ceiling blurred, snapping in and out, closing in, whipping away. My head was a Tilt-A-Whirl, spinning and spinning. I clutched Cormac's hair so I didn't fly away.

He was between my legs, licking me, sucking me, devouring every inch of my pussy like he already knew exactly what I liked, what set me off—like he knew my body better than I did.

The scrape of his stubble, the heat of his mouth, the slow, deliberate way he touched me, overwhelming in the best, most terrifying way.

I wasn't used to this.

Not like this.

Not having my pleasure treated like the main event. Like the most important thing that could possibly happen today...or ever.

My thighs trembled around him, and my free hand fisted in the sheets, desperate for something solid. Everything else felt like it was dissolving.

"Cormac—" I choked out. There were a million other words on the tip of my tongue, none of which I could identify or make sense of. His name was the only thing that was clear, and I said it again and again.

He answered with a low sound that vibrated straight through me, sending another dizzying wave over my body. My back arched off the mattress, chasing the sensation, chasing him. I wasn't thinking. I couldn't. There was only the heat coiling low and bright and impossible.

Once wasn't enough for him. He brought me over and kept going until I was writhing wildly, sweaty, hoarse from crying out for him—until I was oversensitive and so wrung out, my arms and legs went limp. Only then did he crawl over me and drop his forehead to mine.

"Okay?" he whispered.

I nodded. "So okay. You're really, really good at that."

His laugh was a warm gust across my chin. "I really, really like doing that to you."

Moments passed, and my affection for him bloomed so big in my chest I couldn't lie still. I wrapped my arms around his shoulders and my legs around his waist, trying to pull him down on me.

He chuckled into my neck. "I'm going to crush you."

"I don't care."

"I do. I happen to like your body. I don't want it flattened."

I nipped at his ear. "Roll us over. I want my skin on yours."

He shifted to his back, taking me with him, and I lay my head on his chest, over his rapidly thumping heart. He stroked along my spine, up and down, then lower, cupping my cheeks. He was rock solid under my belly, but he didn't ask me to do anything about it.

I wanted to, though. He'd made me feel so good I needed him to have that too.

Bringing my knees up, I rocked against him once, twice. Cormac sucked in a breath and clutched my thighs, stilling me.

"No, Zara." His jaw was tight as he looked up at me, his gaze imploring. "We can't."

"We can." I cupped his cheek, rubbing his bottom lip with my thumb. "You won't go inside. I just want to feel you and make you feel good. Let me?"

He stared up at me, his brow furrowed, then slowly exhaled. His grip on my thighs loosened, but his hands remained, like he didn't quite trust me to keep my promise.

Fair.

I wanted nothing more than to feel him inside me.

I wouldn't do it, but I was sorely tempted.

Instead, I kept rocking over him, aligning him in the center of my slick, swollen flesh. He'd made me so wet I was dripping. Our bodies met and slid easily, the head of his cock bumping against my sensitive clit.

"Fuck," he whispered, his fingers digging into my thighs. "Zara, god, that feels so good."

"Yeah," I murmured against his lips. "So good. You're going to make me come again, you know that? We keep doing this, there's no way I won't."

"Let me see it." One hand moved to my ass, his fingers delving along my crease and lower, finding my entrance. "Can I?"

I nodded, my forehead knocking lightly on his. "Fuck me. *Please*."

Without a stutter in his rhythm, he thrust a long finger inside me, and I gasped, throwing my head back as I rode him harder.

"More?"

"More," I panted.

He added another finger, hooking it to press my front wall, and my body shook like an earthquake. Out of control, I gave in and let him move me. He ground me down on his thick length, hitting my aching clit again and again. Cormac had control over my body, inside and out.

I couldn't stop shaking. My limbs vibrated. My inner muscles twitched and clenched in time with the plunge of his fingers. His grunts in my ear as he rocked his hips and speared me with his fingers made me hotter, turning me on to a level I hadn't known existed.

I grappled with his shoulders, his sides, his scruffy face, kissing his lips and jaw and neck, then licking his sweat-dampened skin. We moaned each other's names, staring at one another in the dark. His jaw was tight, but his eyes were wild with wonder.

I leaned down to kiss his eyelids and whisper his name. His groan was a violent thing, a crash of thunder running through his body, shaking me. Hips pumping under mine, unleashing a torrent on my clit. I was falling, and he was rising, meeting me in a sharp upheaval. My body heaved and hollowed as I cried for him, and his gave me groans and violent jerks, coating my inner thighs and swollen lips with his pleasure until I was soaked through.

I fell, and he caught me, one arm wrapping around my back. His fingers lingered inside me for a long time until he carefully slid them out, leaving me achingly empty.

I lay on him until I caught my breath. He didn't say a word or seem in any hurry for me to get off, so I relaxed, tucking my head beneath his chin, soaking up every second of having him like this.

My Mac.

Eventually, he rolled me onto the mattress and went into the bathroom, returning a minute later with a warm washcloth. Kneeling on the floor by the bed, he parted my legs and cleaned the mess he'd made off me, then placed one soft kiss on my cleft before disappearing back into the bathroom.

I thought maybe he'd leave, especially when he threw on his shirt and briefs, but he sat on the bed beside me, his long legs stretched out in front of him, fingers wrapping around a lock of my hair.

"I should probably get home," he said after a while.

"Probably," I agreed, in no hurry for him to leave.

"I want to take care of your tattoo before I go."

That made me smile. "Of course you do."

He cocked his head. "Should I read into that comment?"

"Not at all." I pushed myself upright, my shoulder bumping into his. "You've always taken care of me. I'm not surprised you want to take care of this."

"Ah." He nodded. "I suppose I can't help it when it comes to you."

My heart slammed against the wall of my chest, fighting for the chance to get even an inch closer to him. But he was already off the bed, gathering supplies from my bathroom. While he was gone, I shuffled to my dresser, finding a baggy T-shirt and a fresh pair of panties.

When he came back, he paused for a second at seeing me dressed, then he was all business, flipping on a light so he could inspect my tattoo. He knelt in front of me, his brow furrowed, and removed the bandage as carefully as possible. After cleaning my skin, he slathered on a thick ointment, lightly dragging his finger along the words. Before he stood, his lips ghosted over my hip, right above the ink.

"What about yours?" I tugged on his sleeve. "Who's going to take care of your tattoo?"

"I've been through this a few times. I've got it." He palmed the back of my head and pressed his lips against my forehead. "Thanks for looking out, though."

"How'd you take care of the one on your back by yourself?" I followed behind him like a shadow. He bent to tug on his jeans, and my stomach sank with each inch they rose.

He paused when they were all the way up, still unzipped and un-buttoned, and I nearly forgot my question. Then his cheeks flushed pink, and I was enthralled.

"Uh...my grandmother, mostly." He gripped the back of his neck. "Not the sexiest thing to admit, but it's the truth."

With a laugh, I stepped into his space, throwing my arms around his middle. "I love how you are with your family. It's sexy as hell."

It took a beat, but he hugged me back, and I felt his smile against the side of my head. "Do you want to run with me in the morning?"

I tilted my head to look at him. His eyes were crystal clear and locked in on me in a way that nearly took my breath away. I couldn't help but wonder if that was new or if I was just noticing.

"To the river and back?" I asked.

His exhale brought a grin with it. "Always, Zara. To the river and back."

Chapter Twenty-five

Zara

C ORMAC ARRIVED THE NEXT morning before I was ready for him. I was yawning and holding my sneakers when I swung open the door, finding him jogging in place and more alert than ever.

"I'm out of shape," I warned, bending over to stuff my feet into my shoes.

He chuffed. "I doubt that. You spend your days climbing mountains and going on hikes."

"But not running." I looked up from tying my laces. "I remember running with you being pretty intense."

"We'll go slow," he promised.

We started down the gravel drive, sneakers crunching in rhythm before easing into a jog once we hit the packed dirt road looping the family side of the ranch. The morning air was cool and clean. I filled my lungs so deep with it; it almost hurt.

For a few strides, I was acutely aware of him.

Of everything.

How just last night, his mouth had been on mine. His hands had been everywhere. Of how his T-shirt brushed my arm now as we ran side by side, close but not touching. Of the quiet space between us that felt...different.

I waited for it to feel awkward.

For one of us to trip over it.

"So," he said easily, glancing at me, "still think you beat me on our last race around the south fence line?"

Relief loosened something in my chest. "Oh, please. You willingly forfeited that race. I won fair and square."

"I twisted my ankle in a prairie dog hole. You left me crying in pain on the ground."

I laughed. "First, you weren't crying. Whimpering, maybe, but not crying." I bumped his arm with mine. "Second, I came back for you."

"After you declared victory."

"It was my only chance of ever beating you. I couldn't let it pass me by."

We settled into a steady pace, the rhythm of our footfalls syncing without us trying. That had always been our thing: we found each other's cadence without effort.

"I forgot how pretty it is this time of day," I said, softer now.

Cormac's gaze found mine. "Most people don't see it. They're still asleep."

"Or working."

He huffed a quiet laugh. "Or avoiding runs any way they can."

"Rude."

He bumped his arm lightly into mine, and the bare brush sent a spark through me. The tension I'd woken up with had begun to unwind. He wasn't distant. He wasn't being overly careful. He wasn't pretending it hadn't happened.

He was just...Cormac.

Talking about the new guests arriving this week. Teasing me about the time Hannah had convinced me to try barrel racing and I nearly took out three fences. Asking about a trail I'd hiked last week and whether the wildflowers were in full bloom.

At one point, he surged ahead a few strides then turned to jog backward in front of me. "Still with me?"

"Barely," I shot back, though I was fine. Mostly.

His eyes dragged along my face, checking me over for himself. Then he faced forward again and slowed without comment.

We rounded the far pasture, where the land opened wide and rolling, the mountains rising blue and hazy in the distance. A cloud of dirt drifted up every time our shoes scuffed the edge of the road. A hawk circled overhead.

I realized I was smiling.

And a big part of me suddenly felt like it had been righted.

This was why I'd come here. Not only to start over, but to return to the beginning, where everything had been fresh and easy. Where I'd felt most like myself, with all good things in front of me, and people who loved me beside me. Where summers lasted forever and friendships never died.

And Cormac was central to all of it.

"I'm glad I came back. Glad we found each other again."

He turned, his eyes bouncing over my face. Something was there, words unsaid, but he kept them to himself and just nodded, the corners of his mouth curving into the barest smile.

"I'm glad you came back too, Zara."

He took it easy on me, leading us on a route I was certain was much shorter than he usually ran. When the guesthouse came into view, I slowed to a walk, my hands on my hips as I sucked in air. Cormac slowed beside me, breathing as easy as always.

The jerk.

We slowed even more when we neared my door, but my heart was a speedy rabbit in my throat. I never got nervous around Cormac, but suddenly, I wasn't sure how to act or what I should say. I knew I wanted to kiss him again, but I wasn't sure if I should, or if he'd want that.

We spoke at the same time.

"What are you—?"

"I should probably—"

He laughed and held his hand out. "You go first."

I stopped, turning to face him. "I was going to ask what you're doing the rest of the day."

His mouth hitched. "I was going to tell you I promised to help my granddad with a project, so I should probably get going." His eyes drifted down my body. "Is your tattoo feeling okay? Did you apply more ointment when you woke up?"

Brushing aside my disappointment, I nodded. "It's fine, and yes, I did. I want it to heal well, so I intend to follow all Giselle's instructions."

"Good. That's good." He scuffed his toe in the dirt. "What are your plans for the day?"

"I'm meeting with Phoebe, Hannah, and Alice later to plan the booth for the market."

His eyes flared. "They're really putting you to work, huh?"

"They are, but they're going to be sorely disappointed if they expect me to craft." I laughed and shrugged. "I'm looking forward to hanging out with them and doing something for the town."

"They'll make it fun and painless."

When he glanced away, I stepped forward, my toes hitting his. His breath caught, and he turned back to face me, a brow lifting. I pressed my palms to his chest, feeling his heart jump.

I wasn't the only one who was nervous.

"Was last night a one-time thing, or can I kiss you before you go?"

Cormac's expression shifted so fast I almost missed it. His brows lifted, mouth parting like I'd knocked the wind out of him, then something heated slid in from behind.

His hands settled on my waist, drawing me closer.

"Zara," he said quietly, my name rough in his throat.

I held his gaze. "I don't want it to be one time. It's up to you."

His fingers tightened at my hips, and he walked me backward until my shoulders hit the door. His body followed, caging me in, and his breath came hard.

"Do you actually believe I've been able to think about anything else since last night?"

My pulse stuttered.

"Cormac—"

He kissed me, and there was nothing tentative or unsure about it.

His mouth moved against mine with the kind of urgency that stole the air from my lungs. I fisted my hands in his T-shirt, pulling him closer, needing his weight. His hand slid up my side, careful when it brushed near my tattoo and firm everywhere else, fingers splaying to cover more of me.

I tilted my head, deepening the kiss, and he groaned low in his chest. His thigh pressed between mine, and I gasped into his mouth, the sensation sharp and sweet and overwhelming.

I took a moment to acknowledge how natural this was. There was nothing awkward or wrong about kissing this man I'd known all my life. Every time our mouths touched, I only wanted more.

Kissing Cormac Kelly was another extension of our connection. Maybe this had been inevitable; we'd just needed it to be the right place and the right time.

Everything faded with his mouth on mine. I had no idea how many minutes had passed. There was only the scrape of his stubble against my skin, the steady slide of his lips over mine, the way his hands kept adjusting, like he couldn't settle on just one place to touch me.

Finally, he pulled back enough to breathe, his forehead dropping to mine, his chest rising and falling hard against my palms.

"Zara," he said again, but this time, it sounded like a warning.

"Cormac." I smiled against his lips. "You should come in."

His eyes opened, dark and wrecked. "I want to, sweetheart. God, do I want to. But I can't. Not today."

But he didn't go anywhere.

He kissed me again, slower this time, deeper in a different way. Less frantic. Like he had all the time in the world to map the shape of my lips and feel of my tongue.

When he finally forced himself to step back, it looked physically painful. His hands dragged down my arms before letting go entirely.

"If I don't leave right now," he said, his voice rough, "I'm not going to."

My breath was still uneven. "But you have things to do. Important things."

A flicker of temptation crossed his face, but he shut it down as quickly as it had appeared.

"Right. Promises I made. Can't let my granddad down."

"He seems pretty forgiving," I argued, knowing I wouldn't win.

Cormac huffed a laugh. "He is, but I'm still going."

He took one step back, then another, like each one required effort. His gaze lingered on my ponytail he'd undoubtedly messed up with his wayward hands, my hot cheeks, kiss-swollen lips.

Then he shook his head, tearing his gaze away. "I'll see you later."

"Later, Maccie."

He turned and jogged down the path toward the main house. Halfway there, he glanced back.

I was still standing exactly where he'd left me.

And I was smiling.

I touched my mouth again, warmth blooming through me.

Yeah.

Definitely not a one-time thing.

Chapter Twenty-six

Cormac

A LONG TIME AGO, my dad had built my mom a kitchen table out of old barn wood. A heavy thing, solid enough you could probably park a truck on it without a sliver of complaint.

When I was a kid, the six of us fit around it fine. We'd scoot over when my grandparents came over, and it'd worked.

Then the family had started growing.

Caleb had Jesse. Hannah brought Remi home, and a couple years later, Silas showed up loud and wild, followed by mellow little Brooks. Phoebe married Deke, then came little Abigail. Caleb married Alice, and now we had Desmond too. We'd more than doubled in size but continued scooting over, laughing when we bumped elbows.

One by one, chairs got dragged in from other rooms, another place setting got laid out, and soon, it was like it had been there all along.

The table hadn't changed. Same boards. Same burn mark from when Hannah had forgotten a hot pan. Same gouge Caleb had put in it with a pocketknife. And it kept holding more of us.

Tonight—a random Wednesday, no special occasion—it would be full again.

My siblings, the kids, and their spouses were spread around the kitchen and spilling into the living room when I arrived. Silas was chasing Jesse with maniacal glee. Brooks was building wooden blocks with Caleb and Remi on the rug. Desmond was snuggled up with Phoebe on the couch, reading a book.

Silas whizzed by, making me jump out of his way so I didn't get run over.

"Hi, Uncle Mac," he called. "Bye, Uncle Mac!"

I laughed, waving at the back of his head. "See ya, kid."

Remi chuckled. "He's on a tear tonight. Watch out."

Caleb shook his head. "Lucky for us all, Jess has the energy to spare."

I tilted my head toward the kitchen. "I'm gonna see if they need help in there."

They turned their attention back to building towers with Brooks, and I gave Phoebe's cheek a kiss and squeezed Desmond's chubby little hand before venturing into the kitchen.

The sliding door was open, and my dad was out on the back patio with Deke cooking something on the grill. Mom and Hannah were at the island, chopping up fruit and prepping side dishes. And at the table, Alice was sitting with Zara, who held Abigail in her lap.

Zara turned her head when I walked in, the smile she'd already been wearing growing brighter.

"Hey, Maccie."

I put my hands on my hips. "I didn't know you were going to be here."

She wiggled her fingers. "Surprise. Here I am."

Since our run Sunday, I'd only seen her in passing. A quick visit to my office yesterday, waving from a distance out on the ranch, passing each other in the lobby. This week had been busy for us both, but the fact of the matter was, I'd needed some space to recalibrate.

Seeing her now, I questioned why I'd been avoiding this. Her long, glossy hair spilled down her back, and my fingers itched to sink into it. And her smile...Christ, I knew exactly what it tasted like. How it felt on my skin. How *she* felt and tasted everywhere.

What was there to think about? I was already in deep. Not a chance it was going to be an easy recovery, even if I avoided her for the rest of the summer. Why the hell had I thought it was a good idea to waste what little time we had?

My mom waved a wooden spoon, drawing my attention. "Do I have to run my guest list by you, Cormac Kelly?"

"Nope. You always invite the best people." I crossed the room, giving her cheek a kiss. "I didn't know everyone was coming tonight."

She lifted a shoulder. "They just started showing up. You know how it is."

"I do. Your kids like to eat you out of house and home."

Hannah held up a grape. I opened my mouth, and she tossed it in. "If we stopped showing up to glom off Mom and Dad, they'd be lost."

Mom snorted a laugh. "As long as my grandchildren keep coming around, I'll be just fine."

Hannah gasped. "I'd be insulted if I didn't know that was a bald-faced lie." She snaked her arm around our mom's waist. "You're obsessed with us all."

Mom resisted for all of two seconds before she lay her head on Hannah's shoulder. "Obsessed might be too strong of a word, but you're not far off. You didn't have to be such incredibly delightful people, did you? It's not fair to everyone else."

Abigail let out a squeal, stealing our attention. Zara had her standing in her lap, laughing at the silly faces she was making.

My mother sighed.

Hannah gave me a shove. "Go see what they're doing, Maccie."

I glanced at her over my shoulder. "You don't need help?"

"Absolutely not," she said, pushing me again.

Giving in, I crossed back to the table, bent to kiss Alice's cheek, and took the chair beside Zara. Abigail waved at me, her round cheeks pink with joy.

I poked her little belly. "Hello, Abby-wabby. Whatcha doin', angel?"

"Zara," she cooed.

Alice smiled. "She's fallen for her Aunt Zara. I'm a little bit jealous."

"It's only because I'm shiny and new," Zara said. "You'll be back to being her favorite in no time."

"Zara!" Abigail shouted. "Hi, Zara!"

"Hi, Abigail." Zara slid a glance my way. "Do you want Uncle Cormac to sing you a song?"

Her eyes grew wide. "Yes! Maccie, Maccie, Maccie, peeeeze."

There was no way I could turn her down. I didn't know a lot of child-friendly songs, but I was pretty adept at singing my ABCs and "Twinkle, Twinkle, Little Star," which was all Abigail needed to be satisfied.

By the time I finished the second round of "Twinkle, Twinkle," the house had shifted into dinner mode. My mom announced it was time to eat, and chairs began scraping across the floor. Little feet pitter-pattered into the room. My dad came in carrying a platter of grilled chicken, Deke behind him with corn wrapped in foil.

Everyone else filed in, and within a minute, the table was filled to the brim.

Zara handed Abigail over to Phoebe, but she stayed right beside me. Our knees brushed under the table, and our elbows bumped as we passed dishes around to fill our plates.

Conversations broke out in layers.

Caleb and Dad discussed fencing on the north pasture. Hannah told Mom about a client who'd tried to pay her in homemade jam. Silas loudly said something about dinosaurs to Jesse, who patiently explained why Silas was wrong.

Through the chaos, I noticed Zara kept glancing at my plate.

I leaned closer, not wanting to raise my voice over the noise. "Why didn't you get any mac and cheese?"

She shrugged, trying to pretend she wasn't eyeing my plate. "I didn't think I wanted it."

"Are you regretting your decision?"

She tipped her head to the side. "Maybe…"

Without thinking much about it, I slid my fork through the corner, scooped up a bite, and held it to her.

She blinked at it, then me.

"Go on," I said. "Eat."

A slow smile spread across her mouth as she leaned in and wrapped her lips around the fork, then pulled back, her eyes staying on mine.

"More?"

She swallowed. "Please."

I fed her another scoop, something deep in my gut immensely satisfied by her hum of pleasure and little wiggle of happiness.

"Want me to get you some of your own?"

Biting down on her lip, she shook her head. "It tastes better from your plate."

Who was I to argue? I scooped up another bite when I noticed the silence. The conversation around us had died down, the only sounds the scrape of my fork against the plate and the babies' babbling.

I glanced up.

Every single person at the table was looking at us.

Caleb leaned back in his chair, arms crossed, trying and failing not to grin. Hannah's eyebrows were somewhere near her hairline. Phoebe looked like she might tear up. My mom had both hands clasped under her chin like she'd just witnessed a proposal.

Even my dad was watching over the rim of his glass.

Silas squinted at us. "Why's Uncle Mac feeding Zara? Is she a baby?"

Heat crawled up my neck.

Zara didn't even flinch. She smiled sweetly at Silas. "Because I asked nicely."

Silas considered that. "Can I have some please?"

Laughter broke out around the table. Caleb ruffled Silas's hair, and Hannah rolled her eyes at her son.

Grabbing the serving dish, I shoved it toward him. "Get your own, you little animal."

When I looked back at Zara, she was smiling at her plate, cheeks pink.

Our knees were still touching.

And despite all the eyes on us, neither of us moved away.

Chapter Twenty-seven

Zara

I walked into Cormac's office without knocking, and he didn't seem to be surprised to see me. Fingers stilling on his keyboard, he leaned back in his chair, a smile pulling at his lips.

"Hey, you," he crooned.

"Hey, Maccie." I kicked the door shut behind me. "I have five minutes before I have to meet a group for a hike."

"And you're spending it with me?"

"Yep." I wound around his desk, and he took my hands, tugging me down onto his lap, exactly where I'd hoped to be. I sat sideways on his long legs, tucking myself against his chest. He held me close, one arm around my back, the other draped over my thighs.

"Glad you came to visit." He spread his fingers wide, dipping beneath the bottom of my shorts.

"I wanted to ask if you'd like to go to the hot spring with me after work. I meant to ask last night, but things were crazy, and your family was—"

"Watching us like we were on the verge of eloping?"

I laughed. "Yes. That about sums it up."

Last night was my first time experiencing all the Kellys in one place, and it had been glorious. The babies, the big kids, the siblings and spouses, and Elena and Lock all together made it feel like home.

It should have been chaos, but it wasn't, even with Silas spilling his drink, Abigail getting overtired and crying, Lock and Caleb disagreeing about some ranch matter, and all eyes on Cormac and me. It made me homesick for something I'd never had.

"The hot spring, huh?" He let his head fall back against his chair.

"Yeah. I haven't been there this summer, and after the week I've had, I could really use it. I thought maybe you would want to come with me."

"Sure I would. Are you sore?"

"I'm okay. It's just been a really physical few days."

His palm slid down to my knee then back up in a slow drag. "We'll get you sorted. Pick you up at your place when I'm done here?"

I nodded, leaning in. "I have two more minutes before I really have to go."

The hand on my back moved up to my nape, gripping me there. "Can I kiss you for a while?"

"For two minutes."

His nose touched mine. "Not long enough, but it'll have to do."

Then his mouth covered mine in a sweet collide and we made every second of the next two minutes count.

The river running through the ranch had a handful of thermal seeps where hot mineral water sprang from the ground. Years ago, Connell Kelly had added a ring of rocks around one of the seeps, turning it into a natural mineral pool. They said the minerals had healing properties, and while that might've been true, I was more interested in relaxing in the water with the clear sky above me and Cormac by my side.

He drove us out to the spring in one of the ranch's side-by-sides, the wind whipping too loudly for us to carry on much conversation. I settled in with my feet on the dash, enjoying the ride.

When we arrived, I hopped out and wandered down to the river, my heart lodged in my throat. It had been so long since I'd been here, but it was exactly as I remembered.

I looked back at Cormac as he slowly approached. "Guests still don't come here, right?"

He shook his head. "Just family."

"And me."

"I think you qualify as family, Zara. No one else gets to know our secret spots."

It seemed impossible, but my heart leaped even higher.

I turned away from him and kicked off my slides to dip my toes in the spring. Warm water enveloped my foot, the faint scent of sulfur tickling my nose. I pulled off the T-shirt and shorts I'd worn over my bikini, leaving them on top of my shoes.

Cormac was behind me, his clothes landing on mine. Then his hands closed around my hips as he helped me into the spring.

The late evening air was warm, and the water was even warmer, melting my tired muscles into a heap. Cormac took me in his arms and settled me in his lap, letting me drape myself over him. His fingers stroked back and forth along my bare stomach, and his nose nuzzled the side of my head.

I closed my eyes, allowing myself to float in the moment. This place, this person, the water lapping around us, the breeze blowing over us, distant animal sounds, the wide-open sky above—I breathed freely for the first time today. Even though parts of my job had been stressful, I'd enjoyed every moment. I hadn't been counting the minutes until the end or wishing I were somewhere else. God, I hoped my next job would fill me with even half those feelings.

Cormac's hand stilled. "You tensed up. What are you thinking about?"

"Leaving. My next steps."

His breath came out in a heavy whoosh. "Right. Are you applying for jobs?"

"Not yet. I probably should, but no part of me wants to think about it." I turned my head, pressing my face into his throat, feeling him swallow. "Let's talk about something else. Anything else. Tell me how many girls you've brought here."

His laugh was sharp and biting. "None. This is a family spot."

"Not even Victoria?"

"No, Zara. No one."

I swiveled a little more sideways so I could see his face. "What happened with her? Why'd you break up?"

He puffed up his cheeks and slowly exhaled. "We weren't together long, and it quickly became obvious to me it wasn't going to go anywhere. I shouldn't have tried dating someone I worked with anyway." His brow furrowed as his gaze swept over me. "I don't regret ending it."

"That's good." I cupped his cheek, his scruff scratchy against my palm. "I feel a little greedy for being glad I have you all to myself this summer."

"Be as greedy as you want with me."

I kissed his chin before laying my head on his shoulder. "You can't tell me that. I'll do it."

His soft laugh rumbled beside my ear. "I dare you."

Dare or not, I would be spending the rest of this summer in his face. Now that I had him back, there wouldn't be a moment when I felt I'd had enough.

After a minute of idly rubbing his thumb over my stomach, Cormac asked, "Did you ever get to any of the national parks you wanted to see?"

"No, not yet."

I didn't need to say Jackson hadn't wanted to go. In truth, it hadn't been his fault. I'd allowed his wishes to become more important than mine. My eyes had been wide open when I'd entered a life with him. I'd known it would mean giving up the things I'd always wanted to do, and I'd said yes anyway.

The person I was even a year ago seemed so far off, I couldn't quite understand her.

"If you didn't have to worry about jobs, where would you go first?"

I tipped my face up to the sky, already picturing it. "Glacier. Or maybe Zion. As long as there are miles of trails and sketchy cell service." I smiled. "I want blisters and sore calves and to wake up in a tent that smells like dirt and pine needles."

He huffed a quiet laugh. "That's very specific."

"I've thought about it a lot." I shifted so I could see his profile. "I love places that make me feel like I'm a part of something bigger than me. You could come with me."

"I'm not a hiker, but I'd go, even if you had to drag me up a mountain."

"I wouldn't have to drag you. I'd encourage you—there's a difference."

He snorted. "Encourage. Okay. I imagine there'd be a fair bit of glaring every time I tried to rest."

I twisted in his lap to poke his ribs. "Fine. I might glare you up a mountain. But you'd secretly love it."

Cormac's mouth curved against my temple. "Probably would."

"And you? If you could go anywhere..."

He was quiet for a moment, turning the idea over carefully. "I'd probably save my vacation days to tag along on your adventures."

"Really? You don't have anywhere you long to be?"

"Not really. I'm right where I want to be."

My heart kicked. "With me?"

"Yeah."

So simple. Right here, right now...it was all he wanted. When I thought about it, when it really came down to it, there was no place I'd rather be either.

I shifted again, turning fully toward him, my knees bracketing his hips under the water. My hands slid up his chest, water beading along his skin, then over his shoulders and around to his nape.

"That's a really sweet thing to say. I'm really happy to be right here, right now, with you." I dipped down to kiss his cheek. "You really can't think of a place you want to go? I want to know."

Humming, he ran his nose along my cheekbone. "There was a guy I became friends with during my hospitality program in college, Masa. He moved to Kyoto when we graduated and runs a hotel there. We've kept in touch, traded stories about guests. He came to visit the ranch last year and extended an open invitation. I've been thinking about it for a while. I just need to bite the bullet and make a plan."

A sudden burst of grief struck me out of nowhere.

But when I thought about it, it wasn't out of nowhere at all. I would always feel the loss of the years we'd missed out on, but hearing him share this small tidbit of his life—a life I could've been part of but chose something else instead—filled me with so much regret I didn't know what to do with it. I should have known who Masa was. I should have been able to close my eyes and picture his face. But I'd never gotten to know Cormac's college friends. I'd willingly drifted away because it had been easier than keeping him close and losing him anyway.

There was so much about him I didn't know, and I wanted it all.

"Wow, okay. Japan would be very cool. I never thought about going there, but if you want a travel buddy, I'm in."

His brow quirked. "A buddy, huh?"

"A buddy, it turns out, I really like to kiss."

His fingers wrapped around my hips, holding me close, and he tilted his head back, his eyes darting over my face. I smiled, and he returned it.

"You're so handsome," I murmured. "You always were, but you grew into a really beautiful man."

His breath fell from his lips in a hard puff. "Yeah? You think so?"

"You have to know how handsome you are, Maccie."

"All I care about is what you think."

I pecked his lips. "Well, I don't want to stop looking at you."

"Then don't."

I let my gaze wander over his strong jaw and the long column of his throat. From one side of his shoulders to the other.

To his tattoo.

The words along his collarbone I hadn't seen clearly until now.

Steam curled between us as I leaned in, brushing my fingers over the dark script. His skin was warm from the spring, and the ink stood out in sharp relief.

I traced the letters slowly, my breath catching as they came into focus.

To the river and back

My heart stumbled.

For a second, I thought I'd misread it—the steam and fading light playing tricks on me. Then I leaned closer, squinting, and there it was. Every letter exactly the same.

"To the river and back," I whispered.

When he kept quiet, I pulled back enough to look at him. "Cormac. We have the same tattoo."

He nodded. "We do. Kinda crazy, huh?"

I couldn't stop tracing the letters, each one matching mine. "When did you get this?"

"A few years ago." He cleared his throat. "It was my first."

He glanced away, like he was embarrassed, but I refused to be deterred.

That morning, in the kitchen with his grandparents, I'd asked him about his tattoo. He'd been vague, but I'd remembered his explanation. "You said it was a reminder. What is it a reminder of?"

He lifted his hands out of the water to cup the sides of my neck. His thumb stretched, pressing beneath the corner of my jaw before coming to rest on my fluttering pulse.

"Tell me," I whispered.

"The good times. The *best* times. No matter what happened, I lived it. I felt what I felt and carry it with me." His eyelids lowered, his gaze going hazy and distant. "What we had might've ended, but I didn't want to forget it, so I put those words where I'd always see them."

"Mac." My forehead fell against his. My chest ached so deeply, I thought it might be close to cracking. "I'm sorry. I'm so, so sorry I didn't take better care of us."

"We both made mistakes. We were kids, Zara."

"We're not so old now."

"You're right. We're still young, but we've learned a lot." His thumb stroked my throat, gentle and steady. "The good thing is, we still have time to set it right."

Blinking, I lifted my head to stare at him. "Set it right," I whispered. "That's what my dad said before I came here. I thought that's what I was doing in Sugar Brush. And it was part of it, for sure. But it's also you. I needed to fix things with you. To set it right."

His jaw rippled as he looked back at me. "I think we're on our way, don't you?"

"Yeah, Maccie. We really are."

He was holding back. I felt it. But for now, this was enough. Knowing he hadn't crossed me off his heart when things had gone wrong. Affirming I was in there the same way he was in mine.

For once, we had time.

And I intended to make the most of it.

Chapter Twenty-eight

Cormac

THIS TIME, WHEN I pulled up in front of the guesthouse, I got out with Zara and followed her to her door, taking her keys from her hand, and she pressed close to me while I twisted the lock. Once we were inside, she kicked the door closed and threw her arms around my shoulders.

"Come shower with me," she said against my lips.

"All right. I'm gonna turn on a light first. I still have a bruise on my knee from the other night."

She laughed and leaned around me, flipping a switch, bathing the living room in a warm glow.

"Poor baby. You should have told me. I would have kissed it better." She threaded her fingers through mine. "Come on. As much as I love the hot spring, I'd rather not smell like sulfur."

"You'll get no argument from me."

The bathroom was tiny. A pedestal sink, toilet, and cubicle shower. Zara reached past me to turn on the water then started shedding her clothes.

It took me a minute to catch up. I wasn't used to seeing this woman naked. My brain went offline the second she revealed her perfect teardrop breasts in the bright bathroom light.

She tilted her head when she found me staring. "What?"

"I—" I swallowed hard, dragging my gaze up to hers. "You're beautiful. I'm looking."

She cupped her hands under her breasts, teasing her peaked nipples with her thumbs. "You like these?"

"Are you kidding?" I sputtered. "I like everything."

With a snicker, she stepped forward, gripped the hem of my shirt, and yanked it over my head. Then her hands were on my abdomen, dragging up to my chest and down my sides.

"You're beautiful too. I love looking at you and getting to touch you."

"Touch all you want."

"I will. You gave me permission to be greedy, remember?"

"You think I'd forget that?"

The shower was a tight fit, but I didn't mind being crammed against her. I barely even noticed my elbow slamming into the tile, not with my cock trapped between our wet stomachs.

I pulled her in front of me, giving her most of the hot water. Her hair darkened instantly, flattening against her neck. She turned in my arms, water dripping from her lashes. Her gaze drifted to my collarbone, and I felt it this time—the pause, her quiet thoughts—before she touched.

"I can't believe you did this," she murmured, tracing the edge of the ink with careful fingers.

My hand drifted down her side, settling on her hip. "I couldn't believe it when you got the same one. Can't believe we match."

"We always have." She pushed up on her toes, touching her lips to my ink. "Why didn't you tell me at Jett's?"

"I don't know." I squeezed my eyes shut, pulling her closer. "I didn't know what to think. Truthfully, I still haven't wrapped my head around any of this."

"What—us being here like this?"

"I guess, yeah. Never thought this summer would happen."

That was such an understatement, but it was enough for now. Maybe for always. I was raw enough without baring the entirety of my soul.

I picked up her shampoo and poured some into my hand. "Turn around. Let's get you clean."

She pivoted, nearly slipping when her foot bumped mine.

"Easy," I muttered, catching her waist.

She smiled back at me. "I knew you'd catch me."

"Always. If you let me..."

I worked the shampoo into her hair, massaging slow circles at her scalp. She sighed, tipping her head against my chest.

"That's so nice," she murmured.

"Yeah?"

"Really good."

It was good for me too. Feeling her melt against me, trusting me to take care of her...it was our dynamic. Even when we were young, I'd always wanted to be the one to look out for her, and when that had been stripped from me, I'd been lost. This, though...I understood. This, I could do without thinking.

I rinsed her hair then repeated with conditioner, combing it through with my fingers and rinsing until the water ran clear.

When I reached for the shampoo to wash my hair, she grabbed it first.

"My turn."

"You don't have to."

"I want to." Her eyes lifted to mine. "Let me?"

With a heavy boulder lodged in my throat, all I could do was nod.

She poured shampoo into her palm and pressed up on her toes to reach the top of my head. Even with me bending forward, it was an awkward fit, making us both laugh.

"You're too tall," she claimed.

"I'm so sorry." I smirked against her temple.

"You should be. This was supposed to be sexy. You ruined it."

I rocked my hips, my erection sliding along her stomach. "Still so damn sexy. There's nothing you could do naked that wouldn't be."

Nothing clothed either.

She huffed in exaggerated frustration, then looked at my chest. A slow grin spread across her face as she planted her soapy hands there and scrubbed, deliberately working through the damp curls.

"Zara."

"I like this." She gave the hair a tug before returning to rubbing in the soap. "You didn't have this the last time I saw you shirtless."

"I was a scrawny teenager."

"You were cute then." She looked up at me through wet lashes. "You're gorgeous now."

"You like that I'm a hairy beast?"

She laughed. "I like you in any form, but yeah, hairy beast really works for me."

I couldn't argue. If she wanted to spend the next ten minutes scrubbing my chest, I'd let her. I reached up to wash my own hair while she was busy cleaning the rest of me.

By the time we were actually clean, we were grinning like idiots, foreheads pressed together under the spray. In all the times I'd fantasized what it would be like to turn our friendship into more, it hadn't looked like this. Now, I wondered why. We made each other laugh and weren't afraid to be goofy. This was *us*, but more.

Her fingers drifted to my tattoo one more time. Soft. Thoughtful. "You really did this."

"Yeah." I touched the ink on her hip. "You really did this."

"I really did."

We stood there longer than necessary, water falling around us, bumping shoulders in the steam. Then we dried off side by side, neither of us hiding that we were looking at one another in the bright light.

Zara tossed her towel in the hamper and held out her hand. "Come to bed with me?"

And I took it, letting her lead.

Where she went, I followed.

That was how it had always been.

Chapter Twenty-nine

Zara

It started with kissing. Cormac's lips were my new favorite place. His mouth was soft and warm and tireless. So very giving. His tongue licked along mine, gathering me up and keeping me close.

Kissing him was as natural and familiar as it was exciting. An adventure I knew without a doubt I'd be safe and free to explore—to let loose and be myself.

He pulled me on top of him, skin to skin. His big hands covered my back then roved lower, carving around my shape. I kept finding my fingers dancing along the words on his collarbone—*our* words.

We matched.

It was a heady thing, seeing part of our insides etched like artwork on the outside. And his was so visible to anyone who got close to him.

A swift kick of jealousy almost took my breath away. Had Victoria touched her lips to my words?

Cormac brought me back from my inner spiral, reminding me I was the one touching him, and he was the one touching me. Holding me. Kissing my breath away. Until I was convinced my lungs had always been useless anyway.

Then kissing me more.

My skin crawled and tightened, and my insides swelled to bursting. I squirmed, needing to move, to taste and touch and give. He let my mouth go to inhale deeply, and I slid down his torso, dragging my teeth and lips along his skin, licking his nipples and rubbing my face against the soft hair on the center of his chest.

I followed the trail of dark hair in the divot of his taut stomach, tasting it with my lips and tongue, and Cormac dragged his fingers through my hair, combing it. When I looked up at him, I found him watching me.

"Zara," he whispered.

I pushed his legs apart to kneel between them, taking his heavy cock in my hand. He stopped breathing, the muscles in his abdomen clenching tight.

"Can I?"

"Anything you want. I'm yours," he gritted out.

If only...

Holding his cock away from his stomach, I lowered my mouth over his wide, swollen head, taking him between my lips. A rush of air left him, followed by a low, mournful moan, and it was all I needed to keep going.

My nose hit his nest of curls, and I inhaled, taking in his scent. He smelled like my bodywash, and beneath it, his own unique smell. Fresh and musky. Clean air and the earth.

"Zara," he groaned. "Oh god, sweetheart..."

He jerked in my mouth but kept his hips on the mattress, letting me go at my own pace. It was nice and all, but we'd held back too long; I didn't want that anymore, not with Cormac.

Keeping him in my hand, I pulled off him. "Move with me. I want to know what you like—what makes you feel good."

"Anything you do feels good," he answered tightly.

I licked a line up his length. "You don't want to go deeper—don't want to hold on to my hair and fuck my mouth a little?"

His eyes slammed shut. "You can't say that."

My heart dropped. Had I read him wrong? "You don't want me talking that way?"

He shook his head. "You don't stop, I'm going to come so fast. Seeing you is enough. Hearing you like that...it's too damn much. I'm not strong enough to take it."

Breathing a laugh, I rubbed my lips against his head. "We won't talk about it then. Just know, I want you to move with me. No holding back."

Then I took him deep in one smooth slide. His entire body shuddered beneath me as he leaked and pulsed on my tongue, each drag of my mouth making him groan like he was dying. It didn't take long for his fingers to work through my hair as his hips began to move with me. He didn't get rough. He wasn't demanding. He was right there with me, both of us taking and giving.

I didn't want to stop. I could have kept going all night, hearing his helpless moans, feeling him deep in my throat, knowing how much he was loving it. I pressed my thighs together, trying to relieve some of the ache, but it was no use. I was heavy and wet and half mad, but Cormac's deep thrusts pulled me away from thoughts of my own body to give everything to him.

"That's so good," he panted. "If you don't stop, I'm going to come."

I had no intention of stopping.

I slid my hand under his cock to cup his balls, rolling them in my palm, then dragged a finger along the sensitive skin beneath. He jerked hard, hitting the end of my throat. I sputtered and coughed, but I didn't let him go.

"Oh god, oh god, I'm sorry," he cried, pushing into my mouth. "I'm gonna come, sweetheart. I'm gonna—"

I took him deep, my pulse kicking as he stilled on my tongue. The salty taste of his release flooded my mouth; I swallowed again and again. Stretching my arm along his torso, I lay my palm over his hammering heart. His hand fell over mine, clutching it tight as his orgasm went on and on.

Finally, he went slack, and I crawled over him, pressing my tingling lips to his. He cupped my head, prying my mouth open with his tongue to sweep it inside, and kissed me without mercy, long and wet and thorough as could be.

Without warning, he reversed our positions. His fingers between my legs, his mouth on my breasts, he opened wide, taking as much as he could. He sucked me deep, rolling his tongue over my pebbled nipple as he pressed on my clit, his fingers circling it tightly.

I clutched his head to my chest and rocked with his hand, so close to the edge it was painful. He moved to my other breast, sucking my nipple as far as it would go, and I moaned. My pleasure was his.

"Cormac," I cried, my spine bowing. "Please."

"I've got you." His hot breath hit my throat. "I've got you, sweetheart. Let go."

The vibration of his deep croon running through my body did it. Heat flooded my belly, bursting through like a tidal wave, and I *flew*. Writhing. Shaking. I came on his hand, his body the only thing holding mine down, and clawed at his shoulders, pulling him on top of me, my mouth searching out his.

Connected, our kiss was messy and fierce. Tongues and teeth and puffy lips melding with frantic need.

I opened my legs for him. "Inside."

He shook his head. "Not without a condom."

I flung my arm toward my nightstand. "In there. I got them for us."

He yanked the drawer open, ripped open the box, and snagged a foil packet. Then I had to let him go so he could pull back and roll the condom down his length.

He was back in no time, pressing his tip against my opening. "Ready for me?"

I lifted my legs, giving him room. "So ready. I want you, Cormac. Please give me you."

"You've got me." He pushed inside, and he did not stop until I was so full I couldn't breathe. "You've got all of me, sweetheart."

I brought my hands to his face, cupping his jaw. He went still inside me, my inner walls stretching and fluttering around him. Having him there, deeply connected with my body, was surreal and beautiful and exactly right.

"You feel so good," I rushed out. "So, so good."

His forehead dropped to mine as he exhaled. "There are no words."

And there weren't. There was only the shared heat between us. The way his control was so tight, I could feel it in the tension of his body. The careful stillness, like he was containing something bigger than either of us.

"You don't have to say anything." I pressed my heels against his ass, urging him closer, deeper into the moment. "Just move, please. Let me feel you moving inside me. That's all I need."

He started slow. So slow. A measured shift made my breath hitch and my toes curl as he watched me like I was the only thing in the world that mattered.

Cormac was a big man, but I was so turned on, so present, so wanting, my body bloomed, letting him inside.

I nodded over and over. Lifting up, I kissed his mouth, his cheek, whatever I could reach. I whispered how good he felt, how much I wanted him, my hands roaming his arms, his back, tracing his ridges and planes.

And he never looked away. Not once.

I'd never felt so safe or wanted.

And that made me climb higher, desperate for more.

"Baby," I rasped. "Please, please stop holding back."

He shook his head. "Don't wanna hurt you."

"You won't, you won't, you won't." I clutched his hair, giving it a tug so he could feel how serious I was. "I promise you won't. I want you."

His brow dropped low, and his mouth set into a hard line. The careful restraint in his shoulders fractured. Blue eyes turned from ice into the purest flame. Heat climbed up his neck and into his cheeks until the tremble in his arms was no longer control.

It was release.

He pulled his hips back then snapped forward in one powerful thrust, and my body answered instinctively, gasping, nails digging into his shoulders.

"Yes," I breathed. "More."

He gave me another and another, deep and slow, watching me each time he speared into me, his hesitation lessening with every thrust. Every time I moaned and told him it felt incredible, he moved a little faster, let his hands wander over me, cupping my breasts and down my sides.

Finally, we found our rhythm, moving together at a pace that left us both panting. The bed creaked beneath us, our breathing ragged and uneven, the air thick and warm. Sweat gathered at his hairline and along my spine. The world narrowed to the heat between us, the press of his chest, the way his name sounded falling from my mouth.

Cormac gave up fighting the pull between us and fucked me like he meant it, his hands sliding beneath my ass so he could take me deeper, and everything fell away except our connection.

Meeting, colliding, retreating, coming back together. Over and over. Until we were desperate, writhing together, clutching at each other. Our mouths slid, wet and frantic. My teeth snagged his lip, and his tongue delved deep into my mouth. Tension mounted low in my belly with every sharp plunge of his cock.

I couldn't take my eyes off him.

This man, this beautiful man of mine, had transformed into a magnificent beast, powerful muscles flexing as he held my hips where he wanted them, my body entirely under his control. Rivulets of sweat made their way from his corded neck to his chest, and his eyes were on fire, no doubt that flame was for me.

He pushed back onto his knees, suspending my lower body in the air. His thumb moved over my clit, rolling it in tight circles as he fucked me. Once, twice, three times—was all it took for me to lose it.

A veil of pleasure fell over me. My neck arched, and my mouth fell open in a wild cry. My eyes went hot and gritty as I came and came. Something inside me gave way. Some tight, invisible cord I hadn't known was there, keeping me braced and bound. It snapped clean, and I was unmoored. Weightless. Uncontained. Flying free.

The intensity was frightening, and the bright, electric rush following was dangerous in how much I immediately wanted it again.

"Zara."

My eyes flew open, but my vision was blurry, wet with tears.

Cormac's expression crumpled with concern, but it was too late. He threw his head back and groaned like he was breaking in two, his cock finding my end and planting as he shook, my name cracking from his lips.

I reached for his neck, pulling him until he fell on top of me, then buried my face as he nuzzled his nose against my hair. I'd never thought of myself as a clingy person, but I held on tight to him then.

He turned his head, his mouth beside my ear. "Are you crying?"

"I didn't mean to." I let out a wet laugh. "I don't know what that's about."

"I didn't hurt you, did I?"

"No way. Not even a little bit." He tried to pull back, but I held him tighter. "Don't move yet. I feel a little silly and embarrassed, and I'm not ready for you to look at me."

His sigh was hot and heavy against my skin. "You've got nothing to be embarrassed about, sweetheart. That was...damn, I might've been close to tears myself."

"You were not." I couldn't keep from smiling, even if he was just trying to make me feel better. "I think I've got a handle on myself now."

He gave me a squeeze, and this time when he pulled away, I let him. He didn't go far, though, rolling to his side next to me.

I smiled.

He smiled back.

And everything was right.

Chapter Thirty

Cormac

I PADDED OUT OF the bathroom, my clothes in my arms, and came to a stop. Zara was starfished on the bed, a goofy little smile tilting her lips, and god, was she pretty. My heart wasn't nearly strong enough to take this.

It was time to go. I'd stayed in bed with her as long as I could, soaking in her skin against mine, the scent of her hair, the feel of her in my arms. Now, I had to head out before I sank so far down in this I wouldn't bother getting up when it was over.

This way was better for us both. We'd keep it fun and physical and draw a line before it went further.

"Why do you have your clothes?"

"I was thinking I should put them on before heading out. Don't want to scandalize my grandparents by walking in naked." I turned, shaking my shorts out. Before I could get them on my legs, Zara snaked her arms around me, pressing her body to mine.

"Don't go." Her hands smoothed up and down my stomach. Her lips moved along my back. "You should spend the night here. Then we can do that again. And maybe again."

I twisted my neck to look at her. "Again? You have another round in you?"

"At least one more." She wound her way to my front and tore my clothes away from me, dropping them on the floor.

To be fair, I didn't put up a fight. When it came to her, I didn't know how.

"You want me to stay the night?"

"Yes." She nodded emphatically. "Come on, Maccie. Stay."

Her lashes fluttered, and she pressed her soft breasts against me—and there was not a chance in hell I was going to say no.

And the truth of the matter was, I didn't want to.

I woke up hot, my muscles achy and tired, and it only took a few seconds to figure out why. Zara was sprawled over my chest, her hair half in my face. I brushed it aside to look down at her, and my heart sputtered like a dying engine.

She was sacked out. The clock on the dresser across the room said we had another hour before we had to get up, but I was wide awake despite not getting much sleep last night.

Flashes of her mouth on me, her moving over me, writhing beneath me, sent blood rushing to my well-used cock. My lips were raw from hours of kissing, and my stomach felt like I'd done a thousand crunches.

Later, I'd fault myself for giving in. For now, I stared up at the ceiling, sliding my fingers through Zara's hair, stuck in the awe of it all. How good and easy everything was between us. That this was possible. And no matter how many times we came together, it was never enough. That waking up beside her was everything I'd ever wanted.

"Mmm, that feels good."

I dropped my chin, looking down at her. Her eyes were still closed, but a small smile played on her lips.

"Did I wake you up?"

"Maybe. I'm not sure I'm really awake."

"You can sleep a little while longer." I continued stroking her hair, the silk sliding easily between my fingers. "I'm gonna need to get home so I can shower and get ready for work."

She tossed her leg over mine. "Stay. You're so comfy."

I huffed a laugh. "I gave in last night. It's not going to work this morning."

"Pfft. You're happy you stayed."

I gave her shoulders a squeeze in response.

I couldn't say I was happy.

Not really.

I'd screwed up...but there wasn't a chance I wouldn't do it again.

My granddad was in the kitchen when I got home, pouring coffee in matching mugs, no doubt on his way to give one to my grandmother.

He raised a silver eyebrow when I appeared. "Doesn't look like you're getting in from a jog."

"No. That's next." I leaned against the counter beside him, crossing my arms over my chest. "I stayed the night with Zara."

He hummed as he added a teaspoon of sugar to one of the mugs. "I had a feeling that's where you were. The frown on your face made me doubt myself."

Without thinking, I reached up to touch my mouth. I hadn't realized I was frowning, but it made sense.

"I'm conflicted." I shoved my hand through my hair, giving it a hard tug. "I know I'm setting myself up for getting my heart broken at the end of the summer, but in the same token, I've got my best friend back, so…"

"So you don't want to stop what's happening." He nodded thoughtfully. "Why does it have to end in heartbreak?"

"She's going to leave."

"You'll miss her, but that doesn't equate to a broken heart. Seems maybe you need to have a conversation about where things'll go when she's back in Oregon."

"Things will end."

Chuffing, he shook his head. "You know, your grandmother and I got into our pickle by not having the conversations we should have."

I almost laughed. His definition of a "pickle" was being divorced for a couple decades and at each other's throats. Looking at them now, no one would have guessed they'd ever been apart.

"Your situation is pretty different from mine."

He set the two mugs on a tray, folding two napkins alongside them. "In the details, sure. When it comes down to the brass tacks, it's not so different. You and Zara have always loved one another—"

I nearly choked on my own spit. "What do you mean we've always loved each other? We were friends."

He leveled me with a hard stare, the kind my dad liked to give. Guess he'd learned from the best.

"I'm not blind, Cormac. There's always been something there. We all knew it. The only thing that surprised me was when you let life get in the way. Lucky for you, you got another chance before you got old and gray." He turned his head, peering in the direction of his and my grandmother's bedroom. "Kills me to think how much time I wasted with Lily."

"I don't think you were the only culprit."

He faced me again, a deep line between his brows. "When it comes down to it, it doesn't matter a lick whose fault it was. If either one of us had opened our mouths and put in the work to figure out how we could solve the obstacles in front of us, we'd have had all those years together. Now we only have a handful left. I have to live with that loss for the rest of my life."

I wanted to argue he had a whole hell of a lot more than a handful of years, but the fact was, my grandparents were in their eighties. One look at Zara and all she'd lost in such a short time, I knew how lucky I was to still have them.

And that wasn't the point he was trying to make.

"I hear what you're saying. I'll think about it." I pushed off from the counter and gave his shoulder a squeeze. "Go give your wife coffee before she divorces you again."

He chuckled. "She could try. I'd just chase her down."

"To the ends of the earth?"

His brown eyes twinkled as he grinned. "And beyond."

Chapter Thirty-one

Cormac

Javier knocked on my office door Monday morning, and I waved him in as I scanned a spreadsheet on my monitor.

"Got a minute?" he asked.

"Sure. What's up?"

He took the seat opposite me, steepling his hands between his knees. "I just got off a strange phone call I think you should know about."

That got my full attention. Elbows on my desk, I leaned forward. "What kind of phone call?"

"It was regarding Zara Vasquez. While you're not technically her boss, I know you're friendly, and"—he hesitated—"I figured you'd want to be aware."

My stomach tightened. "What about Zara?"

"The call was from a man named Ryan Mercer, claiming to be a private investigator out of Portland. Have you heard of this man?"

"I have," I said evenly. "I was with Zara when he called her a couple weeks ago. What did he want from you?"

"At first, he asked for basic information about her employment at the ranch." He held my gaze. "I didn't tell him anything he didn't already know."

"And then?"

"He started asking about her schedule. Whether she keeps consistent hours. Who she spends time with outside of work."

Heat crawled up the back of my neck.

"I told him we don't disclose employee schedules."

"Good."

"He asked if we had a current address on file."

My hands stilled on the desk. "He asked for her address?"

"He did."

"For what purpose?"

"He wouldn't say, and of course, I turned him down."

I stood and moved to the window, looking out over the corrals without seeing a damn thing.

"What else?"

"He asked about emergency contacts—whether we verify them." Javier's voice was steady, but there was a protectiveness beneath it I was happy to hear. If he heard from this guy again, he'd shut him down as firmly as he already had. "He wanted to know if she's dependable...and if we've had any issues with her conduct."

A low, controlled breath left me. "That's a hell of a lot of questions."

He nodded, worry creasing his features. "I don't have experience with private investigators, but his line of questioning caught me off guard. It didn't feel right."

"No," I agreed. "None of this is right."

I admired that he didn't press me for further details. He had to be curious, but it was clear he saw this for what it was: a gross invasion of Zara's privacy.

"I gave him nothing," Javier reiterated. "And I won't. I'll let the office staff know any outside inquiries come straight to me."

"I appreciate that."

"I mean it, Cormac." His eyes held mine. "Zara is a good person. A great employee. Whatever's going on, she shouldn't have strangers calling around trying to map her life."

My jaw tightened so hard, it ached. "Did he say who hired him?"

"No. I asked, and he said he couldn't reveal that."

I had a hundred more questions, but Javier had shared all he could. He'd done the right thing, cutting Mercer off without giving anything away.

Turning away from the window, I moved to the other side of my desk. "If you hear from him again, put him through to me."

Javier stood, sliding his hands into his pockets. "Of course. Should I let Zara know about the call?"

"No." I rubbed the space between my brows. "I'll talk to her."

"She's leading a horseback ride this morning then taking a group out climbing. She should be done with her day around four."

"Thanks." I clapped him on the shoulder. "Really, Javier. Thank you for your discretion."

"It goes without saying." He stopped at the door, his hand on the knob. "Zara's great at her job. She knows the ranch like the back of her hand, and she really likes being a guide. We don't get many like her."

There was *no one* like Zara.

Javier shut the door softly behind him, leaving the office too quiet.

I stood there a long moment, staring at nothing.

My jaw flexed.

Zara had fought too hard for her peace. This was her fresh start, and her ex's business was trying to invade.

That wasn't going to happen. Not while I was still standing.

I had some calls to make. Courses of action to consider.

If Mercer or Jackson—hell, if *any*one showed up wanting to map her life, they were going to find out very quickly every road led through me.

Zara picked up her phone then put it right back down. This wasn't the first time she'd done that. Or even the second. But I didn't blame her for her reluctance. I'd dropped this bomb in her lap the minute she'd gotten home from work. She deserved to know what was going on.

Her dark gaze shone on mine. "I never want to hear his voice again."

"I'll talk to him if you want me to."

"No." She let her head fall on my shoulder, and I wrapped my arm around her, pulling her into my side. "Let me complain about it for a minute, then I'll do it."

I smiled into her hair. She smelled like sunshine, sweat, and Zara. "Complain all you want."

I didn't want her to call Jackson, but after talking it over with my dad, followed by our family's lawyer, it seemed to be the right starting point. This was Jackson's problem. He needed to be the one to handle Mercer. And while I sincerely doubted Jackson would do the right thing, there was a small chance he might. So we were going to start with him and go from there.

Zara gave herself a full minute before sitting up and grabbing her phone off her couch. "Okay. I'm ready."

She punched in his number, and a small, jealous part of me relished that Jackson wasn't saved as a contact in her phone. In fact, she'd had to unblock him in order to dial—that was how completely out of her life he was.

She held the phone between us. Two rings before he picked up. "Hello?"

"Hey, Jackson. It's me," she said.

He made a disgruntled sound through the speaker. "Christ, Zara. I've been trying to call you for a while. You had me blocked, didn't you?"

She ignored his question. "I'm assuming you know there's a private investigator looking into you. He's called me and my job asking questions. What are you going to do about that, Jackson?"

"He called you?" He cussed under his breath. "Why would he call you? You have nothing to do with...look, it's all a misunderstanding. There's nothing for you to worry about."

"That's not true, and we both know it. Whose money did you take?"

"It doesn't matter. I'm handling it."

"It doesn't seem that way. The PI called my *job* today—did you hear that part?"

There was a long pause before he asked, "Where are you working? No one checked with us for references."

Her chin jutted, stubborn and proud. "That's none of your business."

"Everything about you was my business for a long time. It wasn't my idea for that to change."

She squeezed her eyes shut. "Look, I'm only calling about this PI. He threatened to fly out here to speak to me in person, and I really don't want that to happen. I need to know you have an actual plan to fix this *misunderstanding*."

I covered her hand with mine, and she leaned into me even harder. That this conversation was difficult for her—that this man had her feeling *anything* still—killed me. But the reality was she had a past, and he was a big part of it. All I could hope for was for him to stay where she'd left him so she could keep moving on.

"You're not in Portland?" he rasped, sounding shocked. "Where are you?"

"I have a summer job in another state. That really doesn't matter. I'm—"

He cut her off. "You're in Wyoming, aren't you? On that fucking ranch? I should've known you'd go there the second you left me. Should've seen it coming a mile away."

Her spine straightened, and her cheeks flushed pink. She opened her mouth, like she was gearing up to tell him off, then clamped her lips together and took a few deep breaths.

"I'm working with a lawyer, Jackson." Her voice changed, losing its tremor and smoothing out, like glass cooling into something solid.

On the other end of the line, Jackson huffed a laugh. "Oh yeah? And what did your lawyer say?"

"He informed me of my options and reminded me I have no obligation to protect you and your brothers since anything tying us was severed the second our divorce was finalized."

Dell Rivers had been handling the ranch's affairs longer than I'd been alive. Hell, he handled most of the legal needs of Sugar Brush.

He was the call I made after speaking to my father. While Zara had been out leading a trail ride, I'd laid it all out for him, and he'd gotten to work, looking into Jackson and Mercer. By the time she was done for the day, we'd come up with a game plan. She'd only spoken to him for a few minutes, but he'd given her the buttons to press when speaking to Jackson. The path of least resistance had been his first choice, and he'd been hoping leaning on Jackson would get him to do the right thing.

I wasn't so sure—especially not after hearing how he was talking to her, but this was only the first step. If Jackson didn't come through, we were armed with a plan on what to do next.

"I don't need you to protect me," Jackson said after a long pause.

"Maybe, maybe not. I do know I'm not *willing* to protect you from the mess you made all by yourself. Well, with your brothers." She flipped her hand over and curled her fingers around mine, holding on tight. "My lawyer and I are preparing a statement for your investor. I don't know much, but I'll tell them what I know."

Jackson let out a sharp breath. "You don't need to do that. You don't know anything, Zara. I made certain of that. What could you possibly have to say?"

"I'll tell them I discovered what you were doing and kept documentation of the account numbers you were hiding—the ones I never had access to. Not to mention the emails I sent to you and your brothers questioning the discrepancies. It's not proof of what you did, but it *is* proof I had no part in it."

"You were my wife," he shot back. "Anything you say makes you look involved."

"I don't think so," she said softly. "It makes me look stupid but honest."

Something fierce and protective lit in my chest. She was far from stupid. She'd trusted her husband. Hadn't she been supposed to? The problem was, she'd married a man who'd never been worthy of that trust.

"You're really going to sell me out?"

"If you don't take care of this yourself, yes, I will. You didn't care enough about me while we were married to be honest, and I sure as hell am not going to throw myself on a grenade for you now that we're nothing to each other. This is your problem, Jackson. You know I had no hand in any of this."

"We both know that," he conceded. "I doubt anyone will believe it, though."

"God!" She tapped her forehead with her fist. "Have you always sucked so much?"

I had to bite the inside of my cheek to keep from laughing. Zara wouldn't have appreciated it, and it would have alerted Jackson to my presence. But damn, I hadn't expected her to say that. She was killing me.

I'd never wanted to kiss someone more in my whole life.

"You used to like me just fine." Jackson sounded almost offended.

"And you used to be kind of charming. Now, you're just...you're a coward."

A pause. Then, "A coward?"

"Yes. A spineless coward. You'd rather your ex-wife get tangled up in your screwup than own up to it and figure your way out. I've had enough. Pay back the money you owe, or I'll take action."

"Zara...I need time." He exhaled hard. "It's not something I can get sorted out easily. You're good with numbers. You have to understand."

She shook her head. "There's nothing to understand. You willingly put yourself in a very bad position. How you get yourself out is your concern. I want nothing to do with any of this."

He blew out a long breath. "You have to give me time. Ignore the calls from Mercer. It's not like he's actually going to show up in Wyoming. And if he does, I'm sure your little buddy, Mac, will protect you. You know that guy tried to talk me out of marrying you, right? He probably wanted you for himself."

Her jaw went rigid. "Shut up. You don't know what you're talking about."

He did. He knew exactly what he was talking about. I'd thought I'd hidden my feelings well, but apparently not from Jackson. The fact that he had figured out she'd come to Wyoming and was with me was the only thing keeping me calm. It meant this place, and maybe me along with it, had been on her mind, despite the silence and distance between us.

He barked a humorless laugh. "That's it, isn't it? You're with him, aren't you? Christ, I should have known. All those times I caught him looking...oh, this is rich."

Hell yes, she's with me. You can eat shit, man. She's never gonna be yours again.

Zara cut in before he could say anything else. "Hey, Jackson? Just so you know, I've recorded this phone call, and I'll be sending a copy to Mercer. I'm sure he'll be pretty interested in the part where you admitted I never knew what you were doing, so he can cross my name off his list."

"What? Are you kidding me, Zara?"

"I'm not kidding. I don't think anything about this is funny."

He chuffed like an angry bull. "I said I need time."

"What you need doesn't have anything to do with me. If I hear from Mercer again, my lawyer and I will be moving forward."

Silence went on for so long, I was beginning to think he'd hung up. Then, he let out a long breath that sounded an awful lot like defeat.

"We'll have to ask Mom and Dad for money."

Zara didn't seem to feel any pity for him. "Then do it. I'm sure they'd rather give you a loan than see your kneecaps get broken or you get thrown in jail."

"Probably," he muttered. "Don't block me when we hang up so I can let you know when I've taken care of it."

"Text me. Don't call."

"It goes without saying you don't want to hear my voice," he bit out.

"You're right. It does."

She ended the call before he could say another word, tossing the phone on the cushion beside her.

I held my arms out, and she crawled into them, melting like wax on my chest. She was quiet, and I let her be, running my fingers through her hair and holding on.

Maybe this was going to be over soon. Maybe not. Either way, I would be here with her—standing beside her, behind her, or wherever she needed me.

Chapter Thirty-two

Zara

"You want something to eat?" Cormac asked, gentle as a lamb.

I sat up in his lap so I could look at him. *Really* look at him. His face...I couldn't get enough of his face. His perfect, pink cupid's bow, a jaw that could cut glass, and little glimmers of red and blond in his dark scruff. It was his eyes that did me in, though. They should have been icy and cold, but this was Cormac, and everything about him was warm. His cool blues were a summer day, bright and clear. I could have lain down and basked in them forever.

The way he was looking at me now, like he wanted nothing more than to take care of me, if only I'd let him, made me want to kiss every inch of his perfect face at least twice.

My chest was bursting with the need to give him *something*. He wasn't in crisis. I couldn't swoop in and rescue him the way he kept doing for me. But I needed to show him.

"In a little." I shifted to straddle his legs and took his face in my hands. "I'll make us something."

His hands came to rest on my waist. "You okay?"

"I'm fine. I wish you hadn't heard those digs he made about you, but—"

He shook his head. "It didn't bother me."

"It bothered me." I leaned in, kissing the tip of his nose. "You're such a good person, Mac. You always have been. And you're so good to me."

I kissed each of his cheeks then his eyebrows.

"I want to tell you to go run into a door or trip and skin your knee so I can take care of you, but I really don't want to see you hurt." I kissed his chin then along the sharp line of his jaw. "I just want to take care of you the same way you always take care of me."

"You do." He caught my lips with his as they passed, pressing a fleeting kiss. "Come back here."

"You're the sweetest man alive, you know." I squeezed his cheeks with my palms and kissed his eyelids. "I'm so happy you're in my life again. Like, super, very happy."

His mouth hitched, and something in my chest fluttered. Not my heart, but something close by. It felt like a pile of snakes slithering around so much I could barely stay still. What was that?

"I'm super, very happy too," he said, making me groan.

"God, Maccie." I squeezed his face a little harder and kissed him all over his forehead. "You're so cute, I can't stand it."

His laugh was sharp and sudden. "Cute? Is that the kiss of death?"

"No, no, no." I tipped my face to kiss beneath his ear then dragged my lips down the long column of his throat. "I love that you're cute. If you were just sexy, I might be able to resist you. The cuteness is what clinches it for me. I can't stay away."

His arms banded around me, flattening me against his chest. "You can call me whatever you want, as long as you keep coming back for me."

I lapped at the beating pulse in his neck. "Show me your tattoo."

He tugged his shirt to the side, revealing our words. "Here you go."

I fell on them, rubbing them with my lips, then kissed each letter. By the time I got to the end, Cormac took my head in his hands, bringing us eye to eye.

"Tell me you're okay."

"I'm okay." I looked back at him, steady under his blue sky. "I really am. We have a plan, and a small part of me is relieved Jackson's going to his parents. I want him out of my life, but I don't want him hurt."

"I get it. You're human. It makes sense you care, even if you're done with him." He carved his fingers through the sides of my hair. "You are, right? Done, I mean."

"So done," I whispered. "My feelings for him were trampled so thoroughly I don't think I'd recognize them if I ever ran across them again."

I scooted closer, settling my core over his. "You spent your day putting out my fires, Cormac."

"It's what I wanted to do, sweetheart."

I dropped my lips to his, pressing a long kiss there. "I know that. It's who you are, and why you're the best friend I've ever had."

"You'd do it for me," he said simply.

"You're so sure."

He nodded. "I am."

"Lucky for us, you'll never get yourself into trouble. I won't be tested."

"No." His fingers tangled, guiding my face down to his again. When our lips grazed, he murmured, "I don't need you to be tested. I know what I know."

Then he kissed me hard, his tongue sweeping between my lips to claim mine. His hands tightened at my waist, not rough, just sure, like he knew he had every right to touch me this way now. I kissed him back with all the squirmy, slithery need inside me, urging me closer and closer to him.

I broke away just long enough to breathe, "Bedroom."

His eyes darkened, that warm summer blue turning deep and intent. "Yeah?"

"Yeah."

Cormac stood in one smooth motion, and I wrapped my legs around his waist, laughing into his mouth as he carried me down the short hallway. He nudged my bedroom door wide with his foot and set me on the edge of the bed. I threw my T-shirt off and lifted my hips to tug off my shorts and panties. For a second, Cormac watched me, his eyes raking over every inch of my body.

"Come here," I said, tugging him by his belt loop.

He yanked his shirt over his head, toed off his shoes, and crawled over me, bracing his weight on his forearms so he wouldn't crush me. I slid my hands into his hair and kissed him again, slower. We smiled against each other's mouths, bumping noses, trading small, breathy laughs between kisses.

"You're smiling," he murmured.

"So are you."

"I can't help it."

"Good," I whispered. "Don't."

Every time he kissed me, it was like he was checking in, like he needed to make sure I was still with him. And I kept answering. With my hands. My mouth. The way I pulled him closer even when he was right on top of me.

"I like you so much, Maccie. So, *so* much."

His eyelids went half-mast, and his mouth fell open with a whoosh of air. "Christ, Zara…I don't know what to do with you."

"Just be with me. That's all."

He lowered himself the rest of the way, chest to chest, and let his weight settle carefully over me. I wrapped my arms around him and held tight.

He exhaled like he'd been carrying something heavy all day.

"There," I whispered, kissing the corner of his mouth. "I've got you."

He groaned softly as I kissed his neck, and the sound carried all the way through me. Every brush of his body against mine made my breath hitch, but it wasn't frantic. We were moving together with intent. Building piece by piece instead of chasing an ending.

Cormac cupped my face, slowing us down when things threatened to tip into urgency, and pressed his forehead to mine.

"Still okay?"

I smiled, brushing my nose against his. "Super, very okay."

That made him laugh before he kissed me again. Deep. Unhurried. He shed the last of his clothes, our skin seeking and finding. Every touch was a question, every kiss the answer to everything.

Any time he wasn't kissing me, he was looking at me. I was over him now, taking him between my legs. He held on to me, helping me fit him inside and roll my hips against him.

"Zara," he whispered, for no other reason than to say my name.

"I'm here," I breathed. "You feel so good."

I traced his face with my fingertips and leaned in to kiss him everywhere I could reach. His fingers slid over my hip—over the words we shared.

"I love this." His forehead crinkled.

I touched his collarbone. "I love this more."

He pulled me down and buried his face in my neck, and I held him there, stroking his hair as I moved over him, the snakes in my chest slithering to the point I could barely breathe. I gasped as he plunged to the end of me and exhaled when he retreated.

My fingers dug into his skin, and I stared at him like I could find the answer to this...this unknown question he'd stirred within me. The question that didn't make sense but plucked at my mind. Words that wouldn't form. A thought I couldn't quite gather.

Cormac looked back, guileless and so stunningly beautiful, it was all I could do not to yell it out.

He'd riled me up, and there was no settling. No matter how deeply I took him or how much I quickened my pace. I plastered myself against him, breathing in the scent of his skin. He held me close, bringing me with him when he fell. Releasing deep inside me with a shuddering groan as my inner walls closed around him, we were one sweaty, smiling, sated heap, holding on to one another for dear life.

"I like you so much," I whispered into his neck.

"Yeah." He brushed my hair off my face, kissing my temple. "You too, sweetheart. Like you so much too."

Chapter Thirty-three

Cormac

A COUPLE DAYS LATER, we both ended our days early so we could go for a ride. It was the first time we'd done this, just the two of us. When we were younger, Zara was always clamoring to get out on the horse she'd claimed as hers. This summer, she'd spent a lot of time on horseback, and just as I'd suspected, she couldn't get enough.

We took a meandering ride down to the river, neither of us in a hurry to get there, enjoying the late afternoon sun and each other's company.

Zara rode a little ahead at first, like always, then slowed her mare until our stirrups nearly brushed.

"I forgot how this feels," she said quietly.

"The saddle?" I asked. "I thought you kept riding back in Oregon."

She shook her head. "No, I mean *this*. All of it. The space. The quiet. Not having to be...anything."

"There's nothing you have to be with me."

"I know, Maccie. That's how it's always been."

The river came into view over the horizon, the water flashing silver as it flowed. A breeze rolled off it, carrying that clean, mineral smell. Zara closed her eyes and tipped her face, soaking it in.

"For a while, it wasn't." I turned to look at her. "But we're back to the old days, huh?"

The corners of her eyes pinched. "I don't think we can ever get those days back. We're different. Things are different between us. We were only friends. Now, we're...more."

My heart kicked at the acknowledgment. It was such a small, obvious thing, but it meant so much to me. I wasn't in this all alone, buried under my feelings.

"Better, you think?"

She lifted a shoulder. "It can't be better than you and me racing to the river without a single care in the world. But it can be just as good, I hope."

"Yeah," I agreed. "Maybe it can be."

She was right. There was nothing like the carefree days of childhood, before responsibilities got in the way and the only goal in life was to have fun. I was glad we'd shared so many of those days. Glad we'd always have that to fall back on. And maybe we'd have snippets of those days again—add them to the storybook of our lives that was already a hundred chapters long.

We reached our spot by the river and hopped off our horses, leaving them to graze nearby. I dropped my backpack on the ground and pulled out a blanket.

Zara raised an eyebrow. "You're not going to let me sit in the dirt?"

I laughed. "You can if you want to, but I'm going to sit my grown-up ass on this blanket and see what else I have in this backpack."

She dropped down on the blanket before I could even fold myself into a sitting position and started snooping.

Gasping, she lifted her head. "Did you bring a picnic?"

"I did. It's nothing fancy, but I figured I could get you to stay longer if I fed you."

She tilted her head. "You don't have to bribe me. There's absolutely nowhere else I want to be."

I nodded toward the water in front of us. "Your favorite place."

With a sigh, she shifted to her hands and knees and crawled onto my lap. Facing me, she cupped the sides of my neck, her midnight gaze trailing up my face to lock onto my eyes.

"My favorite person..." she murmured, "brought me to my favorite place. Why would I ever want to leave?"

"I'm your favorite person?"

She nodded. "You've spent this summer reminding me how stupid I was to forget that fact." She hooked onto the collar of my shirt and pulled it aside, pressing a kiss on my tattoo. "Thank you."

"You don't need to thank me." I wrapped my arms around her, holding her against my chest, dropping my face into her hair. "Told you I had ulterior motives."

Her lips moved against my neck. "I like your motives."

We stayed like that for a while, hugging each other, sharing memories of our childhood. The races we ran. The rides we took. The times my parents had to go out looking for us because we'd stayed out too late. That was how it was with Zara. Time lost all meaning...until I became acutely aware of how quickly the days we'd had together were passing.

It was no different now. I couldn't settle into being with her. Not all the way. Not when each passing day brought us closer to the end. She'd go, and I'd be here. Where would that leave us?

"I should get off you so we can eat," she said after a while, making no effort to move.

Cupping her hip with one hand, I reached out and dragged my backpack closer. "There's no reason for you to get off me unless you want to. I'm good how we are."

She leaned back to look up at me, a smile curving her mouth. "I'm good how we are too."

It was easy, being like this, relaxing against a tree trunk, Zara's back against my chest, eating the simple sandwiches I'd thrown together as the river flowed past. The horses made low chuffing noises, talking to each other more than us. In the distance, a pronghorn paused, looking to see if we were friend or foe, then bounced away, deciding we weren't very interesting. Zara talked about Henrik's ongoing crush on Javier and his dwindling hope it would be reciprocated. I told her about a problem guest staying for the next two weeks and all their demands.

When we were just about finished eating, her phone began vibrating with a call. She tugged it out of her pocket, glancing at the screen.

"It's my parents. Do you mind if I answer? I owe them a call—"

"Answer it."

She stayed right where she was and hit the video-call button. A second later, Amir and Zadie Vasquez appeared on screen, their faces pressed together.

Seeing Zadie healthy was good for my soul. I tried to block out the image of her so sick she couldn't leave her bed, Amir curled around her, holding her through her pain. My mother blowing into town and taking over the care of her friend and forcing Amir to rest.

It had taken a toll on everyone, but Zadie had gotten through it. She'd gotten older, with wrinkles around her eyes and laugh lines bracketing her smiling mouth—exactly how it was supposed to be.

"Hi, guys," Zara greeted.

"Baby girl." Amir's dark gaze flicked upward. "Cormac. Good to see your face. How are you?"

I nodded to him and smiled at Zadie. "Hi. I'm good. How are you guys?"

"We're doing great." Zadie's smile was soft and gentle, just like the rest of her. "It's so good to see the two of you together. This feels like old times. Whenever we called Zara, you were always in the background."

"She couldn't get rid of me," I said, and Zara laughed, settling against my chest.

Amir raised a brow. "Don't think she tried too hard."

"That's true. I didn't." Zara grinned at her parents. "Sorry I haven't been great at keeping up with phone calls. You know how I get when I'm out here. I get consumed, and the days fly by faster than I can believe."

"You'll be better going forward," Amir replied, no question in his tone.

"I'll try to be better," Zara sort of agreed.

Zadie's laugh was light and airy. "I'm glad you're finding what you were looking for, even if you're much too far away."

"At least you have Zane to fuss over," Zara said.

"Pfft." Amir shook his head. "Last night, he implied we're being too needy and can't stop by whenever we like."

Zadie patted his cheek. "He only asked us to call first. I think we might have interrupted something."

Zara burst out laughing. "Oh no. You didn't! Tell me you didn't go into their house without knocking."

"We knocked," he gritted out. "Might not've waited for them to answer, though."

"We?" Zadie blinked at him. "There was no 'we.' You got impatient and used your emergency key against my advice."

He shuddered, his brow crumpling. "I regretted it immediately. There are some things a father should never see."

Despite Zadie and Zara's laughter, I was internally cringing for Zane and Steven. It was a good thing we were too far for them to pop in without warning. Though...I had a feeling they wouldn't make that mistake again.

"We're lucky Zane didn't rescind our key-holding privileges," Zadie said.

Amir threw his arm around his wife. "You were right, Mama. I admit it."

Zadie's cheeks flushed with pleasure. "All it took for you to admit to being wrong was seeing your son's b—"

He covered her mouth with his hand. "Never say it. Please. I'm trying to forget it, and if you say it, that won't be possible."

Zara jumped in to save the conversation, turning the camera around to show them the scenery. She zoomed in on the river, then scanned left and right, showing them the horses nearby and a hawk soaring overhead.

Zadie sighed. "Beautiful as always, my love. And you look happy."

Zara smiled and pressed her forehead against my chin. "I really am."

Her parents exchanged a glance. He scratched his chin. She nibbled on her bottom lip.

"What's going on?" Zara asked. "What aren't you saying? Mom, are you okay? Are you—"

Zadie raised a hand before Zara upset herself. "No, no. I'm fine. I had a checkup last week and got a perfect bill of health."

"She'll live forever," Amir said, like if he commanded forcefully enough, it would come true.

Zadie smiled serenely. "You just...seem so happy, I wasn't sure if now was the time to bring up a job opening I heard about."

Zara leaned forward, putting distance between us. "Oh. A job opening for me?" Zadie nodded, and Zara's shoulders sagged. "I guess I have to start thinking about that."

"You have time, baby girl," Amir said. "But your mama thought this would be a good fit for you. It's an accounting position at Zane's hospital. You might get the chance to see your brother on a regular basis if you're working in the same place, and you know he likes it there."

"He does," she agreed. "Can you send me the listing?"

"Sure," Zadie said. "Though I'm surprised you haven't found it yourself. I guess you haven't been looking?"

"No, not really." Zara threw her hand out toward the landscape in front of us. "You know, with all this, I haven't put much thought into returning to an office. But I need to. I'll definitely check out the listing when you send it."

With every word they exchanged, my stomach dropped. I'd known this was coming. It never left my mind. But the reality of Zara applying for a job that would take her away was a lot different than only the looming possibility.

They talked for a few more minutes while I listened. I liked how tight Zara was with her family. They had an easy, close relationship that reminded me of mine with my parents. Though she didn't tell them anything about Jackson and the PI. I figured it was as much for his protection as it was for her parents'.

Her dad might've been kind and gentle with his kids and wife, but I'd heard things about his past and had a feeling he would not let Jackson's actions stand if he were made aware of them.

They said goodbye, and Zara tossed her phone down on the blanket. She twisted around to look at me, her mouth pressed into a line.

"You're quiet."

"I was listening." I brushed her hair off her face and dragged my fingertips along her cheek. "They miss you."

"I miss them too. After I left Jackson, I spent a lot of time with them. My mom and I went for daily walks, and my dad stopped by my apartment nearly every day with something he'd found for my place or tools to fix something that wasn't broken." Her heavy exhale made her shoulders roll forward. "Things were such a mess between Jackson and me for so long. I'd stopped talking to them as much. Not completely. They would've never allowed that. But I didn't tell them anything real. I was embarrassed by the choices I'd made, and I...well, that's a big reason I miss them so much now. It's been years since I've let myself be close to them."

"I never would have guessed."

"That's the point. I was really good at hiding." She tucked her face into my neck, her breath warm. "And I was miserable. I don't want to ever do that again. If I can't live honestly, then I know I'm doing something wrong and will make it right."

"That sounds like a good plan to me."

"We'll see. So much is up in the air. At least I have a lead on a job."

"There's that."

She raised her head, her eyes narrowed. "You sound grouchy. What's that about?"

Taking a page out of her book, I went for honesty. "Thinking about you leaving at the end of next month doesn't make me the happiest."

"Yeah..." she breathed. "I guess that's why I'm trying not to think about it. I want to enjoy every minute of the time I have here."

"I want that too."

She brought her hands to my face, smooshing my cheeks. "You're cute even when you're frowning. Maybe cuter, since it's such a rare sight."

I groaned, yanking her against me. "Didn't I tell you to stop calling me cute?"

Squealing, she grabbed my hair like reins. "If you did, I didn't hear it. If you say it again, I'm not going to listen."

Despite the deep pit in my gut, I had to laugh. "You're a hopeless case."

"And you're adorable." She tugged my head back and started kissing all over my face. "So, so cute. I could eat your nose and chin for breakfast."

"Only my nose and chin?"

Her lips landed on my temple then my eyebrow. "I'd eat the other parts for lunch and dinner." She caught my cheekbone and the tip of my nose. "I love your face. And your ears. And your hair."

"So much you want to eat it."

"Mmmhmm." Her lips grazed mine. "Am I weirding you out?"

"Nope." I ran my fingers through the sides of her hair, pulling her face away from mine. Her eyelids fluttered open, and a slow smile split her lips. I smiled back. I couldn't help it. "I know you, Zara. I don't think there's anything you could do or say that I'd find weird."

"Even when I want to eat your face?"

"Even then." I chuckled lightly. "Gotta admit, I never considered I'd hear you say that, but it's kind of...sweet."

Her lashes fluttered as she sighed, everything about her softening. She leaned into me, her forehead resting on mine, her palms sliding on either side of my neck.

"You really get me."

It wasn't a question but an acknowledgment of fact. We might not have known everything about each other. Not anymore. But I did know her—deep down.

We were a part of each other.

"Yeah, sweetheart. I get you. I always have."

No amount of distance would change that.

Chapter Thirty-four

Zara

Let it be known, Phoebe Kelly ran a tight ship. When she'd asked me to volunteer at the town market, I'd expected to sit at a booth and sell her baked goods. Over the last couple weeks, I'd been to three planning meetings, painted signs, designed price sheets, and glued hundreds of silk roses to the booth Deke had built from scratch.

This morning, I arrived at the park just after sunrise, the street-lights still glowing. According to Phoebe, this place would be shoulder to shoulder by noon, but we were the only ones here.

That might've been because we had the most elaborate setup. I couldn't imagine anyone else had had a master carpenter build their booth for them. Phoebe was determined we'd raise as much money for the library as we could, so she'd gone all out.

As time went on, one by one, folding tables were set up and white tents bloomed across the park. Farmers with crates of tomatoes, a woman selling jars of pickled vegetables, another with a myriad of jellies, a high school kid arranging bouquets of sunflowers in mason jars, and a couple food trucks lined the curb.

By eight, the park began to swell. Locals showed up, walking with purpose, like they knew exactly where every vendor would be and what they'd planned to buy. Phoebe had left Alice and me in charge while she ran back and forth between the market and her café. We didn't have to do much to sell the individual boxes of cinnamon buns and little baggies of cookies. They went so fast, we were out before Phoebe could restock us.

Tourists trickled in later. Families in hiking sandals and sunburns, couples wearing matching cowboy hats, and older people studying the printed maps they'd picked up at the five-and-dime that doubled as the information center.

"Are these really for the library?" an older woman asked, peering at our sign.

"They are." I straightened a stack of napkins that didn't need straightening as Alice jumped in to explain.

"We're hoping to add to our children's section this year. I have big plans for a weekly story time and after-school program."

"That's lovely," the woman said, handing me a twenty and picking up a cookie. "The rest is for the children. I hope you raise lots and lots of money."

The woman walked away, and Alice and I grinned at each other. We hadn't spent much time together, but I liked her a lot. She had been quiet at first, but once I'd spoken with her a few times, it'd become clear how smart she was. She'd read more books than I would ever get to in my entire lifetime, and she'd written a series of her own. She also had a sneaky sense of humor and was a great listener. Caleb had gotten lucky when she'd agreed to be his wife.

"The kids of Sugar Brush won't know what hit them," I said, slipping the twenty in the lockbox. "They're going to be buried in new books."

Alice giggled lightly. "Well, I hope not. Burying children is pretty frowned upon—no matter what it is they're under."

I mimed writing on my palm. "Noted. Do not pile books on top of kids. Put books on shelves instead."

She laughed harder. "That's the spirit. You're basically a librarian now."

"If I can't find an accounting job, I know where to go."

She leaned close, her shoulder bumping mine. "You really don't want to keep guiding? I was under the impression you enjoyed it."

"Oh, I love it. But I went to school to become an accountant and studied my butt off to become a CPA. I think I just have to find the right job this time. Besides, guiding isn't really a career."

"It isn't?" Alice slowly nodded. "I suppose it's not a *common* career, but I wouldn't say it doesn't count. You have a regular schedule and get paid to complete a task."

"There's no nature guiding major in college."

"I don't personally know that to be true, but I'll trust you on that." She rubbed her lips together before continuing. "I imagine becoming an expert guide is accomplished more through experience than books. And if you look at it that way, with all your years of exploring the ranch, you've put more time into being a guide than getting your degree in accounting."

Another customer arrived before I could respond, and I was grateful for it. I didn't really know what to say. She was right. Of course she was. Henrik guided full time. He moved around from country to country depending on the season, never forcing himself to sit in an office.

But we were different people walking very different paths that just happened to cross this summer.

By midmorning, I'd gotten the hang of running the booth. I handed out change, tucked brownies into paper sacks, and explained that, yes, Phoebe's lemon bars were as life-altering as they looked.

Eventually, Lily arrived to give Alice a break. She more so held court with everyone who stopped by than did any real work, but that was okay. She attracted attention, which made us money, and I was determined to make as much as we could for the library.

Two women approached the booth, and it took me a moment to recognize them. Melanie, I was most familiar with since I had to pass by her every time I visited Cormac's office. The pretty blond I saw less often, but knew was Cormac's ex, Victoria.

She really was pretty, and so well put together, I felt a little like a slob in my ball cap, no makeup, and a simple sundress. But that was unfair to us both. If I put in the effort, I could make myself just as presentable, and Victoria had done nothing to deserve my scrutiny.

It was just that I was jealous of her.

That was easy enough to admit. To myself, at least.

"Hi. Can I help you pick out a treat?" I asked.

Melanie scanned the table with a slight sneer, and Victoria pinned me with a hard look.

"Are you just here for the summer?"

"I—" Hadn't expected that, so it took me a moment to respond. "Yes. Just for the summer. How about you? Do you live in Sugar Brush full time?"

She lifted her lovely chin. "Yes. I moved here two years ago. It's my home."

"It's a great place to live."

She placed her hands on the table and leaned forward, her face inches from mine. I was too surprised to move away.

"We had a really good thing going, you know."

My brows rose. "I'm sorry. I don't know what you mean."

Her bottom lip quivered, and she quickly hardened it. "Cormac and me. We were good together. I thought—" She shook her head. "Then he ended it out of nowhere. Well, I felt like it was out of nowhere, but Melanie told me you've been spending every second together. You're the reason he broke up with me. It's just...I can't figure out what you have that I don't. What makes you so special?"

My stomach sank, and heat crawled up my neck. I disliked confrontation. Even more, I hated the tremor in Victoria's voice. I felt terrible she was upset, but she had it wrong.

"I don't know anything about Cormac and you," I said quietly. "Whatever happened between you had nothing to do with me."

She crossed her arms and straightened. "I'm not stupid. One day, we were fine, and the next, you showed up and he told me it was over. And now you're spending all your time together. I can do the math, can't you?"

Melanie wrapped her hand around Victoria's arm. "Come on. We don't want anything here. There's much better stuff at the other stands."

They walked away without a backward glance, leaving my head spinning. What was that? How could she think...?

Lily touched my hand. "Are you okay, darling?"

I turned to her, my heart thumping. "That can't be right."

She rose from her seat, taking both my hands and squeezing them. "I think you'd better ask Cormac what's right and what isn't. He'll tell you."

I squeezed my eyes shut. "I should, but I can't leave you here by yourself."

"Hannah will be here any minute, and Phoebe is on her way. I can handle myself for a little while." She placed her hand on my back, giving me a light shove. "Go. It's well past time the two of you had this talk."

To help Phoebe out, Cormac had volunteered to clean Sugar Rush's kitchen, so when I burst through the back door, he was scrubbing the stainless counter.

"Hey." His eyes swept over me, and I knew I had to look about as frazzled as I felt. "Are you okay?"

"I'm fine." I took my cap off and squeezed it with both hands. "Is the shop closed?"

"Yeah." He tossed his cleaning cloth aside and approached me. "Phoebe left a few minutes ago. You just missed her."

"Lily had said she was headed to the park. She made me take a break." I forced my feet to move until I was right in front of him. "Why did you break up with Victoria?"

His brow dropped low over his eyes, but he didn't hesitate to answer me. "It wasn't going to work out."

"It had nothing to do with me, did it?"

His lips parted, and for a moment, he said nothing. I held my breath, waiting for his answer, not knowing whether I wanted him to say yes or no. All I knew was I couldn't breathe until I heard the truth.

He stepped forward and brushed his knuckles along my cheek. "Yeah, Zara, it did."

A whoosh of air punched from my chest. "How? In what way?"

He gripped the back of his neck, turning away. "Because it wouldn't have been fair to keep going out with her after I saw you again and realized my feelings hadn't gone away. If she feels I wronged her in some way, I'm sorry for that, but I did the best I could by her."

"What does that mean?" I pushed up on my toes, trying to get him to look at me. "What do you mean your feelings hadn't gone away?"

He finally turned back to me. "I was in love with you when we were younger."

"What?" I rasped.

He continued like I hadn't spoken. "It had never been the right time to tell you, then you met Jackson. I'd missed my chance, if I'd ever had one, and had to let it go. And I really thought I had. Then you showed up, and that first night when we had dinner at my parents' house, I knew it was still there. So I left their house and went directly to Victoria to let her know I couldn't continue things with her."

"You loved me?" My throat was so thick, I could barely push the words out. "Cormac, you loved me?"

"I was in love with you, Zara." He laid his hands on my shoulders and slid them down my arms. "I still have very strong feelings for you."

"You do?" He was going to make me cry. "You did? God, Mac, you didn't tell me. You should have told me."

Arms wrapped around me, he brought me into his chest, touching his lips to my forehead. "You were too young. Then there was the distance. I was happy to have you as my friend. I promise you, I treasured what we had, Zara, and I never wanted to mess that up. I thought once we got to college together, we'd have the time, but it never happened."

"You should've told me."

He held me tighter. "I'm not sure it would've worked out. You weren't in the right place to hear that from me—"

"You don't know that." I pushed on his chest without much force. I didn't want to be away from him; I just wanted my point across. "How could you know that?"

"I don't. Not for sure. But it's what I think. You were pushing me away, finding yourself on your own. If I'd come in guns blazing, telling you I was in love with you when you were falling for Jackson, I don't think it would have ended well."

I slumped against him, all my fight fleeing. "I hate myself."

"No." He tangled his hands in my hair, pulling my face back. "No, no, sweetheart. There's nothing to hate. Look where we are. We're standing here together. We're *together*, Zara. If I'd told you back then, I don't know that we could be this way now."

"But we missed so much time together," I argued weakly.

"And we still have so much ahead of us."

"I can't believe you've been carrying this on your own for so long. I—" I rubbed my forehead against his soft T-shirt, inhaling the scent of his skin mixed with the sugar floating around the bakery. "It feels like I missed something important, and I'm so mad at myself for not seeing it."

"I'm not mad at you." He stroked along my back, still holding me so close. "For me, it was a fine line between loving you as my friend and loving you as...more. I can't even say when it changed. It feels like it's always been that way."

"Cormac," I cried softly, overwhelmed by what he was saying and the snakes waking up in my chest. I shuffled closer, my feet sliding between his, but it wasn't enough. If I could have opened his rib cage and folded myself inside, that might have done the trick.

"Shhh, it's okay." He dipped down to kiss my cheek. "Love that freckle," he cooed. "So pretty."

I couldn't think of what to say. This was too big for me to comprehend, but I knew it was impossible not to be angry with myself. If I'd been less selfish...if I hadn't taken him for granted, things could have been so different.

At the same time, I understood the fine line. I couldn't look back and see when his feelings had changed. There was no shift. He had always been *this*. So kind, loyal, and attentive. That was who he was.

He nudged my chin with his knuckle, forcing my face up to his. "I hear you thinking. It's okay, Zara. My feelings aren't your responsibility. You were never required to reciprocate them, especially when I never told you I had them. You didn't do anything wrong."

I huffed. "That isn't true, and we both know it." Then my nose crinkled. "I've always loved you too, you know. I'm not sure if it was *that* way. The love has just been there since we met. If I hadn't been so consumed by my mom's illness and the years of grief that followed, I think I would have gotten brave and tried to kiss you."

He pressed his thumb against my bottom lip. "Now, see, we don't need to do that. Playing the 'what if' game isn't going to win us anything but regret. You *were* consumed with grief. *I* let you go too easily. You *did* overhear me talking to Jackson the night before your wedding. Those are things we can't change. But I've got you in my arms right now, and I'm finding myself not too upset about anything."

"I'm not there yet."

"That's all right. We've got time."

The backs of my eyes burned, and panic welled in my chest. We didn't. We had this summer...then what? I had to leave when we were only now discovering this new facet of our love. Would it just be over?

Chapter Thirty-five

Cormac

ZARA'S EYES WERE SHINY black diamonds. "We don't, though. We don't have time."

Frustration rose, but I tamped it down. She didn't think the way I did or see what I saw. But how could she know what was going on in my mind if I didn't tell her? I'd made that mistake with her too many times. It was high time I learned from the past.

"Zara," I sighed. "Come here."

Instead of waiting for her, I scooped her up and carried her over to Phoebe's desk, sitting down in her chair with Zara in my lap. I'd come to learn she liked it there, and since there wasn't anything I liked more than having her close, getting to touch her and learn the feel of her in my arms, that worked for me.

"We can make time."

Her brow creased. "I don't think that kind of physics has been mastered yet. I wish..."

I laughed softly, leaning down to kiss her trembling lips. "Not what I mean, sweetheart."

"Then tell me what you mean."

In the past, I would have considered her feelings before speaking. I would have turned it over and over in my head until I talked myself out of saying anything. I was through doing the same thing on repeat and expecting a different result. I knew what I wanted, and I was going for it.

"If I have my way, we're not going to be finished in September. I want us to have a chance at making this work. If that means doing long distance, I'm willing to give that a try. I have no intention of letting you go unless you tell me I have to. And even then, it might be tricky."

Her eyes darted between mine. "You want to try long distance?"

"I do."

"I...think it would be really hard."

"No harder than giving you up."

A puff of air escaped her parted lips. "That *would* be hard."

"Impossible."

Her chin quivered as she stared at me. "I'm so sorry."

"Stop it." I took her chin between my thumb and forefinger. "None of that. We're not talking about the past anymore. We're moving on to our future."

She blinked, and a tear rolled down her cheek like it was trying to run away so it wouldn't be seen. I didn't miss it. Catching it with my finger, I wiped it away.

"It's not fair we're just getting here," she said.

"Pretty sure my dad told us plenty of times life isn't fair."

That made her laugh. "Oh, he definitely did. My dad too."

I grinned, hope stirring in my gut. "What do you say? Should we keep going like there's no end in sight? That's what I choose. I'm no stranger to hard work. I will do it gladly if it means I get to keep you."

Her lips rolled over her teeth as she nodded.

"Is that a yes? Do you want to give this a real try?"

She nodded again.

I dragged my knuckle along her damp cheek, ending at my favorite freckle. "I want to hear you say it."

Her words came out wobbly but sure. "Yes, Mac. I'm scared, but there's no chance I want us to end."

"I'm scared too," I admitted. "I think this is it. Our do-over. We have to get it right or…"

"We won't get another chance." She squeezed her eyes shut. "I don't want to lose you."

"Then do your best, and so will I."

She huffed a wet laugh. "Bossy."

"Not usually. I'm pretty protective over us."

"I am too." Her palm slid up my cheek, and her eyes opened to meet mine. "I'm protective over younger Cormac who had all these big feelings he couldn't share. I wish I could go back to hug him and tell him I'm so sorry. Since I can't, I'll tell you. Even if you don't want it, please let me say it."

It was on the tip of my tongue to object, to tell her there was nothing to be sorry for, but I just nodded, letting her have it.

"I'm sorry, Maccie. I wasn't a good friend. I could make all kinds of excuses, but that's what it boils down to." She pressed firmly against my cheek. "I see you now, and I want to be good to you. I'm terrified long distance is going to be a hellscape, but I never want to give you up, so I'll walk through it with you."

"No one else I'd walk through hell with."

She fell against me, her arms circling my neck. "Hold me, okay?"

"You never have to ask." I banded my arms around her and buried my nose in her hair, telling myself this was good. I was getting what I'd asked for. We were going to give this a real try.

But the pit of dread in my gut was impossible to fully ignore. Sooner or later, she was going to be a thousand miles away, and I wouldn't be able to hold her in my arms whenever I wanted.

If I had my way, if I was allowed to be selfish and get exactly what I wanted, she'd stay here come September. We'd face the harsh winter, maybe get snowed in together, and she'd still be here when the ground began to thaw and determined buds pushed up through the unforgiving terrain. And we'd have summer after summer of racing to the river and back.

I didn't know if any of that would happen, but I was unwilling to give up on the possibility. If two people could do long distance, it was us. We had experience loving each other from afar. Maybe not the same kind of love, but still a love we'd nurtured. And we were older now. So much wiser too.

We could do it. I'd get used to not having her in my arms every minute, and maybe I'd stop missing her popping into my office all hours of the day. As long as I got to hear her voice and know she was mine, I'd make it work.

I had to. The only other option meant losing her forever, and that was no option at all.

A while later, after Zara helped me finish cleaning the kitchen, we both ventured to the market, hand in hand. It was something of a coming out for us. My family had suspected and hinted they'd known something was going on between us, but this was the first time we'd confirmed it. My sisters and grandmother noticed, and their happiness was evident, but they didn't make a show of it.

We hung around the market, taking turns manning the booth and strolling around to check out the other vendors. Phoebe's baked goods sold out before it was over and we helped break everything down.

Phoebe grabbed Zara's hand once we were finished. "You have to come back for the evening concert. Deacon and I are bringing Abigail, and Hannah's family is coming too."

Alice raised her hand. "Cay and I will be there. Des is going to hang out with Grandma and Grandpa."

Zara glanced up at me. "Do you want to?"

"Yep. I do." I pulled her into my side. "I'm told there's often dancing at these things."

Phoebe grinned. "We usually make our own dance floor. It's always a good time."

Zara leaned into me. "Then I guess we'll see you there."

We parted ways after that, most everyone heading home to clean up or take a rest, and Zara and I drifted.

Main Street still hummed with the lazy warmth of late afternoon. We took our time, no hurry to get anywhere, our hands linked between us. Zara paused at the window of the bookstore, leaning in to read the handwritten staff recommendations taped to the glass. She'd left her hat in my truck, so when a breeze made the hair around her face dance, I reached out and tucked it behind her ear.

She looked up at me and smiled. "Always taking care of me."

"Can't help it."

"You're cute."

"You keep saying that."

We kept going, stopping once or twice to talk to friends of my parents and grandparents. I introduced Zara as my girlfriend, earning my hand a squeeze, and when we were alone, a lingering kiss.

"You called me your girlfriend."

"Aren't you?"

"Yes, but that was the first time you said it." She pushed up on her toes to kiss my chin. "I feel a little claimed."

"You are." I raised our joined hands to rub my lips along her knuckles. "I'm claiming what I've always known was mine."

Her eyes danced. "The next people we meet, I'm telling them you're my boyfriend."

I chuckled, even as pleasure struck me deep. "Have at it. I'd like to see how you work that into a conversation."

We ran into Dell Rivers next, and Zara managed to do it. Dell seemed a little perplexed to be introduced to me when I'd known him my whole life, but had taken it in stride.

Zara was pleased with herself. "See? I did it."

"I never should have doubted you."

She bumped her shoulder into my arm. "When my mind's made up, I don't change it."

"I've noticed that about you, sweetheart. I noticed it a long, long time ago."

"I figured you might have." She bumped me again. "My mind's made up about you, Cormac Kelly. I'm claiming you too."

"That's the best news I've heard in years."

We'd never had a slow afternoon like this. Decades of knowing her, we'd always been racing—against time, our feelings, each other. Now we were finally slowing things down, walking side by side, out in the open and plain as daylight.

By the time the sun had started sinking low, we made our way to Joy's. The bar was already half full, the familiar smell of burgers and fried onions wrapping around us the moment we stepped inside.

We slid into a booth near the dartboards. Zara ordered a chicken sandwich, and I got my usual burger and fries. We talked about nothing important and filled the few silences with smiles we couldn't seem to hold back.

After we ate dinner, dusk had settled over town. The sky was deepening into navy blue, and the first stars were starting to show.

By the time we reached the park, it looked entirely different from how it had this morning—almost like a dream.

Twinkle lights had been strung from the trees and lampposts. The grass was dotted with blankets and lawn chairs, families and couples settling in to listen to the band. A pack of kids ran through the open spaces, glow sticks flashing in their hands.

The four-man band started playing a country rock song at the same time we spotted my family spread out on a patch of grass not far from the stage. Abigail toddled between Deacon and Phoebe while Hannah's boys wrestled in the grass. Hannah and Remi were on their feet, taking turns making sure Silas didn't get too rough with Brooks as they swayed to the music, their arms wrapped around each other.

Alice waved us over. "We were starting to think you weren't coming."

Zara sat on the blanket beside Phoebe, and I dropped down behind her, stretching my legs out. She leaned back against me, fitting on my chest like it was custom-made for her.

We stayed like that through a few songs, talking and laughing, watching Phoebe and Deacon dance. They went out dancing often, so they put the rest of the park to shame.

"I hope you don't expect me to have moves like that," Zara said.

"As long as you let me dip you, I'm good."

After a few songs, Phoebe plopped back down on the blanket, nudging me with her foot. "Go on."

I pecked Zara's forehead. "You want to dance?"

Twisting in my arms, her eyes lit up. "I thought you'd never ask."

I stood and pulled her up with me. The band had shifted into something slower, which was a good thing since I wasn't much of a dancer. All I had to do was pull Zara into my arms and sway. The music wrapped around us, and the lights overhead glowed softly through the leaves.

"I was going to ask you to my prom."

She sucked in a breath. "You were?"

"It had been my plan all along. Then your mom got sick, and I knew there was no way you'd want to leave her."

A line carved between her brows. "You didn't go to your prom, did you?"

"No. Dancing with you was the only reason I'd wanted to in the first place."

Her hand squeezed mine. "At least we have tonight."

"It's not too bad of a consolation prize, is it?"

"Not too bad at all."

Her cheek brushed my shirt as she leaned closer, and I rested mine against her hair. I couldn't imagine taking her to prom would have been any better than this; I'd just had to wait a little while longer for it to happen.

For years, I'd considered the way things might have been different. If her mom hadn't gotten sick. If life hadn't pulled us in opposite directions. If I'd said something sooner. If I'd been brave enough or she'd been less stubborn.

Because even when we weren't close, even when years passed with only a few words between us, Zara had always been there, woven through every memory and place I spent my days. She was never too far from my mind.

It used to feel like we'd missed our chance. Like the window had closed before either of us had known it was open. Standing here now, though, her in my arms, the music and night swirling around us, I could see I'd been mistaken.

It hadn't been the wrong person or wrong place.

It had been the wrong time.

Now, everything was clicking into place. Like every road I'd taken, every mile and mistake and second-guess, had led me right back to this patch of grass, twinkle lights overhead, her arms looped around my neck.

Right person.

Right time.

Finally.

I pressed a kiss into her hair, and she smiled against my chest like she knew exactly what I was thinking and agreed with all her heart. God, I hoped she did.

When the tempo picked up, and the spell was broken, we just stood there in each other's embrace.

She smiled up at me. "That was the best first dance ever."

"Not even a contest."

Chapter Thirty-six

Zara

The barn's fan blasted directly onto my overheated face, cooling the sweat on my skin leftover from a long trail ride. Dust clung to my jeans and the edges of my boots, and my fingers were creaky from hours of holding on to my saddle.

The mare I'd ridden leaned into the brush I ran along her flank, one back hoof cocked, her eyelids half-closed like she might fall asleep standing up.

Behind me, Henrik made a dramatic groaning sound.

"Remind me why I signed up for this job."

I didn't turn around, smiling to myself. "You love it and can't get enough."

"These are lies. I've never loved anything about this job." Something clattered loudly. Probably a brush hitting the floor. "These horses are getting heavier. I am sure of it."

"That's because you let yours eat half the trail."

"That is a lie too," he said indignantly. "Only the green parts."

I switched hands to brush down my mare's shoulder. "Have you heard back from the resort in Switzerland?"

There was a pause. "They offered me the job, but I am weighing my options."

"Really?" I finally turned to look at him. "I thought you were dying to work there this winter."

"Mmm. Maybe." He shrugged, not meeting my gaze. "There might be something better."

This was strange. My entire first month at the ranch, Henrik had been talking nonstop about his next guide job in Switzerland. He'd dreamed of working there and finally had a way in.

"What's with the switch up?"

He waved me off. "I might be tired and need a rest. I'm thinking about it."

"Okay. Keep your secrets."

He hummed. "I will, thank you. And you, liebchen? How are your prospects? Will you soon be chained to a desk like a boring person?"

"Quite possibly. I have an interview next week."

It wasn't something I wanted to think about. Just what I needed to do. My mother had been right. The job sounded like something I could handle, but when it came down to it, anything would truly be better than working with Jackson and his brothers.

Scheduling that interview put me one step closer to leaving Sugar Brush, though. And Cormac. Which was why I wasn't thinking about it.

Henrik stepped into the aisle beside me, his boots scuffing the concrete. "Next time we go on a shorter trail, okay?"

I huffed. "Next time you complain less."

"Impossible."

I laughed softly, giving my horse a firm pat. "*You're* impossible."

"Impossibly lovable, right?"

Footsteps sounded at the far end of the barn, and Javier stepped into view. I straightened, brushing my hands against my thighs as I glanced down the aisle.

"Hey, Zara." He nodded to Henrik. "Henrik."

I waved, and Henrik ran a hand through his blond hair.

"Hello, Javier," he crooned. "You're looking well this afternoon."

Javier stopped in his tracks, and it might've been a trick of the light, but I swore his cheeks flushed.

"Uh...you as well, Henrik. Good ride?"

Henrik crossed his thick arms over his chest and beamed. "The best. I love long, hard rides."

Javier's jaw went slack for a fraction of a second before he cleared his throat and poured all his attention on me. "Good. That's good. Zara, do you have a minute? I'd like to talk to you about something."

"Sure," I said. "I just need to finish up."

He nodded once. "I'll be in the office."

I waited until he disappeared then whirled around to face Henrik. "What was that?"

He pointedly examined his nails, buffing them against his shirt as if they weren't filthy dirty. "I have no idea what you could mean."

I walked up to him and gave him a shove. "You made Javier blush, Henrik. Are you...is he...?"

His eyes lit up like the Fourth of July. "You saw him blush too, right? Isn't it cute? Oh my god, he's—" He bit down on his lip, cutting himself off.

I jabbed a finger at him. "Are you and Javier having a thing?"

He nodded toward the door. "Don't you have to go? He's waiting for you."

My hands parked on my hips. "I wouldn't want to keep your salt-and-pepper daddy waiting, would I?"

This time, Henrik blushed, telling me everything I needed to know. Before I left to talk to Javier, I said, "I promise I won't say anything to anyone."

He looked left and right. "Anything about what?" Then, quieter, he said, "Thank you, liebchen."

That night, Cormac fed me, made me come, then gave me the stars.

All I had to do was tell him how much I loved the sky at night here, and he sprang into action, moving cushions and blankets onto the small deck at the back of the guesthouse.

The way he cared for me was incredible to me, and like second nature to him. I was tumbling constantly, headfirst, wild and crazy. Falling and falling in love with him. I couldn't help it. It was inconvenient, but there was no way to stop it.

Not that I wanted to.

Cormac made it so easy. We already had our rich history and a once-in-a-lifetime deep friendship. But I was seeing another side of him. He was showing me what it would be like to be his. And it was...so beautiful.

We'd started our stargazing lying side by side, Cormac pointing out constellations and planets, things his granddad had shown him as a kid. Eventually, he rolled onto me, his head on my stomach, his arms and legs slung over me. My own Cormac-shaped blanket.

Absently, I threaded my fingers through his thick hair as I counted the stars above us. Frustration curdled my gut. I didn't have enough time to count them all. Not enough time to do anything I wanted. And each star I counted meant there was less and less of it.

"I thought you'd relax out here," he murmured against my belly. "I hear your thoughts churning."

"Just counting the stars."

And thinking about my conversation with Javier. The impossibility of it. Wishing he'd never said anything at all. I was tempted, oh so tempted.

"It's more than that." He lifted his head, his forehead crinkling as he looked at me. "Are you okay?"

"I'm fine." I wasn't ready to share what Javier and I had talked about. Not until I came to a decision. Maybe that wasn't fair, but it was the way it had to be.

I ran my fingers along his cheek and jaw. "So cute."

I caught his mouth curving as he dropped his head back down to my stomach. "You say 'cute.' I hear 'devastatingly handsome.'"

"That too," I agreed. "Definitely that too."

He hummed, snuggling his body into mine. It was perfect. The stars and Cormac all around me.

So, of course, I had to go and poke at it. I couldn't let perfection stand without trying to pick it apart to see what was underneath.

"What do you think it would take for you to love me again?"

He went so still, he stopped breathing. "What?"

"I guess that's probably a silly thing to ask. How could you know? I just...I keep thinking about how I missed it. Something so great, and I had no idea. And the thing is, I don't know if I was in love with you back then, but I'm pretty much head over heels for you now."

"Head over heels," he repeated roughly.

"Yeah." I continued sliding my fingers through his hair as I blinked up at the sky. "I do love you, Mac. I always have. But I've fallen *in* love with you. I can be patient. I'm not demanding anything from you. But I hope you can get back to the place where you're in love with me too. If there's something I can do to reassure you, to help you along, I want to do it. I want you to feel safe falling in love with me again."

He said nothing for so long, fear rose in my chest. I was certain I'd screwed up irrevocably and he was about to tell me there was nothing I could do or say that would make him feel safe. I was close to launching into orbit when he finally lifted his head and pushed up on his elbow, looking down at me.

His eyes glimmered in the moonlight. "There's nothing you need to do."

"Oh."

He took my chin between his fingers, not allowing me to turn away from him. "Because I do love you, Zara."

"You do? Again?"

He paused, sucking in a deep breath, his gaze never leaving mine. "Still. Always. It's never waned. To tell the truth, I haven't tried very hard for it to. You are the love of my life. That's just a fact."

The backs of my eyes burned, and my nose twitched, but I refused to cry. Not now.

"I love you," I whispered. "*Love* love."

His exhale was shaky, and his eyelids lowered halfway. "Never thought I'd hear you say that."

"I'm sorry it took me so long to get here, but I *am*. Right here, Maccie. With you. I love you very much."

His forehead dropped to mine, his warm breath fanning across my lips. "Thank Christ, sweetheart. Everything else is details, as long as we agree on loving each other."

I circled my arms around his neck, pulling him so most of his weight was on my chest. It made it hard for my lungs to inflate, but I didn't care. I just wanted him as close as I could get him.

"We agree," I said softly, my lips next to his ear. "We so agree."

And since neither of us had put on many clothes after making love earlier, it didn't take much to get rid of the little we had. Skin on skin, we pressed together, kissing like we had all the time in the world.

And maybe we did.

It might not always look like this. We might live far apart and only have short visits and long phone calls, but if we loved each other this way, distance wouldn't matter. We could stretch this love a thousand miles then beyond to wrap it around the world if we had to.

I would have welcomed him inside me bare, but Cormac would never take a chance like that. Not with me. He was always so careful with me. So we just kissed and rocked against one another. His mouth never tiring, never becoming sated from mine. He sought me out each time he moved away, again and again.

My slick flesh slid over his swollen length as I held him so tight my muscles trembled. Eyes open, I stared up at the sky I'd missed almost as much as the man in my arms; I'd never experience another moment that would come close to touching this one.

Even if, by all rights, I hadn't deserved it, his love for me had never died. Knowing that was as heady as it was terrifying. I needed to deserve it now.

"I'll cradle it," I said, my lips on his jaw. "I'll hold it in the palm of my hand."

Of course he understood me right away.

"You do," he replied, sucking my earlobe. "You don't know it, but you always have."

Tipping my head back, I cupped his cheeks. "I love you and your beautiful heart."

He shuddered, shoulders going tense. "I don't know how to hear that yet."

"Then I'll keep saying it until you do."

His mouth covered mine, so I said it in my head. In the way I touched him and ground my core against his. Drawing him toward pleasure. Making him feel as good as he would allow. I desperately wanted him inside me, but I didn't push. His needs mattered just as much as mine, and it was important I showed him that.

He reached between us, rolling my clit under the pad of his finger and lowered his mouth to my breast, sucking greedily. I wrapped my legs around his hips and followed the rise of his tide until we were panting, hot and needy.

My mind was a hazy maze, but I managed to keep my words clear as a bell. Whispers of "I love you so much" floated up to the stars like a wish. Even when he brought me over, the cries I released were his name and love and promises of my heart belonging to him.

It didn't take long for Cormac to follow. Hot spurts of pleasure coated my belly and his when he collapsed onto me.

We held each other through it. Naked and spent, the wide-open sky above us.

He nuzzled into my hair. "Say it again."

I rolled to my side, bringing us eye to eye. It was dark, but the moon was bright enough for me to see him as clearly as I should have all along.

"I love you, Cormac Kelly. I really do."

His eyes threatened to close, but he kept them open and pinned on me. "You have no idea...never thought I'd hear that. I thought I'd be in this alone. I'd accepted it."

"You're not." I touched the patch of scruff beneath his bottom lip. "You're never going to be alone in it again. I *love* you."

His lips grazed mine. "About time."

Then his mouth hitched in a smirky little grin, making me laugh.

I gave his shoulder a hard shove. "Shut up and tell me you love me too."

That got a real laugh out of him. "I thought I didn't have to say it back."

"That was before. Now you do."

Still chuckling, he scooped me into his chest and buried his face in my hair. "I love you, you stubborn, gorgeous woman. Now I'm going to take you inside, clean you up, and show you just how much."

"Again?" I squealed as he climbed to his feet with me in his arms.

"Still." He hoisted me over his shoulder and smacked my butt. "Always."

Always. That sounded like almost enough.

Chapter Thirty-seven

Zara

THE FOLLOWING WEEK, I used my day off to meet with Dell Rivers. He'd taken over dealing with Jackson and Ryan Mercer, and it appeared this ordeal was coming to an end.

Jackson had dragged his feet until Dell sent an official letter to him and his brothers. Miraculously, things began to move swiftly then.

Not swiftly enough for Mercer and his client. He'd called Javier again, and me as well. But while I was in his office today, Dell spoke with Mercer on the phone. For a nice old man, he really put the screws to him.

When he hung up, he grinned at me, his wrinkled cheeks pink with delight. "Well, that was fun. Not often I get to throw my weight around like that anymore."

"No? Ranchers don't give you trouble?"

He waved me off. "Pfft. They're pussycats compared to your PI. He was all business until I brought up the law codes he was breaking, then he backpedaled like a scared little girl."

I arched a brow. "As a person who was once a fearless little girl, I resent that remark."

He laughed with delight. "Sorry, darlin'. I take that right back. If Mercer were forced to face you down, I have a feeling he'd be scared of you at any age. Lucky for him, he seems to understand the people he needs to lean on are Jackson and his brothers."

"I hope you're right."

Because I was beyond done with that part of my life.

Unfortunately, I would never be able to forget my first marriage. I'd learned too many lessons from those years to even want that, but everything else about it—including my ex-husband—I wanted far, *far* behind me.

It was the middle of the day when I left Dell's office, and Sugar Rush was having a lull in customers. Phoebe greeted me with a hug and helped me pick out a muffin while her employee made me a coffee.

We sat together by the front window, and she told me about a club where she and Deke like to go dancing with their friends, inviting Mac and me to join them the next time they went. Through a knot in my throat, I had to tell her it would have to be sooner rather than later, since I was supposed to be leaving in a few weeks.

She didn't question me on that, but I couldn't miss the doubt mixed with sadness in her eyes. I was sure the same emotions were in mine too.

It wasn't just Cormac I'd miss. I'd let myself forget how great a friend Phoebe had been to me, and how warm this town's embrace was.

As I strolled along Main Street, popping in and out of the cute little shops, my heart ached. It wasn't just for what I was leaving. I missed my family back in Oregon too. I couldn't wait to squish myself between Zane and Steven, to get lost in a really good hug from my mom, to feel my dad's hand on top of my head as he called me his baby girl.

I'd left them once. I'd sacrificed our relationship for a man who had demanded it. Never in words, but subtle shoves that caused me to become further and further adrift from the people who'd always anchored me.

I picked up a postcard in the five-and-dime. It had a picture of the Kelly ranch on it. Cattle dotted the rolling, craggy landscape in front of the mountain looming like a giant in the background. And through the middle ran our river.

It was beautiful. I loved it so much, I could barely stand to look at it in pictures, knowing I would be leaving it soon. Yet it wasn't the land making my heart crack.

It was him.

Even if Cormac had lived in a concrete jungle or a barren desert, I would feel like I was splitting in two leaving him. I belonged with him. He was who I'd longed for when the summers were over. I might have convinced myself it was our adventures or the places he'd shown me, but at the core of it all, it was him.

If we were going to make this work—and we *had* to make it work—eventually, one of us would have to give something up. There was no other option.

I was certain Cormac could find a job anywhere. He was talented and smart. Everyone liked him. And there were countless hotels and resorts in the Portland area. If he came with me, he'd land on his feet, and we'd be together.

And if I asked him, he'd come. I didn't doubt for a second he would.

But how could I ask him?

He hadn't asked me to stay. Maybe he didn't think he had the right to. We were new, but at the same time, decades old. There'd always been an "us." Our parents had pictures of toddler Mac holding newborn baby me. He was as much a part of me as the marrow in my bones.

My thoughts were filled with every possibility on my way home. Then on my walk by the river. Through cooking dinner and a brief phone call with Cormac, who was spending his evening hanging with Caleb's family.

Just when I thought my mind was going to explode, Zane called me.

"Hey, you."

I smiled at my brother's face. His pretty eyes and achingly familiar smile. "Hello, Zaney. Where's your other half?"

He crinkled his nose. "Can you believe he joined an indoor soccer league? He's currently at his first practice. He was nervous about playing with his new friends. It was all kinds of adorable."

"Aw, everyone loves Steven. I'm sure they'll be nice to him and pass him the ball."

Zane's humor was quickly replaced with a look so sharp it could have cut glass. "They better. Maybe I should have gone and sussed these guys out."

I laughed. "Steven can handle himself. You can look threatening at his first game."

"Don't worry. I'll be there with deadly, spiky bells on."

I sighed. "Like father, like son."

Zane lifted his chin. "Can't help it. I learned from the best."

"We both did." I carried my phone outside, plopping down on the Adirondack chair Cormac had stolen from his grandparents' deck so I'd have a place to sit. "I really miss you guys."

"Same, but you'll be back soon. You know you're going to have to come with me to these soccer games, right? I don't think I'll be able to bear them otherwise."

"You'll get to watch Steven running around in little shorts. I think you'll be okay."

His eyes narrowed, and he pointed at me through the screen. "What's that face about? Why do you sound like that?"

I shook my head. "I don't sound like anything."

"You do. You sound...resigned."

"I'm sad, all right? I want to see you and keep you company at Steven's soccer games, but I'm kind of in love with Cormac Kelly."

His jaw dropped for a split second before he started muttering curses and tugging at his hair. "I knew it. I knew this would happen. Of course you're in love with Cormac Kelly. No one could believe it when you came home from college with a boyfriend who wasn't Cormac. *Jackson.*" He scoffed bitterly. "But I was sure that ship had sailed. I mean, you married a whole other man."

"Can we not talk about that?"

He stopped and stared right at me. "Does he love you back?"

I nodded. "Oh yeah. Big time."

"Fuck. This is a disaster."

Then I told him the thing I'd been trying really hard not to think about since my conversation with Javier last week.

"My boss is planning on moving on to a new job in September. He wants me to replace him."

Zane's head fell back with a loud groan. "I knew you weren't going to come back. I *told* you."

"I haven't accepted." I nibbled on my bottom lip until Zane focused on the screen again. "I have an interview at your hospital tomorrow morning."

He rolled his eyes. "Why bother? You love guiding. You love that godforsaken state and you finally pulled your head out of your ass and fell in love with the man who was always meant for you."

"I haven't decided anything, that's why. Cormac and I are so new. I do love him, more than I thought possible, but what if we move too fast and screw it all up? It would be smart to get a job in Portland and see where things stand then. We've already agreed we'll do long distance when the summer's over."

"Sure. I'm all for that plan." He nodded a few times. "You come back here, live with Steven and me until we get sick of each other, then move into the house next door."

"You've got my future all planned out." Elbow on the arm of the chair, I rested my cheek on my fist. "Is the house even available?"

"Not at the moment, but I have my ways."

I burst out laughing. "You sound so much like Dad."

"He knows how to get things done."

"He does." I tipped my head back, peering up at the stars. There were a million pinpricks of light in the dark, inky blanket of the sky. "It's right, isn't it? Doing the interview?"

He let out a long sigh before answering. "I don't know, Z. I'd be happy as a clam to have you back here, and I think you could build a happy life this time around. If I had my way, that's what you'd do. But...I have to wonder, do you even *like* accounting?"

"Of course. I worked really hard to get my degree and certification."

His brows shot up. "That isn't much of an answer."

"It's the answer I have. Do I have to love my job? I don't think most people do, and it's not like I can just throw away all the work I've done to get here. That's years I'll never get back."

"Mmmhmm. And I'm sure on your deathbed, you'll be thinking how glad you are to have spent your life making spreadsheets."

I tore my gaze from the sky, focusing on the screen. "I thought you wanted me to come home."

"I definitely do. I just question your future plans once you get here. I wish you'd think about what you really want to do and not get stuck in a sunk-cost fallacy."

"I don't know if that's what I'm doing," I argued weakly.

"You don't?" This time, he only raised one skeptical eyebrow. "To me, that's exactly what this is. You did it with Jackson—rode that sinking ship all the way to the ocean floor because you'd invested so much time. And it sounds to me like you're doing the same thing with your career. You can abandon ship, Z. You know Mom and Dad and me and Steven will keep you afloat if you need it."

"I know." I sucked in a shaky breath as a seed of terror bloomed in my belly. "It's the only direction I have, though."

He chuffed. "You're being stubborn, as usual. Didn't you just finish telling me about a job offer you have there?"

"Are you trying to convince me to move?"

"No. No way. But if you're qualified for that job, who's to say you couldn't find one like it here?" Turning away from the camera, he scratched the side of his head. When he spoke again, it was quieter. "I want you to be happy. If that means moving, I won't like it, but I'll support you."

With each word, the terror grew, climbing out of my gut and clawing up my lungs.

"I don't want to make a mistake."

Zane stayed steady, even as I wobbled. "If you do, you can always fix it. There's nothing that can't be undone."

Fear wrapped around my heart, holding on tight. "Do you think you could go outside and show me the stars?"

My brother didn't even hesitate, the phone jostling as he made his way out to his patio.

"Here you go. Look up," he said softly, turning the camera up to the sky.

Through gray clouds, dots of light shone. Here and there, scattered like confetti. It was a beautiful sight, no doubt. And there was a time I would have lain on my back to gaze up at them...to count them for hours and try to pick out constellations. I would have been satisfied.

But now...

I looked up, and I almost couldn't breathe. There was so much. Endless. Countless. No clouds or light pollution blocking the glow. The stars spilled across the sky in thick rivers of light, crowding close together like they were pressing down on the earth. The darkness between them wasn't empty. It felt deep, alive, stretching on forever. It made me feel small, yet like I was a part of something vast and meaningful.

I looked at the phone screen again, and it was beautiful. The clouds, the trees on the horizon, the little snatches of light blinking through the breaks. The sky looked soft there, muted and close. Comfortable. Like home. If I hadn't known something else was out there, I would have been content to look up at it every night.

"It's not enough," I whispered.

Zane pointed the camera at his face again, took a long, assessing look at me, and said, "Well, fuck."

Chapter Thirty-eight

Cormac

I WAS WAITING FOR my coffee at the café when Javier slid up beside me.

"Morning."

"Good morning." He rested his elbow on the counter, glancing at his phone. "How is your week going?"

"Ah, it's fine. I'm sure you know the Kellers are returning tomorrow."

He chuckled. "Yes, I'm aware. Mrs. Keller has already scheduled herself on every hike and trail ride Zara is leading. She won't go with anyone else."

"Believe me, she let me know her preference as well." The barista slid my coffee onto the counter, and I grabbed it, tipping it toward Javier. "Let me know if she gives you any trouble. I'll try to redirect her."

"I'm used to her, and we both know Zara can handle her." His coffee arrived right after mine, and he fell in step with me as we made our way across the lobby. "I was hoping you would have a word with Zara, actually."

"What kind of word?"

"I'm going to need an answer from her as soon as possible. If she's not going to take the job, we'll have to put a notice up soon so I'll have time to train my replacement."

I stopped in my tracks so suddenly Javier took two more steps before noticing.

"Wait. Back up. You're leaving the ranch?"

He turned toward me, confusion flickering across his face. "Oh no. I assumed…you and Zara are friends."

A cold prickle spread across the back of my neck.

"We are," I said slowly. "What job?"

His expression collapsed into dawning horror. His mouth opened then shut.

"Oh." He rubbed a hand roughly over his mouth. "I thought she'd told you."

The words landed like a dropped stone in my chest.

"She hasn't."

"I'm sorry, Cormac." He shifted his weight, suddenly restless, his gaze darting away like he was looking for an exit. "HR is aware of my plans to depart at the end of the season. I approached Zara about taking over for me, but she hasn't given me an answer yet. I shouldn't have said anything. Truly, it's my mistake."

She hadn't told me. Not on any of our early morning runs down to the river. Not when we ate dinner together. Not when I held her in my arms. Not when she told me she loved me. Not when I was screaming on the inside, begging her to just stay.

Not a single word.

My head was going in a whole other direction, like the fact that Zara was currently at home, interviewing for a job back in Portland.

I forced myself to take a deep breath and clapped a hand on Javier's shoulder.

"Don't worry about it. I'll be incredibly sorry to see you go."

"I will too. I've enjoyed my time at the ranch, but my knee is stopping me from being as hands-on as the job requires. I've found a more suitable position in Spain."

I forced a smile. "Going back home, huh?"

"Yes. It will be nice to be near my family again."

"Of course."

Abruptly, I spun on my heels. "I just remembered something. I'll talk to you later."

I didn't wait for a reply.

On my way out of the lobby, I dropped my untouched coffee into the trash without breaking stride. The glass doors slid open, and a rush of warm air hit me, but I barely felt it. My shoes struck the pavement faster and faster as the knot in my chest tightened.

By the time I reached the parking lot, I was half running.

I fumbled my keys out of my pocket and hit the unlock button before I reached the truck, the sharp chirp sounding too loud in the morning quiet. My hands felt clumsy, useless, as I yanked the door open and climbed in.

I turned the key, and the engine roared to life.

I needed to talk to Zara.

I pulled out of the lot faster than I should have, heading straight for her place. It didn't take me long to get there. Not nearly enough time to gather my thoughts or plan out what I was going to say.

My blood was thrumming in my veins as I hopped out of the truck, slamming the door behind me.

Before I made it to her porch, she was there, in the doorway, one tan foot stacked on top of the other, her golden legs bare beneath one of the T-shirts she'd stolen from me.

A look of surprise flashed across her face. "Hey. What are you doing here?"

I didn't stop when I got to her. My arm banded around her middle, lifting her right off her feet. She let out a yelp, but that was all the objection she made, melting against me as I carried her to the couch and dropped her on the cushions.

Falling onto my knees in front of her, I laid my head on her stomach and wrapped both arms around her back. Her fingers carved through my hair as her breath came in erratic spurts, matching my own.

"Don't go," I gritted out. "I need you to stay with me."

I wasn't supposed to ask for this. I'd given her the levelheaded option. Go long distance. Make it work with visits and phone calls like we used to. But that wasn't even half of what I needed from her.

The thought of her driving away in a few weeks eviscerated me. Every day we got closer to the end was like walking over jagged glass, cutting me down to the quick. Every moment of beauty and pleasure was shadowed by dark washes of dread.

"Cormac," she whispered carefully. "What's going on?"

"Don't go, Zara." I squeezed my eyes shut, desperation riding me like a wraith.

God, I had to convince her. She needed to understand I'd do anything for her. I'd love her all the way to the end and beyond if she let me. It could be so good. We could have everything.

She just had to believe it.

"Zara, Zara, Zara." I kissed her belly and rubbed my face against her. "Please, Zara."

Gathering her shirt, I lifted it so I could get to her skin. She gasped as my lips moved across her abdomen and my teeth raked over her hipbones.

I couldn't think of any words that would be convincing enough. So I lowered her panties and drew patterns over her silky flesh with my tongue, pressing her thighs wide. She opened for me, her fingers never leaving my hair.

"Let me." I drew my nose along her cleft. "Give me this."

"Okay." She petted my cheek, her thumb rubbing my lip. "Okay, Cormac."

I was all need when I buried my face between her thighs, finding her wet for me. Wild, frantic thoughts made my head dizzy—thoughts I couldn't grasp but understood were mournful and filled with fear.

She cooed my name as her hips lifted, riding my tongue. I slipped two fingers inside her, careful at first. When she welcomed me with no objection, I went harder, deep as she could take me, thrusting into her again and again, lapping at her clit and rolling my fingers along her sensitive walls.

Taking her ass in my hands, I dove deeper, eating her like this was my only chance. And maybe it was. Maybe she'd tell me she was leaving and we had to end this.

I couldn't let that happen. This couldn't be the end. We were so damn good. She had to see that. She couldn't just tell me she loved me and think I'd be okay with her being out of reach. I could barely stand her sleeping under another roof. A thousand miles was incomprehensible.

"Cormac," she breathed. "What...? Please, baby, what's happening?"

If she was talking, I wasn't convincing her enough. I curled my fingers, pressing against her inner wall, and wrapped my lips around her clit, giving it pulsing sucks. Her words cut off into moans, and her fingers made fists in my hair, tugging like reins.

Then she was coming, slicking my fingers and painting my lips with her pleasure.

It wasn't enough.

Not even close.

I kept at her, lapping up her flavor and inhaling her scent, bathing my chin and lips and cheeks each time she released. She writhed beneath me, the sounds coming out of her throat less and less human. Her hands batted at my shoulders then dug in, gripping me urgently.

"Enough," she panted, pulling on my shirt, forcing me up so she could yank it over my head. "Inside me. Please, please, please."

She slid off the couch, landing on my lap, and I fell back, taking her with me. Her hair hung in ribbons over her shoulders, falling onto mine as she leaned forward and licked my lips.

"That's you," I said.

"And you."

She reached between us, freeing my throbbing cock from my pants, and gave it a few hard pumps. Almost like she was angry.

Maybe she was.

Without warning, she positioned me at her entrance and sank down until she bottomed out.

I couldn't breathe.

Couldn't think.

Could barely move.

Zara sat back on her knees and rode me hard, her hair wild around her face. Wisps flying like tumbleweeds, inky waterfalls flowing over her bouncing breasts.

I held on to her waist and stared up at her flushed cheeks. Her bitten lips. The untamable wonder in her eyes.

"I love you," burst out of me like a geyser, rising hot and high above us without warning.

Her blown-out gaze found mine, and her lips formed the words, "I love you too," without sound. But I knew. It soaked into me like rain after a summer of drought. My cracked, parched heart drank up her love and stayed open, thirsting for more.

Always, always hoping for more from this woman.

Her inner walls were swollen and so wet, it was an easy, euphoric glide. Her ass hit my thighs, her breasts moved with the rest of her, and her eyes stayed on mine. It was all I could do to watch her, hold her up, take what she wanted to give.

"I'm so close," I rasped. "Fuck, sweetheart, you gotta—"

She was off me and kneeling between my legs before I could finish my sentence. And when her hot mouth covered my cock, I couldn't remember what I'd meant to say in the first place.

It didn't take much. Oh god, only a few slides of her tongue along my shaft, her palm splayed on my belly, the other cupping my balls, and I hit the end of the road. My hips arched off the ground as I rooted myself deep in her mouth. She went still, drinking my release like she wanted it, humming around me, her eyes fluttering with pleasure.

A beautiful thing.

A sight I wanted for the rest of my life.

"Zara. C'mere." I took her hands and pulled her onto my chest. "Gimme a kiss."

Her lips were warm and soft on mine. I swept my tongue inside, tasting myself and sharing her flavor with her, passing it back and forth until we were breathless, panting into each other's mouths.

She dropped her head on my shoulder, burrowing her face into my neck. As we lay there, any ounce of calm I'd gained inside her ground into the dust beneath the boot of the monster that was the desperate need to keep this woman.

"I need to talk to you."

"Okay. I need to talk to you too." She lifted her head, her eyes darting between mine. "Let's put on our clothes first. I can't concentrate when you're naked."

Despite myself, I laughed. "I figure you're speaking English right now, but I can't be sure when your tits are against me and my hands are on your ass."

Laughing with me, she pushed off my chest and went in search of her clothes. By the time I'd yanked up my pants and pulled my shirt on, she was back in my tee, sitting cross-legged on the couch, looking like a picture.

Like the love of my life.

Taking a deep breath, I sat down beside her and put my heart in her hands.

"I want you to stay."

Chapter Thirty-nine

Cormac

SHE LICKED HER LIPS, eyes shining bright. "You do?"

I took her hand in mine. "That can't be a surprise."

"It isn't. Not really. But...well, you were adamant we could make long distance work, so I'm wondering where this change of tune came from. Not that I'm mad about it, it's just a complete one-eighty."

"I know."

And the fact that she wasn't immediately saying yes and leaping into my arms landed like a dull blade between my ribs. I'd prepared myself to fight for us. I hadn't prepared myself for the possibility I might be fighting alone.

I had to tread carefully. One wrong word, and I might push her further away.

Keeping my voice steady, I said, "A long time ago, I waited for the perfect opportunity to share my feelings, and it never came. I've lived with that regret ever since."

"Cormac—"

I shook my head. "No, let me get this out. I have to say a few things first."

She rolled her lips over her teeth and nodded slowly.

"Here's the thing, Zara: I want to build a real life with you. We could start out doing long distance. I'd rather settle for that than nothing at all, but it isn't what I want, and I need to say that. If I don't tell you I want you here with me, I'll regret it, and I've already got a mountain-high stack of regrets when it comes to you and me. I won't add anymore."

Her fingers closed around mine, tighter with each word, but she didn't try to speak. She listened with intent, her breath bated, her back ramrod straight. If she'd given me a hint of pulling away, I might've lost my nerve. But she was giving me the opposite, so I laid it all out.

"I know you had a job interview this morning, but I don't want you to take it. Going back there, slotting yourself into your old role won't make you happy. I've watched you bloom this summer. Every hour you've spent outside, doing what you love, has made your smile get wider and brought back the glow I've always loved about you."

My throat worked around the boulder lodged in the center of it, and my eyes burned hot, but I managed to keep going.

"You're going to miss your family, but we'll find a way to see them as much as we can. I'll make sure of it. And my family will wrap their arms around you and hold you when my arms aren't enough."

She couldn't hold back a response. "Your arms are always enough."

I exhaled, dropping my forehead to our joined hands. "Javier told me about the job. He offered you a reason to stay. A real reason, and I have no clue if you want to take it. You're not letting me in—"

Fear cracked through my voice before I could stop it.

"Oh no, Maccie." She scrambled to her knees beside me, cupping the side of my face. "No, I wasn't trying to hide it from you. I had to think about it on my own before I brought it up. It's a lot. A big decision. I needed to wrap my head around it. I don't want you to think I'm not letting you in. That isn't why I didn't say anything."

I rubbed my jaw against her hand, warm and soft. "Please stay. I'll give you a good life. I swear I will. Stay and let me love you like I've always needed to. Stay, and *please*...just love me back."

"I do love you back." She climbed onto my legs, taking my face in both hands. "Cormac, I *love* you. Please look at me. Look at what I'm wearing."

That got me to open my eyes. I scanned her tangled hair, loose T-shirt, and nothing else. My heart thumped, but it confused me. What was I supposed to be seeing other than the most beautiful woman in the world?

"I see you."

She pecked my nose. "Think, Maccie. Do I look like I'm all dressed up for a video call?"

It hit me like lightning.

My head jerked. "I sure hope no one else saw you this way."

"No one did. I canceled the interview, but since I had the morning off, I was being lazy about getting dressed."

"I love seeing you in my shirt."

She gave me a pleased little smile. "To tell the truth, I love that I'm in the position where I get to steal your clothes. It makes me giddy."

She had no idea how it made *me* feel to see my clothes draping her body. It wasn't just proprietary. Clothing the woman I loved settled some ancient, caveman instinct inside me—an instinct that only came to life around Zara.

"You really canceled the interview?" I wasn't going to allow myself to hope. Not yet. She needed to say the words.

"Yeah. Zane and I talked last night, and he had a lot of things to say."

I gripped her thighs, holding back my impatience. I'd waited this long. What was a few more minutes?

"Like what?"

"I was telling him about the interview without much enthusiasm, and he knocked some sense into me, reminding me there was no reason to drown just because the ship I'd chosen to set sail on was sinking. It was really hard for me to hear. I don't know why I'm so stubborn, but I'm working on not getting in the way of myself. That's why I canceled the interview. I didn't want that job, even if, on paper, it was perfect for me."

"Paper doesn't tell the whole story." I turned to kiss her palm. "Why didn't you tell me you'd canceled it?"

"Because I hadn't decided what it meant yet...and I was scared."

"Scared?" My brow furrowed. "What were you scared of?"

"Screwing up. Making the wrong decision about my career"—her voice dropped to a whisper—"us. I'm afraid it's too soon to uproot my life and go all in with you, but I'm even more terrified if I don't, we won't work out, and I'll lose you all over again."

"Zara, I—"

"There's more, Mac. I'm afraid to take Javier's job and not like it. And what if I'm not good at it and you have to fire me? What if I'm great at it, but working together every day is too much? And do I love Wyoming because it's a vacation, or is this where I really belong? I've been asking myself a thousand questions, searching my brain and heart for the answers, and I didn't want to pull you into that until I was clear on where I stood."

"Are you clear? Do you need help talking it through?" I asked, barely daring to hope this might be going where I wanted it to.

"I wasn't really clear until you showed up and asked me to stay."

I almost laughed. "Don't think I did much asking."

"No, but you were very convincing anyway." Her arms circled my neck. "I realized all my questions don't matter. The job will work out or it won't. That isn't what's important, and when it comes down to it, it's not really a factor."

"What *is* a factor?"

"You, Cormac. You're the only factor."

My heart gave a wild thump, sending my pulse skittering. "Tell me what you're saying. Give it to me plainly."

The smile she gave was the sweetest thing I'd ever seen, like sugar and Christmas lights and down feathers.

"For me, it's always you. You set it right. "

"Set what right?"

"Everything. Me, my mind, my heart, my soul." Pausing, breathless, she nibbled on her bottom lip. "I mean, I don't know for sure souls are even real, but around you, I feel like mine is."

Blood rushed in my ears as heat climbed up from my chest. "I...set your soul right?"

"You do." Her fingers slid into the hair at my nape, gentle as a breeze. "When we were apart, I was off balance. Like I was missing an important, integral piece that keeps me steady. When I'm with you, I feel the most complete. It's always been that way. I think that's probably because you're my soulmate. Our souls know each other, and they fit because they're supposed to. We set each other right."

I didn't know what the fuck to say. "Zara—Christ. You're killing me."

"I hope not. We're going to start our life together, Mac, so you can't die." Her smile was bracketed by twin tears trailing down her cheeks.

My eyes were burning, my chest so heavy, it was like breathing underwater.

"You're staying?" I asked, testing the shape of it.

"Yes. I'm staying with you." She wiggled closer, putting us chest to chest. Her heart rattled and leaped for mine. "I want the job, but it's not the reason. You are. I want the same thing as you: to build a real life together. The one we were always meant to have, if only I could have seen it."

"No." I shook my head. "No, we're not gonna put blame on either of us. It doesn't matter. We're here, and you just told me I'm your soulmate. Everything else is behind us. Got it?"

"Yeah." Another tear fell, and damn if it didn't pull one or two from me with it. "I got it. It's behind us."

Relief flooded me so fast my hands started shaking. I pulled her against me and buried my face in her neck, taking my first deep breath since I'd walked into this house, and it was filled with her.

I hadn't realized until that second how certain I'd been that she might choose differently.

It was going to take some time to sink in, but I'd let it.

"You're here," I murmured. "You're really here."

"I'm not going anywhere."

For the first time since she'd shown up in town, I wasn't braced for it to end. I had her in a very real way I was determined to make permanent.

Breath to breath, soul to soul, we held each other.

And for a moment, everything was right.

Chapter Forty

Zara

THE MINUTE I TOLD Zane I'd decided to stay, he'd hauled Steven on the next flight to Wyoming. If he had intended to talk me out of it, he must have changed his mind the moment he saw Cormac and me together.

We were standing in front of the guesthouse when they pulled up in their rental, Cormac's arm around my waist, my head leaning against his chest. For the last week, this was how we'd been. Touching, embracing, as close as we could be. And relaxed. So very relaxed in each other's presence.

This was it. We were finally getting something we'd both longed for, even if we hadn't known it. Once we'd decided this was what we were going to do, it had been so simple to settle into it, looking forward instead of back.

And when Zane hopped out of the car, he took one look at us, threw his arms out, and shouted, "Fuck!"

So that was that.

Zane and Steven were taking the guesthouse. I'd spend my days with them, and my nights with Cormac. Zane wasn't exactly enthusiastic about coming along while I guided, but Steven was all in for new adventures, and where Steven went, so did Zane.

The first day, while Cormac pointed out the family's houses to Zane, Steven put his arm around me.

"You look good, Z."

"I'm the best I've ever been." I nudged his side with my elbow. "Don't let him freak out too much, okay?"

He chuckled, eyeing his husband. "Don't worry about Zane. He just needs to get used to the idea of you being here for good. And in the meantime, I've got him."

"I know you do."

"It's gorgeous here. The resort, the houses...wow." Sighing, he scanned the horizon. "I expected the ranch to be more rustic."

I snorted a laugh. "You actually trusted Zane's description? Come on."

Crinkles burst from around his eyes. "You're right. I should have known."

Later, we took them to dinner with the Kellys. Most of the family showed up, and we found space for Steven and Zane at the table. Silas decided to be best friends with my brother, and Abigail parked herself on Steven.

Zane was confused by Silas's intense, unwavering attention and boundless questions, but he answered each one with enthusiasm.

Steven was bewitched by Abigail's sweet little hands all over his face and her tinkling giggles at his deep voice. All he had to do was say her name, and she was set off.

It was adorable.

I loved seeing my family blend with Cormac's. It made my heart believe this was real. Our life would be this way, and it would be beautiful.

It was late. Cormac and I were in his bed, his head was on my stomach, his arms banded around me as I stroked his hair. It was nice spending nights with Cormac. More than nice. I liked sharing the house with his grandparents. They kept to themselves most of the time, but their presence was peaceful and comforting.

The empty spot in my heart left by the death of my grandfather, who'd lived with my family most of my childhood, was getting filled in just a little bit. It wasn't the same, nothing ever would be, but some of the ache from his loss had been soothed.

"I heard Steven's taking to ranch life," Cormac said.

I snorted a laugh. "He is. Zane is vacillating between being apoplectic at Steven's betrayal and gaga over how hot he looks throwing bales of hay."

That afternoon, we'd found Steven out with Caleb in the stables, doing manual labor. Steven had looked right at home, and he and Caleb had bonded through grunts and sweat. It was kind of cute.

I felt his grin against my skin as the tips of his fingers danced over the tattoo on my hip. "Sounds like a tough life your brother leads."

"Oh yeah. Crazy in love with a hot husband. Real tough."

He flattened his palm over our words. "I'm sorry for taking you away from them."

"You have nothing to be sorry for." My hand froze on the back of his head. "This was my choice. *You* are my choice. And did you see how easy it was for Zane and Steven to get their butts here? I have a feeling we'll see more of them than we even want to."

Pressing his forehead to my navel, his breath was warm as he exhaled. "I don't believe they have a shot of ever overstaying their welcome."

I smiled. "You're right. I'll never get enough of seeing my brother. It'll suck sometimes not living nearby, but we'll be intentional about staying close. Zane and I are locked in. We'll be okay."

"Yeah, you will." He propped himself up on his elbows so he could look at me. "You know who else is locked in with Zane?"

I snickered. "I heard. Mrs. Keller is his number one fan."

"That's right. I had coffee with her this afternoon, and she told me all about the dashing young man she met while on a river hike with you. She said he even looked at a spot on her arm and assured her it was only a bruise, not cancer."

A laugh burst out of me. "Zane didn't mean to charm her. He couldn't help it. Now he's stuck going on a private trail ride with us tomorrow."

That got Cormac laughing too. "Oh god. He's never going to come back to visit us."

"Not when the Kellers are in town."

"Knowing Mrs. Keller, she'll pay someone off to inform her of his arrival and hop on the next plane."

I traced the bottom of his smile with my thumb. "And Zane will love the attention, even if he pretends not to."

"Yeah." He let his head fall back to my stomach and sighed. "I love seeing you happy."

"I love feeling this way." My fingers slid through his hair. "You know you have a lot to do with it, right?"

He kissed my hip. "It's good to hear you say it."

"Are you happy?"

A choked grunt rumbled up from his chest. "That doesn't even touch how I feel. But yeah, we'll go with happy for now, until they come up with a better word."

We'll go with happy.

I liked the sound of that.

Chapter Forty-one

Zara

FOR ALL HER MONEY, lavish lifestyle, and constant need for attention while she visited the ranch, Mrs. Keller was a damn good rider. It was my own brother slowing us down.

"It's no wonder cowboys are bowlegged," Zane whined as his horse meandered along the trail. "My ass is not cut out for a saddle."

Mrs. Keller laughed airily. "That's because it's far too bony. Come visit me in Monterey. My chef will fatten you up."

Zane scoffed. "My husband thinks my ass is just the right size, thank you very much." Then he straightened his shoulders. "I won't say no to a visit to Monterey, though. You can *try* to fatten me up, within reason, of course."

I laughed. "Of course."

When we arrived at a shaded area along the river, the three of us slid off our horses to give them a break.

The leaves of the trees whispered in the subtle breeze. The river moved with purpose beside us. The horses lowered their heads gratefully, reins loose, tails flicking at flies.

Zane groaned as his boots hit the ground. "Holy hell. Muscles I didn't even know I had ache. If I ever agree to go horseback riding again, please slap me."

Mrs. Keller arched a perfectly groomed brow. "I'd be honored, darling. Though I must warn you, I'm stronger than I look."

He pressed a hand to his lower back. "A verbal slap will do fine." Nostrils flaring, he took a deep breath. "God, what is that?"

"It's called fresh air." I pulled a small canvas bag from my saddle horn. "Very exclusive. We make it in Wyoming."

Mrs. Keller accepted the bottle of water I handed her. "Darling, I grew up in Montana. I had fresh air before it was fashionable."

Zane perked up at the sight of the wrapped sandwiches. "If that's turkey, I take back every complaint I've made about this ranch."

"It's turkey," I confirmed. "And I packed some of Phoebe's cookies."

He made grabby hands. "Now, please. I need them."

We settled near the bank, boots in the grass. The horses shifted lazily behind us, content. The air smelled like sun-warmed earth and river water. It was one of those afternoons that felt suspended—no rush, no edges.

Mrs. Keller chewed thoughtfully. "I agree with your decision to make this your permanent home."

"You do?" I asked, unsurprised she was aware of my plans and had an opinion.

"I do. I seem to recall saying you could do anything you wanted, and look at you now. You have a handsome beau, and you're excellent at your job. Easy as pie once you got out of your own way, wasn't it?"

"Maybe," I hedged. "It was the getting out of my own way that was difficult. I'm really good at that."

She flicked her manicured nails. "Aren't we all?"

I leaned my head back on the trunk of the tree behind me and listened to Zane and Mrs. Keller banter, a smile curving my lips. My brother could talk to a brick wall if that were his only option, and I was certain Mrs. Keller had never met a stranger, so their conversation well never ran dry. She told him all about her house, the people who worked for her, and her wayward son George. Zane shared stories about his patients at the hospital, the neighbor who kept putting their trash in his garbage can, and how he and Steven met and fell in love.

While my eyes were closed, the horses decided it was an excellent time to drift farther down the bank in search of better grass.

"Hey—nope," I called, grabbing my reins and jogging after them.

By the time I'd gathered them back, one had managed to tangle a rein around a low branch. It wasn't a big deal, but it had taken a few careful minutes to untwist the leather and calm a mildly offended gelding.

Mrs. Keller checked the sky. "What time is it?"

"Later than I meant for it to be," I admitted.

The sun had shifted lower, the light turning richer, thicker. It would still be a comfortable ride back, but between the conversations and chasing down the horses, we'd lost more time than I'd intended.

"Mount up," I said, brushing grass from my jeans. "Let's get you back before the dinner bell rings."

Zane made a show of bracing himself before climbing into the saddle again. Mrs. Keller swung up with effortless grace, and we turned the horses toward home.

The ride back was easy at first. The river curved away from us, replaced by open stretches of prairie and rolling hills rippling gold in the lowering sun. The breeze shifted cooler against my cheeks.

Halfway up a gentle rise, something caught my eye. At first, I thought it was heat distortion, but when we crested the hill, a thin ribbon of gray in the far distance rose straight into the sky before drifting sideways.

I slowed my horse without meaning to.

"What is it?" Mrs. Keller asked, following my line of sight.

"Probably nothing," I said automatically. "There's smoke. It isn't thick, so I'm not too worried."

But I didn't look away.

Zane squinted. "Is that from the ranch?"

"No. That's the opposite direction," I said, relieved Zane didn't have to find his own way back. Otherwise, he'd be lost for good.

I watched the smoke as we rode, curious about the cause. It was wildfire season, so seeing smoke wasn't out of the realm of normal and didn't spell danger. Not out here, anyway. The ranch sprawled over twenty or thirty thousand acres. Smoke could be miles away and still seem close.

It could be anything. Most likely, a small brush fire caused by the dry conditions.

Mrs. Keller's voice lost some of its playfulness. "Should we be concerned?"

I kept my smile as bright and steady as I could. "If it were close, we'd smell it. And we'd hear about it over the radio." I patted the walkie clipped to my saddle. It was as silent as it'd been most of our ride.

"We'll head in at a quicker pace," I said lightly. "Just in case."

Zane made a sound, a mix between a scoff and a whimper. "You sound calm for someone who just said 'just in case.'"

"That's because I *am* calm."

When we got back to the ranch, I'd check in with Cormac to find out what was going on, but I was certain they were on top of it. There was no use expending mental energy over something I couldn't do anything about.

I nudged my mare forward. "Let's keep moving."

We'd barely gone fifty yards when Mrs. Keller's gelding gave an odd little hop.

She adjusted easily in the saddle, but her hand dropped to her thigh. "Hmm."

I turned in my seat. "What's going on?"

Her brow furrowed beneath the brim of her hat. "My saddle moved."

That pulled me to a stop.

Zane groaned. "Please tell me that's a perfectly okay thing to happen."

"It's not," I said, swinging down from my horse.

We were on a slope—not the ideal place to have tack issues. I went to Mrs. Keller's side, one hand on the gelding's shoulder.

"Lean forward just a bit," I instructed.

She did without question.

The problem was obvious as soon as I checked the cinch. It wasn't undone, just looser than it should've been. Between the horses wandering at the river and us remounting on uneven ground, it must've shifted.

"That's on me," I muttered.

Mrs. Keller waved a hand. "If we blamed ourselves for every minor inconvenience, we'd never leave the house. Wouldn't that be a tragedy?"

Zane blinked down at us. "Speak for yourself. I enjoy my house."

The leather creaked as I tightened the cinch another notch. The horse stomped in annoyance, but settled quickly when I rubbed his neck and cooed at him a little.

I stepped back to check the back cinch and frowned.

"Well, damn."

"What?" Zane demanded immediately.

"The back cinch slipped."

Mrs. Keller sighed softly. "Oh dear. We don't want that."

"If it swings too much, it can make them cranky," I said.

"And we don't want cranky," Zane said solemnly.

"No, we don't," I agreed.

I crouched, readjusting the strap properly this time and tightening it enough to keep the saddle balanced. It wasn't a difficult task, but it took time I really didn't want to spend, considering we were already behind schedule.

When I stood, I brushed my hands off on my jeans. "Okay. Try shifting your weight."

Mrs. Keller rolled her hips gently side to side. The saddle didn't budge.

"It's perfect," she declared.

"Good," I said, remounting. "Let's head in."

We rode on, the smoke still a faint smudge against the sky to our left. It hadn't grown or changed, which was a good thing.

The delay, though small, had put the sun lower than I preferred. We'd get back before dark, but we'd be late, and Cormac would be watching the clock.

Behind us, the river disappeared from view as the ranch waited ahead.

And far off in the distance, that thin ribbon continued to rise into a perfectly calm sky.

Chapter Forty-two

Cormac

I CHECKED THE CLOCK one more time.

Still late.

Not worryingly so, but Zara was pretty good about keeping on schedule, and I wouldn't expect Zane to be willing to stay out any longer than he had to. They should've been back an hour ago, and Zara wasn't answering my calls on the walkie.

Javier wasn't in his office when I checked, the lights shut off for the night. I was too antsy to sit and wait for them to come back, so I decided to head down to the barn and meet them.

Just as I turned from Javier's doorway, Melanie started down the hall, a clipboard clutched to her chest. Her steps stuttered when she spotted me.

I moved to the side, holding my arm out. "Go right ahead."

"I'm just returning the schedule to Javier's office," she said, tucking her hair behind her ear.

"He's not in."

"Oh, I know." Her tone was as dry as the desert, but she'd been angry with me since I'd broken up with Victoria, and there was nothing I could do about that. As long as she did her job, we could coexist.

She went on. "He had to leave early for a doctor's appointment. He put me in charge of the guide schedule in case any guests had questions."

"I see." I nodded toward the clipboard. "Zara took Mrs. Keller out on the east trail, didn't she? They're not back yet. I was thinking about riding out to meet them to make sure all's well."

Annoyance flickered across her features as she peered down at the clipboard. "They—" Cutting herself off, she sucked in her cheek, making her lips purse. "Actually, there was a last-minute change. They ended up taking the north trail out to the ridge."

"Really?" I scratched the back of my neck, confused. "The north trail is a lot more challenging."

Zara and Mrs. Keller could handle it, but Zane wasn't a rider. I wouldn't have expected Zara to make a choice like that. It might've been Mrs. Keller's idea. She could be quite convincing when she wanted to be.

She shrugged. "That's probably why they're late, but you should ride out there and check. You know, to make sure they're not in trouble. You never know around here."

"Right." I nodded, tamping down the edge of panic slicing into my gut. It'd do me no good to let my imagination run away from me. "I'm going to do just that. Thanks, Melanie."

She gave me a tight smile. "Of course."

She looked like she had something else to say, but when she didn't come right out with it, I spun on my heel, done with waiting around. I booked it down the hall, through the lobby and out of the resort.

Outside, the air had cooled. The sun hovered low, stretching long shadows across the grounds, but there was still a good deal of light. I wasn't worried.

Well...not really.

When I reached the barn, a couple hands were watering the horses. They noticed me, giving me waves as they went about doing their jobs. I moved straight for Dusty's stall. She lifted her head the moment she saw me, soft-brown eyes alert, ready for anything.

"Hey, girl." I reached for her halter. "We're taking a quick ride."

I worked as fast as I could at securing her saddle without getting sloppy. I checked everything twice out of habit then grabbed a flashlight and clipped my radio to my belt.

Still nothing from Zara on the walkie.

Tom, Caleb's right-hand man, was heading into the barn as I exited. He flicked the bill of his hat. "You headed out on a ride?"

"Meeting up with Zara," I explained. "They should have been back over an hour ago. I thought I'd head out on the trail to make sure they're doing okay."

"You never know what could keep 'em. No doubt they're on their way."

"No doubt," I agreed without feeling it. "We'll probably all be back soon."

"I'll keep a lookout," he said, sending me on my way.

A few minutes later, Dusty and I were moving at a steady lope toward the north trailhead.

A ways out on the trail, I spotted a plume of smoke rising in the distance, though, as far off as it was, it wasn't too concerning. A few years back, a wildfire had burned about four-hundred acres on the ranch, but it hadn't come anywhere near any of our structures or animals.

Fires happened. The land out here was so dry in the summer it became a tinderbox. A bolt of lightning or the smallest spark could burst the tumbleweeds into flames.

Worry niggled at me anyway. Seemed like a bad omen to see that smoke when Zara was out here, running late, not answering on her walkie.

I pushed Dusty a little faster.

If they'd taken the overlook route, I should've seen them by now. Out here, there weren't a lot of places to hide.

I saw nothing. No riders. No glint of tack. Just empty land as far as the eye could see.

"Zara," I muttered, scanning the horizon again.

Maybe they'd slowed down. Maybe Zane had complained his way into a break. Maybe—well, there were a lot of possibilities. More than I could think of.

I rose slightly in the saddle as we crested a small hill.

Still nothing.

I was losing light fast. Dusk always came quickly out here. One minute, it seemed like you had time, and the next, it'd all run out.

I reached for my radio. "Zara, you copy?" All I got was static.

Clipping the walkie to a strap on the saddle, I swallowed the surge of frustration.

Zara was responsible. Smarter and more capable than anyone I knew. If something was wrong, she would've called it in.

Unless she couldn't.

The thought hit hard enough to steal my breath.

I nudged Dusty forward again, angling toward the ridge proper. If they'd run into trouble, they'd likely have stopped near higher ground.

"Dammit," I breathed.

We reached the first bend of the north trail, where the path narrowed between rocky outcroppings. Dusty's ears flicked back and forth, listening. Her nostrils flared, and I suspected she could smell the smoke on the breeze.

"Easy," I murmured.

Dusty was as calm as they came and sensitive to her rider. Normally, that was a good thing, but my being on edge made her skittish. When a bird burst out of the bush beside us, Dusty startled, shying hard to the left. Her front hooves scrambled on loose gravel.

I grabbed for the horn, but momentum had already taken over. Her hindquarters slid, and my weight shifted wrong.

"Whoa—"

My boot caught the stirrup as she lurched, and there was no stopping my fall.

The ground came up, brutal and unforgiving, air slamming from my lungs as my shoulder hit first. My head snapped back against dirt and rock, and my leg twisted beneath me. For a split second, everything went white.

In pure panic, Dusty bolted in the opposite direction, hooves pounding away.

"Dusty!" I tried to shout, but it came out strangled.

She was gone in seconds. Only when she vanished did I remember my walkie was clipped to her saddle. *Dammit.*

I rolled onto my side, dragging in a painful breath. My shoulder screamed. My hip wasn't much better. My leg was—well, I was pretty sure it was fucked.

The sky above me had darkened another shade. For a moment, I lay there, blinking at the first faint star appearing overhead, and thought Zara would have loved how pretty the sky looked right now.

It was the thought of her that cleared my mind enough to realize I couldn't just lie here. But when I tried to push myself up, hot, bright pain shot from my knee down to my toes. Sweat pricked my forehead, and tears blurred my vision.

This wasn't good. This *really* wasn't good.

I'd move. And soon. I had no other choice. I'd just lie here a little longer, save up my strength, then figure things out.

The sun dipped lower.

Smoke continued rising.

And I lay there.

Just another minute.

Chapter Forty-three

Zara

ZANE GAVE HIS HORSE a dirty look as he backed away. "Never again, Ranger. We're done."

Mrs. Keller patted his shoulder and laughed. "You are absolutely adorable. Won't you and Steven join me for dinner?"

Zane glanced at me. "Are you cool with that? I know we're supposed to be doing the whole sibling-bonding thing—"

I shooed him off. "Go, go. Have a nice dinner. I'll just hang out with my boyfriend."

Mrs. Keller pulled a sympathetic face. "Such a hard job."

I dusted off my hands, grinning. "It is, but someone has to do it."

Once they left, I helped the ranch hands take care of the horses. That was when I discovered why I wasn't hearing any chatter on my walkie—the batteries were dead. I should have known it had been too quiet.

Tom, the assistant ranch manager, was finishing up directing a couple hands on a task. When I walked up, he offered me a friendly smile.

"Nice ride?"

"It was. We were out longer than intended, but it was good. I noticed smoke up north. What's going on with that?"

He nodded. "There's a small brush fire. We sent a drone out to get images. For now, it's nothing alarming. We're keeping an eye on it, watching how it spreads. As long as it keeps reading farther north, it'll run out of vegetation to burn and die on its own."

I rapped my knuckles against the wall. "Knock on wood."

That got him chuckling. "Of course. Wouldn't wanna jinx it." He glanced around the barn then back at me. "I expected to see Cormac with you."

I jerked my thumb over my shoulder. "I'm going to go hunt him down. He's probably waiting for me in his office."

Tom cocked his head. "No…he isn't. He went out about an hour ago to look for you. Said you were running late. He seemed worried. You didn't cross paths?"

My jaw loosened in confusion. "He was looking for me—on the trail?"

"Yep." He scrubbed the white stubble on his jaw. "Took Dusty out. You really didn't see him?"

My brow dropped low. "There was no one out there. You know how narrow the trail is. We couldn't have missed him. Are you sure that was where he went? Maybe you misunderstood."

"I didn't." He walked over to the wall, taking the clipboard down, and returned with it. "Right here. He signed Dusty out at six thirty."

Cormac's handwriting was there, plain as day. So why hadn't I seen him?

"Can you call him on the walkie? Mine's dead."

"Sure." Tom slipped the walkie from his belt, holding it up to his mouth. "Cormac? It's Tom. You there?"

Dead silence.

"Again," I pleaded.

Tom repeated his message. When he got nothing back, he fiddled with the controls then tried one more time.

"He might have the volume turned down."

"Or maybe his is dead too," I ventured, not believing a word of it.

"That's likely." Tom pulled the bill of his hat lower over his forehead. "Let me ask around on the channels, see if anyone's spotted him."

"Okay." I staggered back until my heels hit a bale of hay, then I sat, my pulse roaring in my ears.

There was no reason to feel so panicked. Cormac was going to walk through those doors any minute. He wouldn't stay out after dark. He'd lived here his whole life and knew how dangerous it was. One wrong move, and his horse could break a leg, he'd get thrown—

No. I wasn't going to catastrophize.

He'd be back, and we'd laugh about how freaked out I got for all of two minutes. That was what he got for making me love him this much.

No one had seen him.

He hadn't walked through the doors.

It was pitch black out. Countless ranch hands were out in trucks and UTVs with spotlights, searching for him. They'd tried to make me stay back, to wait at the Kellys' house for word, but that wasn't going to happen.

I couldn't sit and wait helplessly.

The thing was, even as we drove the ranch roads, deep down, I knew what we were doing was useless. Cormac had been out on horseback. Any of the trails he could have taken were only passable on hoof. We wouldn't find him in a vehicle, and certainly not when it was too dark to see more than a foot in front of us.

We kept at it for a couple hours anyway. If it were up to me, I never would have stopped looking, but I was too numb to put up a fight when Lock drove us back to his and Elena's house.

When we arrived, Zane and Steven closed around me and didn't move. They were pressed into my sides on the couch, like I might've bolted if they'd moved an inch.

They weren't wrong to be worried. All I wanted to do was go back out there and scream Cormac's name until my throat was too raw to make another sound.

I stared out the window, nothing but black looking back at me. The entire thirty-thousand acres of the Kelly ranch had been swallowed whole by darkness. Even the moon was hiding out, a sliver of silver barely giving off a glow.

It was too dangerous to keep searching for Cormac right now. We'd start again at first light. Hours from now.

Way too long.

I stared at the front door like I could will it to open.

"He knows this land," Zane murmured into my hair. "He grew up on it."

"I know," I whispered.

That didn't help, though. He was out there, thinking I was lost. How far would he go to find me? No matter how dark it got, he'd keep looking. It was in his blood to be my hero, but for once, it wasn't me in distress.

In the kitchen, Elena stood at the sink, though there was nothing in it. Lock stepped up behind her and wrapped his arms around her waist. She sagged into him for just a second before straightening again.

"He's strong," she said quietly.

"I know," Lock replied, his voice low and steady. "He's so strong."

I pressed my hands to my knees to stop them from shaking.

If the moon were full, at least he'd have light. At least he could see the trail. The ridges. The drop-offs. The dry creek beds that twisted without warning.

Instead, it was the darkest night of the month, because of course it was.

A knock on the door splintered the quiet despair in the house. As if choreographed, everyone's heads snapped in that direction.

Lock moved first, crossing the room in long strides. I was already on my feet before he opened it, revealing the last two people I would have expected to see.

Victoria stood on the porch, a sweater thrown over pajamas, her face pale. Melanie hovered behind her, eyes red, shoulders drooping inward.

"What's going on?" Lock asked.

Victoria spoke first. "There's something we really need to tell you. About Cormac."

My stomach twisted at his name coming from her lips.

Victoria turned to Melanie, giving her back a shove. "Tell them, Mel. You have to."

Melanie didn't lift her head. Her hands opened and closed at her sides.

Finally, she started talking. "Earlier, I ran into Cormac. He said Zara was late returning from a ride. And I...I told him there'd been a change of plans and Zara had taken the north trail."

That didn't make sense.

"But there was no change. We were on the east..."

"I know." Her hands twisted together in front of her. "But I told him north. I said it without thinking. If I'd thought—"

"You told him they were headed out to the ridge," Victoria added, her tone tight. "You told him they might be running late because it was harder terrain."

Silence fell heavy, the implication of what she'd done settling over all of us like a lead blanket.

"He asked if they were okay," Melanie whispered. "I said you never know out there."

Lock's jaw tightened, his hand on the door gripping so hard his fingertips went white.

"You sent him north," Elena said, her voice breaking on the word.

Melanie's eyes filled as she rushed to defend herself. "I thought he'd get out there and see they weren't on that trail. An inconvenience, you know? Then he'd turn back."

"But he didn't come back," I finished for her.

He rode toward the fire, thinking that was where I was. And he was still out there in the dark. Because...I couldn't even begin to think why Melanie would have lied. Nothing about this made sense.

Elena pushed forward, her spine steel as she faced Melanie down. "Why would you tell him that? What was in it for you?"

"Nothing." Melanie covered her face with her hands. "I made a mistake. I didn't mean for this to happen."

Victoria shook her head. "She was mad Cormac broke up with me and thought she'd get a little revenge by sending him on a wild-goose chase."

What? I couldn't breathe. That couldn't be the reason Cormac wasn't here. That wasn't possible. It had to be something else. Something bigger, more noble. Because if this was it...if this was why Cormac was missing...

Elena jerked like she'd been struck. "My son is out there, in the dark, because of some petty revenge fantasy? Is that what you're telling me?"

"It was a mistake," Melanie keened, desperate.

If I'd been less numb and had use of my limbs, I would have clawed her crying eyes out. She'd done this. And for what?

Nothing.

"A mistake is giving someone the wrong change," Elena hissed. "This was not a mistake. You purposely endangered my son. If he—if something happens to him, I—"

All her steam wore out in a helpless puff. She fell against Lock's chest, quiet sobs racking her shoulders. Lock held her close, addressing the two women on his porch.

"If we need anything from either of you, we'll call." His jaw rippled. "You *will* answer."

"Of course," Victoria rasped. "We'll do anything you need."

Lock closed the door and ushered Elena into the living room. I could only stare at the glow coming from the porch light as I swayed. There were so many things I needed to do, but I couldn't grasp which should come first.

Zane stepped closer behind me. "Zara—"

"I need to go," I said, reaching for the doorknob.

Steven blocked my way. "No, baby. You can't go anywhere right now."

"He's out there because he thought I was in danger."

"And you *will* be in danger if you ride out blind in the dark," Steven replied, not raising his voice. "You know that."

A ball of furious helplessness burst in my chest, and it was all I could do not to slam into Steven, shove him out of my way, and run into the night—then keep running north until I found Cormac and put my hands on him.

But he was right.

Deep down, under my anger, I knew he was.

The north trail wasn't forgiving, even in the best of circumstances. There were too many drop-offs, too many places for horses to misstep.

"I can't just sit here," I said, my voice breaking. "I have to do something."

"You won't. We're going to make a plan," Elena said softly, crossing the room to take my hands. Hers were cold and shaky, but they held on tight. "At first light, we'll go out. We'll find him."

I wanted to believe her. She sounded so certain. But I was terrified. This was what I'd always been afraid of. I remembered that day in college, when all those people kept coming up to Cormac, and I felt him slipping away from me; knowing no matter what I did it was going to happen, I let him go.

I wouldn't let him go this time. Not without fighting with every ounce of rage I had in me. Thanks to Jackson and now Melanie, I had plenty to fuel me.

"Okay," I croaked. "We'll make a plan."

Zane wrapped his arms around me from behind, and Steven joined, sandwiching me between them. I folded into them, my composure close to cracking.

"He's all alone."

Zane rubbed his cheek against my temple, humming softly. "Not for long, Z. We'll find him."

I lifted my head, looking toward the window again, and the invisible stretch of land beyond it. He was out there because he was my hero. He couldn't help himself. It was who he was and a big part of why I loved him so.

This time, he might need saving, and I'd be the one to do it. I swore to myself I would. Just a few more hours, and I'd find him. Come hell or high water.

"Hold on," I whispered into the night, hoping the wind would carry the words to him. "Just hold on until morning."

Because that was all I could do.

Wait for the sun.

Chapter Forty-four

Zara

I was at the barn before sunrise, saddling up my horse. I hadn't slept for even a second, but I wasn't tired. Determination had lit a fuse in me, pushing me forward.

I *would* find Cormac.

He would be okay.

Our arms would be wrapped around each other before the day was over.

And that was that. I wouldn't accept any other outcome.

I'd let him go too easily once and had regretted it with every breath since. Cormac and I were finished with regrets. We'd decided on happy.

The others might not have been thrilled when they woke to find I'd left without them, but it had been physically impossible for me to wait another minute.

I knew these trails and this land. If anyone could handle riding out there with very little light, it was me.

The sky was still bruised purple, the horizon just beginning to pale. The ranch was starting to show signs of life, but not quickly enough. Soon, they'd be out searching again, teams of determined men and women working their hardest to find Cormac, but every minute he was out there all alone was a slice to my heart.

The ground was uneven in the half-light, shadows stretching long and deceptive. Every rock looked like a hole. Every bush like something crouched and waiting. We went slow and steady. The last thing I needed was for either of us to get injured. We had a mission to complete.

"I'm coming, Maccie," I whispered. "I'll see you soon."

The north trail rose gradually, curving toward the ridge. As the minutes passed, the sky softened from indigo to gray to streaks of pale gold. The sun edged up behind the hills, taking its time, completely indifferent to the panic clawing at my ribs.

The smoke in the distance was thinner now, lazily drifting upward, its shape dissipating as it reached the sky. Whatever had been burning must've been running out of fuel like Tom had predicted.

At least that was one less thing to be concerned about. I hoped Cormac could see it too and was comforted knowing the fire wasn't spreading toward the ranch.

The trail stretched ahead, mile after mile of scrub and rock and open land. I scanned the ground, the clusters of trees, every ridge and hill. There was no sign of him. He couldn't have disappeared. He was out here somewhere. I just had to keep looking.

I crested one rise, then another. My horse's breathing deepened beneath me, her ears flicking as if she sensed my urgency.

Or maybe my horse had heard something I hadn't. In the next moment, I caught movement to the right, and my heart leaped into my throat.

A chestnut coat caught in the early morning light.

"Dusty," I breathed.

She was grazing, and she was alone. I whipped my head back and forth, and it quickly became clear Cormac wasn't nearby.

I swung down before my horse fully stopped, my boots hitting the dirt hard. "Dusty," I called softly, trying not to spook her.

She lifted her head, ears twitching, and let out a soft nicker. She barely paid me any attention as I approached and looked her over. There was no blood, no sign of injury. The saddle was still on, though one stirrup hung twisted, the leather scuffed, and her reins trailed loose.

My hands shook as I ran them over her neck, her shoulders. "Where is he?" I whispered, pressing my forehead to her warm coat.

What could have happened? Dusty was one of our calmest mares. I couldn't picture her reacting in a way that would cause Cormac to get thrown, but the twisted stirrup was a sign *something* had gone wrong.

I mounted again, leading Dusty alongside me, scanning every inch of earth, braced to find him after every turn, disappointed when there was nothing but empty, brutal land.

Eventually, we reached a fork in the trail. One path continued up along the ridge, and the other dipped toward the river.

Which would Cormac take looking for me? Would he think I'd go to higher ground or follow the river?

As soon as I asked the question, I had the answer.

"To the river and back," I whispered.

That was where he'd go. Where he knew I'd find him. We always found each other there. The words were part of our skin.

If he'd been hurt or disoriented in the dark, he'd head somewhere familiar. Somewhere that meant home. Where he'd be certain I'd go.

I turned the horses toward the river path.

The descent was steep and narrow. My heart hammered so hard I could feel it in my fingertips gripping the reins.

The land was more verdant close to the water. A few trees dangled their leaves over the shimmering river. Rough, haphazard bushes clung to boulders, and small patches of cheatgrass broke through the unforgiving dirt.

Blood roared in my ears as I reached even ground.

"Cormac?" I rasped.

It wasn't loud enough. It barely felt real. Like if I didn't shout hard enough, the world might decide he wasn't here.

I swallowed, dragged in air that tasted like river and ash and fear, and screamed.

"Cormac!"

His name split open the morning, ricocheting off the trees and rolling down the water. I waited there, shaking, listening, heart pounding so violently I thought I might pass out before I ever found him.

Please. Please. Please.

Then, just as I'd pulled in another breath to yell his name again, I saw it. Movement beneath the shadows of the trees. And I knew.

My breath left me in a broken sob.

We tore toward the riverbank, and I didn't wait for my horse to stop. I hit the ground hard, stumbled, caught myself, and ran.

"Cormac."

He was slumped against the trunk of a tree, one leg bent awkwardly, the other stretched out in front of him. His hair was damp and matted to his forehead. Dirt streaked his cheeks. A thin line of dried blood tracked from his temple toward his ear.

He looked wrecked.

He looked alive.

"Zara," he croaked, his eyes darting wildly over me. "You're okay."

My knees gave out as I reached him, and his arms closed around me, drawing me into his chest. He smelled like sweat and his shampoo. Like sunshine and the love of my life. I couldn't stop breathing him in.

"You were lost," I cried against his shirt. "We didn't know where you were."

"I'm here, sweetheart. I'm right here." His voice was thin and thready, like speaking was an effort.

I clutched fistfuls of his shirt, needing to feel his solid heat. My hands slid up to his face, over his jaw, into his hair, down his shoulders. I needed to catalog him. Needed to know he was whole. Needed proof.

"You're real," I whispered, half to myself. "You're real."

He gave a faint huff of a laugh that ended in a wince. "Pretty sure."

I pulled back enough to see him clearly. His eyes were unfocused, a little glassy. "Are you hurt?"

"Yeah." His brow crinkled as he shifted. "I fell when Dusty got spooked and bolted. Think I messed up my knee. Definitely can't put weight on it."

I shook my head, tears spilling freely. "I'm so sorry I couldn't find you sooner. They wouldn't let me out here when it was dark—"

"I knew you were gonna come." He swiped my tears with his thumb. "Knew you'd find me, sweetheart. I just had to hang out for a while and wait."

My chest very nearly caved in.

"You're always waiting for me." My head fell on his shoulder, and my heart finally began to calm. "You came to the river."

"This is our spot. If I was going to sit somewhere hurting, I figured it might as well be here."

A sob-laugh tore out of me. "To the river and back."

"Yeah." His eyelids drooped. "And look...you made it. Just like I knew you would."

"Baby..." I kissed his temple, cheek, jaw. "Let me take care of you, okay?"

His head fell back against the trunk, and he looked at me like I was the best thing he'd ever seen. "All right. Do what you need to, as long as you don't leave me."

"Oh no, Cormac. You don't have to worry about that. I won't leave you."

Not ever again.

Chapter Forty-five

Cormac

Lucky for me, with my family, it wasn't difficult for me to take it easy. The trouble was, they were always watching me, so even when I wanted to do something for myself, they wouldn't let me. And I was getting bored with being laid up for the last two weeks.

After taking my second nap of the day, I opened my eyes and nearly had a heart attack.

"What the hell?" I tried to shoot upright but was immediately greeted with a rocketing pain in my knee.

"Sorry, Uncle Cormac!" Jesse jumped back, his hands up. "Grandma sent me to check on you. I didn't mean to scare you."

I groaned, moving more slowly until I was sitting against the headboard. "Maybe knock instead of putting your face right in front of mine."

"I did knock. You were out cold. Did you know when you're sleeping, you kind of look like a corpse? I couldn't even hear you breathing." He put his hands on his hips and looked me over. "Grandma would've been mad if you'd been dead and I just left you lying there."

"What about if you killed me by sending me into cardiac arrest?"

Chuckling, he handed me my crutches. "Yeah, I don't think she would've been happy about that either."

I let him help me up from the bed and into the bathroom, drawing the line at his offer of assisting me to the toilet. There was little dignity in being injured, I had to hold tight on all I had left.

My leg injury turned out to be more serious than I'd initially thought. I now had pins and plates holding my bones together and a long recovery ahead of me. Still, it could've been a hell of a lot worse, so I was trying my damnedest to keep from getting down about it.

Jesse was waiting for me when I was finished, and he walked beside me along the path from the guesthouse to my parents' place to have dinner with them.

The thing that had come out of all of this was moving in with Zara. It'd been out of necessity—climbing the stairs at my grandparents' house was out of the question—but even without the injury, it would have happened. Neither of us had wanted to spend another night apart. Not for a long time.

I'd only convinced her to go back to work a couple days ago.

Me being lost had been harder for her than me. Sure, I'd gone out there looking for her, but at some point during the long hours, I'd come to realize she hadn't been on that trail. I'd known she was safe. Had felt it in my bones.

Those same hours, she'd spent helpless, unable to do anything to find me. Not knowing what had happened or if we'd ever see each other again.

I might've been the one with the broken leg, but part of Zara broke that night too. We were both working on healing.

"What's Grandma cooking?" I asked Jesse.

"Roast chicken and potatoes." He glanced at me. "Grandpa's cutting up a watermelon, and Phoebe sent over chocolate chip cookies."

"She's not coming to dinner?"

"Nope. Grandma said it's time for everyone to give you a break. You need a quiet night, and everyone needs to get back to their lives."

I raised a brow at him. "But you're here."

He crossed his arms over his chest. "Are you saying you didn't miss me while I was at camp?"

I chuckled. Jesse had been gone for almost a month, so he'd been absent during my drama. I was kind of glad about that. Teenage years were hard enough without having to carry that memory.

"I'm not saying that at all. And I'm not surprised your grandma let you be an exception to her rule."

He grinned as he opened the back door for me. "Don't tell the others I'm her favorite."

"Your secret's safe with me."

The second my crutch hit the floor, my dad was on me, helping me into the house.

"I've got it," I protested.

He grumbled, sending me a sharp look. "Let me, Cormac. I need to see you safe."

I *was* safe. I'd been safe the entire time. I never doubted Zara would know where to look for me. It was why I'd used all my energy to drag myself to the river. It was where she'd look—the one place I was sure of.

My parents hadn't been sure. Like Zara, they'd been helpless and terrified. I didn't know what it was like to have a kid, but imagining one of my nieces or nephews out there had my gut roiling in protest.

"Okay." I leaned into my dad, giving him some of my weight. "Help me into my chair, all right?"

"That's all I'm trying to do," he gruffed, his gentle touch belying his angry snap.

More than anyone, my dad had been furious at Melanie for what she'd done. That wasn't to say we all weren't angry. I was leading the pack. But it was taking my dad some time to let it go.

He'd wanted me to press charges, get her locked up and throw away the key.

I'd thought about it, but really, when it came down to it, I just wanted it to all be over. Firing her had been enough for me, knowing she wouldn't find another job in Sugar Brush—not when everyone knew exactly what she'd done.

And while Victoria hadn't really done anything wrong, it'd been a relief when she quietly put in her resignation. Last I heard, she was planning on moving to another town. It would be better for everyone to put all traces of them both behind us.

My dad would get there. Though it would probably take me getting off these crutches 'til he really healed.

It wasn't long before my mother was fussing over me, bringing me a glass of iced water and a cookie.

"A cookie before dinner?" Jesse whined, sounding like the little boy I'd always see him as, even if he was a huge teenager with a voice as deep as his father's now. "How's that fair?"

I waved the cookie at him. "Break a bone, and maybe you'll get one too."

My mother tsked and smoothed his hair back from his face. "Don't you dare." Then she poked a finger at me. "You're lucky I'm not taking the cookie back. It's your job as an uncle to be a good influence."

When she wasn't looking, I split the cookie in half and gave one side to Jesse. My dad saw it, but all he did was frown and go back to chopping up the watermelon.

It wasn't long before the sound of the front door opening made my heart kick. Zara hurried into the kitchen a moment later, setting her bag in the doorway before beelining straight to me.

I had my arms out when she got to me, pulling her into a tight embrace. She buried her face in my neck, her arms banding around my shoulders.

"Hey, sweetheart," I cooed.

"Hey, Maccie." She kissed my jaw, my chin, then my lips. "How are you?"

"Good, now that you're here."

I took her face in my hands, searching. There were new lines around her mouth from too much frowning. A faint indent between her brows from all her worrying. It drove me nuts to see it. All I'd ever wanted to do was make her happy.

She took the seat beside me since my lap was out of commission for now—another thing that drove me up the damn wall. I kept telling myself we had a lifetime for that. In the long run, a few weeks wasn't a big deal, even if it hurt.

"I have gossip." Her eyes shone brighter than they had since I'd gotten injured.

I took her hand in mine. "Oh yeah?"

Jesse leaned in, his chin resting on his fist. "Tell me."

Zara laughed. "I'm not so sure you'll be interested. You might not know who I'm talking about."

He scoffed. "If it's about anyone in this town, I know them."

Her nose crinkled. "Well, it's about my coworker, Henrik—"

"Big German guy?" He nodded. "Yep, I know him. If you're going to say he has a thing for Javier, that's obvious. The whole ranch knows that."

"Duh." She rolled her eyes. "That's not the gossip."

He rolled his hand. "Get on with it then."

"Well, you know how Javier is moving to Spain for a new job?" All of us nodded, even my dad, who was listening while pretending not to. "Henrik just told me he's taking a job in…Majorca—at the same resort as Javier."

Jesse gasped. "Is Henrik stalking him?"

Zara burst out laughing. "Nope. I pressed him hard for more information, and Henrik finally admitted they're officially a couple and crazy for each other."

I could have guessed based on how many times I'd seen Henrik coming in and out of Javier's office, but it wasn't my business. I couldn't say I wasn't happy for them, though.

Even more, I was relieved Zara's smile was reaching all the way to her eyes. I hadn't seen that bright smile in far too long.

I couldn't stop myself from reaching for her face and pulling her toward me so I could touch her smile with my lips.

Her laugh was warm on my mouth. "What's this for?"

"I love you. That's all."

Her forehead rolled against mine. "I love you too."

"I'm glad you had a good day."

"Yeah. I really did." She pulled back, holding both my hands in hers. "Just so you know, I told Henrik we're coming to visit them in Spain as soon as you're healed."

My mom swung by the table to give Zara's shoulders a squeeze. "Oooh, a winter trip to Spain sounds divine."

I nodded. "Wherever you want to go, sweetheart, I'm there."

Zara's fingers skated along my chest and over the words tattooed under my collarbone. She was quiet, curled against me in our bed. I was trying to read but kept getting lost in the middle of the same page.

From nowhere, she said, "I want a life with you, Cormac."

I agreed without a beat of hesitation. "I do too. All of it."

She raised her head, resting her arms on my chest. "Kids?"

"Yeah," I breathed. "Definitely."

"Me too. Maybe in a couple years."

"A couple years sounds right." I put my book down to brush her hair behind her shoulder. "You wanna get married?"

"I didn't think I'd want to again, but yes, I do. To you. What about you?"

"More than anything, yeah. Soon?"

"Maybe in the spring...before the resort gets busy."

I nodded. "You've been thinking about this."

"Haven't you?"

"I haven't really let myself."

Her fingers grazed my lips. "Please let yourself. I'm not going anywhere."

"I know."

She pushed herself up my chest, aligning our lips. "Do you?"

"I do. I'm sure of it." I took her head in my hands, meeting her dark, bottomless gaze. "Do you know I'm not going anywhere? I'm okay, and this leg of mine is going to get better pretty soon."

A shudder ran through her. "I almost lost you," she whispered.

"No, sweetheart. You only thought you did. You might think you're the stubborn one, but when it comes to you, I'm as bullheaded as they come. I've never given up on you. Do you really think I would when we're so close to having it all?"

Her lips pressed into a flat line as tears welled in her eyes. "It doesn't work like that."

"I know. And one day, one of us will have to live without the other, but that's going to be decades down the line."

"Don't talk about that," she rasped.

"No, listen. We're lucky, Zara. We know what it's like to lose one another, right? So we're going to treasure the days we have."

"Years."

"Years. The years we'll have. We won't take them for granted like some people do. Every day I get to have with you will be precious. I'm not going to forget to hold your hand or take you dancing because I'll always remember the years I didn't have the chance to do any of that."

She shook her head. "How can you see the world so beautifully?"

"I've got you. How can I not?"

That earned me kisses all over my face and whispers of being the cutest man alive. Then she settled against me, and we talked about what kind of wedding we might have, imagining the road we were going to walk together, the life we'd finally get to build.

That night, with Zara in my arms, I dreamed of us younger, racing to the river and back. Laughing and getting dirty, days that never ended and summers that flew by.

And something settled inside me.

A last piece clicking into place.

By morning, when I opened my eyes again, finding Zara already smiling at me, I felt it for certain.

It'd taken a while, but here we were.

At last, everything had been set right.

Epilogue

Zara

Four Years Later

"Come on! We're gonna race." Cormac went running at a snail's pace, and Miriam nipped at his heels, giggling like a maniac.

"I win, Daddy!" she squealed.

"You have to catch me," he called, letting her keep up with him.

I chased after them, laughing and recording their race on my phone. Miriam looked back over her shoulder, making sure I was there.

"Go on. Catch Daddy. We can't let him win," I said.

"Me!" she cried, raising her chubby arms over her head. "I'm gonna beat you, Daddy!"

Miriam was just a month away from turning three, and everything was a race to her. She lived by the motto "Why walk when I can run?" Luckily, she had almost infinite space to roam and a horde of cousins to exhaust her. Her dad was her favorite partner in crime, though.

It didn't take us long to make it to the river, but I was out of breath all the same. Cormac and Miriam celebrated her victory with a little dance then he came over to me to check in.

"You're panting," he said, resting his hands on my shoulders.

I pointed to my big belly. "Your son is compressing my lungs."

His smile was so tender my eyes immediately stung. I would have blamed it on the hormones, but that wasn't really it. Cormac was just...wonderful. He loved me so well it regularly sent me into fits of emotional upheaval. And seeing him with our little girl was just as I'd always imagined. He had bottomless wells of patience and energy, and he was so loving I knew she would never doubt she was safe in his arms.

Just like me.

"You're beautiful, even when you're breathless," he said, cradling my belly.

I cupped his cheeks, bringing him to my level, and kissed around his mouth before he got fed up and stole one from my lips.

Laughing, I squeezed his face. "You're so cute, I can't stand it."

He growled. "Not cute. Devastatingly handsome."

"That too, of course."

He really was, and it was for that reason I got pregnant with Miriam before we had planned. We also hadn't been careful in our prevention, so the truth was, we'd been fine with having a surprise, and once she came along, it had been clear the timing had been exactly right.

My little blue-eyed, raven-haired girl. A rancher from birth, she'd ridden horses and milked a cow by the time she'd turned two. She was an outdoorsy girl like her mama, and easygoing like her daddy.

She did like lots of attention, though. When she decided Cormac and I had loved on each other enough, she'd squeeze between us and hold her arms out, and Cormac would scoop her up, squishing her between us.

She patted my belly. "Baby brother."

"Yes. He's in there. Are you excited to meet him?"

She gave me a different answer every day. This time, she thought about it, tapping her little round cheek and humming.

"Is he gonna be like Avie?"

Avery was her youngest cousin, Phoebe and Deke's third child. They'd had her a year after their boy, Anderson, was born. She was a wild handful like her cousin, Silas, but she was a teeny-tiny, adorable little imp too, so she got away with most of her mischief.

"Maybe," I said. "We have to meet him and let him show us who he is."

She hummed again. "Okay. I'll meet him."

Cormac grinned at me. "Good thing she's willing to meet her brother."

I swiped my forehead. "Phew. I was worried there for a second."

They raced back to the house, with me trailing slowly behind. Miriam ran inside, and Cormac circled back for me. If I'd let him, he would have carried me the rest of the way, but I wasn't at the point in my pregnancy where I was ready to give up walking.

Inside, Miriam had found her great-grandparents. They were sitting together on the couch, Miriam snuggled between them, jabbering away about her day as they nodded along attentively. Cormac and I stopped at the living room threshold to watch, leaning against each other.

When we got married, Lily and Connell had offered to move to the guesthouse so we could have this house for our family, but we hadn't even considered accepting. This was how I'd grown up, with extended family close by, and what I'd wanted for my kids. Besides, I loved my morning chats with Lily and asking Connell questions about the ranch whenever one popped into my head. It wasn't the same as my relationship with my own grandparents, but it was close enough to soothe a part of me that had ached since their loss.

I looked up at Cormac, and he turned to peer down at me. His eyes were soft, but deep down, there was sadness brewing. Because one day, in the not-too-distant future, this would be gone. Lily and Connell were healthy, but they were almost ninety, and no one lived forever. We'd love them and treasure them as long as we had them, and I tried my hardest not to mourn them while they were still here, but carried a pit of dread in my stomach for the day that they weren't.

"We'll be like them one day," he whispered.

"I really hope so," I whispered back.

Lily turned our way, assessment sharp in her blue eyes. "Are you keeping secrets over there?"

"As if we can have secrets in this family," I said.

I pulled Cormac into the living room with me, and we sat beside each other on the sectional. Well, I was half in his lap, where he'd tugged me. If we sat here long enough, I'd end up fully on his lap, one way or another. That was just how we were.

Lily pinned me with a stern look. "Don't do that."

My eyes widened. "What do you mean?"

She lowered her chin. "You know."

Miriam kicked her feet, her hands on her great-grandparents' knees. "What is Mommy doing?"

Lily tucked Miriam's hair behind her ear and smiled. "She's being silly and worrying about things that are inevitable. Do you know what inevitable means?"

Miriam shook her head.

She took Miriam's hand in hers. "Well, inevitable means something that is meant to happen. Like your mommy and daddy falling in love and getting married. That was inevitable. And like you"—she poked Miriam's tummy—"being born. Inevitable and wonderful. And things coming to an end when they're supposed to. That's inevitable too. So worrying about them is just plain silly."

Miriam nodded like she understood, which I doubted. "You're silly, Mommy."

Connell's laugh was still a deep rumble. "She has a point, darlin'."

Sucking in a breath, I smiled. "Then I won't worry, since I don't want to be accused of being silly."

Cormac had told me a long time ago we were lucky to have known what it meant to lose each other, so we would treasure the time we now had.

He'd promised to hold my hand and me in his arms as often as he could, and he'd kept that promise.

In my heart, I'd promised to stop focusing on what we'd lost and look forward to all we would have.

We already had so, *so* much. Nieces and nephews, parents and grandparents. Our children, each other. Health, sunshine, happiness.

I wished I saw Steven and Zane and their twins, Zak and Sophie, more often. I wished my parents lived in Sugar Brush full time and not just during the summers. I wished I could erase the years I'd wasted when I could have been with Cormac instead.

Those were things I could not change. And what we had, how we grew, tipped the scales so far in our favor, it was hard to dwell on any of it for too long.

Cormac brushed his thumb over my knuckles, reminding me he was with me, like he always did. Miriam's laughter rang out, bright and unbothered, as Lily and Connell hung on her every word.

Life would keep moving. Seasons would turn. Babies would be born. Goodbyes would come when they must.

But right now, the house was full. My husband's arm was around me. Our daughter was safe between generations. Our son kicked beneath my heart.

And this love-soaked moment wasn't something to mourn or wish different.

It was inevitable.

And it was ours.

The Parents

Do you want to read Zara and Cormac's parents' stories?
Amir and Zadie's love story begins in Bright Like Midnight
https://mybook.to/BrightLikeMidnight
Elena and Lock's romance blooms in Sweet Like Poison
https://mybook.to/SweetLikePoison

Many Thanks

I CAN'T BELIEVE THIS is the end of this series! When I first wrote about this town way back in Sweet Like Poison, I never imagined what would come of it. But once I introduced the first two Kelly kids in Sincerely, Your Inconvenient Wife, I knew I had to write about this family.

Joy's Elbow Room came to be a couple years ago when my family and I stopped to charge our car across the street from a cute little bar with a similar name. We started spitballing ideas (imagine the craziness two preteen boys and a teenage girl can come up with) and the rest is history. So, my kids get my first thank you.

I have to specifically shout out my daughter, Maya. She's my artist, and had created all the character art for this series, along with the Kelly Ranch logo. Each piece she makes is even more beautiful than the last.

This series wouldn't be what it is without the stunning covers. My girl, Kate Farlow really knocked all of them out of the park. She saw my jumbled vision and returned with masterpieces.

As always, my editor, Monica, and proofreader, Rose, made my words shine. I couldn't do this without them.

And Amber, my PA. Who knows my books like the back of her hand, and predicts what I need before it even pops into my mind.

Cormac is officially in her top 3 book boyfriends (#1 is David from Watch Me Unravel, #2 is Ivan from Jump on Three). So we'll just say this book is dedicated to her and all her loveliness.

I can't forget about you, lovely reader, for always being here with me. Whether you joined me in this series, or all the way back in the beginning, I see you, and I appreciate you!

More Books By Julia

MILE HIGH BILLIONAIRES

In The Details

By The Letter

To The Chase

The Kelly Ranch (small town romance)

See It Through

Hold The Line

Hit The Ground

Set It Right

The Harder They Fall (Billionaire office romance)

Dear Grumpy Boss

Sincerely, Your Inconvenient Wife

P.S. You're Intolerable

Not So Truly Yours

The Seasons Change (Rock star romance)

Falling In Reverse

Stone Cold Notes

Faded in Bloom

Where Waves Break

Savage U (college romance)

Soft Like Thunder

Bright Like Midnight

Sweet Like Poison

Real Like Daydreams

Savage Academy (academy romance)

Save One Thing

These Two Wrongs
Jump On Three

Blue is the Color (Rock star romance)
Times Like These
Watch Me Unravel
Such Great Heights
Under the Bridge

Unrequited (Rock star romance)
Unrequited
Misconception
Dissonance

Never Blue Duet (Angsty rock star romance)
Never Lasting
Never Again

The Savage Crew (dark high school romance)
Start a Fire
Through the Ashes
Burn it Down

About Julia

Julia Wolf is a bestselling contemporary romance author. She writes bad boys with big hearts and strong, independent heroines. Julia enjoys reading romance just as much as she loves writing it. Whether reading or writing, she likes the emotions to run high and the heat to be scorching.

Julia lives in Maryland with her three crazy, beautiful kids and her patient husband who she's slowly converting to a romance reader, one book at a time.

Visit my website:
juliawolfwrites.com